D1259214

BOOKS BY JACQUETTA HAWKES

Archaeology of Jersey

Prehistoric Britain
(with Christopher Hawkes)

Early Britain

Symbols and Speculations
(Poetry)

A Land

*A Guide to the Prehistoric and Roman Monuments
of England and Wales*

*A Woman as Great as the World
and Other Fables*

Journey Down a Rainbow
(with J. B. Priestley)

Man on Earth

Providence Island

Man and the Sun

King of the Two Lands: The Pharaoh Akhenaten

KING OF THE
TWO LANDS:

The Pharaoh Akhenaten

KING OF THE
TWO LANDS:

The Pharaoh Akhenaten

JACQUETTA HAWKES

 RANDOM HOUSE

New York

CONTENTS

BOOK I

I	9
II	24
III	37
IV	70

BOOK II

V	105
VI	137
VII	160
VIII	182
IX	214
X	249

FOREWORD

It seems all wrong for a novel to have a Foreword. The sight of one may well make readers suspect that this is not a novel at all, but an archaeological treatise disguised by a few patches of dialogue. Nothing could be further from the truth. It is precisely because so considerable a part of the story comes out of my head that my publishers and I thought I should do my best to distinguish between this and what is at least supposed to be true according to the latest interpretations. Readers may also like to have a few dates, and to be told what happened to some of the surviving characters after the end of my book.

First of all I should like to say that although I hope to have avoided anachronisms, I have deliberately used familiar English words for measures of time and distance, for seasons, and in other places where Egyptian terms would have been more precisely correct. I have extended this practice to proper names: Heliopolis, for example, was known as On in Pharaonic times. I have done this because I have always found numbers of strange terms to be irritating and—more serious—alienating.

Akhenaten came to the throne in about 1367 B.C. as number ten in the line of the great Eighteenth Dynasty of Egypt. He was first made known to the public by the American historian J. H. Breasted—who wrote of him in glowing appreciation. He called him a "God-intoxicated man", and proclaimed him as "the first individual in history". By this he meant that he was the first man known to have used his personal ideas and conviction to try to change the mindless drift of tradition.

Since then there have been many hostile interpretations of Akhenaten's character and achievement, and he has become one of the most controversial figures in history. In particular certain scholars who seem to have an over-developed respect for 'manliness' and good health have condemned him as sick, deranged, effeminate, a feeble ruler who betrayed an empire for the sake of self-indulgent idealism. It has also been denied that his teaching of the Aten was either original or truly monotheistic. The first of these latter points has some justification—there are already hints of a new universalism in the days of Akhenaten's father. But such thoughts led to no kind of action to modify the extravagant welter of traditional Egyptian polytheism.

I cannot accept the good faith of anyone who denies that Akhenaten was moved by a vision of single and universal deity far in advance of his age. It is evident in his actions: in his suppression of the old pantheon and the sweeping aside of idolatry and all the familiar jumble of spells and charms and other magical practices—particularly those associated with the cult of the dead. But far more eloquent and unmistakable are his words in the magnificent hymns to the Aten discovered at Akhetaten. There he speaks of his god as universal, eternal, the loving creator of all men and all nature. Again and again he emphasizes the solitariness of the self-created Aten, how he shaped the universe while he himself was alone. It is a far simpler, clearer monotheism than that which has been taught in the name of Christianity.

In my own assessment of Akhenaten I have relied very largely on these hymns. We can all have our prejudices about Pharaoh, but his poetry is there—fresh, fine and irrefutable. Its thought and feeling are in harmony with its author's acts in so far as we know them.

I have relied on the hymns not only for evidence of his greatness and genius, but also as giving a hint of the error that betrayed him. In the last verses of the best preserved version of his sun hymn he claims for himself a unique relationship with the deity. "There is none other who knows you save Akhenaten your son; you have given him insight of your purposes, he understands your power." And: "You established the world for your son, he who was born of your body.... The Son of Re, Living in Truth, Lord of Diadems, Akhenaten great in his length of days." (It is only fair to add that he continued: "And for the King's Great Wife, She whom he loves, for the Lady of the Two Lands, Nefertiti; may she live and flourish for ever and ever.")

This conviction is natural enough in a young man who must have had to struggle daily against the incomprehension of others, and who had ascended the throne in a land where the king was no mere steward of divinity but a living god. That it led to the royal pair being worshipped by many of their subjects at the partial expense of the Aten is suggested by texts and by the household shrines. On the other hand there can be no proof either that the King's divine hubris was heightened by his visionary fits, or that it was one of the main causes of his estrangement from Nefertiti.

I have developed the view that Akhenaten's failure to defend the northern empire, consisting of a large number of vassal states, was due to a hatred of war and to his belief that all men were equally children of the Aten. Many authorities have accepted this interpretation—although my belief in the extraordinary topicality of Akhenaten's situation, in his precocious realization of so many of the greatest problems that confront us today, may have led me to heighten it still further.

That he refused or neglected appeals for help from his vassals is well known from the famous Tell el Amarna letters found at Akhetaten in 1887. These tablets, which represent foreign office archives from the reigns of Akhenaten and his father, are the source of most of our knowledge of the endless wars and intrigues involving the Hittites and the collapsing Egyptian alliances in Palestine and Syria. There is no doubt that some more or less loyal rulers in the north felt that Pharaoh had betrayed them; I have made Haremhab give forceful expression to what may have been their point of view. But there is no doubt either that most of the kings and regents, great and small, were involved in plots and treacheries for which Akhenaten had no direct responsibility.

As evidence that his policy was due to positive principle rather than to weakness or religious preoccupations I have again trusted largely to the hymns. 'You created the strange countries Khor [Palestine and Syria] and Kush, as well as the land of Egypt. . . . Men speak with many tongues, in body and complexion they are various, for you have distinguished between people and people." This is one passage that shows his acceptance of 'strangers' as the equals of the Egyptians; several times he insists that the Aten made "all men, all creatures that walk upon feet", and there is the charming passage in which, having described how the god made the Nile for the common folk of Egypt, he continues: "How excellent are your purposes, O Lord of eternity! You have set a Nile in the sky for the strangers . . ."—that is to say, have provided them with rain.

That a man with thoughts and feelings such as these could not have been an imperialist is plain enough. His pacific ideals are corroborated by the fact that he never had himself portrayed striking down or trampling enemies or captives as his predecessors and successors loved to do.

Turning to the characters in my story, I can say that nearly all of them have an historical origin. Records at Thebes and Akhetaten give their names, their callings and some of the events in their lives, and several of the more important are portrayed on tomb walls or in sculpture. The only considerable characters supplied by me are the villain Mersure and the harim ladies Mina and Ninsun. Among the minor characters named at Akhetaten, only Taty and Gilukhipa's major domo are entirely fictional. No one will doubt that I have added to what is known: for example it is vividly recorded that Mahu was devoted to Pharaoh, that he ran in front of the royal chariot when Akhenaten drove his family through the streets, and that he was fat. But there is no kind of record as to how he came into Pharaoh's service.

The ages and some of the relationships of leading characters are uncertain, and the subject of endless argument. In making Ay to be Queen Tiye's brother I have followed a suggestion made by one good authority, but for making him the father of Tutankhamun I have no authority at all. As Ay was the power behind Tutankhamun's throne, it seems not implausible. Smenkhkare's parentage is also quite unknown. The only certain thing about Nefertiti's background is that Tey was her "Nurse" or foster mother. Most people seem to think that she was

a daughter of Amenophis III, but in choosing a Cypriote
moon priestess as her mother I have given myself excessive
licence. There is even a trace of positive evidence against
my invention—but it suits my idea of Nefertiti, and I hope
will be forgiven.

As for Akhenaten's age, it is much disputed. The question is complicated by the related debate as to whether or
not he had a co-regency with his father. It is known that
he made the move to Akhetaten in the sixth year of his
reign, and he must still have been quite young at the time.
As for Nefertiti, although she had by then borne two children she was probably no more than a young girl in our
reckoning—I would ask readers to remember this when
reading my dialogue.

While there is very little evidence for Akhenaten's
activities at Thebes except for the shattered stones of his
Aten temple now piled up among the greater ruins of
Karnak, it is clear and abundant for the years at Akhetaten.
The city of god flourished for so short a time that there is
no confusing overburden from later periods. The inscriptions on the boundary stele record Akhenaten's speech and
the drive in the electrum chariot, and suggest his preoccupation with the idea of enclosure—which I have further
developed as it seems to me psychologically significant.
The speech also mentions some unspecified evil doings of
the priests of Amon at Thebes. In addition to the light
they throw on political and military doings, the Amarna
tablets provide information about Queen Tiye's importance in the early days of the reign, the dowry sent with
Tadukhipa, Tushratta's demands for gold—and his
indignation at being sent plated statues. The tombs in
the cliffs, many of which were cut and decorated though
few were used, have preserved not only substantial parts
of Pharaoh's hymns, but also a mass of information about
Mahu, Hapu, the Queen Mother's festive visit, the gift
of gold to Ay and Tey—and above all of the royal family:
how the princesses went naked, sat on their parents' knees,
were driven through the streets and prodded the horses.

As for the city itself and the adjacent tomb-cutters'
township, although they were levelled to the ground,

excavation has revealed so much that my account of lay-
out and buildings of all kinds can be accepted as factual.
The high position of artists in the city is proved by the
siting of their studios in the most fashionable quarter.
There is no evidence that Dhutmose had responsibility
for the creation of the city, but his studio with its casts was
found, and the bust of Nefertiti does in fact seem to have
been left standing on a shelf.

When we turn to the at first triumphant and then tragic
events enacted in Akhetaten, clarity at once gives way to
mist. The journey to Ugarit to meet the Hittite king I
devised in order to strengthen the theme of the opposition
of two forms of power which runs through the story. Those
readers who think in such terms will also see how necessary
it is for the underlying myth of the hero. The co-regency
with Smenkhkare is certain, and the fact that he was
assigned Nefertiti's titles suggests he was supposed to take
her place in the symbolic relationship of the divine love.
There is evidence that he soon went to Thebes, but not
of what happened to him there. It is reasonably sure that
Nefertiti retired with Tutankhamun to the North Palace;
Merytaten's name was substituted for hers at Maru-
aten. Absolutely nothing is known of how Akhenaten and
Nefertiti died—an ignorance for which I am thankful. A
mummy put into a hastily converted coffin in a tomb at
Thebes may be Akhenaten's body, but this is hotly disputed by archaeologists and anatomists alike.

As to the events that were to happen after the end of the
present story, they continued the ill luck of the Dynasty.
Tutankhamun died after a seven-year reign when he was
about eighteen years old. He has become famous only
from the chance that his tomb alone among those in the
Valley of the Kings survived almost intact. The sumptuous
grave furniture includes pieces that show the continuing
influence of Akhenaten's revolutionary art—although in
somewhat sweetened form.

Ay, the man whom Akhenaten had honoured and heaped
with gold, had probably controlled the kingdom through
Tutankhamun's reign, and when the young king died he
seized the throne outright. Meanwhile a poignant story

concerns Tutankhamun's widow—the former Princess Ankhesenpaten. She wrote to the Hittite king Suppiluliuma saying that she had no son, that she was loath to marry "her servant" (possibly Ay wanting to legitimize his succession by marriage with the heiress), and asking him to send one of his sons to be her husband and Pharaoh of Egypt. The Hittite was suspicious, delayed, and the opportunity was lost.

Ay, already an old man, reigned for a few years and then, as there was no legitimate heir, was succeeded in about 1335 by the strong-handed Haremhab, who chose his chief priests from the army and seems to have ruled and carried through certain reforms with a military efficiency. Although in fact he belonged to no Dynasty, Haremhab is usually recognized as the last ruler of the Eighteenth— to be followed by the Ramessids of the Nineteenth.

Akhenaten's successors seem to have had no scruples in returning to Amon and all the old religious forms. They boasted of restoring the temples up and down the Two Lands; the city of the Aten was soon abandoned, and its creator was referred to as "that enemy of Akhetaten". His name was omitted from the lists of kings. A new hymn in praise of Amon contains the lines:

> Woe to him who assails thee!
> Thy city stands . . .
> He who assails thee,
> His temple lies in darkness.

By the end of the Eighteenth Dynasty it must have appeared certain to anyone of sound sense that Akhenaten and his works had passed into eternal oblivion.

BOOK I

I

T H E boy hung over the edge of the boat, unsuccessfully trying to reach the water with his finger-tips. The gilded gunwale cut into his thin ribs, and still his hand felt not water but only the heat of the sun. How much better it would be to go in a reed canoe as ordinary people did, then he could have put his whole forearm in, felt the tickle of the water and watched the little wave making patterns on his skin. He flopped back irritably on to the cushions. How sickly sweet the paddlemen smelt. His mother insisted on their using a scented oil because she said all Nubians stank. Yet it was quite untrue. Like anybody else they sweated if they had to work in the sun. Why were there so many untruths in the grown-up world?

"Come here, Prince. My funny gosling." Queen Tiye called to him. Amenophis got to his feet and walked across the deck to where his mother reclined on cushions that were draped with sumptuous cloths brought from some Asiatic province. All court life was like that. Heavy with foreign tribute. Men, women and children as well as other luxuries.

His mother crooked her arm for him and he lay down beside her. It gave him a sense of haven. If only he didn't so often hate her for what she said and did. Her flank and her arm were firm even though the skin sagged a little.

"Don't call me gosling."

"But you're so like one. And goslings are delicious creatures. Are you enjoying yourself, gosling?"

"Yes, Mother, but I wish we were in a reed boat. I like to be nearer to things."

"But then we should be burnt up by the sun."

"I love the sun."

"Yes, I believe you do. But you had better be careful what you say, Prince, or you'll find yourself in politics." Queen Tiye laughed enough for the boy to feel her diaphragm quaking below his arm. She did not really care so much about disputes between Thebes and Heliopolis so long as her men won. "What a perverse child you are. All kinds of wheedling to come out with me in *Aten Gleams.* Then when we've only been once across the lake you begin to want something else. And if we were in a reed boat, you would have to do the paddling. You are hardly built for it." She felt his narrow angular shoulder like a prodding market-woman.

"No," Amenophis succumbed to her, "I shouldn't like to do the paddling and I do like being with you in *Aten Gleams.* She is a beautiful boat—the most beautiful boat in Egypt. Look there, Mother." Amenophis jerked up, kneeling awkwardly on the folds of her gown like a much younger child. "Isn't it lovely? Do watch."

A kingfisher was hovering just below the awning's edge, its black-and-white plumage extraordinarily intense against the dull green line of tousled palms. It dropped to the water, its feet just scratching the surface, shot up again and then plunged down in earnest, quickly reappearing with a fish like a tiny silver tongue hanging from its bill.

Amenophis returned to his haven. He was trembling.

"Heavens, what is the matter? Haven't you seen a kingfisher before?"

"It was so near, and so much alive. But then the fish . . ."

"Well, be thankful it wasn't you, gosling."

"I felt as though it was."

"That's how things are. You can't have fine birds without eating fish." She noticed tears in the corners of his long eyes. "How are you to live in this world, Amenophis? Let alone rule?" She withdrew her arm.

The boy jumped to his feet, rigid now and with a kind of strength. "When I am the god everything will be different. Better. Far, far better. You will see." He went aft and leant on a thwart watching the Nubians while he recovered himself. They paddled very gently on the still waters of Queen Tiye's artificial lake, their muscles sliding softly below the glistening skin. The muscular flow, the rhythm of the paddles, the drops falling softly from the blades and the expanding water-rings; it was soothing. "We'll go back now," he said to them. "We've had enough." The Nubians rolled their eyes apprehensively towards the Queen and her steward of boats came fussily from his place beyond her seat. She nodded her head idly, shrugging her shoulders. Deftly the men turned the barge westward where the columns and roofs of the palace rose from its gardens. It looked brashly new in contrast with the wrinkled crags of the low mountains beyond.

Soon the bow was pushing among the blue cups of the lotus which had been planted by the lake edge. Boat boys with hooks and cloth-covered landing-boards, ladies in waiting, footmen, litter-bearers, were all there bowing. A small obsequious army waiting to carry and escort them the two or three hundred yards to the shade of the palace.

Amenophis lay back in his litter, the calfless legs of which his mother so much disapproved stretched out in front of him. He had cared for a time about their weakness, indeed had wept and prayed and taken silly little images to the shrines. Now he didn't care any more, and what was more boring than running and spear-throwing and playing at battles? As for hunting, he detested it. First he was intoxicated with excitement, then horrified by the mortal fall of the quarry, the beautiful convulsed limbs, the bright eyeball clotted with sand. Not long ago he had been obliged to follow a lion hunt. His father had been in the leading chariot, propping himself up with his spear. Everyone saw how when the cornered animal sprang it was his Uncle Ay who brought him down with a marvellous throw. Yet when they returned to Thebes it had been given out that Pharaoh had slain the royal beast. Dreadful. He wouldn't go again. He was old enough now to begin to choose his way.

Looking at his own idle feet, the boy felt the feet of his litter-bearers padding in the hot dust. He shut his eyes. There were flickering shadows, then a sudden coolness— they must have entered the palace gardens. He kept his eyes shut, for that was the way to see it most intensely. The order of the fruit trees line by line; the brilliance of the flowers brought from all over the world; the neat checker of the irrigation trenches glinting in the sun; the arbours and painted kiosks and the tender-fingered gardeners coaxing new plants to grow. And round it all, of course, the protecting walls. It was his favourite place.

Flick, flick, flick the shadows of the colonnade crossed the litter. Then he heard an unexpected murmur of voices. Still he would not look—why should he?

"Wake up, Prince." His mother's grip of his arm was as commanding as usual, but there seemed something new in the use of his title. The mocking undertone had gone. He sat up abruptly and found that his litter had been drawn up beside Queen Tiye's and that a little knot of priests and palace officials stood waiting for them at the entrance to the private apartments. His newly-opened eyes had a confused impression of the bars of sunlight and shadow falling across the brown limbs and white linen when simultaneously all the bodies bowed towards him.

"Something has happened. You have to go to the Audience Hall. I expect it is the Amonites again." Queen Tiye always used this disrespectful term for the powerful priests of Amon. "Your Uncle Ay will tell you what to do." The square, muscular younger brother of the Queen stepped forward. He held the high office of Master of the Horse. Amenophis knew that his parents relied on his rock-like loyalty and his standing with the military, but for himself he neither liked nor disliked him. He laughed too much and was very dull. This morning, however, he looked grim, and seemed to want to ignore the Second Priest of Amon who advanced at his side.

"Son of the King, Beloved of Amon-Re. The Divine Pharaoh has sent me as his messenger to escort you to his Divine presence in the Hall of the Throne. There you will be proclaimed his heir, successor to the throne of Amon-Re, Lord of the Two Lands, Horus of Gold."

Amenophis stared at Ay's sweating face; it looked like a coconut husk taken from the Nile. How long was it since he had been obliged to order this man not to chuck him under the chin or tease him into military games? Now here he was bowing and reciting honorifics. As he watched, Ay came very close to the litters, and leaning towards his royal sister gave her a reassuring look. Meanwhile the priest was asserting himself with his version of the invitation. While it was correctly worded, he contrived to make it sound like a naked summons to appear before the High Priest of Amon.

Amenophis was allowed barely enough time to change his crumpled linen before being hurried into Ay's chariot. The Hall of the Throne was on the other ide of the river in eastern Thebes, in the heart of the maze-like temple city of Amon. His uncle prided himself on driving the best horses in Egypt, and they were soon away from the palace and galloping along the causeway towards the Nile. They went swaying past his father's funerary temple where the workmen were chanting as they hoisted a limestone block as big as a peasant's house. Seated before the façade were the two colossal statues of Pharaoh brought up river from Memphis by the old architect and sage, Amenhotpe. They had been set up for a year or more, but Amenophis so seldom left the palace grounds that he hadn't seen them since the dedication ceremony. Just as he was gazing up at the sixty-foot towers of gleaming pink stone that were his father enthroned as the god, Ay leant over to him and did his best to lower his voice, formed on the parade ground, so that the charioteer should not hear.

"Your father has had a falling fit. The High Priest Ipy was there and saw it happen. They are afraid of your half-brothers and the Heliopolitans. That is why you have to be openly proclaimed Crown Prince. You need not be afraid."

"I am not afraid. How is my father?"

"He had recovered before I left. No doubt you will find him upright on the throne. He has great fortitude, your Divine Father."

"Except when he has toothache."

"That is when he must suffer as a man. Now he is the god."

Amenophis fell silent. Evidently in his uncle's all-accepting mind this answer seemed as obvious as everything else. But for the boy it stirred up all kinds of dark matters that had been troubling him of late: the torments that go with the emergence of consciousness in an intelligent boy or girl as surely as those that accompanied the cutting of their teeth in infancy. Questions of death and eternity and the gods—but for Amenophis above all of the divinity of his father and, perhaps, some day, of himself. He glanced back through the flying dust to where the twin colossi shimmered against temple and sky, massive proof, surely, of a divine power.

Soon he had left all doubt behind. He always found it easy to glide away from troublesome thoughts into an entranced participation with his surroundings. His sensibility in the face of nature was already extraordinary.

The harvest was good that year, and the plots of corn stretching on for ever beside the Nile seemed almost solid, so close-packed were the ears. Surely one could walk upon them. Golden corn, golden sunlight, golden flesh of the gods—the images fleeted through his mind. Women and children came to their doors, drawn by the rare sight of the tossing feathers at the horses' heads. Little boys scrambled up the bank to get a closer view, rolling down again as the dust cloud reached them. He particularly noticed one young woman standing in a plot of melons with a child by her side. She had just cut a fine melon and held it tucked against her breast. He caught her eye, and before she bowed and signed to her son to do likewise she gave him an affectionate smile. She is just like the nicest of the harim women, he thought, only perhaps rather sweeter.

Now the riverside palms showed ahead, and Amenophis had to bring himself back to his own affairs.

"Does my father wish me to be proclaimed?" he asked abruptly.

"You are his only son by the Queen, Prince."

"But he is not fond of Ipy, and it is Ipy who wants this thing done."

Ay tightened his mouth and stared at the line of palms as though they were an enemy host.

"He is not fond of Ipy, but he wishes you to play your part. Bear yourself well though you are not soldierly." The boy frowned at him with such intensity that Ay muttered a prayer against bad luck. The prince might seem soft, might be correctly rumoured to have fallen foaming with the divine sickness, but he certainly had power of a kind in him. Royal blood was different from mortal blood. He believed this even if his sister, who had married into it, did not.

Until they embarked on the boat everything had come to Amenophis with intensity. The speed, the sights along the way, his imagining of the ceremony to come. But now the day became dreamlike. His consciousness turned into a bubble with scenes and events reflected on its brittle iridescent face. He was no longer a participator, but an onlooker, floating somewhere far above.

As they crossed the Nile, allowing the current to carry them just far enough to bring them to the quay near the Temple of Amon, river and sky were merged into a pale blue haze, milky yet dazzling to the eyes. The rocky mass of el-Quern, sheltering so many of the illustrious dead, had receded and turned to a faint pink. Heavy-laden boats dropping downstream passed in silence as though bound for the Underworld; those struggling upstream creaked and groaned as the heavy sails strained against the masts. As they approached the landing-place Amenophis could see contingents of the Royal Guard drawn up in stiff readiness, while a mob of temple priests was waiting just beyond them. Lines of Nubian soldiers held back the crowd which had come pouring from eastern Thebes as word of unusual doings spread through streets and markets. So many people, so horribly many bodies. The boy floated yet further away. Perhaps he was Horus already, hovering on beating wings.

The processional approach to the temple seemed to last for ever, although the distance was not great. The prince sat upright in his palanquin, staring past the Second Priest of Amon, who preceded him as the bearer of the sacred wand, to the dark heads of the Guard. The other priests had formed a line behind the palanquin, while Ay brought up the rear with another detachment of Guards. The march was set at the slowest pace, and again and again they stopped to pay due honour at shrines along the way. Too many people and too many gods, Amenophis thought. All these bejewelled images with the heads of birds and beasts suddenly meant nothing to him; were

even a little ridiculous. Now they had entered an avenue
of sphinxes of a kind which his father had had carved in
their hundreds to line the sacred ways of Thebes. All identical, the stony eyes in the long, inane faces glared across
the passing column. Amenophis found himself counting
the pairs as slowly he was borne abreast of them and left
them behind.

At last a gigantic gateway rose before them like a cliff,
flags lifting softly on the eight flagpoles. As they passed
through it and on into the temple, leaving the sunlight
behind, for a moment Amenophis could see nothing. Then
he was aware of Ipy the High Priest advancing towards
him. He stopped before the palanquin and made an
almost imperceptible obeisance. No one had told the boy
what he should do. He remained inflexibly upright,
merely raising his hand slightly in what he hoped was a
regal acknowledgment.

This encounter over, Amenophis became conscious of
noise and confusion all about him. Here was no state entry
such as he had pictured. It seemed that only the High
Priest and a few of his followers, who now made a circle
round them, knew that he had arrived. The pillared hall
was surging with the most various crowd he had ever seen.
The columns themselves were gaudy enough, and between
them moved men of every skin colour from pink to black,
in every dress from a loin cloth to gorgeous cloaks. All were
alike in bearing gifts. Panniers of rare fruits, caskets of
jewels, ebony in great chunks, dazzling birds, leopard
skins. Close at hand was a party of Nubians. Two were
stooped below a six-foot elephant tusk; several stood with
gold ingots balanced on their shoulders; while four huge
fellows had a grinning and grotesquely-horned head on a
tray suspended between them. It was the head of a giant
rhino hunted down somewhere far to the south and
brought to Pharaoh for its magic properties.

Just beyond the Nubians a group of black-bearded
Asiatics was leading an Arab horse saddled and harnessed
in crimson leather, and beyond them again, their fair skin
and hair in surprising contrast, were several Mycenaean
youths bearing great painted wine-jars. They had with

them a tall girl in a long flounced skirt; her head hung down so that her reddish hair curtained her face. There was a babble of voices in a dozen languages, a medley of colours and smells; the Arab whinnied and farted, the tropical birds whistled and shrieked. Somewhere far off there was the bellow of a bull.

The throng appeared chaotic, but was in fact slowly moving down the Hall, and there, at the end of an aisle, Amenophis could see one figure seated above the rest, motionless and rigid as the colossi by the roadside, and given an air of superhuman height by the spire of the Double Crown. He was looking at the Pharaoh Amenophis III, Horus of Gold, Ruler of the Two Lands, Son of the Sun: his father who yesterday had smashed an ivory chair because his tooth ached.

"Your Divine Father has determined to receive tribute. This should have taken place before noon, but was prevented by the absence of the Son of the Sun."

Ipy, to his chagrin, was a small man, but with features so perfect that no artist need idealize them. As he spoke his black eyes flashed a disparagement at the host of tribute bearers. The prince did not need great penetration to see that Ipy had been thwarted in the detail of his plan.

"Pharaoh is gracious to the humblest of his servants," said Amenophis, repeating a phrase he had heard somewhere and wondering desperately how to deport himself. At this moment Ay pushed forward. Wherever he was he seemed to be out of doors.

"We can go ahead with the sacrifice to Min. If the Prince will consent, there is no need for the Divine Presence." Ay was an hereditary servant of this god of generation. He offered his hand to his nephew as a sign that he should leave the palanquin. The priestly party quickly re-forming in procession, they moved off through the less crowded side of the Hall, passed through several dim and awkward passages and came out into a small temple courtyard. Even as they entered it, a bellow echoed round the colonnade. A bull white as the milk of the many cows he had sired was the centre of a group of nervous attendants at the end of the court. Behind, a black rectangle in the façade, was the portal of a chapel.

Amenophis was led inside. It was pitch dark save for a shaft of sunlight pouring through a small hole in the roof and striking the statue of Min pedestalled on the floor below. The ray made the black basalt shine in the darkness, and revealed the phallus projecting from the mummy-like body. The impact on his senses of this shrine was so violent that Amenophis did not hear a word of the prayer for the continuance of the Royal House which Ipy was reciting.

Through the incense stole a taurine smell: the beast had been led to the very portal. As the litany went on and the boy found his eyes returning again and again to the potent rod projecting above him, there was the beginning of another roar that ended in a gurgle, a thud, and then silence. Ay entered, holding a bowl of bloody tissues, and handed it to the High Priest. Ipy took Amenophis's hand, dipped it in the yielding mass and applied it to the statue. The warm, the soft, the red; the cold, the hard, the black—and filling his mind's eye a vision of the noble, mutilated bull outside, bound and bloody.

A frightful nausea filled the boy. Surely he would vomit or faint. But Ay was there at his elbow. He must show that a prince did not have to play at soldiers to be in command of himself. He swallowed down the foul juices in his mouth, extended his reddened hand below a ewer poured by the Second Priest, made an obeisance to Min, and stepped back into the sunshine.

The horror of this half-hour had brought Amenophis back into himself, but now he felt more remote than ever. Indeed, afterwards he had difficulty in remembering what took place.

When he returned to the Hall it had been emptied of the former bizarre crowd only to be repeopled by priests. Priests of Amon preponderated, but representatives had been summoned from all the temples of Thebes. The hundreds of white-clad figures moving decorously among the forest of pillars seemed to Amenophis like disembodied spirits. The painted reliefs of gods and battles on the walls oppressed him, closing in on him from all sides. He found himself installed on an ebony stool, and in front of him, raised on the sacred throne of Egypt, was Pharaoh. He noticed that this figure, which seemed to be that of a stranger, was swaying slightly, and that the royal face had been painted to conceal its pallor.

A few stewards were there to maintain the dignity proper to the throne, and the vizier, the King's friend and Ipy's rival, stood on the pyramid of steps below his master. Most of the court officials, however, had absented themselves. Ipy was not to have a full court to increase his small triumph.

The movements of groups of priests, the raising and lowering of arms in unison, the recitations heavy with honorific titles, bored the boy into a torpor. He looked on in dull despair to see a pink sunset cloud framed in one of the lights below the roof. Then at last the preliminaries were over. The bevy of priests nearest to the throne parted and Ipy himself could be seen bearing the diadem of the Crown Prince from the shrine of Wadjet where it had rested. The vizier crossed to Amenophis, took him by the shoulder and guided him to the second step below the throne. Ipy appeared on his other side, and his father was stretching out his hands to crown him, but the hands were trembling and fumbling so much that, forestalling Ipy, the boy himself pulled on the diadem.

He felt the golden band above his brow and the scratch of the plaited tress of gold wire hanging beside his ear. He was the Crown Prince, heir to divinity and a mighty empire. He felt absolutely nothing. Instead the sacrificial bowl, red and steaming, returned to swim before his eyes.

After that he only remembered a childish sense of disappointment and desolation until they were outside the temple, he and Ay and a temple steward and a few of the Guards. El-Quern, so faint and distant when he had last seen it, was now a sharp black pyramid against the afterglow. The scent from domestic fires where humble Egyptian women were cooking evening meals came trespassing among the temples, defeating the incense of the priests. Then Amenophis noticed three figures waiting for them;

they were standing at the edge of the sacred lake near the great, squat sculpture of the god Khepri in the form of a scarab beetle.

"Greetings, Prince Amenophis. The gods protect you, Crown Prince. Wrap this round you, dear nephew, you must be tired and the evening is cold." It was his Aunt Tey, Ay's wife, who had been waiting with her woman- and man-servant. She folded a woollen cloak round him and gave him a homely pat just as she did in the old days when he was a little boy. What wonderful comfort there was in that touch and in the simple, ordinary words. Coming after the surfeit of ritual phrases, they restored him and his senses to life. Tey turned to her husband.

"He can't return to the Palace tonight. He looks half dead already. He must sleep with us. We can send a messenger to the Queen. Would you like that, Nephew?"

"I should like it very much, thank you, Madam. And there is no need to send a messenger." He knew that by this hour his mother would have retired into her apart- ments with the scribe Kheruef.

"Very well," said Ay, "I will send for his bearers. They are waiting at the Nile Gate."

"I have asses waiting. They will carry us more quickly."

"It is not fit for the Crown Prince to ride through the streets. I cannot agree to it."

"But I wish it, my Uncle. It is my will." Even in the dusk Ay could see the implacable look which the boy had turned upon him.

"He can draw something over his head." Tey spoke with a beaming smile as though she had made the cleverest suggestion in the world. Amenophis saw her smile, and her figure now rapidly putting on flesh, and felt a sudden love of all women. How much more sensible they were. How much nearer to the truth of things.

"Very well. It's all out of order. But then everything today has been out of order. Very well. But let his head be covered, or we shall have ten thousand gapers." That evening Ay seemed very unlike the successful commander of men. Tey drew a fine linen scarf from her own shoulders and wrapped it round the prince's head and neck, in the

manner of a Bedouin in from the desert. He could feel the
gentle warmth from her body hidden in the cloth. The
man had gone for the asses and soon the horny tappings
of their hoofs sounded on the paving.

The house of Ay and Tey was on the southern side of
East Thebes, near the river. The distance after they left
the Temple precinct therefore was not very great, yet they
had to pass through a small part of the town. At first they
were on another of the sacred ways where the sphinxes
showed pale in the darkening air. Then they entered a
quarter mostly inhabited by masons and other builders
employed on the many royal projects there on the east
bank. Amenophis, who had seldom been allowed into the
city, and never into ordinary streets, was fascinated by the
lighted interiors of houses and wine shops, the little stalls
in alleyways with torches flickering beside them, by the
bargaining voices of housewives and the sudden wild
scamperings of packs of small children. Soon they came
out on the river bank, and here the drifting sandy dust was
so thick that their donkeys' hoofs trotted in silence. The
after-glow was now narrowed to an intense band; the
shapes of a few late-moving boats were black against the
water.

At the monumental entrance gate servants came forward
with torches to lead them to the house. They went
through a pillared hall, then Ay flung open a door and
ushered Amenophis into a room which seemed brilliantly
lit after their ride through the dusk. The painted walls
glowed from the light of a score of lamps. This was very
much Tey's room, comfortable, warm, abundantly furnished. The couches were piled with cushions, the doorways masked with fine red hangings.

"No need for disguise here! Let me see my Crown
Prince." And Tey unwound the scarf, took off the cloak.
"Still pale. Here, drink this wine. What a day you have
had, dear Nephew. Those priests of Amon have no pity.
How they go on. And you were at the centre of it, poor
boy. You couldn't go to sleep—as I do." As she was
rattling on, the hangings of a door at the far end of the
room twitched for a moment, then parted just enough to

let through a slender little creature who then stood nervously before them.

"Come, my little one. Come to salute the Prince Amenophis who is honouring our house. Today he has been crowned in the Temple, but still he won't cut your head off." As the small girl walked stealthily across the floor, every line of her delicate form visible through the transparent shift, Tey turned to her and with delight in her voice said, "Crown Prince, let me present to you the treasure of our house—our Nefertiti." The small girl made her formal obeisance with grace, and spoke her greeting in a voice remarkably soft and controlled. Amenophis realized with pleasure that she was not shy as he had thought. As she stood there eyeing him, she made him think of the gazelles he had seen in the desert, watching for a moment with a passionate physical intensity, before bounding away with their featherweight strength. He almost expected that she, too, would flee from him. How entrancing she was! He smiled at her, and his face, already lengthening and a little heavy, was transformed. As Tey had long ago discovered, he had extraordinary charm when his spirit was quickened.

"I am glad to meet you, Nefertiti. I have heard of you from the Queen, my mother." He hesitated between formal and informal speech. "I am sorry that you live on this side of the river."

"I have seen your palace. And the lake. And I looked into the garden—it is a lovely garden."

"Yes. It is where I most of all like to be. You must come and be with me there."

When, an hour later, having been fed and bathed and rubbed with oils until all the strain of the day had left his body, Amenophis was left lying in bed, he found himself thinking of Nefertiti. It was true that his mother had spoken of a little girl who lived with Ay and Tey, but who, he seemed to remember, was said not to be their own child. Why in the world had she never told him how pretty she was, and how much more wonderful than other children? In his mind's eye he saw her steeped in a golden light.

The hangings at the door stirred, just as they had done in the withdrawing room. And again it was Nefertiti who slipped through them. Eagerly he raised himself on his elbow.

"May I approach you, Prince Amenophis?"

"Yes, yes. Come to the foot of my bed."

"My mother would blame me for coming, but my nurses let me do what I like. I wanted to let my cat see you." Amenophis looked up at her. She was standing with a silky-haired, yellow-eyed cat in her arms, her own triangular face above the cat's, her pointed chin nestling between its ears.

"I hoped you had come to say goodnight to me. Why do you bother about the cat?"

"All cats are a little divine, and you will be the god one day, won't you, Crown Prince?" She spoke with such seriousness that Amenophis felt quite at ease in replying.

"Yes—unless I die before my Divine Father. But I want to be a different kind of god. I pray for it every day. I believe that the Sun God will guide me."

Nefertiti gazed at him with an awe roused by the feeling in his voice. She was so small that the pendant tail of the cat reached to the hem of her night shift, yet the essence of the future woman was present in her. Suddenly, without a word, she dropped on to her knees and bowed her forehead to the ground, bending the cat with her. It was a homage paid only to Pharaoh and the other divinities at the highest moments of the temple rituals.

The cat escaped from its uncomfortable position and jumped on to the prince's bed, looking disdainfully from one exalted child to the other. Then gingerly it stepped over Amenophis and fitted itself behind his bent knees.

"It knows you," Nefertiti whispered. "Yes, it recognizes you."

Amenophis let his head fall back, and smiled as he saw the curtains move. He had never spoken of these things to anyone before. Now he could sleep.

II

T H E shade of the canopy made an island in the sunlight of the harim courtyard. Amenophis and Mina shared its privacy—happy islanders. Fans swayed above their heads, but to them the young men who wielded them were no more presences than the fish turning and turning in the lily pond at their feet.

The boy leant forward eagerly in the inlaid chair that seemed too large and rich for him. "Tell me what life in Knossos was like. You are different from Egyptian women. Different from all the women in the harim. You are so much just yourself. Was there something very special about Knossos?"

Mina shook her head until the curls framing her face swung across her cheeks. She was barely forty, and by Egyptian standards looked far younger. She still always wore the long, flounced dresses of Crete. They weren't very well suited to the climate, but Pharaoh had liked to see her in them during the days when she was in high favour, and now she clung to the style as a support to her individuality. Besides, young Egyptian women were so boringly straight and slender: her way of dressing helped to show that it was possible to have full hips and breasts and still keep a narrow waist.

"It was all such a long time ago, Prince. I was hardly older than you are when we had to leave. . . . I can't remember. And it makes me sad to think about it."

"I am sure if I had to leave Thebes now I should remember everything. And if it makes you sad to think about Knossos, you can't have forgotten it. Tell me—I command you." To soften his words he smiled up at her, his wide, thick lips, which harim gossip attributed to Negro blood in Queen Tiye, curling up at the corners.

"You are too quick at argument for me, Amenophis, but what can I tell you? Our palace was very much like this in some ways—with courts and gardens. Only less

grand and more agreeable. Then we had flowers and birds
and animals painted on the walls just as you do—"

"No, *no*, Mina. You know that isn't what I want." He
picked up her right hand, plaiting his fingers between hers
and giving an impatient squeeze and shake. "You must
tell me what your life was like, what it felt like to be you."

"I suppose the great difference from life here for us
women was that we believed ourselves to be every bit as
good as the men. Perhaps rather better, for we were the
bearers of life. Daughters of the Great Goddess herself. So
we felt quite independent—we would have been far too
proud to plot and wheedle as you have to here if you want
to get your own way. Then we didn't care much about
morality—women don't if left to themselves, Prince. We
only care about love." A happy look came into Mina's
face as she paused, letting her thoughts play with her
favourite subject.

"But didn't the priests keep you in order?"

Mina giggled. "Priests of the Great Goddess had other
things to think about. And of course a lot of them were
women. Don't forget, Amenophis—though goodness
knows, you're too young, I ought not to talk to you like
this—don't forget that if no one has thought up a sin and
given it a name then it doesn't exist. If there's no word for
fornication, there's no sin. That is how I see it. Oh, I dare
say we were all very frivolous, but we did seem to be
happy. There was much more laughing at Knossos than
here in Thebes. Many of the things I've told you I got
from my mother, and perhaps in the misery of exile she
idealized our old life. But I do remember the laughter."

"And the Goddess was really the chief of all your
divinities?"

"Of course. We saw her as the source of all life on earth
—wild life, garden life, human life. Everything. And of
love too, for that is the beginning of life. That is why we
gave her doves, for they are the most amorous birds."

"I think I should like that," said Amenophis earnestly,
but then his face clouded. "But that would mean putting
Hathor above Re—that couldn't be right."

"But then you make Hathor into a cow. That was the

thing that astonished us most when we first came to
Egypt. The Goddess as a cow!"

"But your Goddess was very fond of bulls—so perhaps
she was much the same really."

"Oh no. We should never have given her long ears and
horns—and a face like a bun." Mina giggled again, but
seeing that the boy looked really upset she went on hastily.
"But don't take any notice of me, Prince. Women never
understand theology. And then in Crete we met people
from so many lands and all of them had different gods—
some of them such very odd ones. I'm afraid we came
to regard it all as rather a joke. I realize now that it
isn't."

The boy fell silent, frowning and fidgeting. Mina picked
up her neglected embroidery and the soft rustle and creak
of the fans was the only sound. Then Amenophis looked
up, still scowling. "I detest some of our gods. I was nearly
sick the day of my coronation. A sacrifice to Min. . . ."

"Oh well, Min!" Mina wanted to be sympathetic, but
she could never prevent her eyes from lighting up at any
hint of copulation. At that moment they heard voices and
scampering footsteps. Several small children ran through
the door leading into the court from the garden, and then,
seeing the awning and the figures below, hastily withdrew
again. After a moment three or four ladies entered the
court followed by their maids-in-waiting, nurses and a
little procession of children, all going on tip-toe, and all
peeping at Amenophis. A tall figure detached itself from
the rest and strode forward. It was Gilukhipa the Mitannian princess, a strong-featured, brown-haired woman a
little older than Mina who stood a forehead above most
Egyptian men. In her wake, making herself as unobtrusive
as possible, was Ninsun, a royal lady who had come from
Babylonia longer ago than most people could remember.
She had once been plump, but now the flesh had sagged,
dragging the skin into a thousand wrinkles. Her lips were
so much gathered into creases that it was said that with
Ninsun it would be difficult to tell the mouth above from
the mouth below—and this observation had earned her
an unkind nickname. She was a poor, forgotten, feeble

creature, but she liked to look after the harim children and was always bribing them with sweets.

Gilukhipa approached, making an obeisance that was hardly more than a nod. "May we join you, Crown Prince? We are sick of our own company, and have had no chance to greet you since your elevation."

"Yes, Gilukhipa, but send the children away—they will disturb me." In some moods Amenophis loved to be the centre of a group of women. The nurses and their charges were waved over to the far side of the court, where they started a nervous and over-decorous game of ball. Several of the ladies approached the awning, while Ninsun hesitated, stepping this way and that trying to decide which party to join. Finally she sat down behind Gilukhipa as the attendants ran out with more chairs and cushions. The ladies and their maids-in-waiting, all in the dresses of their native lands, looked bright and frilly as a flower bed, while the fans bent above them like palm trees in the wind.

"We were talking about women," said Mina inaccurately.

"What a thing to talk about when you've got them all round you—assorted shapes, colours, sizes and habits. Nowadays whether it's for zoological and botanical gardens or for harims, kings collect their specimens from far and wide. And I suppose you were boasting, Mina, about the 'high status of women' in Knossos? Well, Prince, we didn't do badly in Mitanni either. Lord, how miserable I was when I was first cooped up here—once the excitement of the journey was over. Do you remember?" Gilukhipa turned to appeal to two women who had been among the hundreds of girls forming her marriage retinue. They assented dully, having long ago lost all interest in the fortunes of the princess—and indeed in their own. It was Ninsun who responded with unexpected feeling.

"I shall never forget it. You were such a splendid young thing, so free and unceremonious. You frightened me. And although for months Pharaoh had eyes for no one else, that didn't seem to make matters any better for you. But if you had been born in Babylon you would all know that Egyptian women are quite fortunate. Looking back on it now, it seems to me that we had no choice but to be either chattels or disreputable women—harlots almost. It wasn't until you came, Gilukhipa—and then you, Mina—that I realized that women could be anything else. Could have souls, perhaps you might say."

"Poor Ninsun," said Mina unpityingly.

"Yes, poor Ninsun. But frankly, I don't believe you would have had a very strong soul wherever you were born. Anyway, here we all are in Thebes and here we shall die. I've learnt to put a good face on it—but as I used to say in the day when I cared about my looks—the only reward a woman gets for laughing at the world is crowsfeet." Gilukhipa had indeed very deep crowsfeet, which added to her formidable appearance. As so often happened with Amenophis, his imagination had been following its own paths. Gilukhipa's words about the women of the harim coming from far and wide had conjured up an intense picture of the world stretching out to the horizons —of torrid Nubia and the land of Punt, of the long course of the Nile and the ocean and its shores and islands, of the valley of the Two Rivers. And then he had seen all these brides coming to the palace, leaving homes so various, making long, dangerous journeys because their fathers and his father willed it so. Again, as before with his Aunt Tey, he felt an all-embracing love of women, of the way they endured things and got along together with a kind of affection.

"Isn't it extraordinary," he said, assuming that his listeners had been following his thoughts. "You all grew up so far apart and so differently. You all worshipped different gods. And yet now you understand one another and seem very much alike in many ways."

"As far as I've ever been able to see, human beings are much the same everywhere. Neither better nor worse. Men sometimes have to pretend that they are to make an excuse for going to war and cutting off their prisoners' heads and hands and burning cities. But women, who have so many experiences in common—most of them foul ones —know that we're all the same under the sun."

"Yes—and under the same sun. ... " Amenophis slipped

off again in pursuit of his own ideas, though with half an ear alert to the talk of his companions.

"The Prince doesn't know much about harim jealousies," said Mina. "Still, I suppose we have all settled down together pretty well. And I don't suppose there will be any additions now."

"You sound very knowing. But you're wrong," Gilukhipa answered, with one of the wide grins that were still attractive.

"Wrong?" Ninsun craned forward, her little wattles seeming to tremble with curiosity. "Do you mean to say that Pharaoh . . .?"

"I do. I still have contacts with my royal brother, you know. And I hear that he is negotiating with Pharaoh for the despatch of my niece, Tadukhipa. She's about fifteen, poor child."

"Good gracious!" Mina exclaimed, not without a certain delight. "And when will she be coming?"

"There are difficulties. Tushratta feels important now that he's conquered Assyria, and he's insisting that my niece should become Great Wife and what he calls 'Mistress of Egypt'!"

"Evidently he's counting without Queen Tiye." Mina dropped her voice and glanced at the boy, who appeared to be far away. "I don't suppose she'll come at all, then. And what would be the good if she did?"

"He still tries, you know."

"So much the worse. I don't believe anything much has happened for years." Amenophis was well aware that they were talking disrespectfully about his father. He didn't care. Perhaps he saw dimly that no king was a divinity in his own harim, and moreover that morning he felt strangely in tune with the women. He made them glance guiltily at one another when he said, "When did my father last have a child? Would any of these be his?" He pointed towards the ball players.

"Heavens no," Gilukhipa replied. "As far as I know his last child was a daughter born eight or nine years ago. But what a question to ask, Crown Prince."

"Who is she? Why isn't she here?" Amenophis was still

no more than idly inquisitive. Mina foolishly intervened. "We can't tell you that, Prince Amenophis. She was sent away—a long way away."

"Tell me, Gilukhipa."

"Really, Prince Amenophis, I forget. It's not interesting." But the boy was very much interested now he saw that something was being kept from him. He jumped down from his chair, his sandals clapping sharply on the paving. He pointed his finger at Ninsun, looking at the old lady with his extraordinarily compelling gaze, saying nothing. She winced and quailed. "Oh no, Crown Prince. Oh well, now things have gone so far . . . it can't do any harm. It's all blown over now, I dare say. Her name is Nefertiti."

"Nefertiti!"

"Why couldn't you hold your tongue, Ninsun," said Gilukhipa roughly, then turning to the boy, "There's no great mystery. Her mother came from some island in the ocean."

"Cyprus," Mina quickly intervened.

"Cyprus, then. She had been a priestess of the moon there. It was said the temple had been sacked by pirates and they brought her to Egypt, where they knew they would find a good market. Kritas was the most beautiful woman I have ever seen." Gilukhipa seemed reluctant to go on. Now that her tongue had been set free, Mina felt no such scruples.

"Yes, she was so beautiful that she was bound to end up here. But she was pale and bright and disembodied like her own goddess. All spirit. She never learnt to speak a word of Egyptian and avoided us as much as she could. It was like having a ghost in the harim. At first, in spite of her beauty, Pharaoh took no notice of her. But then, suddenly, he did. Perhaps, if you'll forgive me, Prince, more out of cruelty than desire. She got desperate; we hardly ever saw her. Then one night she was fished out of the river, and we learnt that she was with child."

"Of course she lived, and the baby too. If she'd been an ordinary woman wanting a child, no doubt it would have been still-born," said Gilukhipa.

"The rest of the story is almost too dreadful to tell," said

Mina with evident intention of telling it. "At just about the time when Kritas jumped into the Nile Pharaoh had the first of his attacks. Until then he'd been very young and vigorous for his years. Diviners told him that it was due to someone ill-wishing him, and they put the blame on Kritas."

"I am sure she had a great deal to do with it . . . or I was sure at the time." Ninsun nodded her head and went on nodding it.

"Considering how vilely you behaved in the matter, I think you might be quiet about it," said Gilukhipa. "Kritas was had up for some kind of examination. It was said that she had used the moon to cause Pharaoh's sickness, and Ninsun here testified that she had seen her working spells."

"I only told the truth, or so I believed. I was suffering from indigestion as I so often do, and went along to the closet in the middle of the night. Looking out of the window I saw the priestess standing naked in the rays of the moon. Stark naked she was—I was terribly shocked. Then she started slashing her face; I still remember how in the moonlight the blood looked quite black as it ran down her cheeks. It was all just as I described it at the enquiry."

"But then you said that you saw her send an evil spirit into the Pharaoh's chamber."

"Well, what was she doing there if not evoking the moon for some wicked purpose? And I did see a bat fly past her towards the palace." Gilukhipa stared at her with a scorn that might have brought a falcon down from the sky.

"They threatened me with torture and worse," she muttered. "I only wanted to live."

"And so Kritas had to die. But still, Ninsun, I don't suppose you did anything but make it easier for them. The Diviners *know*. They're the same all over the world whether they use birds or livers or falling sticks. Well, Prince, I don't blame you for looking impatient. As soon as the baby was born, the mother was put to death—they couldn't do it sooner because she was carrying the royal seed. I'll spare you the details. Pharaoh would have liked the baby girl destroyed too, thinking her dangerous. But as the royal stock is sacred she was sent away—somewhere far to the south. It was rumoured she was suckled by a Negress. Anyway, years afterwards when Tey went with your uncle on one of his Nubian expeditions, she tracked her down— out of the warmth of her heart—and brought her back. She said nothing, keeping her quietly in the house and saying she was an orphaned relative—which is true in a sense. It was only recently that someone let the cat out of the bag."

"So she is royal," Amenophis cried, his eyes shining. "Re has given her to me. Dear Gilukhipa, darling Mina, you have made me happy." To her astonishment, the boy seized up Mina's hand again, gave it a nip with his teeth, and flung it back on to her lap.

"Then you have met Nefertiti, Prince?"

"I love her." Never in his life was Amenophis to have any desire to conceal his feelings. They were reality and had to be uttered. "She is lovely, and I think she understands god. When I was in Ay's house she came into my room and worshipped me."

The ladies looked at one another, half amused, half solemn. Two of the ladies-in-waiting whispered together.

"I must find my mother. I will send for Nefertiti at once."

"It may be difficult, Prince." Gilukhipa spoke with unusual gentleness.

"The Nile is not so wide."

"But much history flows between you."

"You don't understand. This isn't like an ordinary wish. It is something which can't be prevented." He signed to his attendants and set off for the Queen's part of the palace. As he went the ladies rose all together and bowed with a certain genuine awe.

"So he's in love," said Mina, jangling her curls. "Tiye will be furious."

"I have never felt such a fool." In spite of her words Gilukhipa looked round at them all with some self-satisfaction. "For twenty years and more I've seen myself as the sophisticated cosmopolitan, the woman who has experienced everything and can never be taken by sur-

prise. And I've always sworn that young Amenophis's
interests would lie the other way. Some intelligent, well-
built noble, perhaps, since he's sensitive and doesn't like
soldiers. But now it's a small girl—and the daughter of a
moon priestess too." Her loud, throaty laugh reached even
the children, who stopped their game to stare. "Well, I'm
glad to be proved an idiot if it means the succession will
be secure—though why I should care, heaven knows."

"But he is so young—and the Queen will never allow
it." Ninsun pursed her lips until every little furrow was
visible.

"Have you ever tried to stop Prince Amenophis when
he's in a mood like this?" asked Mina. "He's delicate.
They say he has the divine sickness—though I've never
seen it. But he has a brazen will in that queer head of his."

"And fire, too," said Gilukhipa. "That is his great
virtue. Tiye will be well advised to give way. After all, it
was years ago." Suddenly she looked puzzled, and added
in a different tone, "Does something odd strike you? Why
the sudden ardour? Why didn't he go after her as soon as
they had met? Instead he kindles only when he knows she
is of the royal seed and could be legitimate Queen and
Great Wife. I thought that for once we were going to have
a Pharaoh of fire and feeling. But can he turn his ardour
on and off at will? If he can at his age then he'll soon come
to accept all the old routine that has bored everyone to
death for centuries."

"Poor Amenophis. He has feeling all right. I have seen
him rescue a beetle from a bonfire—and you know how
sweet he can be to us old has-beens. But I think he broods
on his own divinity—on becoming Horus and Son of the
Sun. Who can blame him?"

Amenophis himself, now hurrying through the maze of
the palace, would have been astonished to hear this conversation. He would have seen nothing puzzling in his
conduct. He had been thinking of Nefertiti ever since their
encounter, had been holding her in his imagination, talking to her—even kissing her. But it was only when the
news of her birth penetrated his mind like an arrow that
he had had one of his sudden, blinding convictions that

she was meant for him, that their coming together had been divinely willed.

He went abruptly into his mother's own apartments, a sanctuary of her private life where he was almost a stranger. The Queen always rose late and was just having her face done, but seeing his uncontrollable excitement she sent her maids away. She half turned towards her son, but remained seated at her dressing-table, which was scattered with alabaster cosmetic jars and palettes wet with green and black eye shadow. She felt absurdly vulnerable without her make-up, and irritated by the boy's intensity. Yet she decided to handle him lightly, and quickly mustered her maternal powers.

"I hear she is a very pretty child. And I'm delighted that you fancy you love her—very well, that you do love her, then. That promises well for the future and the Queen we shall find for you. But you can't pretend you're a man yet, Amenophis, and as for Nefertiti, she's no more than a little girl."

"That makes no difference. The gods have given her understanding. And me also. I shall never think of any other woman, however many you find for me. Never."

"Women! It's hardly a matter of that yet, is it, gosling? And if you have understanding, you must know that Pharaoh won't let the child come near the palace."

"It isn't that sort of understanding the gods give."

Queen Tiye, who had been supporting her chin on a rounded but well-muscled arm, now let it drop and her fingers beat on the table. A sensuous woman, she hated passion, especially passionate thought.

"Well then, let *me* have some of your love." She tried to look pathetic and tender. "You know I don't have an easy time with Pharaoh now he's so often sick. If he hears so much as a mention of that woman's name he will go out of his mind and I shall suffer. Have consideration for me. I am getting old and need your help." The boy moved nearer, hesitating, half responding to the familiar ties and his own pity, half suspicious. She turned right round and drew him close to her side, confident of victory.

"Thank you, Amenophis, thank you, my Crown Prince.

I knew you wouldn't hurt me. Try to forget her for my
sake and you won't find it difficult. Why, when I was a
young girl I used to fall in and out of love a dozen times a
year, yet each time . . ." Amenophis stiffened and pulled
away.

"Be quiet, be quiet." He shrank from his mother's
exposure of her quality. "My love is not like yours, and I
cannot obey you even if I would. This is the will of Re, I
know it is, and I must obey *him*."

"Bless the boy!" cried Queen Tiye with a natural exasperation that was only to be preferred to her act as the
skilful mother. "And isn't Pharaoh himself the Son of Re—
don't you have to obey *him*? Pharaoh would not let Nefertiti near us. If I'd had any sense I would have told him
when I learnt that that fool Tey was hiding her over there.
She must be sent away again—back to Nubia."

"You know that you don't care about Pharaoh. You
know that you could have your way with my father if you
wished. What about Kheruef? You have what you
want. . . ."

The Queen leapt to her feet and appeared to be about
to shake the boy. He, filled with blind despair at his
mother's inadequacy, at the beastliness in himself that had
taken him by surprise and by a sense of outrage, burst into
tears. Lights began to float round him like fireflies and he
ran from the room. He blundered almost blindly along,
the fireflies growing thicker. As he went down a passage
he heard a small cry suppressed in a way that seemed to
give it added pain. He paused at a doorway, hearing
heavy breathing just on the other side of the curtain. He
pulled back the embroidered cloth. There, horribly close
to him, was Pharaoh, his face distorted and sweating.
Tied face down on the bed lay a naked girl with curving,
bright weals on her back and buttocks. Amenophis recognized the red hair that fell from the pillow to the ground—
it was the girl whom he had seen among the tribute-
bearers in the temple. Then the fireflies grew larger,
turned into little flames, crowded together, filled the whole
of his vision. He clutched the curtain, pulling it down with
him as he fell.

A disc of fire hung before him supported on vast wings, each feather à flame. It came nearer and nearer until the wings were out of sight—but he could still feel them beating behind him. He was in the presence of the sun. The sun was everywhere and everything, yet he was not consumed. For he stood on the little hill, on the steps of the throne, and the waters were about him. An opening appeared in the sun, a mouth, a crimson cavern, a place of birth. The air was full of a singing tone, a humming, a wire of light stretched tightly in his head. Then a tiny figure appeared within the opening, and motionless they moved towards one another. He saw it was Nefertiti, framed in pale light against the blood-dark cave. They met in the cave mouth and Nefertiti's eyes shone like little suns. There were no words but the cave itself uttered, "My son and my daughter." Nefertiti's face came closer and closer then suddenly they were one. The humming wire of light, the beating wings of the sun god; light, light, tighter and more shrill.

Someone was holding his legs, and there were horrible thick fingers in his mouth. He bit, the fingers were withdrawn and his lips were wiped with linen. He felt weak yet radiant, sick yet triumphant. He opened his eyes and smiled at the crowding faces.

III

F OR several days after his attack Amenophis was confined to his apartments in the Palace. This was at his own wish. While his illness left him bodily weak, the intensity of his vision gave him spiritual strength, and absolute intellectual certainty as well. He spent much of his time reclining among cushions on his day couch, his eyes closed while he rehearsed every phase of his experience. But sometimes he would stare at the ceiling, prettily painted with doves, dreaming of the future and how he would shape it. For he had the blissful sense of accomplishment of a woman who has just given birth to a child, combined with the shining conviction of some great prophet of hope.

The only thing which he wished to forget was the spectacle of his father and the Mycenaean girl. This he consigned to the shadowy places of his mind where it lurked in close company with memories of the sacrifice to Min.

As soon as he was fully conscious, Queen Tiye had come to sit beside him. All that was genuinely maternal in her powerful nature was now aroused, and the two were easily reconciled. Amenophis allowed her to stroke his hair while he described his vision and expounded its meaning. But he held himself emotionally apart from her. He would never again be the boy seeking security and oblivion under his mother's cloak. Nor would he ever again feel quite subject to her will.

Indeed, even at this first visit, when his limbs were like water weeds and his face the colour of Nile mud, he quietly took it for granted that his vision expressed the divine intention and made his union with Nefertiti as inevitable as if it had already happened. Queen Tiye did not oppose him. She hardly could at such a moment, but her acceptance, though grudging at first, became more real as she listened to the Prince's eager words. Against the promptings of her usually triumphant common sense, she was impressed by her son, recognizing the extraordinary strength that was growing in him—even though it was so unlike her own. She was still prosaic, she still did not see a future god lying there on the couch, but she could not altogether resist the poetic force of his imagination.

She visited him several times, but only to ask how he was and bring him offerings of fruit and of scented lotions for his forehead. Then on the fourth day she entered just as Amenophis was dismissing a little band of Palace musicians who had been playing to him for an hour or more. He felt so much better that he had suddenly made up his mind to go out into the garden. The Queen turned and went with him, waving back the servants who as usual were preparing to follow them with fans, a canopy and folding chairs. After so many days in the cool dimness of his apartments, the sunlight struck Amenophis with an impact that made him pause. Quickly he raised his arms in salutation. Tiye said, "So you are greeting the Aten? In a way this is what I want to talk to you about, my son." She took his arm (reflecting that not long ago she would have held his hand) and led him towards a shady walk between pleached sycomores.

"Prince," she began as they walked slowly along, "I can see that the time has come for me to take you into my confidence. You are too young in some ways, but old for your years in others. People who are clever and fond of reading are often like that. Perhaps some part of you will never grow up. But I have enough sense to recognize that already you understand things that I never shall if I live till the River runs dry. In any case you are intelligent, quite intelligent enough to understand politics."

"But, Mother, I am not interested in politics."

"My poor son! And I have just said you are intelligent! You are Crown Prince, which means that you can't escape from politics unless you want to be a feeble puppet, worked by someone else's strong hand. And you know whose hand it will be? The High Priest of Amon's."

"No. I would not allow that."

"Then you'll have to stoop to politics. For more than half my life I've had to struggle behind the scenes to try to stop the Amonites getting the throne under their thumbs. Pharaoh has done his best, but really he was always more interested in hunting and women. I think you have some idea of why Ipy staged your proclamation the other day? He thinks you will always be a weakling and that he can control you. By bad luck I ran to daughters, and you were born late. I have had to work with some of Pharaoh's older sons, and the Amonites are stupid enough to think that I want one of them to succeed his father. I am sure that if you hadn't been ill they would already have been after you, trying to puff you up with flattery and put you against me. That is one of the reasons why I want you to leave Thebes for a time."

"There is no need to worry, Mother." He gave her one of his sudden grins, then stooped to pick up a ripe sycomore fruit which had just plopped down in front of them. He bit into it, then went on, "Re has revealed himself to me and shown what must happen. So I shall take no notice of the priests of Amon. All that is important now is that I should be betrothed to the Princess Nefertiti."

Queen Tiye took a step in front of him and stopped. She saw that Amenophis's lips and hand were stained with juice, which unreasonably increased the irritation she had to conceal. "I see everything as fitting together very well," she said evenly. "Re has sent you a vision, and it is with the priest of Re at Heliopolis that we have to work to keep the Amonites in check. As for Nefertiti" (she could not suppress a flick of the eyebrows), "I am willing to help you to have your way if you will be reasonable."

"I do not admire reasonableness."

"No. I'm aware of that. Well, if you will behave as though you were reasonable, then. My plan is this. It is most desirable that you should be kept out of Ipy's clutches for a time. And I think it good that you should meet some of our allies in Heliopolis. You have been ill—"

"I have not been ill, Mother. It is abominable to say that. It was a visitation from the god." His eyes flared with conviction, yet suddenly he seemed very young again.

"Then such visitations can be as exhausting as sickness. The point is that whatever the cause, you are known to be in need of rest and change. I propose that you should take two of Pharaoh's barges and set out towards the north. We would provide physicians and other harmless companions, then when you are well away from Thebes, probably at Abydos, one of your half-brothers might join you. Of course before you reached Heliopolis Ipy would get wind of what was happening, but he could hardly stop you, and wouldn't think it worth trying. To please you, I am willing for Tey to go with you and to bring Nefertiti. I have no patience with Tey. When you know more of the world, you'll see her for the sentimental goose she is, but—"

"If Tey is a goose, then I don't mind being a gosling."

"Wait and see, I tell you." The Queen flushed with annoyance. "Tey has no notion of the realities of life, or she wouldn't have brought that child back to Thebes. But what I was going to say is that although I find her a fool, I am inclined to let her go with you. The suggestion will be that I have entrusted you to her motherly care, and that she is obliged to take Nefertiti with her. Then you can get to know the child and discover whether this is more than a passing fancy. I will do this on one condition. That you swear to me that whatever happens you will keep quiet about Nefertiti until Pharaoh is dead—that is to say until he has arisen as Osiris. Let us be frank: you may not have very long to wait."

Already Amenophis was imagining himself at Memphis, the ancient capital which still seemed to him more glorious than Thebes, at the pyramids, sailing past the great sun temples by the side of the Nile and then at the great sanctuary of Re at Heliopolis, the holy of holies. Moreover, he saw himself doing all these things in the company of Nefertiti. He was so enraptured that his natural stubbornness melted away. He embraced his mother, kissing her with sticky lips.

"Dearest Mother. You do things for the wrong reasons and you use the wrong words. But I thank you for this plan, and I promise that I will do as you say. And I promise, too, that I will bring you closer to the priests of Re. We shall understand one another. What was it you meant about the Aten?"

"This isn't the time to tell you. It is an idea for a compromise that would bring over the waverers. But really, of course, it would strengthen Heliopolis. I'm afraid, Amenophis, that it's a matter of politics rather than religion." The Prince frowned, but his mind was busy with plans for the journey.

"I shall take one of my tutors with me. I don't know the Heliopolitan texts as well as I should. And, of course, I must have someone learned in the past to show me the monuments. I don't want to miss anything. But, Mother, why aren't you coming yourself?"

"I'm glad you at least thought of asking. But that would be too much for the Amonites to stomach. Besides, I don't know which would be worse, bickering with you, or having to chatter about domestic management and the virtues of my brother with the good Tey. No, I'm always needed here, and more than ever when Pharaoh may have to take to his bed at any time."

Queen Tiye beckoned to the servants who were squatting in the shade of the palace, and they came running with the canopy. The sun in the exposed part of the garden was fierce and Amenophis looked pale, but as always excitement gave him animation.

The sun was still not clear of the palms across the river when the royal litter approached the west bank. Amenophis had the curtains drawn back so that he could see everything that was going on. The royal barge was riding some little distance out, but the bank and the stretches of dried mud beyond were crowded with people and animals and the small craft which had brought them. Although there was still a coolness in the air, clouds of dust rose from the scuffling feet and hoofs. What seemed like a cloud of sound also came drifting from the throng, a medley of voices and calls of men, women and children, much quacking and cackling of ducks and geese, the plaintive bleating of calves and the troubled lowing of cows, and even, just once, the laboured braying of a donkey straining for its grotesque crescendo. It was the voice of

Egyptian everyday life—vigorous, cheerful and common-place.

Strings of donkeys and a few gawky mules were waiting to carry the vegetables, flowers and crated poultry up to the Palace, and to the booths of western Thebes. One string was already approaching at a trot, the leading animal ridden, behind huge bundles of onions, by a cheeky-looking small boy. Amenophis's attendants, who had been running before the litter, brandished their staves and started shouting to the boy and those pressing up behind him to make way. The donkey kept on, but swerved, and the boy who had been balancing easily on its haunches was tipped to the ground. He was near enough for Amenophis to see the scowl on his face as he picked himself up, but then as the young peasant looked up, and his eyes fell on the royal insignia, an expression of utter awe transformed his face. Letting his charges go, he remained on his knees while the litter went past.

Amenophis now called to his attendants not to force back the people. "I like to see them," he said, "and it is right for them to see me." All the same, most of his future subjects had scrambled out of the way, and had fallen silent so that now only animal noises could be heard. Then, just as the litter-bearers were stepping on to the rough causeway leading across the mud to the river, a filthy old man pushed forward and gripped one of the poles. His legs were covered with ulcers, and one arm ended in a puckered stump. He was half blind, and only dimly aware that here was some lord who might have something put into the bowl that he held in his one hand. He thrust his face, the clouded eyes pale among the dirt and stubble, to within a yard of the Prince's, then begged for help in the name of half a dozen gods. As he spoke the spittle frothed in the corners of his mouth. Suddenly Amenophis cried out in a shrill voice, "Take him away. Take him away. Don't let him touch me." The old man was hustled roughly off the causeway, and, when out of sight behind the litter, given a parting kick. Amenophis heard the whimper and seemed to come back into himself with a sense of dismay that contracted his throat and stomach. He stared fixedly ahead as the litter moved on, and then, as it was put down at the water's edge, he pulled out one of the small gold rings with which he had provided himself as tokens of royal favour, and ordered a servant to run and give it to the old man. Even now, however, he could not make himself look back to see that his order was carried out. So Amenophis stepped on to the barge and began the journey which he had expected to be one of unbroken bliss filled with self-disgust.

Soon, however, he began to revive, and soon all his misery dispersed. It was a radiant morning, the barge, built of finest cedar wood and with its bright awning supported on slender columns in the form of lotus flowers, seemed a little palace of delight. His favourite tutor, Meryre, was bowing at the entrance to his tented cabin. Inside was a large casket of papyrus rolls, which Amenophis still imagined he would read, and the equipment he would need for drawing and painting.

Brushing aside the enquiries of an obsequious doctor who would dearly have loved to start dosing him as soon as he had stepped on board, he approached the tutor and asked, "Where are the Lady Tey, and the Princess Nefertiti?" The young man smiled, for talk of the Prince's passion had spread from the harim to all parts of the court in a matter of hours.

"The gracious Lady Tey is embarking in the other barge which is attending her on the east bank. If you would care to look you can see the vessel there below the great gate of the old temple. As soon as we cast off, Crown Prince, her boat will follow ours."

"But I wish to have them here. If they are on another boat they might as well be a hundred miles away."

"The Queen gave instructions that they were to sail on the *Breath of Amon*. But she also instructed me to tell you that no one can see down the river as far as Memphis, and that no doubt some adjustments will prove to be necessary."

"Then let us cast off as soon as possible." Amenophis smiled happily, full of the contentment that he still felt when he found himself in sympathy with his mother. "Call the captain to me."

The ship's captain was brought up to the Prince. He was plainly very nervous indeed, for although as commander of a royal barge he had carried divine passengers on many occasions, he had never before had to confront one. He looked at the ground, murmuring, "Life, prosperity, health to your Divine Majesty." Amenophis replied:

"Greetings. May our voyage be a safe one. Give immediate orders to cast off. And as soon as possible sign to the captain of the *Breath of Amon* to bring his ship abreast of ours."

The captain began to back away—always a difficult thing to do on a boat—when Amenophis raised his hand.

"One thing more. My cabin here is comfortable and well fitted, but there is no view from it. I do not wish to miss any of the temples and tombs and other monuments of our ancestors which I have had described to me and which are among the wonders of the world. Some I shall wish to visit, but others I can see well enough from on board. Have a shaded seat fixed for me in the bows where I can command a view of the banks."

"It shall be done, Divine Majesty," the captain said with a hunted look. "I have to say that at this time of year the waters are falling, and the shoals are dangerous. I have to mount a look-out in the bow."

"A boy will not seriously block my view of the Nile banks," said Amenophis with apparent gravity, although he knew that the man was really afraid that it was sacrilegious for a mortal boy to be stationed near the son of Pharaoh.

"And now let us cast off," he concluded, giving a sign of dismissal to the captain. The poor sailor left the royal presence as best he could, picturing a voyage spent zigzagging to and fro across the river, attempting royal landings through mud and reeds, having to stop in impossible currents to exchange passengers with the *Breath of Amon*, and all manner of other trials. He had just discovered that the boats were carrying extra musicians, an artist, a scribe, learned men, painting gear, papyrus rolls, and even lumps of rock for some carving fellow. It was all very irregular, and some of it was certain to be unlucky. The captain had never before sailed with anyone with tastes of this kind. Then he was worried by the order to prepare a seat in the bows. Although it was never mentioned, that was the place reserved for the goddess. What happened if a visible god offended an invisible goddess? It was all too much for a man who only knew about ships and the Nile. "I always heard that he was a strange one," he thought to himself, "and for once rumour hasn't exaggerated."

At that season the flow of the current was no longer very strong, and with the steady northern wind that could be expected, oarsmen would be needed. They stood ready with their long sweeps, six on either side of the steersman, whose huge oar was secured to the stern. The ropes were let go, the sweeps bent under the strain of the start, and then the royal barge began to slip towards mid-stream, the little straw canoes that were still coming in with their loads of produce getting out of the way as best they could. Across the river the captain could see the *Breath of Amon* beginning to move.

As soon as he felt the boat travelling at full speed, Amenophis waved aside his various attendants and made his way into the peak, where he leant on the carved lotus flower that tipped the curving prow. He did not at once look forward, but across the water to where the sun had now lifted well above the palms and the distant mountains. The surface was still glassy in the early morning calm, and he could see the other barge showing black against the glitter. As it approached an intense emotion filled him. There coming nearer and nearer to him was a part of the golden fate which, ever since his visitation, he felt certain awaited him. There in fact was his partner in this fate, his god-appointed love and the sharer of his divine throne. He hardly saw her as the small girl he had met, but as the radiant figure of his vision. Now the waters of the River, the whole flow of life, were supporting them and bringing them together.

Slowly the courses of the two vessels converged, and the

Breath of Amon came abreast. Amenophis had to wrench himself back from his ecstatic imaginings to look at reality. For a moment he was disappointed. He saw a comfortable-looking, homely matron with her arms round the shoulders of a little girl. But then this small figure detached itself and ran forward. Nefertiti had seen that Amenophis was in the bow of his barge, and was sure that she should take up the same position in her own. The boy's heart leapt, stirred now by the true Nefertiti, the girl he had loved on sight. Yet as she reached the prow and stood there separated from him by some thirty feet of moving water, he was prompted to raise his arms in the same formal greeting with which he hailed the sun, and she, like his mirror image, did the same. Then, still seeming to move by a single impulse, both turned to face ahead, gazing solemnly down the river along the course their boats must take. The stiff folds of the Prince's head-dress blew back in the wind of their progress, while Nefertiti's white pleated shift streamed steadily behind her. Everyone in the vessels behind them looked on in awe. It was the beginning of a journey.

After a few moments Amenophis suddenly relaxed, waved in a normal fashion, signed that Nefertiti should join him, and turned back towards his cabin. His eye was caught by Nefertiti's cat, which was standing on some rope looking distastefully at the water and fidgeting its paws angrily up and down. He smiled, feeling a prick of precise amusement and delight. But he was so tired that he must lie down.

The cruise soon developed into an altogether joyful affair. It was not only Amenophis and Nefertiti who were happy, almost everyone on board felt all the time as though they had just drunk several cups of wine. One cause undoubtedly was the escape from Thebes with all its religiosity, extravagance and intrigue. But far more truly responsible was the presence of the two young dreamers who seemed to move among them as the hero and heroine of some enchanting legend.

Amenophis, indeed, opened to a situation which for him was one of pure bliss like a lotus bud in the sun. He was away from the trammels of the parental court, he was king of the small realm of the two ships—a realm peopled by his chosen favourites. This gave him an altogether new confidence, and his nature was of a kind which confidence and success could only sweeten. With a quick instinct he contrived to reduce the painful etiquette surrounding his person until he had achieved an easy informality that embarrassed no one. This did not mean, however, that he was willing to surrender any of his right to command. He was not in the least imperious but utterly compelling.

If Queen Tiye had allowed herself to hope that being constantly in Nefertiti's company would dim his passion and make him see her as an ordinary little girl, she was to be disappointed. Many sensitive children have the same poetic quality in their whole being that manifests itself in their art. Nefertiti had it to an extraordinary degree. Her broken and often unhappy upbringing had given her a prevailing seriousness that was poignant. But it had also given her self-confidence: it was impossible to imagine any situation that she would not calmly accept and emerge from with grace.

Amenophis was so happy that he often became lively and voluble, arguing with his tutor and the young sculptor Bak, and teasing his dear Aunt Tey. While he was in these moods Nefertiti looked silently on, smiling a little when Amenophis laughed, and gazing at him with the eyes of a worshipper.

It was when he resumed his more normal moods of thoughtfulness and abstraction that she seemed to come closer to him. Then they would sit together in the bow, talking a little, watching the palm groves and the villages slip past and the birds that abounded along the river banks. From the heavy, handsome wild geese to the exquisite pure white egrets rising like clouds of butterflies, they delighted in them all.

When evening approached with its strange intensity of light, Amenophis would watch the girl's small, triangular face, so delicate and yet catching a glow from the sky, and see in it the embodiment of all his dreams and ideals. She was the perfect human creature, the natural queen of an imaginary land. As a small boy he had spent much of his time in this country of his, but now he began to believe that he was destined to create it in actuality, and to teach all who were worthy how to live there.

Even after Tey had come to take Nefertiti to bed on the *Breath of Amon* (for she insisted on keeping up this proof of decorum), Amenophis still seemed to see the girl's face floating in the dusk, riding moon-like above the fiery horizon.

Of all the cheerful party sailing from Thebes, Tey was in her own unexalted way probably the best satisfied—and certainly the most grateful. She could still hardly understand what had happened. When Queen Tiye's private scribe had arrived at her house with a message that she was to be ready to accompany the Crown Prince on a prolonged cruise for the sake of his health, she was altogether astonished. Tey was not a woman who troubled herself deeply as to whether people liked her or not, but her sister-in-law's antagonism and contempt had been one of the set facts of her life ever since her marriage to Ay. Why this sudden favour?

Then, as the scribe stood stiffly before her reading from his papyrus, she heard something still more extraordinary. The Great Queen had directed her messenger to say that as she understood that it might be difficult for the Lady Tey to leave her young ward Nefertiti unattended in Thebes, she was graciously willing to allow the child to accompany the royal party—should it prove unavoidable.

Tey was dumbfounded. Not long ago her husband had worked himself into a frenzy of alarm when he discovered that someone had given away Nefertiti's identity, and that talk at the Palace had reached as far as Queen Tiye herself. He had reminded her of how he had been strongly opposed to the adoption, and how she had all but outwitted him in smuggling the child out of Nubia. Now if the news reached Pharaoh's ear he would be dismissed, and they would all most likely be banished or worse.

For a short time Tey had been alarmed, and had kept Nefertiti always by her side. She had come to love the child so much that she was quite prepared to fly with her.

KING OF THE TWO LANDS

However, nothing had happened, the Queen had kept her own counsel and the little surge of Palace rumour had died down. That was why she had been so bold as to present Nefertiti to Amenophis when he had come unexpectedly to her house.

The extraordinary message aroused her fears once more. Was this some plot to lure them both away from Thebes and from Ay's protection in order to destroy them? Tey's imagination was not nearly so strong as her common sense —so all she did was to start packing. Then that evening when her husband came home the mystery was explained in the happiest possible way. Ay had heard, though later than anybody else, that the Crown Prince had announced his love for Nefertiti and was contending with his mother over her. Some even said that this was the cause of his fit.

This invitation must be a proof that he had won. Tey never for a moment thought that the voyage could weaken Amenophis's feelings. She herself not only doted on Nefertiti, but was dispassionately convinced that she had quite exceptional qualities. After all, she had known a score of little girls, but never one with anything like her intensity of being, her individuality or her promise of beauty. She believed that some of the power of the Moon Goddess must have entered into her at birth. The Prince could only love her more every day he spent in her company.

So Tey had embarked in the conviction that she was the most fortunate of women, and moreover that, as she had always tried to believe, the world was a place where the good prospered. She had never liked the idea that they had to wait for death and judgment by Osiris before they had their reward. As for what she expected from Amenophis, she told herself that she would not even allow herself to speculate. But in fact, of course, she saw Nefertiti as Tiye's successor. She trusted Amenophis's single mindedness and extraordinary tenacity of purpose. Had not Ay complained to her year after year of his complete failure to rouse the boy's enthusiasm for manly sports or for the glories of the battlefield? In the end the Prince had forbidden any further mention of these matters in his presence —and Ay had been obliged to surrender.

Soon after the barges had drawn up for Tey, Nefertiti and their attendants to return to the *Breath of Amon*, both vessels would draw in toward the more sheltered bank and there anchor for the night. Amenophis, as he lingered in the bow with his images of love, liked to picture to himself how all the shipping on the Nile, from the largest cargo boat coming in from the ocean to the smallest craft carrying a family to another village for a wedding or funeral, would be coming to rest at this same moment. It gave him a sense of tranquillity, and a sense, too, of how all the people of the River were as one, and he himself one among them.

While the afterglow was still bright he would make his way back to his cabin and be joined for supper by his tutor and by Bak—for these two were quickly established as his favourite companions. As they reclined in their little cave of light drinking wine and talking, Amenophis felt for the first time that he was a man at home among men. Bak, indeed, began to make a strong impression on him. They had met because Bak's father, Men, was his father's chief sculptor. Men had spent years in the Red Mountain quarries near Heliopolis carving the two colossi for Pharaoh's funerary temple, but after that had often been at the Palace working on various commissions. When Bak was old and skilful enough, his father brought him to work at his side so that he could show him the final secrets of the sculptor's craft.

One day when young Bak had been entrusted with the carving of a small panel in an inconspicuous place on a large bas relief, he had dared to vary the accepted way of treating the subject according to some notion of his own. His father had lost his temper and struck him (for the panel once cut could not be changed), whereupon Bak had flung down his tools and marched away. It so happened that Amenophis had been watching the sculptors at work from an upper floor of the Palace, and, feeling an immediate sympathy for the rebellious son, had sent for him and asked him to explain his ideas.

This Bak had failed to do—except to complain of his father's tyranny—but afterwards he had come on several

occasions to give the Prince some elementary lessons in
sculpture. Amenophis had asked that he should come with
him partly because of this acquaintance, and partly because Bak knew his way about Memphis and Heliopolis
very well indeed. He had lived there while Men was
working on the colossi, and as already he had a passion for
art, he had spent most of his time poking his nose into
every building and monument that was open to him—or
where by using his father's name he could beg his way past
the custodians.

Bak's mother had Semitic blood, and he was more
robust and of warmer complexion than most Egyptians.
He had recently grown a short but very dense beard along
the line of his jaw and on the point of his chin. He was
immensely vehement, but really rather inarticulate. He
always seemed about to say something of revolutionary
significance, yet in the end his listeners (if at all inclined
to be sympathetic) felt that they must have missed a few
crucial words or failed to recognize his point. Still, for
Amenophis, he had one great appeal. He was dissatisfied
with things as they were—not for his own sake but because, elusive and ghostly, he saw the shapes of a different
world.

Meryre, the tutor, was not only considerably older, but
an altogether different type of man. He was very thin, and
a life spent among papyrus rolls had left him without
muscles. Amenophis noticed that when, in his little cabin,
Meryre's legs were stretched out beside Bak's, they looked
like the legs of a heron against those of a well-fleshed
young bull. His head was shaven, and he had the fixed
eyes and remote expression of a man much given to intro-
spection. He had served as a priest of Re at Heliopolis in
his young days, and was especially well versed in the Heliopolitan theology. But he had also studied the rival Mem-
phite system, and had found it appealing to his natural
mysticism. It was this mysticism, together with his pro-
found learning and his preoccupation with problems of
deity that had made Amenophis turn towards him during
the past year.

On the evening of the fourth day after leaving Thebes,

the ships were anchored off shore at a point near the short road to Abydos. Amenophis, Meryre and Bak had just finished their supper and were talking over their wine cups.

"In Egypt everything just goes on and on," said Bak. "Think of all those wretched peasants we see on the banks every day working their shadufs. They let down the empty pot, they heave it up again full. Hour after hour, day after day, season after season. Their fathers and grandfathers did the same, and so will their sons and grandsons. It makes me sick."

"But the water flows into the channel, and the channel flows on to the field—and we are nourished," Meryre replied with his usual seriousness.

"Yes, but that's all part of it," Bak replied, swilling his wine round in the cup. "The corn sprouts and dries and we cut it and sow it again. The Nile comes up and recedes again; men are born and men die; the sun rises from the Underworld and returns to it again. Round and round, round and round!"

"But that is the glory of Egypt," the tutor replied. "We maintain Ma'at—comeliness, justice, unchanging order and the beautiful cycle of death and resurrection."

"What is it you want, Bak?" Amenophis broke in. "How could things be different?"

The sculptor dipped his forefinger in his cup and flicked so that a drop of wine flew up into the air, sparkling in the light of the lamp flames.

"That is what I want," he cried. "I want to catch that drop in the air. That instant. For me that is life, that is art."

"But Egypt puts her trust in the eternal, in the unchanging essence of things. No man can alter that, or should ever attempt to do so." Meryre gazed earnestly and a little reprovingly at the younger man.

"That is what is so insufferable. We men are like asses tied to the threshing-pole, trotting round from birth to death."

Suddenly Amenophis raised his hand authoritatively, as though he were about to address not two people but a multitude.

"A man cannot change the order of things. But you must know that a god can."

Abruptly the sound of the crew talking together, of rustling water and even of mosquitoes, could be heard in the royal cabin. Meryre started nervously, swayed his thin body to and fro, nodded his head slowly and looked at Amenophis with a new reverence that was almost comical. Bak began to knead his beard, allowed a self-conscious smile to make a brief appearance, then seemed to feel a surge of excitement, his eyes brightening. It was the tutor who at last broke the silence by saying formally:

"You have spoken, Crown Prince who shall be Horus. We are your servants."

"And spoken well," said Bak. "Perhaps the deadly round will be straightened at last." Amenophis, who was trembling, signed to them to go, but as they rose the steward approached, bowing with every step. This man, whom Queen Tiye had charged with management of the expedition, was in fact full of disapproval of the way things had turned out. In particular he was shocked that the Crown Prince should hobnob with commoners—and lowly commoners. He had pictured his royal charge remaining inaccessible to everyone except himself—who would be in constant attendance. As it was, he had to spend most of his time with the captain.

"May I be heard, gracious Prince? Word has just reached us from the shore that the Lord Mersure is hastening to join your servants, but cannot reach Abydos while the sun is high."

"Then we must wait for him," said Amenophis wearily. He was not inclined to welcome his half-brother's company. "I wish in any case to see Abydos and visit the tomb of Osiris. But do not send word of this. I shall go privately." Again he made a sign of dismissal and Meryre, Bak and the steward retreated while the Prince's night attendants came up to prepare him for sleep and to watch over him until dawn.

Amenophis was woken by a penetrating and unfamiliar sound. At first, while half asleep, he thought it was a mosquito in his ear, then that it was some great flock of

unknown birds. But it grew louder, more shrill and weird.
"What is it?" he called out to the young watchman he
could see squatting outside in the early sunlight.
"A funeral, my Lord Prince. And a second is following
behind. It is always the same at Abydos."

Amenophis wrapped himself in a long gown, slipped his
feet in sandals and went outside. The air was still fresh,
and the wide panorama of the river seemed alert and
hopeful—unconcerned in death. The leading boat of the
first funeral party was almost abreast of the royal barge.
Amenophis could see the mummy case, like a hugely
bloated body, lying on a bier with a woman, probably the
widow, crouched near its foot. The bier was confronted by
two priestesses, personifying Isis and Nephthys, eternal
mourners for the murdered Osiris. If the priests gathered
in the stern were reciting a litany, their words were
drowned by the din coming from the boat behind. The
entire forepart of this vessel was crowded with women.
Their breasts were bared, dishevelled hair fell down their
backs and round their faces, and they were beating their
brows while emitting the frightful wails that had woken
Amenophis.

It seemed to him that if all the cats in Bubastes were
caterwauling together they could not make a more horrible
noise. Some of the women clutched small children by the
hand—and these little ones were weeping in good earnest.
In the rear boat was a party of substantial-looking gentle-
men, relatives and associates of the deceased, who were
holding lotus and other funeral flowers with a slightly
awkward air. This boat also carried a statue of the dead
man and a pile of his worldly goods—an ornate chair and
many inlaid caskets, some alabaster vases and the frame
of a large bed. They were expensive possessions—only the
well-off could afford burial at Abydos—but they looked
utterly poor and forlorn as they lay untidily exposed to
the sunlight.

Amenophis turned to the attendant, who seemed
neither troubled nor interested.

"They make a great noise, but does anyone care?"

"No, Lord Prince, but it is the custom."

"And do you think that it is a good custom?"

"If you can afford it, Lord Prince."

"Would you like to have all those women screaming behind your bier?"

The attendant shifted his feet; the last thing he wanted was to be forced into what sounded like an argument with this peculiar Crown Prince. Why could he not behave like Pharaoh's son? His voice sounded sullen when he replied:

"What is always done must be a proper thing, Lord Prince. And a man with a proper funeral here at Abydos will find it easy to join Osiris and live for ever."

"Don't you believe, then, that it is what you have done in life that will count for most? Every man's soul must be weighed and may be found wanting."

"I don't know, Lord Prince, but I have noticed that it is always right equipment that wins. A poor man shuffled into the sand won't have the equipment to reach the Kingdom."

Amenophis, who didn't know himself whether his questions had been entirely serious, now felt an undoubted twinge of exasperation.

"Go and rouse Bak," he said hastily, "and tell him that I want him here as soon as he is ready." Hearing shouts, he looked towards the jetty where the funerary boats were now tying up. Evidently gangs of Abydos porters were competing for the job of carrying the grave gear up to the cemetery. There was an interlace of muscular brown bodies pushing against one another, sticks and fists were raised, and a man fell flat into the water accompanied by noisy jeers. Amenophis frowned, then for comfort looked at the *Breath of Amon* anchored near at hand. The knowledge that this comely boat, riding as comfortably as a duck on the softly moving current, held his Nefertiti sweetly asleep, filled him with tenderness. He gave a little private sign of greeting towards the silent vessel before going back into his cabin.

Later that morning Amenophis himself climbed on to the jetty. Ahead of him went the steward and his servants, and behind him came Bak. He had intended to slip away alone with the sculptor, but Tey had come upon the scene and had absolutely forbidden him to go up to Abydos unless he were properly attended. Indeed, although she was no lover of ceremonial etiquette, she would have liked to have insisted that if he were to venture at all into the teeming City of the Dead, he should go publicly as Crown Prince. This, however, he absolutely refused—with all the charm and will-power that he could turn upon his friends. The truth was that after long confinement within the artificial, monotonously safe and luxurious world of the Palace, he was now suddenly filled with dreams of escape. He saw himself mingling with the people of Egypt as at once their brother and their god. A galling memory of the incident of the Theban beggar only made him more eager to experience his true self.

The crowds had thinned out, and porters and other hangers-on were sitting on the platforms set up to support waiting coffins, eating bread and onions and taking squirts of beer out of bulging goat skins. They went past two large and lifeless statues showing Osiris with the crook and flail and Osiris in the shape of the ancient Jackal god of the region whose cult he had absorbed. The heads of both—manhead and doghead—had white chaplets of bird droppings.

As soon as the party stepped on to the dusty road leading in to Abydos they were beset by vendors of religious knick-knacks. There were little pottery figures of the god in various forms, others, more costly, in blue faience; there were all manner of plaques inscribed with prayers and charms for the comfort and help of the dead; there was a vast choice of jars and bowls containing food and drink for the dead to help out those pilgrims and visitors who had not been able to bring their own. The only attractive merchandise among all that was being held up to them by eager children and sad old women were the huge bunches of lotus, papyrus and other approved funerary plants.

The steward, whose disapproval of the expedition showed not only in his face but in his every movement, abruptly ushered the party into a rambling roadside farmhouse. The only way, he declared, by which they could possibly get to Abydos with propriety would be by hiring donkeys.

The farm was a pleasant place, with a little terrace shaded by ancient vines and enlivened by gaudy flowers growing in jars. Two huge, soft-looking oxen were waiting patiently with their heads slightly bowed by the yoke, while a flock of geese was parading fussily about the yard; through a window Amenophis could see a darkened room where wide bowls of milk showed like moons. Strong wafts or manure came from the cattle byre. It was the first time that the Prince had ever encountered this smell, and he thought it delicious.

He sat down on a bench below the vines and signed Bak to a stool.

"How nice it is! I think I could live here."

"You prefer manure to myrrh?"

"Everything seems simple and more real. Look. I like the feel of the wood here." He ran his hand along the edge of the bench, glossy yet heavily grained from the wear of generations of wine-drinkers. "I like it far better than ivory inlays."

"But I hope you wouldn't want to live without art? A prince must patronize us poor artists."

"I don't like banter, Bak. You know that. Speak honestly or you will offend." He flashed a look of scornful disapproval that made the sculptor wince. "We could live closer to nature and still have art."

"You are counting without the tax collectors." Bak argued, partly to wipe out his discomfiture. "It may seem very agreeable and peaceful here at the moment, but the farmer could give you quite another picture. When he and his sons have laboured from dawn to dusk to raise fine crops, your taxmen come and leave him only just enough to get through the winter. You can't build palaces and temples and maintain the imperial armies without the people being bled."

At this moment the farmer's wife appeared, carrying a jug of wine and some slices of cream cheese. With his usual directness Amenophis immediately asked her, "Is it true that the tax gatherers oppress you?" The woman, who was

stout and comfortable-looking and supported her weight
on broad, dusty feet, reached up, picked two vine leaves
and laid them on the table to receive the cheese. Then she
answered with a confidential smile.

"We don't do badly. My husband has come to a satis-
factory arrangement. The taxmen have to live, too, you
know, sir. Then we were lucky enough to own a piece of
land up at the edge of the cemeteries and we sold that to
great advantage. But there are many who are crushed.
Look over there." She pointed across the road to where a
small house of mud brick was plainly fast returning to the
dust from which it had been raised. "Last year when we
heard that the tax gatherers were on their way the family
disappeared in the night. They took the few beasts they
had left and plenty of seed and went off somewhere. The
man wasn't clever like my husband. He used to talk of
justice and to rage against all officials. So of course they
pillaged him. Often and often before harvest the children
used to come across for our scraps."

Amenophis jumped up. "But of course they should have
had justice. Every man must live under Ma'at." As he
spoke his eyes filled with tears.

"There, young lord. I hear you are of the nobility and
rich so there is no need for you to distress yourself. You will
be well looked after and able to enjoy all the blessing of
Ma'at. And there is no need to feel sorry for a fellow like
our neighbour. He was against the authorities and caused
trouble in the town. I never heard of any man who went
against *them* coming to any good. Don't they teach that
obedience is the greatest virtue in the eyes of the gods?"

"Yes, but only obedience within Ma'at. No Egyptian
should be abused because he demands justice."

"The man across the way was a rebellious fool and
deserved what he got. I was sorry for the children, though.
Now here come your donkeys. I can see that my husband
has brought out his best saddle for you. If you're going
into the city, young lord, look after yourself. Like all places
where there's a lot of religion, there's a lot of wickedness as
well. My husband always says that the gods attract cheats
and robbers, and there are plenty in Abydos."

"Thank you for your wine, madam, and for what you have told me." Amenophis fumbled in his belt and brought out another of his small pieces of gold. "If your neighbours return, help them for my sake. And tell them that there are those in authority who care for them." The woman looked at him incredulously, then shot a questioning glance at Bak. When he nodded and smiled, she bowed as low as her stoutness would allow, murmuring thanks and promises.

The successful farmer had hired them fine large asses, and with the modest height and speed they provided the little party was able to brush off all the touts and vendors. Amenophis rode in silence, seeming hardly to notice what was going on around him. Had he not been so preoccupied with thoughts that made him frown and mutter to himself he might have objected to the way his steward was behaving. Riding ahead with a servant on either hand he saw to it that his master had the crown of the road. A large party of pilgrims who had come all the way from Elephantine was forced to string out along the verge, while some of their black Nubian porters were jostled into the ditch. Then a group of mourners, including many widows, all carrying offerings of food and drink and preceded by a dark sacrificial bull, was made to scatter. Only the bull failed to show a proper docility, and by snorting and swinging its head induced the steward to bend his course a little from the centre of the road.

It was this bull, whose wet muzzle appeared within a foot or two of his leg, that finally roused Amenophis from his difficult thoughts. They were already passing through the last of the irrigated fields and the outskirts of the town were beginning. Most conspicuous was a large mason's yard crowded with stone slabs to be set up in the tombs and cenotaphs of the necropolis. Some were already carved with the appropriate texts and symbols and only needed the insertion of the name of the deceased; others were blank and would be carved to the order of the family. There were also a few statues of men and divinities standing in a haphazard knot, staring blankly at space or one another. Bak pushed his donkey up to the fence and gave the establishment a professional scrutiny.

"Dreadful stuff!" he said as he jogged back to the Prince's side. "This donkey could carve as well. What a confounded waste of stone."

"Nearly everything here seems to be shoddy. And I hated the touts, and the porters fighting to carry a man's goods to his grave. What is wrong with this place?"

"The head of Osiris, Prince, nothing else! Because people imagine it's buried here, and everyone nowadays thinks about life in the Underworld before anything else, they are willing to give half what they have to get themselves and their dear ones safely into the Barque of the Dead. And where you get a lot of people in that mood you'll get others ready to rob them."

"You said 'imagine it to be buried'. Don't you think it is true, then?" Bak felt embarrassed at what he had let slip. After all, Amenophis was committed to all this. Before very long he would have to accept himself as a living god. Still, the boy always demanded openness, so he went on a little apologetically.

"You know how it is, Prince. I spent half my boyhood running wild in Memphis and Heliopolis, and up there you meet all kinds of people. Not god-fearing people. Refugee artists especially, men who have worked for half a dozen different priesthoods and believed in none of them. But I have a faith of a kind, and I am sure that Egypt's gods must be true for the Egyptian people."

"Mina said much the same thing of the Cretans. So the more one sees, the less one believes. There is something wrong, and I must understand what it is." He broke off and exclaimed, "What can this be?" They were approaching a compound shaded by a few trees, and from it were coming yaps and howls and a powerful smell of dog. It was the enclosure of the sacred jackals kept in honour of Khentamenty. Their house took the form of a miniature temple, and the palings of the enclosure were crowned with recumbent jackals, the standard of this canine Lord of the Dead. Naturally the little beasts would have fed at night, but the minor priests attending them kept them hungry so that their feeding hour could entertain the pilgrims. A crowd was gathered now, watching the sacred captives, many of which were mangy, fighting over stinking donkey bones.

Amenophis pushed ahead and led the way towards where the columns of the great temple of Osiris-Khentamenty showed above its precinct wall. His heavy lower lip was thrust out and he looked fixedly ahead, ignoring the crowd, trying not to hear its laughter. The wide temple precinct was hardly less swarming with people, but here most were earnest and devout. There were women with tear-stained faces, whole families that seemed to be united under a pall of grief. Some had come only to pray and leave offerings before the many images of Osiris, but others attended corpses that were to receive last rites within the temple before their journey to the tomb. Among the pillars of the inner hall the mummies lay in a long line on their biers, their cases bright with colour and gilding, the moulded and painted faces gazing patiently at the roof.

Bak took Amenophis aside to admire some beautiful reliefs known to have been executed for one of the first Pharaohs of Amenophis's lineage. Then the two of them penetrated into a dark inner chapel where there was just enough light to see a sculptured figure of the jackal god and the thousands of paintings that filled the walls from greasy floor to dim ceiling. Here, cramped and teeming, were depicted in endless monotony the inhabitants of the Underworld and the painful journeys of the dead. Among the stiff little black figures of Underworld deities, of Osiris and of the birds representing the souls of the dead, there stood out countless monsters, sinuous reptiles rearing their many spiteful heads, long undulating serpents walking on human feet, snakes twisting their necks in venomous ropes.

They seemed to Amenophis infinitely horrible, but not in the least awe-inspiring. The whole chapel exuded a kind of evil that was essentially mean and sordid. The two trespassers slipped out as quickly and secretly as they had gone in.

"It reminded me of a scullery full of black beetles," said Bak, laughing with relief at escaping to the open air. "But what marvellous monsters *I* could devise if I wanted.

They'd really be terrifying. Beasts of darkness that the dead would fear to pass. . . ."

"If you are going to be a painter of monsters you will not work for me," replied Amenophis softly but with intensity. This was the first time that any word about their possible future had ever passed between the prince and the artist. Once again Bak was checked and chastened by the realization that this odd young creature at his side might soon be master of half the world.

They went back to where the steward was waiting with the donkeys, and were soon headed for the Tomb of Osiris, the most popular shrine in all Upper Egypt. The route took them along the processional way, scene of many of the festivals of the god. Amenophis tried to imagine what it would look like on the day of the Great Going-forth, when the god and his sacred barque were carried to the tomb, and thousands of people thronged into Abydos to take part in the mysteries. At the moment, although they met a funeral party straggling back towards the river and there were priests and pilgrims in some numbers, the road was not crowded and they could see the vast cemetery that lay all about them. It was indeed a city of the dead, with their houses packed along the narrow thoroughfares and twisting alleys. Their presence seemed to produce a disturbing silence that made itself felt even along the frequented processional way.

In some quarters dilapidated mastabas and little brick pyramids, set as close as teeth on a threshing board, were powdering into decay; in others new tombs and cenotaphs were being built. A few priests and mourners moved softly along roads ankle-deep in drifted dust, and once Amenophis heard distant wails such as had wakened him that morning. He felt an inner shiver of apprehension. It took the sacred place of the god of resurrection to shake his absolute confidence in the after-life.

After about a mile they left the cemetery behind, while the traffic of pilgrims began to thicken as they approached the holy place. On the fringe of the crowd two dwarfs were doing comic turns and tumbling tricks; a huge Nubian was leading a sad, greying, withered pygmy on a rope, and there were dozens of stalls offering such things as chips of stone from the Tomb, little pots of sand from the floor and leaves from the sacred grove. At the centre of it all was the entrance to what was evidently a very ancient vault. Priests stood before it, some reciting prayers, others blessing the pilgrims who were pressing up with jars of wine and oil, myrrh and precious unguents, as well as humbler offerings of meat and fruit and flowers. Scribes moved about making an inventory of this stream of tribute. Amenophis saw one woman, a recent widow, suddenly unclasp a necklace and thrust it on to an offering table.

"What becomes of all these things?" he asked Bak suddenly.

"They are left on the tables for a day or so and then taken to the temple repositories. And I suppose most of the food finds its way to the priests' larders—if it's good enough."

"But surely that is wrong. . . ." The prince looked frowningly into his friend's face.

"Why? The woman back there said that tax men must live. Well, so must priests—and there are thousands of them in Abydos. And what's the use of letting good things waste? Or did you think that the god came out at midnight to empty his offering tables?"

Amenophis shook his head without speaking, recognizing that in a hazy, unquestioned way he had believed something of the kind. Bak was feeling contrite at his brutality and lack of respect. There was something in the innocence of the boy that provoked him. Perhaps after all there was much to be said for the restrictions of etiquette.

"I am sorry, Crown Prince," he said, "perhaps you had better take some of the holy sand. It is said to be a salve for all ills." An old woman was shaking a little flask before their eyes.

"It won't cure the wounds I have suffered today," said Amenophis with a sad smile. Then he went on. "All this is abominable. Let us get away from it and visit the sacred grove. Perhaps we shall find holiness there."

Bak, wanting to please the prince, followed him out of the crowd and through a gate in a boundary wall. At once they saw more tombs, and Amenophis went up to one with a collapsed roof to examine the inscribed stone at the entry. The hieroglyphs were so archaic that he found he could read only a few, but he could tell that they included royal titles. They must be immensely old, older than the great pyramids themselves. He had a deep poetic sense of the past, and particularly of the past of the throne that he would occupy. He ran his fingers over the symbols of the royal names, freeing them from dust. For the first time that day Amenophis was seized by the excitement, the expansion of spirit, that made him feel that the universe and his consciousness flowed into one another, and that both were transfused by the same light. Beyond the tombs he could see the clustered trunks of the Osirian grove.

They went on in silence until they came to the irrigation dyke enclosing the palms. The trees were perfectly tended, their trunks straight and diapered like snake skin. The ground beneath them was carpeted with young grass of a greenness that struck the eyes with incredulity at that season of the year. It was absolutely quiet except for the faint creaking of a sharduf being worked somewhere on the far side of the grove, and the rustle of the palm fronds overhead.

Amenophis told Bak to wait while he went among the trees. The vistas between the trunks, the hushed shade of the place, lured him irresistibly. There, surely, he would encounter some spiritual presence that would wipe out the painful impressions of the morning. The palms were close enough together for Bak soon to be out of sight, then, as he went deeper, placing his feet as lightly as he could to avoid tearing the delicate skin of grass, he had a glimpse of a tall, motionless figure that must be standing in a clearing at the heart of the grove. He stopped, for he did not wish to see it more clearly, to be made aware of its stoniness. He bowed his head and held out his hands above the grass as though he were warming them at a fire. He began to think he could feel life running into his fingertips, the life that was concealed in the waters of the River, in the seed and the egg, the life that was Osiris.

A woodpecker flew shrieking away and some large black

birds clattered off from the treetops. Two men appeared, moving swiftly towards him, priests who had been on duty at the shrine. Their faces showed amazement and horror as well as fury.

"Out, out at once!" the older man said in a low, angry voice. "This is sacrilege. Do not speak. Go back."

"I am here of right," Amenophis said softly, keeping his ground. "It is less sacrilege for me to commune with the god in his grove than it is for you to abuse me."

"Impious brat, you look as though the gods had cursed you already." Both priests advanced as though to take hold of him. That was something Amenophis could not allow, and against all intention he moved back a pace and cried: "I am here by right, I say. I am the Crown Prince Amenophis. I came to the grove to cleanse myself of the beastliness and corruption you have made out there. My ancestors gave you land and treasure, but you have turned Abydos into a market of cheats and lies, a place where Ma'at is dishonoured and the people abused and misled. I came here to meet with the god whom I know, and who knows me." As his denunciation mounted his eyes blazed and his thin legs shook.

The younger priest raised a whistle to his lips. "He is mad," he whispered. "He is possessed. We need help against this demon."

"Yes, that is true—I am possessed. Do not care to come near or I will burn you up." Amenophis backed away, holding them with his eyes, then suddenly turned and ran —for as his passion ebbed he foresaw the inevitable indignities, the explanations, the necessity of involving Tey and Nefertiti. As he darted through the maze of trunks he heard the whistle and imagined gardeners, custodians, even the sharduf worker, coming in pursuit.

He fled over the little bridge where Bak was waiting and made the sculptor follow him without a word. As they reached the gate, they looked back and saw the priests leading a group of men, some carrying hoes and rakes. They stopped running but walked rapidly towards the crowd of pilgrims, hoping to rejoin the steward and ride away. Amenophis was still tense and silent, unable to

speak of what had happened. Bak felt his misery and
paused a moment in his stride.

"The only thing is to laugh, Crown Prince. You ran like a
gazelle from angry farmers, you who will be King of Egypt."

Tears came into the prince's eyes and he was still only
on the brink of hysterical laughter, when a fearful din
broke out behind them. Inside the portal leading into the
cemetery, two groups of men and women were fighting.
Almost at once the crowd of pilgrims began to stream
towards the combatants, mindlessly eager to see what was
going on. Bak, who had noticed the priests and their
henchmen coming through the gate still in determined
pursuit, thought it best for the prince and himself to be
carried along with the mob. As a result they found themselves in the cemetery in the front line of gapers.

It was an astonishing scene. One large group of kinsfolk,
mourners, priests and priestesses had evidently been leaving a tomb after an interment when they became embroiled
with another cortège, still grouped round a bier, that was
trying to enter it. From the abuse being hurled by both
sides it appeared that the cemetery agents had sold the
same last resting-place to two customers. Bak shrewdly
guessed that the agents had been caught out in what was a
piece of regular business sharp practice by bad luck or bad
management.

Several of the relatives in each party were lunging at
one another and some had drawn knives. Most noise came
from the women mourners, who were tearing at each
other's already flowing hair and screaming personal
insults. Even one of the priestesses had begun to utter a
formal curse at the top of her voice. Distraught officials
were trying to induce the leaders of the incoming funeral
to withdraw, but their efforts had a contrary effect. Several
strong young men who had been carrying the bier quickly
put it down and dashed together into the mausoleum. In a
few moments they struggled out again, embracing a
mummy case. Immediately the outraged relatives hurled
themselves on the young men to rescue their dead, while
those of the incoming party who were not already fighting
rushed to their support.

The mummy case rode higher and higher as the raiders tried to lift it out of reach. Above the angry faces of the living, the impassive painted face stared first one way and then another as the mummy lurched from hand to hand. At last Amenophis saw it swaying above him, a young man stretching up to support it by the feet. The youth himself tripped, the mummy case flew into the air and then crashed down on a small granite obelisk at the edge of the roadway. The smooth, rounded form shattered into a tangle of coloured splinters, the mummy itself was thrown out and its cocoon of bandages burst open by the fall. A stump of bone showed among pickled flesh, and a smell more sickening than that of normal putrefaction exploded in the hot air.

Amenophis turned green, and Bak looked desperately round to discover how to extricate him, when to his relief he saw the steward and servants pushing their way through what had now become a battle involving every man and woman of the two funeral parties and many of the pilgrims as well. With four men to force a path, Amenophis was able to walk out of the cemetery without further indignities. He still looked sick and badly shaken.

"His Royal Highness cannot continue," the steward announced in a voice meaty with condemnation. "Over there behind the trees is the house of the High Priest of the shrine of Osiris. I am acquainted with his major-domo and spoke to him just now when I was seeking for His Highness." He glowered at the sculptor. "There he can be properly received, and conveyed back to the royal barge."

The bronze doors in the thick walls clanged to behind them. The dust and din were cut off so sharply that they seemed unbelievable. Amenophis found himself passing through a cool, watered, well-tended garden to a house of columns and bowing servants. The floors were polished, the hangings rich and some fragrance hung in the air.

The major-domo hurried ahead to where at the end of a long aisled hall two men on a couch were talking earnestly together. Startled by the announcement of an extraordinary visitor, both jumped up and moved towards Amenophis. He saw that while one was evidently the High

Priest—for whom at that moment he felt nothing but anger and contempt—the other was his half-brother Mersure.

"My brother Mersure says that we have to be on good terms with the priesthood of Osiris because we need their help against Amon. Have you ever thought about politics, Nefertiti?"

"Never. But I know that my foster-father doesn't like politicians."

"No, but only because he likes soldiers, and they are worse. All the same," Amenophis went on hurriedly, seeing that he had wounded her, "I agree with him. I don't intend to do wrong things and make friends with hateful men to get my way. I shall assume that all men are with me because I shall do what is right."

"I am sure that they will be," said Nefertiti, looking up at him with her ready admiration. "I wish that I had been there when you rebuked the High Priest for the evils of Abydos." They were sitting in their place in the prow of the ship, the girl leaning against the prince's stool. It was evening, and the barges were moving along the east bank at a place where the cliffs receded from the river, enclosing a semicircular stretch of almost desert land. As they came abreast of one small wadi, with a trickle of water still meandering down it, which cut across the desert, the crew began the usual preparations to anchor for the night.

"Yes. But my brother says, and Bak seems to agree with him, that where thousands of ordinary people go there are bound to be abuses—and that they like false relics and trumpery amulets and effigies. As for the idea of selling tombs over and over again and hiding away the bodies in old vaults, they seemed to find it funny."

"I hate people with a sense of humour," said Nefertiti quite simply.

"Yes. And I am sure they are wrong about the people. If those who should lead them are true to Ma'at and act justly, then the people would follow them and do as they do. How can the people be righteous if the officials cheats and the priests are irreligious? I learnt a great many things, Nefertiti, during that horrible day in Abydos, but only one good thing."

"And what was that?"

"When I went into the sacred grove, the god I met there was the same god I met in my vision. I am sure of it."

"But Osiris is the god of the dead, of darkness, and Re is light?"

"So it has always seemed. But Abydos has made me think that the Underworld with its serpents and monsters comes from the nightmares of human beings. From our guilts and fears. The god I met in my vision and in the grove was a god of life."

"Or of love, Amenophis? My foster-mother has told me that all women worship love."

"The Great Goddess." Amenophis looked down at her, smiling. "Yes, the Great Goddess, Nefertiti my dearest." He fell silent and looked beyond her to the river. He watched the smoke rising from the fires of some Bedouin come in from the desert to camp by the wadi, then followed the movements of a duck guiding her brood into the reeds. "Yes," he repeated, "love and life, the divinity that all men have everywhere. And all creatures, too." They held themselves perfectly quiet, as though they were guardians of the evening stillness. When they spoke again, it was Nefertiti who murmured, "I shall always remember this place, Amenophis. I think I should feel quite safe there where the wanderers are camped. The cliffs wall it round. It is like a little kingdom. And look—now the sun is blessing it for us."

Amenophis turned his head towards the other bank, where the setting sun was balanced on the horizon.

"The Aten, the great disc of the Aten. I shan't forget this place and this moment, either, Nefertiti." Again he turned his head, at the sound of Tey's familiar footsteps.

IV

QUEEN TIYE waited impatiently inside the palace. She knew that Amenophis had arrived, and that the vizier and all the other functionaries were at the entrance staging a formal reception. Almost to her own surprise she found that the return of her son after so long an absence warmed her with a genuine emotion. He was back a little sooner than expected, for the wind had suddenly strengthened and swept them upstream. A murmur went through the hastily assembled court: there he was coming up the hall now, escorted by Ramose, the vizier. He seemed more strangely formed than ever, for the thin legs were longer, and his hips seemed to have broadened rather than his shoulders. His face had lengthened, too. He was certainly going to have a very long chin. But those lips, what did they mean? Perhaps after all he was sensual. No, it was impossible with eyes such as he had. They had many expressions, but were never greedy or appraising.

She stepped quickly forward and embraced him. "Dear son. How you are changed. And now I have to look up at you." It was true that Amenophis was taller than his plump little mother. Because he was aware of her emotion, the ordinariness of her words delighted him. He returned her embraces ardently, but with a new confidence and control. After a correct greeting to the Great Queen he said privately, "Of course I have changed, dearest Mother. I have been away ten months and have seen a thousand things. But you are the same, except that you look better than when I left."

"Come to my apartments. Your clothes can be changed there if you wish. My Lord Ramose, I expect you will wish to wait until Pharaoh can be summoned from his Audience. A mother must be allowed half an hour." The vizier bowed and withdrew.

As soon as they were settled in her favourite room, the prince oiled and in fresh linen, Queen Tiye began.

"I have missed you, Amenophis, which I did not expect. But I was certainly right, when your father made such a good recovery, to send word to you to stay in the North until after the inundation. Ipy and his friends were angry, but had to put a good face on it. Now, tell me of your doings."

"The journey back has been wonderful." Amenophis's mind loved the immediate or the ultimate rather than those intermediate affairs which preoccupied the Queen. "Travelling so soon after the subsidence of the waters made us slow, until these last days, but it was worth it. All Egypt seemed like a garden with everyone sowing and planting, and the banks already green. Then in the evenings each village we passed had its festival. We heard singing and the sound of flutes and harps coming across the water. At several places, after we were anchored, decorated boats put out and sailed round our barge while musicians played and sang to us. Nefertiti liked that most of all. She is very fond of music." Queen Tiye realized that however much her son had changed she would still have need of patience.

"Ah, yes," she said, "I thought you would enjoy a spring journey. But how were Memphis and Heliopolis?"

"I was very happy. Often in the mornings I went sightseeing with Bak, and in the evenings I studied with Meryre. Nefertiti studied, too. She is very quick and can already read all but the most difficult texts. Her tutor said that she was the best pupil he had ever had—though he had always taught boys before. Then, when we visited Heliopolis, I was often in the Temple of Re itself. You never told me that the temples there are open so that the sun strikes on to the altars. That is how it should be. I know now that I have always loathed our dark sanctuaries. I shall build for the sun. The Aten should be master of his own house."

"So you have talked with Mersure?"

"Of course." The glow left the prince's face. "I do not like him. He is always in the company of priests, but is quite without god. In the end I had to order him not to speak to me any more of the worship of the Aten. For god has shown me more light, Mother, and I cannot serve the lord of the sun in order to outplay the priests of Amon. Those men will fall because they are evil and do not know the truth."

"So you have not changed your mind about politics?" Tiye asked rather glumly.

"No. I have moved even further the other way. What I saw at Abydos—and I don't want ever to talk about it— has made me quite sure that one must live by Ma'at and deal only with those who do the same."

"If you apply this to the affairs of state, then we are in for trouble."

"Don't all the inscriptions about my ancestors declare that they served Ma'at and lived in righteousness?"

"Inscriptions! Such things are right and proper for a funerary temple. But while he is alive Pharaoh is a ruler and must behave like other rulers."

"Didn't the Wise Imhotep say, 'He who wills a right end must act rightly'?"

"I only know that if I had been above politics you would not be Crown Prince at this moment." Her indignation was so lively that Amenophis gave her a quick grin and said, "Never mind, honoured Mother. I spent much time with the priests of Re, and they are my friends. The Greatest Seer himself explained many theological matters to me, and I told him of the visions vouchsafed me by the god. Together we agreed on the creative power of the light and of Pharaoh as the son of light on the throne of Re. The Greatest Seer and his priests are full of godliness and learning, but naturally they must condemn the priests of Amon for usurping the power that was given them in the beginning."

"You are an extraordinary person, Amenophis. I don't pretend to understand you in the least. But if you can use theology to strengthen our alliance with Heliopolis, so much the better. Perhaps after all you are cleverer in these matters than I am."

"I do not 'use' theology, and I do not wish to be called clever. I am speaking of the truth, and I believe in the truth. Re was the first king of his created world, and

Pharaoh has always been his son and the inheritor of his throne. So there need be no question of an alliance, but of the god and his priesthood being reunited." Tiye nodded her head as though reflecting on these ideas, then, after a pause, said abruptly, "And Nefertiti? Tell me more about her."

"Nefertiti understands everything." His face softened as he spoke. "She is wonderfully quick at learning, as I told you, but also she knows from within. She said when we parted just now, 'You are my light, and soon you will be the light of the world'."

Tiye laughed. "No wonder you are so fond of her company. You are sure you love her, then, Amenophis?"

"Every day I love her more. I have discovered how delightful it can be when another person's happiness is your own. I will tell you of an instance. We went to see the great pyramids north of Memphis. They are amazing —and the god must have given great strength to build them. It made us feel sad when we saw how all the pyramids rose from among desolate ruins. Then, while we were still there, the sky became grey and thousands of drops of water fell from it. Rain. I had heard of rain, of course, and know that water often comes in this way to lands across the ocean where they have no Nile. But I had never seen it, and the greyness seemed to make everything sadder than before. I went into the tent that had been pitched for us. But Nefertiti saw at once that all water is a gift of life, and she stayed outside and did a most beautiful dance, with her hands cupped to catch the drops and her face laughing and streaming with water. I had never seen her in such a mood before. Watching her I felt such delight, Mother, as I think you could hardly imagine. And afterwards it seemed to me that this had been one of my happiest days. I believe this is how it will always be."

Queen Tiye rose quickly and took a few paces to divert the small pain of senseless jealousy. "But you will keep your promise to me?" she asked in an even voice. "There is no knowing, now, how long you will have to wait."

"Yes, certainly I will do as I said. I don't mind how

long we must wait if I can see Nefertiti whenever I wish. That is all that matters."

The Queen scrutinized his face, found it calm and innocent, and gave one of her little shrugs. "Very well. You relieve me of a great deal of worry. And we can't be sure how long the improvement in Pharaoh's health will last. The doctors attribute it to all their drugs and incantations —and mountains of cattle have been sacrificed. But I claim much of the credit for myself as I persuaded him to eat and drink less—and not to think about women. There I have another anxiety. Do you know about Tadukhipa?"

"Gilukhipa's niece from Mitanni? Yes, I heard that she might enter the harim, but that her father the king demanded that she should be Great Wife."

"That was sheer nonsense. Living right over there he understands nothing. Did he really suppose that I should yield up my place to a half-grown girl after thirty years of keeping things together here at Thebes? She is coming all the same. They've made some compromise about her title —but there will be none about her position. Still, as I say, it adds to the uncertainty." She smiled mischievously. "Now, by the sound of it, Pharaoh is returning. You had better go and greet him and give him your news from Heliopolis."

"Yes, dearest Mother, I will tell him what I can." While he and the Queen had a way of wounding or annoying one another when they talked together, they still liked to talk. On the other hand Amenophis had always found conversation with his father to be virtually impossible.

Looking back on this year afterwards, it seemed both short and hazy. This was because nothing of importance happened to him in either his inner or his outer worlds. He saw it as a pause in his life, an interval between the implanting of the ideas and convictions that had brought about his sudden emergence from boyhood, and the next period of growth and change that was to begin when he mounted the throne of Egypt.

Perhaps everyone at court felt much the same. It had

been whispered about that Pharaoh was mortally sick and that his return to Osiris could not be long delayed. Inevitably there was a feeling of dullness and disappointment when he was once again to be seen in the audience chamber and fulfilling every one of his divine offices.

The Great Queen, too, was known to be resuming her control of state affairs and her ruthless, underground contest with the priesthood of Amon. The third priest, one of Ipy's ablest and most ambitious supporters, was sent on a mission to Kush and was reported to have fallen from the boat and been eaten by crocodiles. No one believed in the accident. But most people were inclined to feel in sympathy with Queen Tiye now that they saw her as holding a shield to protect her vulnerable son. Moreover, whatever had happened to the priest took place a very long way away, and could not be allowed to disturb the ordinary pleasures of Thebes. Yet there was a sense that this familiar tenor of court life could not last. It was a sluggish time of waiting.

In fact Amenophis was neither bored nor impatient. Each week Nefertiti and Tey were quietly brought across to the Palace early in the morning. They had been given apartments near the harim where they spent the night, returning to East Thebes the next evening. These two days of Nefertiti's company were all that he asked, and they seemed to bring a delightful and sustaining rhythm to his existence. He, who before had been so completely self-absorbed, took an intense pleasure in watching her develop, and in listening to her as well as pouring his own ideas into her ear. In spite of her own devoted admiration for her foster child, Tey was astonished at the sensitive respect with which he treated her—not just as a girl he loved but as a growing person. He seemed to regard her as an equal: Tey had never known anything like it.

Soon after his return, Amenophis sent for a priest whom he had heard about from Mersure. He had the title of Steward of the Mansion of the Aten, and presided over a small, modestly-endowed temple which the Queen's party had set up as part of their plan for a new cult to wean Thebes away from Amon without openly committing anyone to his rival at Heliopolis. The Prince found the priest agreeable and polished, but when he tried to make him understand his intuitions about a divinity of light and life and love he got no response worth listening to. It was not that the man did not want to respond—he was desperately anxious to make a good impression—he was simply incapable of it.

For this Steward of the Aten, religion was the correct and punctual performance of prayers, sacrifices and other prescribed observances. These he attended to quite conscientiously, but he was more truly interested in winning an increase in his establishment and in pleasing the Great Queen through small triumphs over the priests of Amon. He finally left the royal presence as much disappointed in his hopes of great patronage, as the Prince was disappointed in his hope of finding someone who could share his understanding of the godhead.

After this failure, Amenophis decided to return to his own meditations, helped out by occasional discussions with Meryre. He spent a good deal of time in the Palace garden, sometimes sitting in the shade, sometimes pacing with his odd stiff gait in the sycomore walk, most often distracting his thoughts by looking intently at something that caught his attention—eggs lying among feathers in a bird's nest, a butterfly uncoiling its long tongue to plunge it down a flower, wasps stripping wood for their nest or ants streaming in their tireless, busy processions. He found that he still went out to these tiny experiences as completely as he had done in childhood. Now, however, he saw each one as celebrating, in its own exquisite particularity, the divinity of life, the universal power he was struggling to understand.

Even in the Palace garden he could not fail also to see the ruthlessness of nature. He saw caterpillars writhing as the ichneumon maggots burst from their sides; he saw wasps and spiders paralysing other creatures to devour them at leisure. And in the spectacle of black swarms of ants slowly dragging a beetle to exhaustion and death he seemed to be watching a symbolic drama, for was not the scarab the symbol of self-creative life, and as Khepri one

of the aspects of the Sun God? Amenophis no longer
attempted to intervene in these cruel struggles, for he knew
that it was useless. He had, instead, formed the habit of
looking hastily away. But he was honest enough to make
himself think about them, and he found it hard indeed to
reconcile them with the trend of his beliefs.

In one direction Amenophis made an altogether new
effort during that year of waiting. Bak's talk, and much of
the ancient sculpture which he had seen in the north, had
fired him with desire to liberate artists from their traditional bonds. He often recalled the drop of wine flashing
in the candlelight of his cabin and Bak's cry for an art of
the instant. Would not this way of looking at things be
closer to his idea of Ma'at? Closer to the living truth. He
determined first to try for himself.

He persuaded the Queen to allow him to make use of
her barge, *Aten Gleams*, and he went out on the lake with
only his usual attendants. He had sheets of papyrus mounted on thin boards and specially treated so that they would
take quick strokes of the brush, and armed with these he
had the barge rowed softly round the edges of the lake or
allowed to drift past the reed beds, hunting for subjects.
He tried to show kingfishers in the act of diving or alight-
ing on a reed, a goose reaching back to bite its rump
feathers and a heron struggling with a frog. Sometimes he
tried to catch the movements of his paddlemen. He was not
very successful at first, for he could not use any of the
tricks and set forms he had learnt in the past.

Then one evening when he had told the men to let the
boat drift, a gaudy drake came hurling down on to the
water only a few yards away. He saw just how the bird
checked itself at the last, bracing its wings and sticking its
webbed feet out in front so that little plumes of water shot
out from them. In a kind of frenzy he dashed it down on
his board without a thought of anything but capturing
that checked speed. The result delighted him. The drake
looked distorted and a little grotesque, but there was a
heavy bird coming from the sky and striking the water.

In great excitement he showed his painting to Bak, and
the sculptor almost seized it out of his hand the instant his

eyes had scanned it. He gazed intently at it for a minute, moving his lips almost as though he were spelling out the lines. Then suddenly he let out his breath in a kind of whoop. "Forgive me, Crown Prince, but it is just as though you had winded me. There it is: you have caught the moment. I have been your subject in all other things and now I must bow before you as an artist. Of course my father would think it frightful. Perhaps nobody but you and I in all Egypt could understand what you have done."

The next day they went out together in *Aten Gleams*, and Bak tried his hand at the new method. He was even less successful than Amenophis had been when he began, because, in spite of his bold ideas, the old forms were more firmly in control of his imagination.

"It's hopeless," he exclaimed after his third attempt had turned into nothing more than a neat study for a Palace mural. "I'm no good on the flat, anyway. I must try it in stone." He tore the papyrus off the board, crumpled it and threw it into the water.

"Yes, when the time comes that is what I shall want of you. Thebes is full of statues of Pharaoh which are as nearly identical as all those of Amon—or even of Sekhmet the lion-headed. Perhaps a longer or rounder face may be allowed, or the shape of the nose varied. But everyone knows that my grandfather had one leg much shorter than the other, and I've heard that my famous ancestor Tuthmosis had lost an ear. As for those two staring giants on my father's funerary temple, they might be anybody, yet Pharaoh has a very distinctive, ugly face. Ma'at has many faces, and I have seen that for the artist it means showing life as it is—that kind of truth. It is another way of looking at your 'art of the instant', because it means the truth of the moment as well as of form. When I am Pharaoh I want to be shown not only with my thin legs and all the other oddities I know I am developing," he grinned and stretched out his feet as he sat on the folding stool, "but I also want to be shown when I am happy and when I am sad—while I am young and when I grow old. . . ."

"You would allow this, Crown Prince? You would have such portraits put up in temples and public places?"

"Certainly: indeed, I should command it."

"But—my Lord—would the priests consent to it? Can the divine king of the Egyptians be seen by the people to have thin legs?"

"Pharaoh is Pharaoh. Let us have some wine." The barge was tied up and wine poured. Amenophis left his stool for some cushions, and Bak sat cross-legged beside him. They drank in silence; then the Prince smiled into the little red pool of his wine cup and said, "There is only one person who couldn't be flattered by any artist, who would only be more beautiful if seen with the eyes of Ma'at. . . ."

"That is true—I have tried. I can't approach the loveliness of Nefertiti. And it will increase." Bak emptied his cup, then emboldened he turned his full, bright eyes on Amenophis. "Crown Prince," he said, "I have watched you now for more than a year, seen both you and the Princess Nefertiti growing and changing. You spend so much time in her company. Do you never desire her— many would say she is old enough . . .?"

Amenophis held himself very still, and for a moment Bak thought that he had angered him. But when the Prince spoke it was as quietly as before. "I do not desire her except as a part of loving her. I know that men speak of possessing women, but no one could ever possess Nefertiti. I believe that Re will give the sign. Meanwhile I am content to watch—sometimes I feel I am holding her soul in my hands almost as I am holding this wine. . . ."

Bak picked up another papyrus board, and now began to sketch calmly but swiftly. Amenophis followed his quick glances and saw two grebes engaged in one of their strange courtship rituals. The birds were so intensely preoccupied with one another that although they were quite close to the barge they took no notice whatever of their human audience. For a time they had been bowing, beak to beak, but now the male rose half out of the water and curved his long, snaky neck above his mate in a way that seemed half beseeching, half imperious. The female moved her head sideways with a small, deft response.

Bak laid down his brush and laughed as he looked at his

own handiwork. He had shown the grebes with a few broad lines, yet the interplay between male and female, the tension and feeling that united them, was perfectly expressed.

"You see they are *together*, Crown Prince. Now as an artist I can lift up my head again in your presence. See the life flowing between them."

Amenophis nodded his head, and his face lit up for a moment. "Yes, I understand. That is the third thing we need. Truth of the moment and of the individual, and now the feeling between one thing and another."

"Yes," Bak cried, "and what we can do for birds we can do a thousand times more powerfully for human beings. I see it now. At last there is going to be change."

Again Amenophis nodded, but he looked dejected and weary. "Tell them to take us back," he said, and went to his couch where he was hidden by a low awning. When they reached the landing stage he took a formal farewell of the sculptor, and for some time afterwards saw much less of him.

It was spring again, and all Egyptians were able to forget their burdens at the sight of fields shimmering with the first green blades. Everyone made offerings to Osiris, whose presence in the flood waters and in the seed corn had brought about the annual miracle. A messenger arrived at the Palace, and was at once admitted before Pharaoh. Within an hour the court, and most ardently the ladies of the harim, were discussing the arrival in Egypt of the Princess Tadukhipa with a great retinue and a shipload of splendid gifts.

In the harim Gilukhipa was the centre of curiosity, because it was known that the messenger had brought her a letter from her brother, the Mitannian king.

"What does he say?" asked Mina, her face alert with inquisitiveness. "Is he going to insist on her being Great Queen, and will you have to support him?"

"Heavens, no. Tushratta has enough sense to know that I am of no use to him any more. Besides, I'm against the whole thing. It will be abominable for the girl, and I can't

see it doing Mitanni any good politically. Probably quite
the opposite in the long run, for Amenophis won't give a
damn for alliances of that kind, while Tiye, who's bound
to be immensely influential, will be antagonized. However, kings don't ask advice of half-forgotten sisters in
foreign harims."

"Does your brother say what Tadukhipa is like now?"
asked Mina, eagerly following her favourite scent.

"No, of course not—what an idiot you are sometimes,
Mina. All the same I did have a private word with the
messenger, and he says she's not exactly beautiful, but
that she's become wonderfully attractive in rather a virile
sort of way. Very much as I was, I suppose." Gilukhipa
gave one of her throaty laughs, screwing up her eyes in
the way that deepened her crow's-feet.

"What do you think will happen with Pharaoh? Will
he . . .?"

"I should think it will be the death of the old man," said
Gilukhipa.

Amenophis, who still occasionally went to talk to his
favourites in the harim, felt only a mild interest in the
expected arrival. He did, however, feel very indignant on
her behalf. His faith in Pharaoh's divine throne was absolute—any doubts he had felt about it had been swept away
by his own vision of Re. On the other hand, he had come
to separate this divinity from the human aspect of the
ruler. The god, as he now saw it, was incarnate in a man
who remained a man, and whose acts should conform
with a human ideal. That a young girl should be sent
thousands of miles from her home to be put at the mercy
of an old man as part of a game of politics seemed to him
abominable. One day he said to Gilukhipa, "I know you
feel sad about your niece. Do you think that a woman can
be happy in a royal harim?"

"It depends on the kind of woman, Crown Prince. The
very feminine ones, and the girls who have been brought
up in subjection, are happy enough. They have every
luxury, and companionship of a sort. They don't have the
feeling, as I used to, of being no better than spoiled prosti-
tutes and slaves. For you know, Prince, we haven't the

dignity and independence of an ordinary Egyptian housewife—or that is how I see it."

"Do what you can to protect Tadukhipa, and I give you my promise that when I am Pharaoh I will have her sent home if she wishes."

"When you become Pharaoh—if it is at all soon—I don't doubt that my niece will be passed on to you. My brother would insist on it." She almost added, "and perhaps you might like her very much", but thought better of it.

"That would make no difference, if she wishes to go. Would you like to go with her, Gilukhipa—back to Mitanni?" There was a moment's silence, then she drew a very deep breath and her tall, powerful body seemed to shiver.

"You won't believe it, because you are young, dear Amenophis, but our possibilities wither; things can happen too late. I'm an old horse, though a tough one, and it's too late for me to go back to my youthful pastures. But we'll do what we can for Tadukhipa."

"And I will do what I can for you also." He was a little aware of the pain he had caused her.

On the same day another messenger announced that the princess's boats should reach Thebes within five days, and preparations for their reception had to be rushed ahead. Queen Tiye had determined on her course of action, and had no difficulty in persuading Pharaoh and the vizier to fall in with it. They would receive the girl and her retinue with great honour and magnificence, quickly stage a marriage ceremony to give her the status of wife, and see to it that her escorts went back to Tushratta not only laden with gifts but also with reports of the splendour with which Egypt had received his daughter. Tadukhipa would then be installed with a decent suite and establishment and be left to discover that she wasn't very important after all. Privately, of course, the Queen prayed that Pharaoh would not be attracted by his young wife, but there was nothing she could do to prevent it, except to pretend that he looked ill again, and to try to fill him with anxiety about his health.

Amenophis had to play his part as Crown Prince in the Palace reception arranged for the Mitannian party, but he excused himself from the banquets and other celebrations that were to follow. He sat on his lower seat beside Pharaoh and Queen Tiye—who firmly took her place as Great Wife—and listened to the swelling cheers as the procession approached through the crowds gathered from West Thebes. (They came out readily enough, but had been encouraged by the provision of free beer and wine.) As the princess, escorted by her father's ambassador Nahramassi, came up the aisled hall, Amenophis, who had hitherto been divided between boredom and disapproval, was seized by a conviction that this entry, this surge of richly-clad and bejewelled figures between the brightly-painted lotus columns, was going to cause an impact that would set his life moving once more. The pause, the quiet interlude, was at an end.

The leading couple advanced from among their followers, mostly young ladies-in-waiting supported by a few well-born Mitannian pages, who looked amazingly stalwart and fair-skinned against the background figures of the Egyptian court. The ambassador was a huge fellow, with a domed cap on his head that made him appear even taller; he was wound in a richly-woven cloak with a massive border of gold thread that was making the sweat break out all over his face. Amenophis was interested only in the girl, observing her intently as she mounted the lower steps of the throne. She was strongly built, though not so tall as her aunt, and riding had made her too muscular for the Egyptian ideal. But she had a glorious pale golden brown complexion and a pile of wavy red-brown hair. Although her features were boldly cut and could easily have passed for a boy's, there was at that moment something purely female in her face which took Amenophis by surprise. Gilukhipa was certainly not lacking in femininity, but her expression was proud, frank and absolutely fearless. Her niece also had a proud—indeed almost arrogant—carriage, but as she raised her eyes to Pharaoh's there was something abject in them.

Pharaoh, with his lofty headdress and heavily painted

face, appeared remote and impersonal, but as he looked down on to the girl's face and saw the expression there, his own gaze kindled with a sudden recognition. His slack body stiffened and drew up, and for an instant Amenophis had the illusion that the sacred Uraeaus serpent on the royal brow had darted out its tongue.

Leaning forward very slightly, Amenophis could just see his mother. She looked startled, and her small fingers were racing on the arm of her throne—a thing which only happened when she was agitated. Very quickly, however, she recovered herself, made the little shrug he knew so well and was receiving the princess as befitted the Queen of Egypt welcoming an honoured but inferior newcomer to her court. In another moment Nahramassi was directing pages to bring forward gifts, and the encounter seemed to fade into unreality in the swirl of formalities.

Tushratta had sent three lapis lazuli caskets for Pharaoh, Queen Tiye and the Crown Prince, and these Tadukhipa, herself put into their hands. Pharaoh's contained a massive gold ring with his royal cartouche carved on the blood-red bezel and his name in cuneiform on the back. The Queen had a lapis and gold necklace, by Egyptian standards inferior in workmanship and design, while in Amenophis's casket lay a small jewelled dagger with a silvery-dark blade. He felt the deadly sharp edge and point and knew it must be made of the rare Hittite metal, the charcoal-baked iron. He imagined the dreadful power of an army equipped with such weapons, and hastily shut the lid of the casket. Evidently Tushratta did not know how much he loathed all thoughts of bloodshed and war.

The Mitannians had also brought a big cedar chest full of pretty gold leaf ornaments and pearl-embroidered slippers for the ladies of the harim, and outside were great quantities of oil and bronze vessels, as well as spices and bales of fine cloths from their Indian trade. But chief among all the gifts which Tushratta had despatched to show his power of lavishness to his promised son-in-law were a superb golden chariot, heavily built and probably not suited to Egyptian conditions, and a string of magnificent riding horses. These beasts, Nahramassi declared,

were so well trained that even the most delicately nurtured
lady could learn to ride them. He hoped that Tadukhipa
would be able to introduce this delightful exercise to the
royal household.

All these gifts, unusual even in cosmopolitan Thebes,
together with the presence of so many foreign visitors,
would have caused quite a stir in the court even without
the celebration that followed. Queen Tiye had spared no
expense, and for a week there were banquets at night and
all kinds of informal festivities during the day. The pretty
girls who danced and sang and played instruments began to
feel quite worn out, while the royal wine stores were
dwindling. It seemed like a return to the best of the old
days before Pharaoh's illness. And running through all
the excitement, and all the exhaustion too, was a very
special nervous tension.

Everyone belonging to the inner circle of court life
knew that Pharaoh was spending a great deal of time with
Tadukhipa. The marriage, which had been celebrated in
East Thebes quickly and without great public ceremony,
was proving to be no mere formality. As the harim ladies
passed languid mornings sipping fruit juices and recover-
ing from the excesses of the night before, they exchanged
any rumours they had gathered about the progress of the
affair, and more particularly of Queen Tiye's reactions
and likely counter measures. Some held that Pharaoh's
passion would not last, some, like Gilukhipa, that he would
kill himself, while others again gleefully declared that
Queen Tiye, the Great Wife, was going to be robbed of her
power at last.

Amenophis kept out of everything so far as he could. He
felt a strong antipathy for the Mitannian Princess, and was
happy to tell Nefertiti that she was in every way Tadukhipa's opposite and that the contrast made him treasure
her more even than before. One day they were both
together in a secluded part of the gardens feeding goldfish
and speculating on what it would be like to be a fish, when
Gilukhipa arrived quite unattended. She drew Amenophis
aside.

"Crown Prince," she said, "I have heard something

which I want to pass on to you. Probably it's a matter for the Queen, but it's not easy to talk to her just now."

Amenophis looked at her impatiently, for he resented being made to leave Nefertiti. "Very well," he replied, "but you know that I'm not likely to be interested."

"As you'll have heard, Nahramassi is leaving tomorrow. Well, last night the High Priest went very privately to see him. I have learnt about it only through a lucky chance. The ambassador has been using as a translator the son of one of my ladies-in-waiting—he grew up with her here and then returned to Mitanni. All right, Prince, I'm coming to the point." Amenophis's attention had wandered, and he was watching Nefertiti as she leant over the pond, allowing the fish to nibble her fingers. "Anyway, I'd naturally got to know this young man, and this morning he confided in me. It seems that Ipy told Nahramassi to take a message to the king that he and his priests rejoiced to see how quickly Tadukhipa had won her due place at court, and that, if by any misfortune Pharaoh should be called to return to Osiris, they would wish to see her transferred to you as Great Wife and Queen."

"That, of course, is impossible. I cannot even feel angry, it is so far out of the question." He looked at Nefertiti again.

"And it is not the worst. Ipy ended with a sentence that was to be precisely repeated to my brother. He said 'that in addressing the royal father of this beautiful and already well-loved princess he knew he could depend upon his understanding and interest'. Which, as I understand it, was as good as telling Tushratta to use the threat of his military power in Asia to force his daughter on to the Queen's throne—whether it is beside you or your father."

"I have long ago decided to dismiss Ipy as soon as I am able. I am not afraid of him. The seat at my side is already occupied: Ipy cannot alter that—nor Amon either." He spoke the last words defiantly, looking round as though he half expected to be struck down. The garden was very peaceful.

"The priesthood of Amon is powerful and abominably rich—and many of the nobles of Upper Egypt are behind them just because they feel they must be against Helio-polis. And there is no doubt that the present situation with Tadukhipa looks dangerous. Well, Prince Amenophis, it is no longer my business. But you know that I am devoted to you, and I thought I should tell you what passed—then you can decide whether to speak to Queen Tiye."

"Gilukhipa, there is something I wish to say to you. I was, as you know, very sorry for your niece and promised that I would help her. Now I don't feel at all the same." Gilukhipa looked at him intently, then nodded.

"I am afraid I have to agree with you. It seems that you understand women of all kinds, Crown Prince. Tadukhipa is more than a little rotten at the centre. It must be her miserable Babylonian mother. Women who are like that can't help themselves—that's all I can say on her behalf."

"One other thing. Did you hear that Tushratta sent me a Hittite iron dagger?"

"One hears everything in the harim."

"I thought he would have known that I am not fond of such things."

"Yes. I was surprised, then I began to think that he may have intended to send you a message. That you will have to fight."

"I shall have to fight, Gilukhipa, but not with iron. I wonder if your brother can understand that?"

A little later Amenophis sought out his mother and repeated the whole of Gilukhipa's story. Queen Tiye was nothing if not a fighter, and opposition made her seem admirable. She was angry at the news of Ipy's treachery, but declared that she was not in the least surprised.

"His scheming against us goes on all the time. It is that which has become the breath of life to him, not Amon. However, he is often not so clever as he imagines. I have better sources of information than Ipy, and I hear that Tushratta is getting worried about his neighbours the Hittites. Their new king is able and ambitious, and of course likes to look eastward. No, I am sure that Tushratta will want to remain on good terms with us—and that he will be satisfied with the reception we have given to his daughter—far better than she deserves. He has a passion for gold, and seems to think our mountains are made of it. We'll send back his messengers tomorrow weighed down with the stuff, and then I think we can be sure of his loyalty. To say the truth, Amenophis, I'm far more worried about the situation here. I haven't been able to talk to Pharaoh once since the girl arrived."

"I don't think it will last, Mother. He will tire of her."

"You begin to talk as though you had a vast experience of women, Amenophis."

"I don't know how it is, but one can have understanding from within. I have watched Tadukhipa . . . and I have some knowledge of Pharaoh. . . ."

"Yes." Tiye tightened her lips and looked grimly at him for a moment. "In fact I agree with you. It is most likely that either Pharaoh will tire of her, or he will kill himself. And if it is the second, you will stand by me, won't you, my son?"

"When I am Pharaoh, I trust that you will stand by me, Madam Mother." He said this seriously, then added with a grin, "I don't want another Hatshepsut."

"Do you see me putting on a beard? It wouldn't become me in any way." Queen Tiye went off to supervise the final selection and packing of gifts for Tushratta, feeling much more cheerful and confident. Perhaps after all her freakish son was going to be a comfort to her. She must be patient, but meanwhile it was galling as well as worrying to catch glimpses of Pharaoh going about with brighter eyes and a firmer step, and to receive reports from her informers among his body servants that he was trying to return to many of the habits he had had as a younger man.

The Mitannian ambassador was honourably embarked with great rings, ingots and figurines of gold for his royal master, and pleasing presents also for himself, and the life of court and Palace began to return to normal—all, that is, except for the private life of Pharaoh. He remained so preoccupied with Tadukhipa that Amenophis no longer took any serious precautions about his meetings with Nefertiti. One day he had taken her out with him in *Aten Gleams* and was expounding the theories of art which he and Bak had developed, while at the same time trying to sketch her and her favourite cat.

Nefertiti, so much alive to music and poetry, had very little feeling for the visual arts, but she was always absorbed in anything Amenophis had to say.

"So you mean that painting and sculpture aren't just ways of showing the gods, but are really a part of religion and goodness?" She looked up at him with the wondering admiration which Amenophis found so irresistible.

"If they are truthful, if they are done according to Ma'at as our new art will be, then they are a part of divine creation. The more I think about things, all the countless things that there are"—he waved his arm and paintbrush as though to sweep in the whole world—"the more sure I am that there is some single force holding them all together. Re of Heliopolis is the sun god who created everything from the primeval hill when it rose from the waters, and he made it all of the same stuff. And he made it all with the same power. That is why you and I, who are open to Ma'at, feel so much at one with birds and animals and flowers—and even with the rocks and sands of the desert. Often we imagine we can feel them in our bodies. And sometimes I think that the power is more the divine thing than Re himself. You said it might be love, and I think that the source of all love is the sun. It is a great divine furnace of love which feeds all life and without which things turn ghostly white and die. Perhaps it is the creator burning himself up with love and power. This is what I shall call the Aten, and this is what I shall find burning in myself when I mount the throne, and it will be in you, too, Nefertiti, as you sit beside me."

"But isn't it in all people—and all things too? I am sure it is in my cat?" She did not say this quite innocently, but looked at the prince with a mysterious smile. He was startled at anything but complete acceptance from Nefertiti—more particularly as he had expected to delight her with his picture of their shared glory.

"I was in earnest," he said gently but reprovingly. "I meant what I said."

"So did I—although perhaps I mentioned Sekko to

tease you a little. But I do think there must be divinity in all things, and especially in all men and women."

"Yes: I said myself that everything is made of the same stuff and by the same power. But Pharaoh is the son of Re, and through the throne and the two crowns divine power burns in him as in the god. He must be the presence of the Aten on earth, linking all earthly things with the heavenly power that gave them life." Seeing that she still looked a little troubled, he went on, "But Nefertiti, don't think that I want to appear as a being set apart as other Pharaohs have done. I wish to mingle more with the people, to lead a family life—and to be shown always as I am. That is why I am determined to teach the new art, the truthful art." Nefertiti nodded and looked at him with her old childlike devotion.

"I wish that you could begin soon. I wonder how long you must wait before you can put all your ideas into practice. How everyone will love you." They had drifted for a few moments in such silence that Amenophis could distinguish Sekko purring under Nefertiti's skilful caresses, when they heard someone cry out at the Palace, then an outburst of voices; through a gap in the reed beds they saw guards—and even gardeners—running towards the royal apartments. Before the barge could tie up several house servants had come down from the Palace and were gesticulating excitedly as they told some spicy news to the royal bearers. Then Tey appeared, hurrying along and anxiously pursued by one of her ladies. She had been in the Palace gardens awaiting her charge's return from the lake. Amenophis held Nefertiti back until Tey arrived, and it was her hand (slightly muddy because she never could resist pulling up any weed that caught her eye) that helped them ashore.

"It's Pharaoh," she said, drawing Amenophis quickly aside. "He's had an attack, and some are saying he is dead. It seems that the Princess Tadukhipa came screaming out with almost nothing on and looking quite wild. Of course her noise has roused the whole Palace. I thought she would have had more sense."

Pharaoh was not dead, but survived his attack paralysed

and unable to speak intelligibly. Tey's mild censure of the way in which Tadukhipa had lost her head was generous when set beside the comments of Queen Tiye. She pretended to think that the girl had done it deliberately in order to show her involvement in the affair. "If only she had behaved with decent discretion," she declared, "as any peasant woman would have had the intelligence to do, we could have hushed up Pharaoh's illness and prevented news of it spreading through the country. Now it will be whispered to infants in their cradles and shouted into the ears of deaf old men—and there will be trouble. Tadukhipa deserves to be buried alive."

The news did in fact spread up and down the Nile with remarkable speed. Within a few days it was being discussed by Negroes in the markets of southernmost Kush, while it overtook Nahramassi well before he was ready to embark for Ugarit. And it did cause trouble and distress. While there was probably no one else who agreed with certain tribesmen in the extreme south beyond the Third Cataract who said that a sick king must be returned to the fields, almost everyone felt ill at ease and exposed to bad luck. Their god at Thebes, who cost them so much, was needed to preserve Ma'at and the goodwill of the other gods. If he were sick things were bound to go wrong.

And things did go wrong. There were crop failures, plagues of locusts, and, in Kush, ruinous depredations by hippopotami. Many villages had epidemics and many mothers had monstrous births. There was a rumour that thousands of snakes had invaded the streets of Elephantine, and prophets of all kinds foretold that the flood would fail that year.

Queen Tiye and the vizier Ramose thought of declaring a regency, but decided at last that Pharaoh's life could hardly be sufficiently prolonged to justify it. Instead they arranged for Amenophis to take his father's place in receiving tribute and giving audiences. It was spread about that the prayers to the sun of the inspired Crown Prince were almost as efficacious as those of Pharaoh himself. Ipy, acting as usual without consultation, sent proclamations to all cities that the Crown Prince, beloved of Amon, was enacting many of the rites of the god and was under his special protection. This gave great satisfaction in Upper Egypt, but provoked minor rioting by fanatic groups in the north. They held that Pharaoh's sickness and all the ills of Egypt were due to this honouring of the upstart god of Thebes.

Meanwhile in Thebes itself week after week the afflicted Pharaoh continued to live. The doctors fed him on honey, wine and infusions of herbs administered with the appropriate spells and exorcisms. In his temple hundreds of priests delivered thousands of prayers, and the pens of the sacrificial animals seemed as crowded as a market.

Amenophis loathed the ugly sight of his father and his suffering, and visited him rarely. Nevertheless, even in the absence of love, his powerful imagination made him share in Pharaoh's torments. His sleep was often broken by nightmares where black serpents from the Underworld lay in wait for the dying. He was troubled to find the crooked, wet-mouthed figure on the bed, with his occasional pitiful attempts to speak, seemingly all stricken man and no immortal god.

He was troubled also by lesser questions, for he had now formed a habit of mind which, whether he wished it or not, made him question everything. One day when he had forced himself to attend his father, he found him apparently asleep and snoring painfully. Several doctors were there, but for the moment were not attempting any ministrations. Pharaoh's head was propped on a bare wooden rest, and his body was now so emaciated and rigid that it appeared to Amenophis as though the whole figure were carved in wood. Tears came into the prince's eyes, yet at the same time the sweet smell of burning frankincense mingled with the stink of the sickbed greatly disgusted him.

Perhaps encouraged by the quiet arrival of the Crown Prince, one of the doctors placed a scarab on the royal forehead and began to exhort the spirit said to be gripping Pharaoh's tongue and limb muscles to depart to the dark realms from which he came. Amenophis listened, then found himself recalling the words of Tey and his mother and everyone else who in the first frantic hours of the seizure had taken it for granted that the cause lay with Tadukhipa.

He was about to ask the senior physician, now bowing before him, whether in truth he attributed Pharaoh's condition to an evil spirit or to exertions with the Princess Tadukhipa, when footsteps and voices could be heard outside. A servant held back the curtain, and Queen Tiye came in. Seeing Amenophis, she checked her quick walk and said, "Prince, I am glad, as well as surprised, to find you here." Then, turning to the doctors, "Sirs, you have heard it rumoured that our royal brother the King Tushratta had again despatched the divine Ishtar from Nineveh. She has now arrived, and her priests, hearing that Pharaoh is sick, are asking that she be admitted at once into the presence." The Queen spoke with unusual formality, contriving, so it seemed to Amenophis, to convey all her feminine scepticism in her tone and face.

The physicians, while exchanging glances of annoyance, could only express their happiness that the great goddess of the Assyrians should be begged to exercise her healing powers upon their divine master. Amenophis stepped back into an alcove to watch what would happen. The servant lifted the curtain once more, and in paced two priests, their curling black beards and long hair gleaming with oil. Both immediately prostrated themselves before Pharaoh's bed; as he fell to his knees one of them ventured to look directly at the sick man, and Amenophis saw a look of intense horror and dismay transform his face before he hid it by touching his forehead to the ground. In spite of the solemnity of the moment, he could not help noticing, too, how difficult the priests found the full obeisance because of their long, tightly-wound skirts which stretched across their buttocks like drums. Then the lofty doorway was blocked by a golden shrine borne on a stretcher on the shoulders of four sweating Assyrians; it swayed as the bearers crossed the threshold and for an instant it looked as though the towering, gem-encrusted edifice were going to topple on to the helpless monarch.

The men recovered themselves and lowered their burden

so that the shrine stood on the short legs of the stretcher facing the royal couch. Finally there entered a third priest, whose hair and beard were thin and grey and who was evidently worn by the long journey from Nineveh. He was leaning on a staff, and although he bent his head and shoulders until Amenophis could see the rayed star which formed the crown of his cylindrical hat, he did not attempt to prostrate himself. Instead he tottered up to the shrine and opened the inlaid doors of the central arch to reveal a squat figure completely hidden by a cloak of pearls and set between two golden lions, the eyes of which glowed redly in the shadowy interior of the shrine.

The elder priests addressed her. "Divine Lady of Nineveh, Ishtar, Lady of the Star, Great Mother of All! Through me your priest and lowly servant, Tushratta, King of Mitanni, overlord of Assyria, beseeches that you look favourably upon the divine Pharaoh, Horus, Son of Amon, Son of the Sun. Great Goddess, you who have brought back life from the Underworld, command this demon to return to the darkness, that the divine Pharaoh, King of Upper and Lower Egypt, lord of all peoples, shall be set free from his sorcery and live for ever."

There was a hush in which the snoring breath from the bed seemed more than ever heart-rending. Then suddenly its painful rhythm was broken, there was utter silence, a little harsh sound, then Pharaoh's body contracted and fell back again, the head knocking over the wooden rest and falling awkwardly on one side. Amenophis III, sovereign of Egypt and her Empire for as long as most people could clearly remember, was one with Osiris and the souls of his ancestors.

Afterwards even Queen Tiye agreed that the king's Ka must have sprung from the corpse and filled the room with its power, for all there knew that Pharaoh was dead and all uttered a groaning cry. The old priest stumbled and clutched at the shrine, causing it to lurch, then threw himself on the ground. He was, in truth, in a blind terror lest he should be blamed for the Goddess having struck down Pharaoh instead of healing him. The young priests and doctors followed his example, and in an instant everyone was prostrate except for Amenophis and his mother. She fell on her knees beside the bed, removed the rest and straightened the head. Amenophis stood at the foot of the body, tears flowing down his long face, and yet possessed by a kind of joy. It was the first time he had seen a man die, and that had torn at him, but the power of the Ka in the room assured him that even in the sick and tormented man the godhead had been present, and now, surely, he could feel the divinity waxing in himself.

Amenophis stood there a full minute, while the corpse seemed to relax and assume a kind of gaunt repose; he took a deep breath and his emotion was abruptly followed by a feeling of detachment. He turned, and found himself looking through the open doors of the shrine. The jolt had made the image of the goddess tip over sideways, lose her headdress and protrude from her cloak of pearls. He saw a clumsy female figure carved in a greasy-looking black stone; the enormous eyes stared straight ahead, quite without expression, while stiff little feet jutted out from an almost conical body.

The old priest was just rising on his knees, and he looked fearfully up at the young Egyptian who now had power of life and death. On a sudden impulse Amenophis lifted the naked statuette of Ishtar from between her guardian lions, and held her out feet first to the priest.

"I do not doubt the power of the Great Goddess and Lady of Nineveh, but I believe it does not reside in this image. Take it at once from the Palace, and when you are rested pack it in your baggage and return to your fine city. I will send gifts of gold and my thanks to my brother King Tushratta, and will see that you and your companions do not leave empty-handed. One other thing. Tell your master that I esteem his friendship, and that it is my purpose that there shall be peace not only between our peoples, but between all peoples." Amenophis embraced his mother, then went out to look for Nefertiti. He knew that he had not many more hours that would be his own.

Amenophis found her together with Tey in the simple withdrawing room of their apartments. Tey, as so often, was busy embroidering a cushion, while his love was frowning over an exercise in cursive script. The room was furnished in ebony and white and smelled strongly of lilies: it seemed to Amenophis a place of perfect bliss after the death chamber he had just escaped.

Tey stuck her needle in the cloth. It was largely owing to her tactful persuasion that the Prince had overcome his reluctance to visit his father, so she asked in what was perhaps a rather complacent way, "Did you find the Lord Pharaoh any better, Crown Prince? Did he recognize you . . .?" As he approached she saw that he had been weeping, while at that moment wailing could be heard from the harim. Nefertiti jumped up and ran over to him, fondling his hand between her own; her head did not quite reach up to his shoulder. Amenophis nodded sadly.

"Yes," he said, "the god my father has returned to the source of light. His Ka was very strong." Tey no longer dared hug him as she used to do, but she put an arm about him impulsively. Then she drew back. "But I am forgetting. We are now in the presence of Pharaoh. We cannot treat our dear Amenophis in the familiar way we have in the past." Nefertiti continued to fondle his hand, and his face was transformed by one of his sudden grins.

"Tomorrow I shall go to the Eastern Window to address my prayer to Re, and during the day the accession will be proclaimed—this is how it is always. But at least until sunrise I can still be your Crown Prince."

"And afterwards? Will you be so changed?" Nefertiti stepped back a little, though keeping her fingertips in his palm.

"Not to you, Nefertiti, nor to my dear Aunt Tey. But there must be one great change between us. Tomorrow, before the accession, we must celebrate our marriage. Then the people will know from the first who is to be their Great Queen—and can rejoice with us."

Tey looked horrified. "But, Crown Prince, that is impossible! There is no time to get ready. . . ."

"No time is needed. And if you want all kinds of dressing up and ceremony, that can be at the time of the coronation. Meanwhile, dear Aunt, I will see that all my subjects honour you as Great Queen's Nurse."

"But then Nefertiti is so young, young even for a royal marriage. Don't think I am not overjoyed by what you propose, by the thought that my dearest treasure is to sit at your side. But she is young, not in mind, I know, but very young in body. . . ." She broke off, looking at him pleadingly.

"I do not intend that there shall be any change in our relationship except that Nefertiti shall be with me always. In her body, as you say, she is still almost a child. And I . . . I am not ready either. My Father has not yet spoken." As she heard him, Tey suddenly flopped on to her knees, rather heavily as she was now very stout. She reached for his knees, but at that moment, to the Prince's relief, a scribe arrived to say that the vizier Ramose begged an audience as soon as he was able to grant it. Amenophis raised Tey and kissed Nefertiti on the forehead.

"Our time has come at last," he whispered to her. "But at first we shall have to endure many wearisome things. Rise early tomorrow and keep yourself in readiness."

Two days later Amenophis was resting on a couch, with the Queen Mother sitting beside him and Ramose hovering near. The evening was intensely hot, and he was exhausted by the extraordinary exertions of his accession. The emaciated remains of Amenophis III had been solemnly handed over to the priests of Anubis for embalming, and the new king had moved into the royal apartments. He had just returned from East Thebes and his face looked very weary, but a triumphant smile seemed to give it light.

Tiye felt some genuine sorrow for the death of a man she had worked with for over thirty prosperous and splendid years, but she evidently did not intend to appear as the broken-hearted widow. At this moment she was speaking with the most cheerful animation. "Fortune is with you in every way, Amenophis. We have just had word from Elephantine that the inundation will be a good one— that your accession should come at this moment is the greatest of luck. It means, too, that there will be enough time for your visitations of the cities before returning at the New Year for your coronation. The people will see it as perfectly auspicious and forget all the uneasiness they felt during Pharaoh's illness."

"Then, if I may be permitted to address Your Majesty," Ramose said, "Your marriage to the Princess Nefertiti could not have been more wisely conceived. At the present time it is far more valuable to have her upon the throne of the Great Queen than it could be to have any foreign princess. The noble Ay is immensely influential both with the army and with the great lords of Upper Egypt. And because of his wife's sway over him, and his own attachment to their foster child, his loyalty is even more absolute and active than before. Ipy is correspondingly weakened. All his plans have miscarried."

Amenophis gave one of his rare laughs. "I am happy that you find my marriage diplomatic, my lord Ramose. Yet when you first heard of my love for the Princess Nefertiti, I should be surprised if you did not throw up your hands. Now you must admit that your judgment has been at fault in another matter. Were not my appearances before the people today proved to be right? I intend to make myself known to all my subjects—to let them see that I am fellow man as well as god."

"Your reception throughout the city was certainly a triumph, Your Majesty. Two hundred thousand people must have hailed and bowed down to you and Queen Nefertiti as you showed yourselves in your chariot. Such a thing has never before happened in Thebes—or indeed in all Egypt."

"Yet I can tell that the Vizier has reservations," Tiye interposed. "But now, my son, we wish to receive your commands as to the work of the Palace. When your father was in health, the Vizier and the Chief Treasurer had audiences with us every day. They reported on the cases in the royal courts, on the state of the provinces and the army and on the prospect for taxes. And of course news from our ambassadors abroad. The affairs of Egypt are endless. Does Pharaoh intend to be present at the daily audience?"

"Honoured Mother! You are clever and experienced in all these matters, and my wish is that, for a time at least, you should look after them on my behalf. I have to be free to devote myself to what are, for me, much more important things."

"And what, Your Majesty, will these be?" Ramose was so astounded by his new master's words that he failed to check his abrupt question.

"I have to show the way towards the art which will truly serve Ma'at. And I have to create a temple of the Aten and its priesthood so that the truths that have been revealed to me can be made manifest. I intend to instruct both artists and priests, but first I must seek more light for myself."

Ramose looked so bewildered that the Queen Mother laughed and said, "You must learn to know Pharaoh, my lord Vizier. Both as man and god he is unlike all others." Amenophis went on as though nothing had been said. "Although there is no time for me to listen to reports each day, I am much concerned about the government of my people. In particular, you are to instruct the Chief Treasurer to take proper control of the tax gatherers so that they do not oppress some and take bribes from others. And the High Priest of Osiris and the Governor at Abydos are to be dismissed and the city management reformed. This must be done at once or I cannot make my visitation there." Ramose bowed. After a pause he added, in quite a different tone of voice, "And one other thing, noble Ramose. Are you interested to know more about the art which is about to change all our old traditions?"

"Your Majesty's interests are mine, although my understanding may be weak."

"I have been told that you are having your tomb prepared in the cemetery of the nobles. You may hand it over to Bak, now appointed King's Sculptor, to complete the reliefs. Then you yourself, and in your own tomb, will be able to see with the fresh eyes with which we look on the world. And your sepulchre will become famous throughout Egypt—and beyond." Amenophis looked at the vizier with a flickering smile which the anxious official could not interpret. The whole situation was beyond his experience. "Your Majesty, I am not worthy of such an honour," he babbled. "The gods have left me witless in these matters. I have only some poor knowledge of business and the law—which I lay at your feet."

"But I find you worthy, my lord Vizier. You shall have your tomb as I have promised. I will supervise the drawings myself."

Amenophis no longer felt like himself. All that was individual and private about him seemed to have rinsed out of him by the months of ceremonial through which he had lived. After the rituals, the passion plays, the endless purifications in which he had figured, he seemed himself to have become an idol, a holy presence remote from thought and feeling. Even Nefertiti, so faithfully at his side, had become ghostly to him.

Now, in the great Theban temple, he had just been subjected to a final long purification and led to offer incense before the sacred image of the god. Now he was led on to where two little wattle buildings stood incongruously among so much splendour. They were the Dual Shrines of Upper and Lower Egypt, where the ancient standards of the gods and the spirits of his ancestors lived and presided over the Two Crowns housed in their golden shrines.

The Greatest Seer of Re guided him into the Shrine of Lower Egypt, tall, narrow, dim and strange enough in its rustic simplicity to touch his feelings. There in the depths hardly to be seen, were the shadowy effigies of the wolf, the ibis and the falcon. The priest went to the shrine and took out the Red Crown, which was itself the goddess Wadjet with her hooded cobra poised above the circlet. He held it aloft and chanted:

> "*The doors of the Horizon are opened, their bolts are slipped.*
> *He comes to thee O Red Crown, he comes to thee O Fiery One.*
> *He has purified himself for thee, mayest thou be satisfied for*
> *him,*
> *Mayest thou be satisfied with the words he will say to you.*"

Then Amenophis himself addressed Wadjet:

"O Red Crown, O Fiery Snake!
Let there be awe of me like the awe of thee.
Let there be love of me like the love of thee.
Let me rule, a leader of the living.
Let me be powerful, a leader of spirits."

Here he ceased, for he had told the Seer that he would not pronounce the last line, which evoked his sword against his enemies. Now the Red Crown was to be placed upon his head; there were many more rites to be enacted—the presentation of the White Crown of Upper Egypt, and of the Crook and Flail, the Circuit of the Walls—it seemed that they stretched endlessly into the future, even as rites already enacted stretched back into the past. But this for him was the supreme moment, and as he felt the gold on his flesh and knew that the Uraeus, the very being of kingship, was reared above his brow, he thought he heard a voice which was not the priest's. He gave a low cry as though of greeting, and then staggered where he stood. Nefertiti, who was standing close behind, tried to support him, the Seer stretched towards him the hands which had just relinquished the crown, and Mersure and others of his royal kinsmen also rushed forward, thinking that he would fall with an attack of the divine sickness. But he remained upright, leaning on Nefertiti's shoulder, shaking. Then he opened his eyes and whispered ecstatically into the girl's ear. "I have been shown it, the symbol of the Aten that we have tried to find. There was a clear disc of light, and from it there flowed such an abundance of life and love that it was as though hands were offering them to us—yes, the rays seemed to have hands. This is how we shall proclaim the Aten. This is how he will be made known to all men."

BOOK II

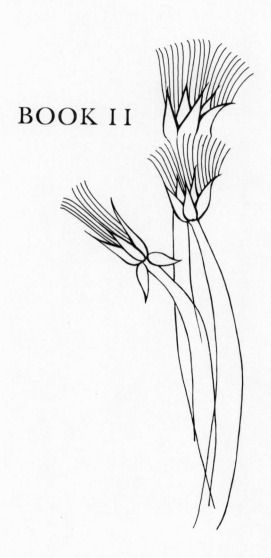

V

"WHEN I brought my father in here and showed it to him, the old man spat. Yes, actually! I don't think he meant to, but he loathed it so much that he had to spit just as a dog has to bark or a snake to hiss." Bak laughed heartily, throwing his head back so that the pouch of flesh which had grown below his chin was smoothed out and his curly hair, which he now wore much longer, slid between his shoulder blades. "He shouted at me, 'It's blasphemous, Pharaoh should have you thrown to the crocodiles.' Then the poor old chap had a fit of coughing, and I tried to help him—he's getting very feeble—but he pulled himself away and said, 'You are no son of mine. From this day I disown you. I taught you all the skills and secrets of the generations and now you bring disgrace on us with this abomination.' He looked as though he were going to pick up my hammer and try to smash any part he could reach, but then he thought better of it and shuffled out as fast as he could. I haven't seen him since."

Amenophis said nothing and looked troubled, leaving it to Nefertiti to speak. "I am sorry about Men; it is dreadful to make an old man unhappy and set him against his son. But why is it he can't see the beauty of the work you are doing now—and of this in particular. It is your masterpiece."

Amenophis and Nefertiti, with a few of their chosen friends, were gathered in Bak's studio outside the Palace gardens. They were all standing round a huge figure of the king which Bak had just finished carving from a thirteen-foot block of limestone. The posture, upright with hands crossed high on the breast holding Crook and Flail, was traditional, but everything else about the sculpture was revolutionary and strange. "Enough," said Ranufer, the handsome young man whom Amenophis had recently made his chariot driver, "to bring back the spirits of the dead from the Underworld—or even from the western

stars." The body faithfully reproduced the young monarch's thin, angular shoulders, tapering to a slender waist
and swelling out again to wide, curving thighs. It showed,
too, the belly which he had developed from lack of exercise
sagging a little over the top of his tight-fitting loincloth,
and the spindly legs. Yet in spite of these odd, almost
grotesque, proportions, the whole body was graced with
immediate life. Unlike the traditional statues which
showed men and women frozen into timeless attitudes,
this one suggested a youth of spiritual power who had just
risen to his feet, clasped his sceptres of office and lifted his
head to gaze across the fields or along the shimmering
surface of the Nile. Rather against Amenophis's own
wishes, Bak had insisted on portraying him in a full wig
and ritual beard. These lifeless masses he used to bring the
mobile face into intense relief. Bak had obviously enjoyed
carving the large, full and strongly-shaped mouth and the
heavily-lidded eyes, and had contrived to embue them
with an expression that was authoritative and yet nervously vulnerable, absorbed and serious yet with some
faint curl of irony.

"Do you agree it is a masterpiece, Amenophis?" Bak
asked eagerly. "Are you really satisfied with it at last?"

"Yes, I think it is what we want, and the head is
masterly. For my own taste, as you know, I prefer the
everyday figures you have carved of us. It is easier to catch
the instant in wood than in stone."

"Yes. I wish we had back those pieces we sent to
Mitanni—where they certainly weren't appreciated. What
a failure that was!" Again Bak roared with laughter.
Amenophis smiled too, though at the time he had been
upset and angry. Soon after his accession Tushratta had
sent him letters demanding golden statues which he said
had been promised by his father. It so happened that he
and Bak had recently completed some lively figure carvings in wood, inspired by their new theories, which seemed
to him of surpassing value. Thinking that Tushratta must
share this opinion, and wishing to propagate the new art
in other lands, he had the wooden figures lightly plated in
gold and despatched them to Mitanni. The result had

been two rambling letters, one to the Queen Mother and one to himself, in which Tushratta complained bitterly at being fobbed off with plated statues and openly demanded those in solid gold which he declared that his envoys had witnessed being prepared for him while the old Pharaoh was alive.

Amenophis had been disgusted by the implication that he had cheated his "brother" over the statues, by Tushratta's failure to recognize great works of art and by his implication that the King of Egypt owed him something more for taking Tadukhipa into his harim—a step to which he had been persuaded by his mother. As for Queen Tiye, she had of course foreseen the outburst over the wooden figures, and was greatly amused. With things as they were in Egypt, and with news of further Hittite pressure, she felt there was no hurry to pacify Tushratta and satisfy his appetite for gold. Personally she did not feel any gratitude to Tadukhipa's father, and determined to keep him fuming for a year or so longer.

Recalling the affair now, Amenophis found he no longer cared. "It is a pity," he said, "that Men is as blind as Tushratta was. But we must forgive him, because old men cannot get new eyes. But when my temple is ready I will teach the court and the priests—and perhaps the people, too—the beauty and significance of our work. How soon will you be able to have the other statues ready?"

"Much more quickly than this one. I shall put my apprentices on to roughing them out and give most of my time to finishing the heads. I want to vary them and to catch your different expressions—you have a fascinating face, Amenophis."

"Indeed he has," cried Nefertiti. "And I love to think of so many likenesses of it watching over the Aten Temple. It will be the most wonderful building in Thebes."

Bak shouted to his servants for refreshments, and soon two graceful Nubian girls (whom Bak preferred to Egyptians) were pouring wine and passing honey cakes. Ranufer was there, and also a Syrian friend of Bak's called Tutu, who was very intelligent and also well versed in Asian affairs. He had further endeared himself to Amenophis by his well-judged praise of Nefertiti. Another member of the circle who was not, however, present at the viewing of the statue, was Meryre. The ideas that he and Amenophis were developing about the proper worship of the Aten, and the social life he now enjoyed among the young King's friends, were making him much less austere and scholastic than before. He already held high office in the growing priesthood of the Aten.

Amenophis depended upon this circle of intimates to make his life acceptable. Within it he had decreed that there was to be a complete relaxation of the etiquette and ritual observance that weighed so heavily upon him in court and temple. All titles and other formal modes of address were discarded, and although members of the group usually had the sense not to treat them with familiarity, Amenophis and Nefertiti went among them as friends and equals. Occasionally they were joined by Gilukhipa and Mina, for whom Amenophis kept his old affection, while the Queen had drawn in a lovely Cypriote girl whose father was at court on an embassy. Nefertiti was first attracted to Lasia because she was a native of her mother's island, but soon both she and Amenophis came to admire her for her talents. She sang and played excellently, and composed poetry which the King recognized as expressive of the spirit of the Aten.

In many ways these first years of Amenophis's reign had gone very well indeed. Certainly he had become popular throughout the length of Egypt—for reasons both spiritual and material. He and Nefertiti had continued to make occasional tours of the streets and market-places of Thebes, blessing the people and sometimes listening to grievances. Then one day, when they had stopped their chariot for a moment in the fruit market, Amenophis noticed an elderly woman squatting behind a few melons and a little heap of figs, with a handsome youth stretched on some straw beside her. One of his legs was withered, and crutches lay near to his hand. The woman looked up and saw the great Pharaoh looking with pity on her son. At once she got up, helped the young man to his feet and led him hobbling over towards the chariot. "Lord Pharaoh, Divine One," she cried out, alternately bowing and looking up at her sovereign, "I beg you give a blessing to my fine son who has been stricken through no fault of his own. We believe it was my husband's sister down at Coptos who ill-wished him. I beg of you, Lord Pharaoh, drive out the evil so that he may worship you with whole limbs." Her son also looked up, and Amenophis found himself staring into eyes that were both strained and sullen, then suddenly a look of hope came into them. Acting on impulse, he stepped down from the chariot, his attendants having some difficulty in holding back the crowd. He turned his steady compelling gaze on the cripple, and raised his own arms towards the sun. "Take his crutches, Mother," he commanded. "And Boy, run to the heap and bring your mother a fig." The youth put his bent leg firmly on the ground, ran almost easily for the fruit and brought it back, skipping with delight. A vast sigh rose from the crowd, and immediately children went scuttling to spread the news of what they had seen.

From that time, Amenophis's public appearances became more and more difficult for the city guard to control, as wherever he went sick men, women and children were brought out by relatives determined to obtain the god's blessing if they could. Amenophis, however, only rarely gave of his power, choosing out individuals intuitively. He never had any failures. His subjects did not so much marvel that he could work these miracles, for it was recognized that a divine king could do whatever he willed, but they thought it wonderful that he was ready to save the humblest of his people.

They loved him for this, and they loved him because at this time he did succeed in having the burden of taxes lightened. His court was less extravagant than his father's had been, Egypt was at peace and he did nothing to strengthen the army. Although he was intent on building his temple of the Aten, he had no such grandiose architectural projects as those on which his father had poured out his treasure. Moreover, for the time being at least, the princes of his Asiatic Empire continued to send their tribute to Thebes as obediently as before. All this made it possible for his Chief Treasurer, who was an honest and able minister, to assess taxation at a slightly lower level, and to instruct his lieutenants to be lenient when they encountered cases of hardship. In spite of this the royal treasury grew steadily fuller—a fact which particularly delighted Tiye, who, like most queens, took a woman's satisfaction in good housekeeping.

Indeed, the Queen Mother had reason to be satisfied with the way things were going. She with Ramose and the Treasurer controlled most public affairs successfully, seldom finding it necessary to refer them to the King. On the other hand Amenophis exercised his traditional function of giving judgment on the cases that reached the central courts. If he was inclined to view all plaintiffs other than soldiers with extreme leniency, his generous decisions did not appear to be undermining authority. She was astonished at the patience with which he suffered his ritual life —the invariable series of services and purifications which marked his days from sunrise to sunset. He did, it is true, have some cut short, and occasionally pleaded ill health when expected at the Temple of Amon, but in general he could only be admired for enduring observances that tired his body and tried his active mind and imagination almost beyond endurance.

Undoubtedly the reign had begun in popularity and plenty. But there were two small areas of trouble that might easily spread and shadow the whole scene of a smiling kingdom. The first was the old one of the Amon priesthood. Amenophis had fulfilled his obligations towards the Theban king of the gods and his human representatives. He reigned outwardly as the chosen of Amon. But he had made it clear that he had no intention of adding to the enormous royal endowments which already gave the priesthood their power and enabled them to rule a kingdom within the kingdom. Then he had chosen titles for himself which emphasized his greater regard for Heliopolis and the royal kinship with Re. Worst of all, the whole court and everyone in authority throughout the land knew that the young Pharaoh was devoting himself to the development of some mysterious and towering idea

centred on the worship of the Aten, and that the establishment of the new temple near the precinct of Amon would
bring matters to a head. His mother and those who knew
him intimately were aware that he was becoming so
exclusively devoted to the new worship that he found the
service of the other gods, particularly Amon, Min and
Osiris, more and more distasteful. Each year until now he
had reluctantly taken his place in the Min celebration
before the harvest, which was the chief popular festival of
Thebes. This season it seemed he might refuse his presence.
Queen Tiye very greatly feared it.

This question of the Min Festival was related to the
second shadow on the throne. While at the time of their
marriage Nefertiti had indeed been young to be taken as a
wife, now, though still not quite fully grown, she was
universally considered old enough, and everyone in Egypt
from the highest to the most humble longed for an heir to
the throne. The Festival of Min, held at a time when all
life would soon be parched to death and assurance for its
resurrection had to be sought, was the occasion when the
royal pair should lie together and the divine impregnation
be assured.

Amenophis's devotion to Nefertiti was extraordinary—
beyond the comprehension of most of those who saw it.
Exquisite and full of grace as she was, it seemed to some
men quite improper that the Pharaoh should show so
exclusive a passion. Yet the rumour grew until it was
accepted as a certainty that the marriage was still uncon-
summated.

The situation in the royal harim was equally extraordinary. Amenophis had taken over the establishment,
and in consultation with his friends there had appointed
his own officials. He had agreed to take Tadukhipa into it,
much as he disliked the girl, and had even consented, at
the urgent request of Queen Tiye and Ramose, to go
through a marriage ceremony with a Babylonian princess.
But all he ever did with any of the ladies of his harim,
whether young or middle-aged, was to talk to them.

The Queen Mother was almost in despair, yet she still
did not believe that her son was impotent. When she tried

to question him about it, he did not seem in the least disturbed, but merely said that he was not ready, that the god had not revealed himself, and ordered her not to speak of it again. After this Tiye sought out Gilukhipa, knowing that she sometimes went into his circle of intimates.

"Gilukhipa," she said, "I am wondering if something has to be done about an heir to the throne. I'm still full of energy, but I can't last for ever, and I want to see the succession made safe. Everyone is anxious."

"I'm told that when Pharaoh and the Queen appear in the streets of Thebes there isn't a man or woman who doesn't scrutinize her figure."

"You see Amenophis when he is with Bak and all his artistic and intellectual friends. Have you noticed anything suspicious there? I have heard of a young man called Ranufer, and Bak himself has always seemed to me an unpleasantly flamboyant creature."

"I have watched, because I must confess I used to have my own expectations in that direction. But I think you have no cause for alarm. Pharaoh is certainly aware of Ranufer and likes to have him about, but I'd be astonished if there is anything more in it than that. He is always entirely absorbed in Nefertiti—or in himself and his ideas. But, Queen Mother, why do you ask? What would you have done if my report had been a worse one?"

"If Amenophis fails to provide an heir, I may have to make some arrangement. It is for Egypt. I do not want Mersure on the throne, and now that he is married to a royal daughter I suspect he is full of ambitions. Such things must have been arranged before now."

"If you are depending on co-operation of that kind from Nefertiti, I'm sure you won't get it. But wait for a time. I have a feeling that our Lord Amenophis, like any god, has his own seasons. He is full of fire and spirit and, strange though he is, I don't believe he lacks ordinary potency."

Tey was as distressed as anyone else, and sometimes wondered whether she might be partly to blame. She tried in her mild and simple way to get Nefertiti to talk about her marriage, but without success. The girl appeared not to understand what she was asking about, declaring with great intensity that hers was the supreme marriage in all the world. Nevertheless, Tey got the impression that her foster daughter was fully conscious of the situation and often thought about it. So she concluded by saying, "The Festival of Min is at the next full moon. Pharaoh says that he is waiting for a revelation from the god. Can you not pray to the god to be with you at the Festival, then perhaps he will give you a child?"

Nefertiti only replied, "You don't understand. Pharaoh himself may not attend the Festival this year."

Nevertheless, when a few days later she was with Amenophis and he was resting after his prayer to the setting sun, she said to him very softly, "Dear Lord Amenophis. I hope that you will celebrate the Min Festival in spite of what you have said. It is true, isn't it, that for this occasion Min stands above all for the divine power in yourself, and for the renewal of life? That is not against the spirit of the Aten."

"You know how much I detest the worship of Min—and although it is true that in this Festival he is identified rather with my divine power and the promise of spring, we have to walk in procession with his idol. And it has been shown to me now that all idols are abominable to god, and this one in particular. I believe only in the divine radiance, and not in the dark things." He looked at Nefertiti almost pleadingly, for she seldom asked any favour and he hated to oppose her. But now her slender body which she usually carried so easily became awkward, and she looked at him almost fiercely. "I loathe the dark things of evil imagination. The serpents and dragons and all the vile black creatures with which men have filled the Underworld. But there is another kind of darkness without which the radiance could not shine—which feeds it like the root the flower. Sometimes as I am falling asleep I have seen it as a dark sun. Women understand it, Amenophis, as they understand the darkness of earth and deep waters. But you should understand it, too. You saw the sacred stone of the sun at Heliopolis, the *benben* . . ."

"It represents the sun's rays and the place of renewal of the phoenix of light. . . ."

"It is capped with gold, it is true, but, my dearest lord, you must see that it also stands for this dark root of life and of love. Without it all the life that we worship, all the natural world that rejoices in the light of the Aten, would never be. Amenophis, my love, you must accept this kind of darkness." Amenophis remained silent and brooding, though he reached for her hand. At last she got up and said quite lightly, "There is another thing in favour of the Festival of Min. It is the only one where you and I, the King and the Queen, must appear together . . . where our union is celebrated. That makes it dear to me. . . ." For a moment it seemed that he was going to pull her down beside him, but then he let go of her hand saying, "Goodnight, Nefertiti. I hope to be shown what I must do. Goodnight."

For days before the full moon Pharaoh was hardly seen at all except by his officiating priests. He had not made any announcement about his participation, and no one dared talk openly of so appalling a possibility as Pharaoh's withdrawal from what was for Thebans the most crucial festival of the year. Yet everyone had somehow heard of the danger and was uneasy. The priests of Amon and of Min, always closely related, were known to have held a secret meeting.

The night before the Festival, Amenophis had still not made up his mind. Neither could he sleep, but lay watching the patch of moonlight moving across the marble floor. Then he rose and went to the window and stared back at the moon, which was so bright that he could hardly detect the thin paring missing on the left-hand side. He knew that the priests and their servants would be up all night making their preparations, and that East Thebes would be crammed with country people come in from the whole Thebaid. Every roof and alley would be tangled with their bodies asleep. He looked down on the sharp, geometric shapes of moonlight and shadow in the courtyard. Certainly this was a beautiful form of darkness, and from it the day would rise . . . like a flower from its roots. . . .

When his personal priests arrived for the purification before the sunrise prayer, they found their Pharaoh asleep with his head on his arm and his arm resting along the sill.

With his skin still wet from the asperge and the room in the House of the Sun swirling with incense, Amenophis climbed the steps to the great eastward-facing Window of the Sun. Already the sky was very bright behind the eastern hills, and some high flown feathers of cloud were within the reach of the sunlight.

Yet down below the garden still seemed veiled in grey, and there was no morning freshness at that season. The day lilies of yesterday hung withered on their stems—the gardeners had not yet removed them—while the new day's buds were still furled. All the foliage looked a little dusty, for unlike himself, it had not as yet been sprinkled. But the birds were stirring, and one or two were even splashing in the shallow basin he kept filled for them. He thought he saw a movement of white linen in the garden pavilion confronting him towards the sunrise—were the maids up early at work? Then he saw the earth of a flower bed darkening as water flowed on to it. Somewhere a gardener had stooped to open a channel. Withdrawing his attention from these small matters, always so sweet to him, Amenophis raised his arms and began his prayer.

> "*I turn my face towards you, Re-Herakhte, Lord of the Horizon.*
> *I salute your majesty on the threshold of your day.*
> *All your creatures are stirring; cattle in the marshes,*
> *Birds among the reeds, men in their dark houses,*
> *All will rise with your rising, answering your rays.*
> *I am your son, and lift up my arms in praise of you.*
> *Glorious Aten on the threshold of your day.*"

As he spoke these words above the silent garden, the rim of the sun showed above the hills, and the rays began to dance and dazzle in his eyes. Then he saw a figure standing at the centre of the blaze. The linen shift shone like a faint nimbus, as the fleece of sheep will sometimes shine when the sun is low. The figure at the heart of it remained dark. He recognized its female form, and yet it seemed to him that a sacred pillar had been raised against the sun. Was it Nefertiti or the root of darkness within the Aten? Suddenly he knew that the god was with him and had filled him with a great desire.

He finished his prayer, and then before he turned away from the window he said:

> *"Lord Re, your son asks your forgiveness,*
> *It is the radiance of the Aten that will lead us today,*
> *The power that is the truth of all the gods."*

As he rejoined his priests, who were waiting to cense him once more, he told them, "I must be dressed for the Min Festival. Send word also to Queen Nefertiti to say that she should get ready."

When he and Nefertiti made their entry into the processional ranks drawn up outside the temple of Amon, Amenophis found it easy to view everything round him with detachment. Indeed, instead of the distaste or boredom that often seized him on ceremonial occasions, today he could not help feeling a kind of amusement. There was his Uncle Ay, eminent in the hierarchy of Min, rather portentously marshalling the ranks. (He did not know that the good man was congratulating himself on having secured his presence at the Festival. Ay had, as he thought, sent earnest warnings through his wife and sister, but in fact Tey and Tiye had not breathed a word of them to Amenophis, being quite sure that they would determine him to stay away.) There were the standards of the gods, with their crowning emblems swaying high above the heads of the crowd, and nearby, in an inanimate cluster, the jewelled effigies of his ancestors. And there, taken from its dark chapel into the morning light, was the statue of Min himself, standing on a litter borne on the shoulders of a group of priests. The litter was hung all round with cloths charged with the royal titles, so that only the heads of the priests protruded. The whole contraption looked like a walking tent with the great phallic figure balanced on the roof. Amenophis was astonished to discover that he was regarding it with a mixture of derision and excitement.

In front of Min and immediately behind the royal pair walked a huge, placid, creamy, stupid bull, its wide horns sheathed in gold.

At last the procession reached the temple fields, where the ripe wheat was rippling in the sun. A shrine with a tabernacle behind it stood among the corn, and the Min-bearing priests deposited their burden inside. Ay handed Amenophis a sickle with which he cut a swathe of wheat and presented it to the bull. The soft wet tongue coiled round it, and the beast, playing its part to perfection, steadily chewed the grainy ears. Those standing near saw the delight with which the young King watched the bull, and how he reached out for an instant and laid his hand on one of its horns, before leading Nefertiti into the taber-nacle—the House of Pharaoh in the Field of Min.

Gilukhipa used her long, square-tipped index finger further to emphasize the line of Mina's waist, then clamped the clay she had scooped out on to the breasts of the figure. For obvious reasons the practice of the arts had become very much the fashion at court, and the Mitannian found that modelling sizable figures in clay gave her much more satisfaction than painting flowers and birds as most of the other women did.

"You still have quite a good figure, Mina. How do you manage it?"

"I don't know," said Mina, beaming with pleasure, "I expect it is just because I am Cretan. Although, of course, I am careful about how much bread and oil I eat." Then she added, "I can't think why I bother—what is the good?"

"It gives me satisfaction as a modeller—but I don't suppose you care about that?"

Mina shook her head, and then said a little pettishly, "I'm getting very tired, and my arm is aching—haven't you nearly finished?" Gilukhipa had induced her to stand as though reaching to pick a persea fruit from a tree growing in a tub. "Art of the instant" was the catch phrase which had spread from the royal fountainhead.

"Nearly. I have to do it all at once, the clay dries so quickly in this heat." She worked on pitilessly for five minutes, then sat back. "There, that will do. Thank you, Mina. I think it's good—would you like it for your tomb? Let's have some sherbet."

When the drink had been brought and they were both lying back and sipping it, Mina said, "I still can hardly believe in the change in Pharaoh."

"I can. I was perfectly right when I said that like all gods he has his own seasons."

"But now it seems that both of them are absolutely given up to it. . . ."

"Divinities don't do things by halves . . . they say he's as riggish as a young goat." Gilukhipa gave her baying laugh.

"Do you think that Min did it?"

"I think that Nefertiti did it—though I don't know how."

"We thought them so spiritual. . . ."

"They loved one another before. Perhaps bodily lust with love *is* very spiritual. The god has possession of them."

"So it isn't likely Pharaoh will start visiting the harim?"

"I don't know . . . but one thing is certain, Mina. He won't come for you or me. Except to talk."

"No," said Mina, giggling. "But I wish he'd take an interest all the same. After all, harims weren't intended for painting or modelling in clay. . . ."

The building of the Aten temple and the swelling of Nefertiti with her first child progressed together, so that it seemed that the temple would be ready for dedication just when the infant was ready for delivery. During these months Amenophis was filled with an extraordinary elation. His self-confidence, always strong, now seemed to have a fiery quality; his sensibility was intensified and his imagination reached new heights of vision. All the time that could be won from his duties as Pharaoh he divided between amusing and comforting Nefertiti through the trials of pregnancy, writing hymns and prayers for the services of the Aten temple, and working with Bak and the artists now gathering round him on designs for its decoration. In particular they were engrossed in working out the most beautiful and telling form for the symbol of the Aten which Amenophis had seen at his coronation. In place of figures of the god, he wanted the walls of the new building to be bright with sun discs and rays extending their blessing hands towards all life on earth.

Both his exalted state of mind and body, and his longing for more time to spend as a human being, made Amenophis a little more careless of his ritual obligations. His absences from the temple of Amon became more frequent, and his pruning of all rites not directly concerned to celebrate him as son of the sun more drastic. It was also rumoured that in private he indulged in the rich food and drink that were forbidden Pharaoh. Everyone knew that his father had done the same, but that was in some way different.

Indeed much of the growing opposition to Amenophis among the court and priesthood was caused by dislike of his exaltation of spirit, his display of love and the enjoyment of life. Everything that to the young king seemed most to prove the divinity in him and the especial favour of god shining upon the throne, seemed to these opponents most improper and ungodly.

Certainly the opposition increased and became more coherent. Ipy drew round him not only his own priests and those of Min and others who felt their gods and treasuries neglected, but also many of the senior officials, leading figures with hereditary ritual offices at court, and nobles with large estates and many followers. All these rich and wrinkled enjoyers of privilege, while they would not be heard to speak against their divine sovereign, were willing to agree with the High Priest that something must be done to guide his footsteps back on to the traditional paths.

Queen Tiye, who had hoped that her anxieties were at an end when she heard that Nefertiti had conceived, was now more worried than before. Although she did not think he would come out against the royal party, she even doubted the absolute loyalty of Ramose. She knew that although the vizier had been very willing for her to act as a kind of unofficial regent when Amenophis came to the throne, he felt that Pharaoh ought now to resume the daily councils and to take more direct interest in the affairs of state. He was also vexed by a number of the king's judicial decisions which had gone against his own advice. Perhaps, too, he was more seriously distressed than he could admit about the decoration of his tomb. He detested, and secretly feared, the new art that now, after long delay, was finding expression in his mausoleum. Might it not cause him terrible trouble when he came to die?

Amenophis himself refused to be at all alarmed; he had grown used to the unsuccessful scheming of the Amonites, and was moreover absolutely confident in the rightness of his chosen way and his power to maintain it.

When his mother had brought him another warning and had urged him to do more to reassure the vizier, Amenophis only grinned at her and said, "I have Nefertiti, and a child soon to be born, I have Ma'at and the radiance of the Aten. What more can I want, and what reason can I have to be afraid of anybody?"

"Luckily you also have the army," his mother replied.

About a month before Nefertiti was expecting her child, and when the Aten temple was complete except for the reliefs which Bak and his apprentices were carving on the pale limestone walls, news was brought to Thebes of trouble in Nubia. The viceroy, the messages said, had been on a mission far to the south, and in his absence what had been a small tribal rising in Lower Nubia had been made serious by an incursion of desert nomads.

The plea for immediate reinforcements was met, although Amenophis insisted that Tutu should be attached to the staff and given every opportunity to settle affairs peacefully. He was empowered, much against Ramose's wishes and to the fury of the viceroy when he heard of it, to grant pardons to the trouble-makers if they would disperse and agree to live in peace under Ma'at. The despatch of this force of infantry, coinciding with desert exercises that always took place at that time of year, left the chariots, under the direct command of Ay, as the only active troops at Thebes.

Then Ay fell ill with high fever and his bowels dripping a terrible green sludge. It was a sickness well known and greatly feared—about half its victims died. Tey was distraught, and the Queen Mother, now much more tolerant of her sister-in-law, kept in close touch with her through messengers who crossed the Nile morning and evening. Ay was tough but past his youth; the general expectation at court was that he would die.

One day when Amenophis was in Bak's studio looking at the drawings for the very last panel in the Aten temple, Ranufer came in. Although he stood in the background while the King took up a charcoal stick and made a small change in one of the figures, it was obvious that he was eager and impatient. Bak's chief assistant murmured his admiration of the improvement the Pharaoh had made, but Amenophis seemed to sense his chariot driver's excited presence, for he turned swiftly round and said, "What is it, Ranufer? You are oozing with news like an old wine skin."

"Yes. I have heard something, a very evil tale, brought to me by a young servant of a fellow who used to be a brother officer of mine when I was with the chariots. I never liked him much. . . . But I meet him from time to time when I go to see my old friends. This young man says he has risked his life coming to the Palace, but that he owes everything to you. He seems a nervous, jumpy lad and I don't know whether to believe him. If you would only look at him, I am sure that you could divine . . ."

"Where is he?"

"Quite near. In the little lotus kiosk in this corner of the garden—well screened from view." Without saying a word Amenophis went along the covered way specially built so that he could go privately to the studio, then turned into the kiosk. It was a place with which he had happy associations from the days when Nefertiti used to make her weekly visits. As soon as he reached the doorway, the youth inside knelt and touched his forehead to the

ground. At first Amenophis could not remember where he
had seen him before, but as he told him to rise he saw that
it was the cripple boy from the fruit market. He was full
grown now, very good-looking and with both legs of equal
muscle.

"Divine Majesty," he said, his voice nervous but clear.
"Since the day when you healed me I have dreamt only of
how I could do something to serve you and the blessed
lady Nefertiti whom I saw beside you. For this reason I
joined the chariots, thinking I could fight for you." Amenophis smiled at him and shook his head. "I am already
personal groom and batman to the Third Officer of Your
Majesty's chariots." He said this with a pride that went
oddly with what was to follow. "My master has a great
fault. He drinks too much wine. Almost every night I have
to put him to bed. Perhaps it is because it is so long since
there was any active campaigning. The evening before
last my master had supper with the Second Officer. After
I had filled their cups many times they began to talk of
things other than the spear-throwing contests and the
merits of their horses. It is very easy for rich men to forget
that poor men understand their language. They spoke of
the High Priest of Amon, and of a prince of Coptos whom
they did not name. These two, they said, were angry with
Pharaoh because he sets the Sun God above their Amon.
I did not like the way they spoke as though Pharaoh were
an ordinary man. Then they talked of a day when some
plan was to be carried out." The young man paused,
dropped his eyes, wriggled his toes in his sandals and
fidgeted with his dagger. "The rest of the story, Divine
Majesty, is difficult to tell. But all know that you wish your
subjects to live strictly under Ma'at, and so I must tell it
as it happeed. The Second Officer was staggering when
he left, and my master was still further gone. As usual I
began to rub him with oil before lifting him on to his
couch, and all the time I was wondering how I could find
out more of what they had been speaking. Then he did
something he has never done before—he began to hold me
and stroke me. Divine Majesty, I hope my conduct was
right. I let him go on a little, but all the time talking to

him and giving him sips of wine. In the end I don't believe he knew who was with him. I was able to find out that the High Priest and the prince of Coptos intend to oblige you to humble the Sun God on the day of the consecration of the new temple. He kept saying, 'It is not rebellion. We just have to be blind for a day or two—and aren't I blind already?' All yesterday, when we had a parade and inspection, I tried to think what I should do. At last I decided I must come to the Palace and find the lord Ranufer. It wasn't difficult to slip away and get myself ferried across the River. It will be more difficult to return, but that is nothing if I have served your Divine Majesty."

Amenophis seemed more incredulous than angry. "They conspire against the Son of the Sun, the chosen of the Aten? Against the very Aten itself? I knew there was ill will, but I did not think they could be so impious." He stood in silence for a full minute, now with a frown gathered between his long, level brows. With a deliberate effort he relaxed himself and looked kindly on the youth.

"What is your name?"

"Mahu, Your Majesty."

"You have indeed served Pharaoh well, Mahu. I am only sad that there was cause for such service. And now I must demand more of you. Return to your master as discreetly as you can. If by ill luck you are questioned, you must not say where you have been—whatever they may do to you. I do not want these enemies of god to know that they are discovered. So you may have to suffer for Pharaoh, Mahu. But I promise that if all goes well I will take you into my household—make you one of my bodyguard. Ranufer, see that he is shown the best way out of the garden and the way back to the River across the fields."

Amenophis always remembered this encounter afterwards because it was the first occasion on which he himself took a decision on action in the world of affairs. He had so often been granted imaginative pictures showing what he should do towards god, in the arts and in his private life.

Now, during that moment of his silence, he seemed to see Ipy and his sympathizers directing all their schemes and forces towards his temple on the appointed day of the consecration. He saw them being allowed, even encouraged, to do this, and then being caught in their deed by Pharaoh, as a man catches birds among the reeds with a clapper net. He saw this so sharply that he accepted it without further thought, and the taking of the decision gave him a kind of jubilation.

Amenophis did not return to the studio, but went at once to the Queen Mother. When he had told her Mahu's story and his intention of allowing Ipy to develop his plans to the last, she was in warm agreement. "Moreover," she said, "I have just received news that will make it even easier for us to close the net when the day comes. Tey has sent word that Ay has turned the corner. He has been able to take food, and the fever is less. I must let her know at once that she is to keep quiet about this, and to give it out that he is slowly sinking. Then he can return suddenly to his command."

"You think there will be a need for military action?"

"There is no answer to that. I think it will be a question of feints and counter feints. The mention of the prince of Coptos gives away what they intend. You are so out of touch with your court, Amenophis, that you probably don't know who this must be. He is a man who has contrived to keep up a kind of private army as the nobles did in the old days before our house reunited Egypt. I suppose that his men will enter Thebes in twos and threes and chance to gather in the Precinct at the decisive time."

"And if Ay appears with the chariots they will be out on an exercise? I do not like it—it is not my way. But I see that this is how it must be." He looked stricken, and suddenly his eyes filled with tears, as they used so often to do when he was a boy. "What is worst is that these people think that they can succeed against Pharaoh, against the god."

"Not many people are simple-hearted or single-minded in these days. Horizons are wide and we know too much. And, as you see, even a god must sometimes scheme."

"It can never be the same. I shall feel I cannot trust anybody here in Thebes."

"Dear Amenophis, it is not so bad as you think. You can be sure that most of those who seem to be with Ipy have easily persuaded themselves that they are true to Pharaoh and the god. They say to themselves that some demon has possession of you and that they wish only to save you and set you back on the way you really wish to go. All these men believe that they know what is right, and what is right is what has always been. You see Ma'at differently, but this is how they see it. As for Ipy, I think that he still simply underestimates you. He is not trying to overthrow the throne. It is not in his power even if he would. He thinks he can use this moment of our weakness to frighten you, to show his strength at court. Perhaps, who knows—" she smiled mischievously "—he may even expect that Amon will come to his aid. But as you have seen in your own plan, it is for the best. They are playing into our hands. We can get rid of the leaders and the rest will be sure they never intended anything to happen. . . ." Tiye broke off, for at this moment one of her ladies came hurrying into the room. On seeing Amenophis there the poor woman gave a gasping squeak of dismay, and began to back through the doorway murmuring apologies. "What in the world is the matter? Come back. Our Lord Pharaoh will not eat you. Say what you have to say." At Tiye's impatient call she returned and stuttered, "Gracious Madam, my Lord Pharaoh. Forgive me, it is difficult. I came to tell . . . with the news . . . that the Great Queen, our beloved lady Nefertiti, has started her pains."

Amenophis stood up quickly and began to tremble. "Then I must go to her at once. Come, dearest Mother, let us go at once."

"Go to her? Are you mad? Such a thing is unheard of. It will bring bad luck." Tiye, so little troubled by metaphysical and theological non-conformity, was now outraged to the depth of her ordinary female being. Her attitude to the divinity of her late husband and son might be ambivalent, but this threat to ancient feminine belief exposed long-buried superstition. She turned into a woman

Amenophis had seldom seen before, running to the doorway and throwing out her arms to prevent his leaving the room. The King controlled himself with an effort. He looked at his mother with the extraordinary authority he had always commanded, and which was now at its height. Yet in his gaze at this moment there was also something gentle and understanding. Slowly Tiye grew calmer, her heaving little bosom quietened, and she dropped her arms to her sides.

"Come, dear Mother," he said again, "It is a small thing really. I have not seen Nefertiti since after the sunrise prayer. I must embrace her and bring her the blessing of the Aten."

Amenophis took his mother's arm and led her along the corridors to Nefertiti's room. As they stood for a moment at the entrance they heard Nefertiti's low, clear voice saying, "Take those things away. My Lord Pharaoh would not approve them, and I do not want them in the room." They stepped inside, and Amenophis felt he was in the hell's kitchen of the female world. The air was already thick with aromatic vapours, and women were making concoctions of herbs on small braziers, whispering spells over their pots. He looked away hastily from some form of heavy, legless chair painted all over with magical devices and filled, it seemed, with white linen, to where Nefertiti herself was leaning on a couch while the chief royal midwife was touching her belly and uttering loud incantations. The purpose of the Queen's command was evident, for a younger midwife had approached the couch with two golden images of the goddess Hathor.

It seemed half a minute before all the preoccupied ladies noticed the presence of Pharaoh; then an irrepressible gasp of horror rustled like a wind across the room and then fell to silence. Some of the women went on their knees; all looked aghast at the figure of their divine King who was at the same time an interloping male. Amenophis walked calmly over to the couch, knelt beside it, put his arm about his wife and kissed her on the temple. At once it seemed to Nefertiti as though a tent enclosed them, screening them from the rest of the world.

"How long has it been, beloved?"

"Since soon after you left me. I concealed the pains as long as I could."

"Are they terrible when they come?"

"Not yet." She smiled apprehensively.

"Would you like me to stay with you? Remember nothing is shocking under Ma'at."

Nefertiti hesitated, holding one of his bony hands tightly in hers. At last she shook her head. "At this moment I long to say yes, my lord. But I would not have you suffer with me—nor see me ugly. Besides, the Chief Royal Midwife would surely die." She contrived a small laugh which Amenophis found deeply touching. Then he saw her pressing her lips together and her eyes becoming fixed. At once his horror of sickness and pain seized hold of him, and he was thankful that he was not to stay. She clung to his hand till the bout was over, then he kissed her again and stood at her side. He held his long arms sloping down towards her, with his hands in the position of those they had devised for the Aten rays. He said nothing, but Nefertiti felt that strength and warmth were pouring into her.

In spite of the muttered forebodings of the midwives as to the bad luck likely to come from Pharaoh's visit to her couch, Nefertiti's labour was not unusually long or difficult, and the baby was safely delivered before midnight. It was a daughter. The Queen Mother could not conceal her disappointment, but Tey was delighted. There was plenty of time for a son, and besides, she said—rather tactlessly as Queen Tiye had not been of royal birth—"the throne properly went through Pharaoh's daughter". One messenger had served to warn Tey to keep her husband's recovery secret and to fetch her to her foster-child's confinement. She it was who washed the placenta and cord and handed them over to the priest to be enshrined. Then, reluctantly, she had to return to her own house.

Amenophis himself had expected that his child would be a son, and yet was quite overjoyed by his daughter. He resolved that she should be called Merytaten and so become the first royal child to bear an Aten name. He went to see her immediately after his sunrise prayer and purification. Nefertiti was asleep, but he took the infant, now well-swaddled, and held her up in the shaft of early sunlight that was striking through a window. Afterwards he visited his wife and daughter every day, a fact which further endeared him to the ladies of the court and caused the men, even those who were of the royal party, to shake their heads and ask what would become of Egypt.

So great was Pharaoh's engrossment in his first-born that he did not dwell on the coming trial of strength with his opponents. It was the Queen Mother who posted informers and soon had confirmation of her guess that the prince's retainers would be drifting in from Coptos. Small parties arrived all through the week, some having boarded merchant ships, others attaching themselves to traders' caravans and to the many other groups of travellers that made their way to the richest city in the world.

Amenophis had chosen the site of his temple of the Aten outside the eastern gate of the vast precinct of the Temple of Amon. There were temples of several other deities within the precinct, and the King had preferred to build outside not as a concession to the Amonites, but so that the rising disc of the Aten could send its rays to strike directly on to its own sanctuary. The form of the building was unusual, for although it was traditional in having outer walls and two rows of columns, each with one of Bak's huge statues of Amenophis before it, running down the middle, the whole of this central area was open to the sky and the eastern wall was pierced by great windows opening towards the place of sunrise. The freshly cut limestone was still almost white, while the figures of Pharaoh and the reliefs of the Aten, with their innumerable beneficent rays, had been coloured a clear saffron yellow. The whole contrived to capture something of the hope and brilliance of early sunlight.

The dedication of the temple was to coincide with the festival of the sowing of the spring corn and with the celebration of the renewal of his powers as Son of the Sun. Amenophis had determined on this addition to the meaning of the festival as soon as he knew that Nefertiti was to bear him a child.

When the day came, Meryre went at dawn to greet the
sun and to install the single stela which was to take the
place of the images of the god. Bak had worked hard to get
it done in time—for it showed the royal parents holding
the tiny figure of their daughter below the spreading rays
of the Aten. It was covered with thin gold so that it should
shine out from the west end of the temple. The consecration itself would take place at noon, when the sun would
be shining almost straight down into the central space.

On his return Meryre reported that he had been left
unmolested, but that he had noticed an extraordinarily
large number of young men praying and making offerings
at the many shrines in the Amon precinct.

Pharaoh and his mother ate their early morning meal
alone together—it having been thought best to leave Nefertiti undisturbed in West Thebes. Neither was nervous,
Amenophis because he was confident in the power of the
Aten being manifest in himself, Tiye because she was
confident that their plans had been well made down to the
last detail. In the middle of the morning one of her men
brought her a message from Ay to say that he had arrived
undetected at his headquarters and had placed his disloyal
lieutenants under secret arrest.

As they had arranged, Amenophis and the priests with
him went very slowly towards the Aten temple. He began
to pace himself by a butterfly that was fluttering idly westward along the flowers which he had had planted along
the processional way. As they drew abreast of the angle of
the precinct he looked along it and saw a winking of wheels
among the palms of a large temple plantation. Then two
horses neighed and Amenophis wondered whether those
awaiting him in the temple heard them too and began to
realize what was afoot. Glancing ahead towards the great
eastern gate, he caught a glimpse of the group of Coptos
men gathered inside.

As soon as he stepped into the temple, he could see that
it was crowded by far more people than those there by
right or invitation. The chief priests of all the leading
priesthoods were there by right, as were Ramose, the
Treasurer and other senior officials and the hereditary

fan-bearers, standard-bearers, guardians of the sacred staffs and all the other holders of sinecures about the King's person. Amenophis had also invited a number of Thebans, not courtiers, who had already shown sympathetic interest in the teachings of the Aten. But now among the crush of faces before him he could distinguish many officials whose positions gave them no religious privileges, as well as a quite undue number of priests of Amon. Above this massed congregation, which Amenophis could feel was full of tension, rose the great sculptures of himself, calm in their poise and remote in their expressions.

The King expected some intervention, but he began to carry out the rites of the consecration, advancing up the relatively narrow way left open along the central nave. It was then that he saw what Ipy had done. In front of the golden stela stood an image of Amon, tall enough for the shadow of the sculptured feathers crowning the head to make a black bar across the stele of the royal parents. And in place of Meryre, who should have led him to make offerings before the Aten, Ipy stepped forward, first bowing low, then fixing his bright eyes on the King's face.

"Majesty," he declaimed in his loud, clear voice, "Lord of the Two Lands, Horus of Gold, Beloved of Amon. Even as you are King of Egypt and of the Lands Beyond the Sea, so is your Father Amon King of the Gods. Even as you love your people, so your Father Amon loves you. Amon gives his most holy breath to all those great yet lesser gods that gather round him, and he has come here this day to bring his blessing also to the Aten. His humble servant, the High Priest Ipy, tenders into the hand of our divine one, Horus of Gold, Beloved of Amon, the offering that he desires to make to his father Amon." Ipy took from an attendant priest the long holder with its little cup of smouldering incense and held it out to Pharaoh.

Amenophis made no movement, and replied to the High Priest calmly and directly, using ordinary speech free from ritual elaboration.

"Ipy, High Priest of Amon, I am your divine sovereign. I and all my ancestors and the endless line of kings before us have ruled over Egypt as sons of Re, heirs of his first throne. Our monarchy draws its light from the sun; we have spread it among the people, bringing them life and prosperity. My father Re has granted me visions of the Divine Aten, the supreme power of love, creation and life. He has shown me that I have been chosen to teach the true worship of the Aten to the world of men. I have built this eastern temple and embellished it under Ma'at, and today have come, the sun shining upon me, to give it to its divine owner and to seek his blessing upon it. I am a man of peace and hate strife, most of all in a holy place. I command you to have this image of Amon returned to the Temple of Amon so that I may do what I have come to do."

Ipy again thrust forward the offering of incense and said, "Divine Majesty, before whom I am as dust, you will see that many of your subjects have come to prove their devotion to you as the Beloved of Amon and their wish to see you make your offering, according to the custom of your ancestors, to the King of the Gods, the most holy Amon." As he spoke Ipy looked beyond Pharaoh towards the open east end of the temple; he was full of the expectation of triumph. Amenophis did not turn, preferring to read events in Ipy's face. Suddenly the High Priest's expression changed, his neat, arrogant features seemed to blur and he took an involuntary step backward. For an instant there was a look of real terror in his eyes: he had seen Ay, whom he believed to be near death. The eyes of every man in the crowded temple followed the direction of Ipy's gaze.

Amenophis could no longer resist turning for a moment to see just what was happening outside. Framed in the high doorway was Ay, standing with his driver in the golden Mitannian chariot. Some of his junior officers could be seen parading their chariots slowly past the windows, while others were leading a contingent at a gentle trot from beyond the Precinct wall. By now, as he knew, his own bodyguard must have blocked the East Gate, probably with no show of force and hardly of hostility. The Precinct of Amon, which the High Priest had used as a lurking place for the men from Coptos, had

easily been turned into a pound for their helpless confinement. The manœuvre had in fact succeeded perfectly,
and no man had raised a spear—or even his voice. Ay and
the Commander of the Royal Bodyguard stepped quietly
into the temple.

The King faced to the south and raised his arms to the
sun in what was now his customary salutation to the god,
before once more confronting Ipy. The little man was
holding his ground. Indeed he could hardly do anything
else with the massive image of Amon standing behind him.
Why, he was asking himself, had he burned his boats by
bringing the thing into the Temple of Aten? It had been a
last-minute decision taken when everything seemed to be
going so well. Now he couldn't escape by pretending that
nothing had happened.

"Former High Priest Ipy," Amenophis spoke solemnly,
but with a hint of a grin on his lips, "I appreciate the love
of Amon as proclaimed through his servant. Now, however, it is time for his image to return to its place. As it is
heavy and the bearers probably dispersed, I will entrust
it to some of the strong young men who seem to have
gathered outside." At a sign the Commander of the Bodyguard slipped out, presently to return with half a dozen of
his stalwarts. Meanwhile the King went on: "When this
consecration has been celebrated, the former High Priest,
and the Second and Third Priests of Amon, together with
the Prince of Coptos whom I believe to be now waiting in
the Precinct, will be taken to the citadel. They have given
and listened to evil counsels. As for our Vizier, Ramose, I
will leave it to his own inner voice to tell him what he
should do, for I do not know whether he listened to these
counsels. And for the rest of you," Amenophis spoke now
with a husky break in his voice, "I ask you to return home
and at the hour of the sunset prayer to examine your
hearts and expose any ill you may find there to the healing
rays of the Aten, the living lord whose purposes I know."

During the minutes when the Amon statue and the three
priests were being quietly removed from the temple, all
the force and light seemed to empty out from the King,
and instead he was filled with disgust. His crown felt

almost unbearably heavy, and the heat and airlessness intolerable. The stunned congregation, the élite of Egypt, began to come round a little and to whisper. When at last Meryre was able to lead him to make his offerings, and to consecrate the building on which he had lavished so much thought and love, Amenophis felt no exaltation whatever, but only a longing to get through the ritual as quickly as possible and return to West Thebes and Nefertiti.

He found Nefertiti in the white-and-ebony room which he had always liked so well. She had turned it into a nursery, and at this moment was holding their daughter on her knees, helping the nurse to wash her tiny body and rub it with ointments. The Queen was thought by most of the harim ladies to be very eccentric to take any part in these tasks herself—but then the madness of the royal pair was a favourite topic of conversation among them, and they could see that this particular oddity of behaviour was in line with the rest.

Amenophis came over to her, walking wearily and his forehead deeply marked where the crown had been pressing upon it. The nurse bowed and then resumed her rubbing; she was growing accustomed to these informal ways, and the sight of Pharaoh kneeling close to her no longer made her want to faint. The little creature was wriggling her arms and legs in the air in the silly way that infants have when taken from their swaddling bands. Amenophis did not try to express the joyful relief that this scene gave him after his ordeal, but said at once:

"Isn't she exquisite—and hideous? Really, my darling, she is just like a new-born mouse. Do you remember that nestful we watched in the garden kiosk?"

Nefertiti smiled at him fondly, and ran her fingers along the red groove on his forehead. "At least she was born with her eyes open—and plenty of hair on her head."

"And she hasn't a tail. But you must agree they are very much alike." He knelt there for several minutes, watching his daughter's every movement and talking idly. Life ebbed back into him. How wonderfully clever Nefertiti was at falling in with his mood. Would not any other woman have started at once asking questions, thinking to please him with her interest in affairs?

He felt so happy in the simple room that he gave orders that their evening meal should be served to them there, while Merytaten should be taken to sleep with her nurse.

"The great thing is," he said as the baby was prepared for the night, "that our Merytaten is a new life, fresh as today's spring sowing. She won't know anything of the evil things of your childhood, or of the hatred of the priests of Amon. We will see her grow in truth and light, the first child of the new world we are creating."

"But can she be so untouched by all that has happened?" Nefertiti spoke out the sad side of her nature. "She is our child, all Egypt is about her—she has to grow up in the midst of things as they are."

"They can be changed. For a long time now, and most of all since we discovered this last scheme of Ipy's and I saw how many there were in sympathy with him, I have found Thebes hateful. It is so heavy with all the things that have been. I know that it is splendid, a great monument to our House, but even that splendour is oppressive, it weighs down on me like the crown itself." Amenophis put his hand to his forehead where the mark was still faintly imprinted. "And it is so full of old gods and their images. Think of them everywhere in their shrines and chapels—hundreds and hundreds of them, mountainsides of granite and limestone, all lifeless and without Ma'at. They make a stone army ranged against me. And the human beings—the courtiers and officials and priests. Whatever their age, they are old, too, for they want only one thing: that everything should remain the same. Unless, indeed, they could grow even richer and more powerful. Now that it has been revealed to me how all this must change, how the truth of all the gods is in the power of the Aten—I know that we can't stay here any longer. Thebes and the Thebans will stifle my teaching. How can we either practice or teach our understanding of love and life with all these stone gods and mummified men opposed to us?"

"It is hard, certainly. They all seem to stand shoulder to shoulder in resistance—those men who have had power so long."

"You did not see them today in the Aten Temple, where in very fact they were shoulder to shoulder—and nearly all with their hearts and feeling embalmed long ago."

"But I think your ideas are spreading—and with the temple and the beginning of a true ministry there they will spread faster. Think of Nakht, prince of Thinis, who has now been enlightened—and all the priests who came up from Heliopolis, and the Theban merchants . . . and, of course, all our real friends."

"Yes. Many are with us—or say they are. Dear Nefertiti, you know how it is that I cannot be as innocent as other men think I am, or as I should like to be. With our own friends it is different, but with these other people who claim to have seen the light of the Aten, how do I know they are not just seeking to please Pharaoh?"

"That is better than seeking to displease him. Like Ipy."

"Yes, perhaps, but not enough. If they had to make a sacrifice, if they had to leave familiar Thebes, that would be a test. I wouldn't fear they were only looking for preferment if they would follow me from their well-filled mangers."

"Oh Amenophis, my dearest lord. I do see how wonderful it would be if we could all be somewhere together, all of us who love the Divine Aten—and have eyes for the new art, and wish to live under Ma'at and enjoy all creation with our eyes and ears and noses. . . . Do you remember how happy and right we were on the boat sailing to Memphis? It was because we were with people you had chosen, there together with the water all round us."

"Water all round us—yes. And I have always been happy in gardens enclosed by walls. Enclosures, outlines, are sacred. The Aten is a boundless fire by day with rays embracing all the skies, but as he goes to meet the horizon he may withdraw within his own outline, revealing his perfect disc. It is then that he seems his most potent and solitary self."

For some time they were silent, Amenophis watching Nefertiti's face. "Now that the child is born she is becoming more beautiful than ever," he thought, "it is almost more than I can bear."

At that moment Nefertiti sat up on her couch and leant towards him. "I know! I have thought where we should go. Do you remember that place where we anchored for the night and watched the sunset? A place where the cliffs enclosed a great half-moon of land? I remember I said at the time it was like a little kingdom. And it belongs to nobody. Oh Amenophis, could we go there?"

Pharaoh swayed his body gently to and fro in his effort to recall a complete imaginative picture of the place and the occasion. A joyful expression broke gradually over his face. "Sitting here in our nursery, I seem to be there again as we were that night. The ducks tracing the bright water-surface, the Bedouin camp with smoke rising in the stillness—and you and I. It was the first time we spoke of the Aten as the divinity of love and life. And I remember how the sun disc stood for an instant on the horizon, lighting the great curve of cliffs. It has been truly revealed to you where we should go, my Nefertiti. There our dwelling of the Aten can grow within its outline, and the cliffs will protect as my arm protects you now." He curved his arm round her shoulders. "We will make it the centre of the world, an earthly disc of the Aten from where the light of our teaching will stream out on to all men. And you and our children will live there in perfection." He began to make love to her, but Nefertiti stiffened for an instant and pulled back her head. "But, my darling, it is only a dream, isn't it? We can't really leave this tremendous city? Thebes which could be as strong as a bull and as angry as a lion?"

"A dream? It will be a dream made real. The imaginary land of my boyhood brought into being beside the River."

"It is possible, then?" She still seemed unable to surrender.

"My dearest, where Pharaoh and his Great Queen are, there is the capital of Egypt. You would not stay behind?"

VI

In spite of the excitement that it stirred in him, Amenophis decided not to make any immediate announcement
about his decision to leave Thebes. Indeed, he did not even
confide in the Queen Mother. His motives for this
uncharacteristic caution were mixed. He wanted more
time for reflection when, as he confidently expected, he
would receive further enlightenment from the god. Then
perhaps two personal matters counted with him. He
enjoyed sharing this tremendous secret with Nefertiti,
while on the other hand he feared the opposition of Queen
Tiye. Finally, there was the practical consideration (and
the young King was by no means unpractical when his
feelings and convictions were not at stake) that Ipy's
conspiracy of coercion had to be fully settled before it was
possible to put a further great strain on loyalty. He and
his mother had closed the net on their enemies, but what
now was to be done with their catch?

The reactions of the court after the happenings in the
Aten Temple were predictable. All those officials, ritual
office-holders and courtiers who had given tacit support
to the High Priest but who were not openly committed,
united to make a great show of horror and shocked disapproval over what had occurred. How could it be that
Pharaoh, who was divine, and divinely guided, could ever
err or should ever be opposed? Many of them sought out
the Queen Mother, Meryre, the loyal treasurer, and even
Bak to express these sentiments to them and to profess their
devoted interest in the teaching of the Aten. At the same
time all avoided Ramose, as he had been named by the
King and his position was equivocal.

The royal party decided to accept this sudden devotion
as though it were genuine. At least half the court was
involved, and it was impossible either to move against
them all or identify any that were more guilty than others.
Ramose's case resolved itself. Queen Tiye had become

convinced during the week before the consecration that the Vizier. knew that something was afoot and that although he had not participated in any way, he had not seen fit to tell her what he had discovered. When taxed with this the unhappy man, who was in poor health and tired out by overwork, admitted that he had heard that Ipy intended some demonstration, but had convinced himself that relations between Amon and the Aten were altogether beyond the responsibilities of his office. He begged to be forgiven and allowed to retire to his estate, which lay some hundred miles away from the capital. This arrangement Amenophis and his mother were thankful to accept, for Ramose was essentially loyal and harmless, and had given devoted service to Egypt. The decoration of his tomb was stopped, and it remained unfinished, with one of the lively scenes drawn by Amenophis and Bak already carved, while a second, intended to celebrate all the foreigners in Thebes, was only sketched on the wall. The King appointed Nakht, Prince of Thinis, to take his place.

What was to be done with Ipy and his leading priests and to the Prince of Coptos—whose conduct had been the most nearly traitorous of all? The Queen Mother wanted to have the high priest and the prince buried alive, and the underlings sent to the turquoise mines in Sinai. She said that wherever the leaders could be sent into exile they would foment trouble—if far away they could work undetected, if near at hand they could still make a rallying point for discontented Thebans. Amenophis saw the force of her argument, but he was determined to show the loving kindness of the Aten. He was fortified in this by the return of the expedition from Nubia. His friend Tutu was able to describe how, as soon as the soldiers arrived in the rebellious province, the desert people made off and the local rebels capitulated, begging for mercy. He, Tutu, had read them Pharaoh's message, and they had all worshipped his name, sworn undying loyalty and promised to live in peace under Ma'at. He declared that when the guilty tribal chief had heard that even his life was to be spared he had burst into tears and had insisted on returning with him to Thebes to swear his loyalty in person.

"You see, my pitiless Mother, mercy does change people. If you try to stamp on an adder it will sting you, if you move gently it will glide peacefully away. I should like Ipy to be made to serve the Aten with hard work. On a farm, perhaps. As for the prince, he has the pride of power and must be made to live for the humble. When I was in Memphis I saw an orphanage which our general Haremhab had set up for the families of soldiers killed in our service. The proud man from Coptos shall be their cook—and Haremhab can keep an eye on him. As for the other priests of Amon, I will have them sent to the temple of Re at Heliopolis to work as scribes for the god. There! I have given judgment." He grinned at Queen Tiye.

"You are taking risks," she said, shrugging. "And I would never take risks for Egypt. But I begin to see that you have to follow your own ways in everything. How did I come to have a son like no one else's son?" She laid her hand on his arm affectionately.

"Because the Aten is my father, I expect, my poor Mother. And then sometimes a thing will produce its opposite."

The King's unheard-of judgments were carried out. Ipy, who for several weeks had been anticipating death, was thankful to be sent to work on Nakht's estate at Thinis. The prince made a half-hearted attempt at suicide before submitting to the life of a cook.

In the end it was the least guilty who paid the worst penalty. Without consulting anybody, Ay had his First and Second Officers executed before the eyes of all the other officers and men of the Chariots. When Amenophis heard of it he was sickened but did not protest. Soldiers, after all, lived to kill one another. Instead he sent Ranufer to make enquiries about Mahu. It proved that the young man was very much alive. His absence on the day he visited the Palace had been noticed, but he found little difficulty in persuading his master that he had been to West Thebes on an amorous exploit (for the moment, evidently, he had forgotten his dedication to the strictest truth). He was let off with nothing worse than confinement to barracks and stable-cleaning fatigues. When he learnt that Pharaoh had remembered him and that he was indeed to join the royal bodyguard he experienced, as Ranufer reported, a kind of adolescent ecstasy. He was full of dreams of saving the King's life.

So the powerful but submerged disturbance, which had broken the surface only for a few minutes in the Temple of the Aten, subsided, leaving the royal party in command. Indeed, once all the passively disloyal courtiers and officials had insisted on their loyalty sufficiently to feel that they were safe, many of them began to drift away from Thebes. Far more of them than usual retreated to their country estates and summer houses, while officials suddenly found duties calling them into the provinces. So Thebes seemed subdued and lifeless, like someone who has offended against Ma'at and must live with his guilt. In the city rumours were circulating as to what had happened in the temple. Some people said that Ipy had been possessed, and had drawn a knife against Pharaoh, while nearly all were agreed that Amenophis had evoked his god and that a disc of fire had descended before him, temporarily blinding the congregation and overcoming the high priest. It was also said that Ay had been brought back from the dead to punish Pharaoh's enemies.

Now that everything was settled and the Amonites crushed, Amenophis knew that he must announce his great decision. His resolve had only hardened as the days went by, for he found the new atmosphere of the court oppressive, and was more than ever convinced that he could never lead the world into the light while he himself lived in the shadow of Thebes with its weighty past and its present deadness of spirit. His mother's control of affairs of state was inevitably weakening now that Ramose had gone. Nakht was his man, an earnest convert to the Aten, and Tiye, although she had to help and instruct him at first, could never feel at ease with him. A little to Amenophis's surprise she seemed quite ready to hand over most of her powers, and she was undoubtedly glad to see him giving more time to state affairs than he had in the past. Nevertheless, he still felt that it was her approval of his plan to create a perfect city that really mattered to him.

The Queen Mother was very much surprised one evening to have delivered into her hand a papyrus inscribed by
Amenophis himself. They had met together in council
with Nakht only that morning, and there seemed no
reason for her son to communicate with her in writing.
She opened it with a twinge of nervousness, but it contained an affectionately-worded request to her to meet
him at the entrance to his father's funerary temple an hour
after sunrise on the next day. It seemed a strange invitation, and an inconvenient one, but she supposed that some
pious impulse must have prompted Amenophis to celebrate a morning sacrifice for his father, and that she had
better humour him. She turned to Tutu, who had brought
the letter and was waiting with his usual air of modest
discretion, and said almost curtly, "Tell my Lord Pharaoh
that I shall meet him at the place and time he has re-
quested." Then she went to take her evening meal with
Kheruef. She was living with him openly now, and enjoying a kind of domesticity she had never known before.

Amenophis and Nefertiti climbed the dark and narrow
staircase of the great building for the worship of the divine
Amenophis III, and presently stepped out into the early
sunlight. They were on the flat roof of the entrance gate
with the heads of the two colossal figures of Pharaoh just
below them. Woven rugs had been spread and stools set
out, while four guards (one of them the proud Mahu)
stood at the corners of the gate as though to defend them
from winged enemies.

Holding hands, they walked gingerly to the edge and
looked down. They had a curious foreshortened view
down the bodies and on to the laps of the statues, where
the huge hands lay along the knees in the sacred posture.
Between the low pedestals they saw the clustered heads of
all the men whom Amenophis had bidden to attend. Ay
was there and Nakht, Meryre and the Treasurer—with
Bak standing rather apart. At that moment a curtained
litter turned in from the road, preceded by one of the
palace stewards.

"She has come," said Amenophis, and without waiting
for the litter to be set down, drew Nefertiti back towards

the three stools. He was obviously very nervous. Nefertiti was disturbed by his mood and puzzled by the extra-ordinary meeting-place. Did this breaking of the news to the Queen Mother matter so much? They stood side by side in silence and were able to hear Tiye's panting breath before the steward helped her up the last steps. The King handed her to the centre stool, and he and Nefertiti sat down on either side.

"It is years since I climbed so many stairs," she gasped, "and I certainly would not have come if I had known of this insane plot of yours, Amenophis. Why have you brought me here? I thought it was to make a celebration for your father."

"For my father? In a way perhaps that is true. For him and for his father and for all my ancestors. I brought you here, dearest Mother, to show you Thebes so that you may understand why I must leave it."

"You are thinking of taking the court back to Memphis? There is much to be said for it."

"First I want you to look at Thebes through my eyes." He made a sweeping movement with both arms, embrac-ing the whole city that was spread out round them.

"Your eyes admire the Aten Temple and I cannot see through them. To me," and she stretched out her legs in front of her with a deliberately comical movement, "to me Thebes looks uncommonly beautiful."

No one could have denied it. In front of them as they faced the River the fields with the crops now well up, the scatter of white farms with their palm groves, the shining irrigation trenches, made a rich carpet of prosperity. Lines of peasants were hoeing between the rows and singing as they went, while egrets, like single feathers caught in the wind, rose up in front of them and settled in their wake. Then beyond the strip of the River the quays and houses and clustering temples showed clearly in the morning light, set off by the tranquil forms of the eastern moun-tains. When they turned to look away from the River, the prospect was even more magnificent. They could see the pleasure lake fringed with exotic trees, the palace with flowers and creepers cascading over its walls and the graceful temple of Tuthmosis III standing next to it, then the houses and gardens of the citizens packed below the foothills and climbing a little way up them, the line of temples along the edge of the town, with their forest of pillars rising above the corn, the little rocky hills where the nobility were buried fretted with pretty chapels. From their vantage point, too, they could see enough of the stately approaches and the wild crags behind to make them imagine how, just out of sight, the great temple built by Queen Hatshepsut would be standing at the foot of the precipice with its long, elegant colonnades steeped in the sun. Further on, below the summit of el-Quern, they had glimpses of the road winding up the valley towards the royal tombs.

In spite of the singing peasants and the stream of busy people passing on the road, it seemed as they stared about them that for an instant they were outside time. Or rather, perhaps, that there on the gate they were perched on the still point of the present with all the past and future of Thebes, of Egypt, of the world, revolving silently, invisibly round them.

Amenophis turned back to look into his mother's face. "I believe we are looking not through your eyes or mine, but through the eyes of the Aten himself." He spoke these words softly, then suddenly using the full resonance of his voice, he said, "Yes, it is beautiful, our city, but it is my enemy."

"Less so now than for years. The people over there," she pointed towards the distant temple of Amon, "are left without leaders and gradually we will confiscate their lands and reduce their power to nothing. . . ."

"I am not thinking of enemies of that kind—although it is hard to serve Ma'at in a court rotten with humbug and deceit. Thebes is my enemy because the whole of the past, and the present servants of the past, are entrenched here. I was born to the throne to lead men out into the light of the Aten. We have to leave behind all the old gods who at best were but aspects of his truth. But here their houses and their idols are everywhere. And under the Aten all men can live in peace, but Thebes is bristling with the pride of conquerors. That of my great-great-grandfather Tuthmosis, for instance. Wasn't I shown his temple out of my nursery and told how I must be like him, spending my life with armies conquering our neighbours? And up there in the valley are the bodies of my forebears, men who have caused the deaths of hundreds of thousands. And all Thebes is heavy with the wealth we have extorted and the people we have enslaved. That, dearest Mother, is why I have to leave it and why I ask your blessing on my going."

"But Memphis has even more of the past, and if the court went there would soon be as wealthy."

"I am not going to Memphis. I have to found a new city on desert land where life can start afresh under the Aten. Nefertiti and I have chosen the place. We shall call it Akhetaten, the Horizon of the Aten." Amenophis spoke positively, and yet he scanned Tiye's face in doubt.

"I see. And why did you make me climb up to this crazy place to tell me what is already decided?"

"It is decided. It has been decided for me. And yet I do not want to leave Thebes against your will." It was a long time since he had spoken to her with pleading in his voice. She was moved and she did not know how to respond. It was a preposterous idea, and yet was not everything her son did preposterous and at the same time proper to him? She escaped into trivialities.

"And this place you have chosen—you say that no one lives there?"

"When we saw it there were a few Bedouin tents and a farm or two along the River's edge. And it is close by the road that leads to the alabaster quarries of Hatnub." Amenophis suddenly grinned as he gave her this useless information. He knew now that his mother's opposition was not going to be painful.

"Then it will be years before you can go there. Or will you live in a tent or a mud hut?"

"We shall live in the most delightful palace in the world. Shan't we, Nefertiti?"

"Yes. And because it won't be in a big city we can bring nature into it—animals and birds and all the most lovely creatures."

"It sounds like children's make-believe to me. Have you really considered this seriously enough, my Lord Pharaoh?"

"You do not usually suspect me of not being serious enough. More often you say I am intolerably earnest." He grinned again.

"Well, I am earnest now. Amenophis, have you thought that where you have enemies, you also have friends? And with your friends you can struggle for what you believe to be for the best—as I have done. In this dream city of yours you will be alone."

"As the Aten is alone. He created all things out of this solitariness. And it is he who has decided that I should build Akhetaten."

"If you were like other men, I should say that you were trying to fly from what cannot be left behind."

"No, no. It is not like that," Nefertiti said eagerly. "As I see it most men of power live as it were in a citadel, with wall behind wall and many towers. But Amenophis must live in a happy dwelling where all the doors are open and where his life can flower and all can see him and receive his light. He can only live in that way where he is quite free and untrammelled."

"I don't know that I can follow your language, Nefertiti," Tiye said with some roughness, "and frankly I don't really understand why he can't flower in our lovely palace here. It is free and open enough. But then, my son, I know that I am a woman without much religion in me. With your father I never could believe that he was a god except through the being of Egypt. But with you it is different. I know that you have divinity in you, and that is why it is useless to oppose you. And yet you are a man, and as a man I am afraid that you are tying yourself to a cross." Amenophis stared at her, wondering if she understood.

"Perhaps. To the cross of the sun."

"This stool is getting most uncomfortable, and I don't like being exposed up here between earth and sky. So, my dear son Amenophis, I give you what you want. My blessing on your Akhetaten. . . ."

Amenophis jumped up, raised her from her seat and

embraced her. But then suddenly he dropped her hands and stepped back. "Amenophis .. . Akhetaten," he said to himself, "How could I have been so deaf? I cannot keep that name . . . that name which is becoming hateful to me . . . the name which I must leave behind." Nefertiti looked apprehensively at him, feeling the excitement that was beginning to shake him. Closing his lids he turnèd his face up to the sun and cried, "Here in the eye of my father who teaches me all things I announce myself as Akhenaten, and pray that he will enable me to fulfil this name that he has granted me. I, Akhenaten."

Nefertiti and Tiye looked at one another in astonishment, but while the girl ran to embrace her husband and try the new name, the Queen Mother gave her inevitable shrug. "I am going down now, my Lord Pharaoh. I have burnt my complexion already." Her servant came over to help her. "Please stay with me while I tell the news to my Uncle Ay and all the rest who are waiting below," Akhenaten called out after her. Mahu came forward, and was allowed to give his shoulder to support Nefertiti. When they had all gone a little way down the cramped, dusty steps, they had to stop for a moment, so intensely dark did it seem after the glare on the top of the gate. "You won't be able to make the move for years," Tiye said in the darkness. "I may be dead before you do."

Through long habit of preparing himself for the sunrise prayer, Akhenaten always woke early. That morning, because of the excitement with which he had looked forward to the day ahead as he fell asleep on the narrow folding bed, he roused even earlier than usual. Seen through the dyed cloths of his tent, the dawn light seemed rosy in one place, blue in another. From just outside came the sound of slow, soft breathing; it was Mahu, who when his spell of guard duty was over, had come to sleep across the tent flaps.

Akhenaten got up and went outside, stepping carefully over Mahu, amused that his watchdog did not even stir. He noticed that the young man's hand was ringed and dimpled like a baby's. Good living at the Palace was making him fat.

Akhenaten looked intently about him. This was his first clear sight of the place chosen for the creation of Akhetaten. The royal convoy had tied up after dark the previous night, for in his impatience he had refused to allow an anchorage to be made before they reached their destination—the north end of the arc of hills. Now in the wan light the scene was desolate. Even the River in its relentless flow had a grey, glum look, and the cliffs that meant so much to him seemed harsh rather than protective. In between the two, the semicircle of desert showed nothing but sand, stones, boulders and stretches of thorny scrub. Only the strip of cultivation along the River bank offered any hope for the future, and that was a slender one.

The encampment itself, though well prepared for them in advance, had a straggling, insufficient appearance in the face of these natural wastes. Beyond the tents were a picket line of drooping horses and a row of chariots with their shaft poles sloping upwards. The largest one, with two spearmen slouched beside it, must be the electrum chariot in which he was to mark the bounds of Akhetaten. Beyond this again were the pens of the cattle and sheep soon to be offered to the majesty of the Aten.

Akhenaten shivered. It all seemed utterly unlike the promised land that he and Nefertiti had been visiting in their imaginations. Could the city be built here on the ground as it had been built in their thought? Could his will prevail against all this nothingness? It seemed to him that his shoulders were already bowed with the weight of the world, and he felt exhausted as though it were the end of the day. Finding that he could neither pray nor meditate, he began to rehearse to himself the words he would speak at the dedication ceremony. Presently he slipped into Nefertiti's tent.

Only a few hours later the whole scene was transformed, and in the sunshine it was impossible even to remember despondency. River and hills were bright, horses and chariots were assembling with a sparkle of wheels, and the coloured tents had a festive air. Ay, Nakht, Meryre, Tutu,

Bak, and all those who from the beginning had been committed to Akhetaten, and who looked forward to being its first and greatest citizens, were standing together, jewelled and serious, waiting for the ceremony to begin.

At the same time a crowd was gathering round the outskirts of the encampment, word of extraordinary doings having spread up and down the River. When they saw Pharaoh and his Great Queen leave their tents, all these people threw themselves on to the ground and then leapt up again, full of chatter and speculation.

Ranufer brought up the electrum chariot, Akhenaten and Nefertiti mounted, and they led a procession to the northernmost point of the encircling cliffs. Although their horses were the strongest in the King's stables, the weight of precious metal made the royal chariot lumber heavily across the uneven desert floor. At the cliff foot, Ranufer wheeled so that Pharaoh could speak from the back of the car, while the other chariots drew up in a half circle round him. The pursuing crowd came to a scattered halt and stood gazing. It is unlikely that anyone except the few nearest to him heard all Akhenaten's words, for the wind carried some away, and the horses fidgeted and shook their ears.

Speaking as loudly as he could, he began: "In this sixth year of my reign I have resolved at last to establish the city of the god in this place which he himself has chosen. He kept it inviolate, belonging to no one, until he revealed it to me, his son, and to my dearest Nefertiti. He set up cliffs to enfold his place and protect his people. My Father has shown me that I must guard this boundary and never trespass beyond it. For the outline is in his likeness, and I shall dwell within it and teach what he has taught me, and the light of his words will shine out upon the world like the rays of the sun. Here we shall show how men and women can live together supported only by love, for I shall impose no punishments nor harsh judgments. We shall leave darkness behind at Thebes, where abominable things have been said and done against the Aten."

Then Akhenaten went on to describe the many temples he would build for the service of the Aten, and the Palace of the King and Queen where he and Nefertiti would exemplify the power of the divine love. Finally, to show his courtiers that he was resolved that Akhetaten should remain the capital of the Two Lands for all time, he declared that whenever and wherever he or the Queen or their children should die, they would be buried in the cliffs overlooking the city.

Just as he had finished speaking, Akhenaten noticed a woman who had stepped out from the crowd carrying a basket of blue lotus blossoms. Probably she had some idea of strewing them before his horses.

"Mahu," he called, "go to that woman, give her this gold and bring me her basket." When it was brought, he held it out to Nefertiti and said, "As we drive round the bounds of Akhetaten, you shall throw a flower wherever you feel a mark should be set up. Where it falls a stone shall be carved with my words—so that all citizens will be able to read what I have said on this founding day of their city."

Nefertiti nodded, and at once tossed a lotus to the foot of the cliff. "I will do as you say," she answered, "and the first one shall go where the words were spoken and where the sheltering wall begins."

Ranufer made a move to take up the reins, but Akhenaten suddenly resolved that he must drive the chariot of the sun alone with Nefertiti. "You shall run beside us, Ranufer, and pile stones at each place where a lotus falls." Then he himself took the reins and they set off round the foot of the cliffs, the other drivers falling in behind them one by one. The surface became harder, glistening with quartz, and their shining chariot gathered speed. As it swayed, Nefertiti leant against the King, clasping a flower ready for the next throw. They began to laugh together, half from childlike excitement and half from a kind of ecstasy.

"Now we know how the Creator exulted on the first day," Akhenaten cried, urging the horses on. "With the wheels below us we are drawing the body of the new capital of the world." Nefertiti laughed again, but she only replied, "I did not know that you could drive horses so well, my lord."

"That is because I have never before wanted to drive them. What I desire, that I can do." Nefertiti tossed another flower, the wind caught it, lifted it in the air and blew it against a crag.

By the time they had completed the arc and were near the River once more, they had sobered and were as tired as their sweating horses. Nefertiti quietly placed the basket with the remaining flowers to fix the southernmost point of Akhetaten. Then, when Ranufer and the other chariots had caught up with them, they all embarked in a barge which had come to carry them back to the encampment.

As they approached, a tall man came out from Pharaoh's tent, followed by a boy. It was Mersure with his son, Smenkhkare, now about six years old.

Soon after Akhenaten became Crown Prince, Mersure had married one of his many half-sisters, a dull, handsome woman born to Amenophis III by a Babylonian princess. She approved his ambition and he appreciated the value of her royal blood. They had settled on Mersure's estate near Thebes, and he was often at court. Although he kept on good terms with the Queen Mother, he and Akhenaten generally avoided one another. The young Pharaoh felt ill at ease with a man who had helped to spread the worship of the Aten before his own enlightenment, but who, as he felt sure, had no religious conviction whatever.

Mersure bowed before his half-brother, at the same time, as Nefertiti noticed, giving a sharp clip to his son to make him prostrate himself.

"Greetings, Mersure. I had not expected you here." Akhenaten made no attempt to sound welcoming.

"Then my messenger must have failed to reach you in time. As you may perhaps know, my Lord Pharaoh, I have been on a mission on your behalf to Amurru and when I returned to Memphis I heard of this expedition. You will forgive me if I longed to see where my future home was to be, and where at last the Aten was to shine undisputed."

"It is my intention that all who are true worshippers of the Aten shall be free to live in his city." Akhenaten stared at his kinsman with distaste.

"I shall count every season lost until I can be numbered among them. And now, my lord, may I present to you my son, Smenkhkare, who is still only a child but who promises to have all the virtues which you find lacking in his father."

Smenkhkare was a beautiful boy. Probably it was from his Mitannian great-grandmother that he had inherited large, dark grey eyes and a coppery sheen in his softly curling hair. He had delicate features, and there seemed to be something withdrawn and poetic about him. Yet he had a full, strongly peaked mouth that any woman might have envied. As he raised his head from the obeisance he looked into Akhenaten's eyes and smiled very sweetly.

At that moment Nefertiti gave a little cry of pleasure as the Cypriote girl, Lasia, came out from the Queen's tent carrying Merytaten. The baby was holding out her arms towards her mother, but on seeing Smenkhkare she immediately lunged her little body in his direction and reached out as though to touch his face. The boy showed the instinct to please which had been his greatest birth-gift. Standing on tiptoe beside Lasia, he took Merytaten's diminutive hands and lifted first one and then the other to his lips.

Nefertiti laughed, but nevertheless was quick to take her daughter from Lasia and go with her into the tent, murmuring that she was tired, and the sun too strong for the baby's eyes. Mersure looked appraisingly at the King and said, "You see that the princess in all her innocence recognizes the truth of what I said about my son. She seemed to love him at once—and he to respond. Perhaps, who knows, they will become playmates when we are happily living here together."

"Or perhaps five years is too great a difference of age. I hope, Mersure, that you have brought some shelter with you, for I fear that all our tents are assigned."

"Thank you, Lord Pharaoh. We have excellent cabins on board—as you see, our boat is a large one."

Akhenaten turned and went after Nefertiti. She was playing with Merytaten on a beautifully marbled giraffe-skin rug which covered half the floor of her tent. Even this charming picture did not soothe him. He sat down beside her, frowning.

"I do not like the thought of Mersure living here." He paused, running his finger along the pale tracks between the russet patches on the fur. "Indeed, I have to confess to myself that I had not thought of people whom I did not want coming to Akhetaten. Yet Mersure is outwardly a devout servant of the Aten. What can we do?"

"We have to love him." Nefertiti looked back at Akhenaten with the same rueful expression as his own.

Still frowning, he shook his head. "I can see that he will have to come—and perhaps you, Nefertiti, will have enough goodness in you to be able to love him. And Mersure said one true thing. Smenkhkare may grow up to bring us happiness—I never saw a more engaging child."

"He is very pretty."

"Yes. But I don't know why we are thinking of *his* prettiness. Send for Lasia to take our daughter away. I want you for myself."

When they had rested and eaten something, Akhenaten determined to survey his realm to decide where the principal buildings should be raised. He had not been in such wild country since the days of his father's lion hunts, and he longed to escape into it with his friends. He sent for Mahu and told him to saddle donkeys for Nefertiti, Bak, Meryre and himself.

The doubts stirred up by Mersure had completely left him, and he was in a jubilant mood. When Akhenaten was in high spirits everyone near him always shared in them, and they set off like any party of young people intending to enjoy themselves. Yet at the same time the purpose of their mission gave them an extraordinary sense of power.

Bak was the liveliest of them all. He was thinking of the great part he could play in embellishing a whole new city in this challenging place. He looked very big and florid as he straddled a small white ass, making it circle round and round his companions while he whistled and sang.

They went southward, parallel with the River, talking of the best positions for some of the buildings and gardens that Akhenaten and Nefertiti had long been devising in their minds. When they had made their choice for the palace of birds and beasts, the terraced gardens above the River, and for the wharves, they turned inland. At once the going became rougher and more thorny. There were so many scrubby bushes and boulders that it was impossible to think of building sites; it was as much as they could do to struggle along. Their spirits were beginning to flag when they heard a clear, resonant tapping coming from some distance ahead. There were momentary silences, but always the sound began again.

"It reminds me of something," said Nefertiti, listening. "Why, yes, of you at work in your studio, Bak."

"Sculptors are mad, certainly, but not with a hermit's kind of madness. We don't rush off into the desert in order to carve its rocks——"

"What is it, then?"

"Maybe, madam, it is a peasant shaping a grindstone, or a giant bird trying to smash open a tortoise, or——" Bak broke off in disarray as they came out from the scrub on to an open space above a *wadi*. A hut neatly built of palm leaves stood on the edge of the watercourse, and outside it were two men. One was a tall, hook-nosed Bedouin, sitting motionless, gazing into space. The other was a thickset Egyptian—and white chips were flying out all round him as he attacked a block of stone with mallet and chisel.

As the donkeys rattled out on to the little plateau, and Nefertiti laughed aloud at Bak's expression of amazed discomfiture, the sculptor stopped work and turned to watch the approaching party. He called out.

"Greetings! You are most welcome if you are from Thebes. I'm wanting news."

Akhenaten scrutinized the artist before replying. He was a man of about forty with broad, heavy shoulders; stout in a vigorous, compact way. His face was in perfect harmony with his body—square, the cheekbones high and strongly modelled, the nose straight and blunt. Yet it was saved from stolidity by a long, convex, almost monkey-like upper lip, demarcated by deep lines running from the nose, which seemed to give a sardonic twist to a calm and serious face. The King felt at once that this was a person as firmly founded as the great pyramid.

"Yes, we come from Thebes," Akhenaten said quietly.

"I saw them all galloping round the cliffs. They were in chariots of solid gold—or so I hear." He nodded towards his model, who had now turned his hawk gaze on to Nefertiti. "Yet you and your friends have to make do with asses."

"So you can suppose we are quite humble people. I do not find it more surprising that a king should ride in a gold chariot than that a sculptor should set up his block in the middle of a desert. What are you doing here, sir, and what is the news you want to hear?"

"I must look like something dropped accidentally from the sky. But in fact I am here for a simple and selfish purpose. I want your master our Pharaoh to be my patron. I heard while I was doing some work for the priests of Re at Heliopolis of the extraordinary plan for Pharaoh to leave Thebes and build a new city somewhere here. Then when I was down-river at Hermopolis there was a rumour of this visit of his. And of course I have known for years about his ideas of Ma'at and 'art of the instant', as those in the fashion like to call it. They excited me, because I'd already moved in that direction myself—though I suspect his sculptor Bak of going too far. I've had to earn my living as best I could as a not very successful traditional stone carver, but I've always done my own work, mostly modelling, for myself alone. Now I see a chance to serve someone who sees things as I do, and to say goodbye to hack tomb reliefs and temple ornaments. Sound men shake their heads over this young Pharaoh, but I say more strength to him. The idea of a new city here in the desert, starting afresh away from all the old men, is magnificent. So what I want to ask, although I don't expect any of you know the answer, is whether the sculptor Bak is here with the rest of them, and whether he is the sort of man I could approach. I don't think he would fear a rival—there will be enough work for twenty of us." While the man had been speaking, Bak had dismounted and gone to look at the half-finished carving. At these last words he grimaced at Akhenaten from behind the sculptor's back, but gave a sign of approval of his work.

"Would you not rather approach the King himself?" the King asked.

"I don't think that would be reasonable at this time— and I am a reasonable man. Besides, he would talk of the Aten, and I should be lost. All gods are the same to me."

"Do you mean all gods are the same god to you, or that all are nothing?" Akhenaten fixed the man with an intent stare. He made a quick movement, grasping the mallet between both hands and looking up sharply. It had dawned on him that these could not be servants or stewards. But he only replied, "I mean that all are one, and all mankind as well."

"Then you need not be so much afraid of meeting the Pharaoh Akhenaten." He paused before adding, "Which is as well, for I am he."

For a moment it seemed as though the river must have ceased flowing from the south and the breeze blowing from the north as they all stood quite still in the sunlight. Nefertiti noticed that the burly man before them was trembling, as slowly he thrust out his arms stiffly behind him and bent his body forward until it was in line with them. He remained so, staring at the ground.

"Your Majesty, I have spoken as I think. I cannot ask forgiveness, only understanding. You are like a lion who has come upon his victim when his head is down to drink."

"You spoke roughly of the Aten. That cannot please me." The sculptor neither moved nor spoke, but Nefertiti pushed her donkey up beside her husband's and said softly, "My lord, it is because he has had no opportunity to hear your teachings. Neither from you nor from anyone who has listened to you. He spoke well otherwise, and we know that what he said he meant." Akhenaten laid his hand on her arm, but otherwise took no notice of her. He went on inflexibly.

"You said that my servant Bak had gone too far. If that is true, then it is I who have gone too far." The man drew in his breath harshly and said in a thickened voice. "I see I have destroyed the greatest chance a man ever had—the life I imagined—" Nefertiti was going to intercede again, but looking into his face she saw that Akhenaten wore his rare but characteristic grin.

"What is your name?" he asked abruptly.

"Dhutmose—of Memphis."

"Then, Dhutmose, you think that Pharaoh is an idiot?" At this the sculptor swung himself bolt upright and shouted with the force of his big lungs, "Sire, I swear that I did not until this instant." He glared at the King, and then, seeing the grin and a gleam from the long eyes, his glare broke into a look of doubting recognition.

"That is well spoken under Ma'at. Every man should be himself. It is I who should ask your forgiveness, but a master must try a new servant." Dhutmose was still gripping his mallet and now, impulsively, he· held it out towards the King. "Then I may dedicate this to your service?"

Akhenaten beckoned Bak to his side. "This is Bak, who is a generous man and will not bear malice. Together you two will help me, and the Queen Nefertiti, to raise Akhetaten, to make it as beautiful as it must be to fulfil our dreams. But now we are hot and tired and have lost our way and would like to rest in the first building of the new city." He pointed to the palm-leaf hut. They all dismounted, and soon an impromptu picnic was in progress, with Akhenaten and Nefertiti seated side by side on the sculptor's rough couch, and Mahu delightedly pouring wine while Dhutmose offered fragments of cold fish and wild duck wrapped in leaves and flavoured with onion. He explained that much of the time he was not at work he had spent fishing or shooting waterfowl, and he pointed with pride at the bow and arrows and rods hung below the roof.

Akhenaten leant back against an antelope skin, enjoying the filtered green light, the soft twangings Bak was making on a harp belonging to Dhutmose, the smell of onion and the feeling of intimacy. It was one of those occasions when he found himself wishing that he could have been born with gifts instead of a crown, so that he could live simply like this, yet with the richness and life and warmth that artists seemed always able to create. But then here at

Akhetaten he would be able to leave behind many formalities and live as the artist-king, offering the patronage of the Aten to men like Dhutmose. He reflected, too, that no doubt before long Dhutmose himself would be building a fine villa to take the place of this hut.

It was not until now that Dhutmose was able to ask what the real purpose of their excursion had been. When he heard, he said at once, "But, Your Majesty, I have been waiting here for nearly a month, and have walked over every part of your half-circle of desert. You can see that I have." He stretched out his legs to show scratches and punctures all over his shins. "I have noticed many promising sites, and could answer your questions. The best thing would be for me to lead you to a vantage point I have found up on the cliffs. From there you could look out over the whole domain, see the lie of the land, and determine how the city shall be built."

Akhenaten got up at once and asked Dhutmose to lead them. "But, Your Majesty, it is surely too late. You will not be able to get back to your camp before dark."

"Mahu can go back now, and order our tents and everything necessary to be moved here. The Queen Nefertiti and I like always to act immediately while the spirit is with us—and we should like to lay our plans for Akhetaten by the light of the setting sun."

So it was arranged, and well before sunset the donkeys were carrying the King and Queen, Bak, Meryre and Dhutmose by zigzag path up the steep slopes. The track brought them to the end of a little promontory on the northern lip of the *wadi* where it ran out from the hills. As they all chose rocks where they could prop themselves without too much discomfort, they saw what a magnificent view the place commanded. The whole territory of the Horizon of the Aten lay below them, enclosed by the cirque of cliffs. Two miles away across the River they could see the rich farming land on the western bank. Akhenaten craned forward and cried, "Look, Nefertiti, the low rays of the sun are showing us the tracks of our chariot, the outline of Akhetaten. And there are two of the places you marked—where boundary stones are to stand." She could just distinguish the cairns the men had built, each with a fading lotus lying on top of it.

"In my judgment, Your Majesty, your royal palaces should stand where the *wadi* joins the River; that is the most pleasing site and has the best soil. Also, as you can see, on this side of it is a level area that could easily be cleared for the great court of the Aten temple. Then the city would grow naturally round palaces and temple. It is bound to keep over on the River side because of the need for irrigation."

"Yes, that is the most important thing. To make as much as possible of this harsh land turn green and flowery," said Nefertiti. "For we are determined that our city shall have no crowded streets and alleys, where people seem to be huddling together for protection from some enemy. Here every house, of whatever size, must have a garden."

"You hope, then, that there will be no poor in your city?"

"Of course there can be no poor. All will be children of the Aten and therefore of Pharaoh. He will care for them."

"Yet you will need very many workmen, first to build the city and cut the tombs, and then to do all the dirty jobs that there always are." Dhutmose spoke gently, knowing his words were against her inclinations.

"They shall have a little town of their own. There is room for all."

Dhutmose turned to the King. "My Lord," he asked, "where will you grow your food? Gardens are good, but they won't yield grain."

"We are going to build wharves. Grain and other food-stuffs will come by boat."

"But then the 'outline' which means so much to you will lose its value. We shall be dependent on the outside world. I think, my lord, that we must take in the west bank where there are miles of fertile land."

Akhenaten frowned, staring across to the trees and fields beyond the River. Soon his face cleared. "You are right, Dhutmose. I have not thought enough of these things. We will draw a boundary on the west, completing the disc. In that way, as you said, we can live secure—" He broke off, then exclaimed, "Look, Mahu must have travelled fast. There is the baggage train coming towards your hut, Dhutmose." They sat in silence watching the tiny black line of men and beasts moving against the reddening sunlight. Akhenaten and Nefertiti were both perched on rather high rocks, and their broken shadows fell far across the wilderness behind them. In the sculptor's eyes they looked terribly frail. "How long, your Majesty," he asked abruptly, "how long will it be before you can hope to live here?"

"A year. Or perhaps two. I do not campaign abroad; I can command an army to make my city of peace. And all can be quickly built and lightly. Except for the Great Temple, I do not want walls and columns that will stand for ever. Here things need only be beautiful and good for living. We can rebuild when we wish, for life must change. There is time enough, Dhutmose, don't be afraid."

Soon after this he and Meryre went a little apart to celebrate the sunset prayer. Nefertiti lingered behind for a moment and murmured to the sculptor: "What a wonderful end to the first day of Akhetaten. That the eye of the Aten should look from the west, while Pharaoh sends down his blessing from the east!"

"Yes," he answered absently. "Yes. And the end to the most wonderful day in my life. But, madam, do you know the world? Do you know these lords and priests and high officials? They love their power, and so they want things as they have always been. Can he stand against them and their incomprehension—which will turn to hostility? It is as though I tried to carve granite with an obsidian blade. . . ."

"There is too much pity and protectiveness in your voice, Dhutmose," said Nefertiti with the slight asperity of which she was capable. "Our father the Aten can break these men of power as though *they* were blades. Our strength is in the Aten."

"Perhaps I am wrong. It is as though my heart were sinking with the sun. My faith cannot be equal to yours. But this I know, we must do great things here so that come what may Akhetaten shall never be forgotten."

VII

"MY dear son, I know you like the truth. I don't care
about animals even when they are in such fine cages as
these. I suppose they are beautiful, but what can one do
but stare at them—and smell them? I still prefer human
beings."

Akhenaten felt nothing but pleasure in Queen Tiye's
small opposition. This was her first visit to the new capital,
and it had gone well. She had admired enough to satisfy
him. Her occasional resistance now seemed to be part of a
game that they had always played together.

He put his hand on her shoulders and made her stoop
until her face was almost level with the antelope's, smiling
to himself at the sight of the slender, quick head of the
animal so close to his mother's plump face and ornate,
beribboned wig. No one else wore such wigs at Akhetaten,
but she would not give up the old fashion. "Look into the
eyes of this doe," he said, "And you are looking into a new
world. A place of feeling and no thought. A place where
the creature worships the creator just by living. There are
so many animals and birds and flowers in the city because
I want this kind of worship to mingle with ours."

"I see," she said, straightening herself. "I suppose that
is what the birds are doing when they wake me at an
unearthly hour in the morning. If I were going to live here
I should have the aviary moved away from my house."

"They are greeting the first light of the sun—as I myself
do. When I stand in my eastern window sending a prayer
to my father, I like to hear their voices with mine. Our
birds and the foreign birds, the harsh and the melodious. It
is all one. If you can't like the shriekers and chatterers,
Madam Mother, then put linen in your ears. Now we'll go
back to the Palace."

Mahu was summoned, and the King's chariot brought
up to the gate. Mahu had been appointed chief of the
guard for the whole city, a piece of good fortune so great

that he still marvelled at himself. It fulfilled all his dreams for serving Pharaoh. When he found that Akhenaten had taken to driving himself and his family about the streets, Mahu insisted on running before the chariot to prepare the way. Yet in spite of all this exercise he was still putting on weight.

As they drove southward from the North Palace where the animals were kept, they went through an area where building was going forward on both sides of the road. There were large stacks of sun-dried brick, vats of white-wash, and, the only expensive item, wooden posts or stone slabs for the doorways. A new suburb was springing up, mostly trim little houses in small gardens.

"I had not intended that houses should be built here," Akhenaten said as they bowled past, "but Dhutmose tells me that we can't have priests and courtiers and artists and scholars, without having traders and all kinds of small officials. Evidently he is right—for here they are."

"Dhutmose has played a great part in the making of Akhetaten?" Queen Tiye asked.

"Dhutmose understands the practical things that elude me. Things about materials and labourers and how they must be rewarded for their work. I understand my father's purposes and know what should be done. Dhutmose sees *how* it should be done. And at the same time he perfects his work as a sculptor, coming nearer and nearer to the truth of Ma'at. When I think how we came upon him, and all that he has achieved, I know that he was sent by the god."

They were entering one of the two main streets of the capital, running parallel with the river. Here lived all those fortunate people whom the King had raised up and given gold in recognition of their loyalty to himself and his teaching. Their houses were large, and stood in spacious walled gardens. Many had lively decorations, for Akhet-aten was full of young artists, most of them only too happy to cure the blankness of a white wall if they were given some wine and freedom to paint what they liked. In every garden, facing the entrance gate, there was a household shrine, and in every shrine a carved stela of the royal family, standing below the Aten with the rays slanting down upon their heads.

Akhenaten was happy to think of himself and Nefertiti enshrined in all these gardens, their love expressing the divine love of the Aten, but he fretted because most of the sculpture was of poor quality. Dhutmose always reassured him, saying that when so much had to be done at once, some of the work was bound to be mechanical. Later on, he insisted, these stele and other popular merchandise could gradually be replaced. Granted long life, he would do it himself.

On the crest of a slight rise, Akhenaten drew in the horses. There was a gap in the garden walls at this point, and from the chariot platform they could see something of the city. There was a view of the building which dominated all the rest—the great temple of the Aten. Even from here it could be seen that the courts covered a vast area, presided over by the sun discs and giant figures of Pharaoh carved and painted on the smooth, sloping sides of the gateways. Behind, the Palace rose on its slight eminence, the gleaming white walls inscribed with praises of the Aten. The glazed symbols were so large that they could be read over half the town—and also from the river, which lay just beyond at the foot of terraced gardens. Near temple and palace were the other public buildings such as the Royal Archive, the House of Life and the Hall of Tribute. These buildings made the points of emphasis, but all the rest of the scene was filled by houses enclosed by garden walls. It was an intricate pattern of white cubes and rectangles, enhanced by the greens and occasional coloured masses of the young gardens.

The King looked at it all greedily, glancing at his mother to see her response.

"You have made a beautiful place, Akhenaten, there is no doubt of that. But it's less like a city than a great collection of country houses. It is amazing how quickly all these gardens have been made out of desert."

"How quickly?" the King exclaimed, possessed by a sudden nervous excitement. "It is far too slow for me. Look how small all the trees and shrubs are. Hardly one yet showing above the walls. And the creepers, still only halfway to the top while they should be cascading over. I long to pour all my radiance into making them grow, grow, grow. In the mornings when I should be attending to affairs of state I find myself thinking of seeds and running water and bursting buds. Or I see myself pouring water from a jar and a flower springing up towards the sun. These images dazzle me, and I can think of nothing else. Then when I see the reality, my impatience hurts me almost more than I can endure. . . ."

"Why should you be impatient?" Standing so close to her son in the stationary chariot, she could feel that he was shaking. "Do you feel that you have little time?"

"I have time. The Aten will grant me years enough. Surely he will. But as a creator I am not worthy of him. It is all not enough and too slow. If I stare at that pomegranate, should it not grow?"

"The sun is fierce this morning, Akhenaten," she said. "Please drive me home." He signed to Mahu, who had come hastening back, to lead the horses, while he himself leant on the front of the chariot. The colours of the houses and gardens melted into one another, but his mother's wig, which was near his face, he saw with such intensity that it seemed to form a magic landscape of its own.

After a few minutes at a walking pace his surroundings resumed their normal outlines, while the wig lost its magic. At that moment he was delighted to see a light, four-wheeled cart with a striped awning standing at the roadside, with only a boy in attendance.

"There is Gilukhipa's chariot!" he exclaimed. "There is nothing else like it in Akhetaten—or in the whole of the Two Lands. She must be visiting one of her unfortunates—although I wouldn't expect any hereabouts. Go, Mahu," he called, "see if you can find the Princess Gilukhipa." The commander of the guard had not gone far before two figures appeared on a narrow path between two properties. Gilukhipa was talking earnestly to Weni, her major-domo, who was carrying a huge basket. She was wearing a long dress of blue linen, with a necklace of uncut turquoise beads. She had aged well. Her face was deeply lined but strong, the powerful bones free from sagging flesh.

Her protective love of Akhenaten had strengthened with the years, and she had become passionately committed to the fulfilment of his dream. Akhetaten must be made a paradise on earth where everyone could live happily under the protection of the Aten. All the scepticism life had given her seemed to have melted away in the light of the new faith.

Realizing that the royal pair and their circle would not remember the existence of the workmen and their families who had been uprooted from their homes and brought to build the city and to cut its tombs, she had appointed herself their guardian. She worked hard to prevent their dwellings from becoming slums that would be a sore on the fair body of the city.

Akhenaten looked on her and her doings with favour and affection. He had gladly allowed her to leave the harim (where she was among a handful of ageing survivors from the last reign to make the move to Akhetaten) and to build her own house. He was even delighted by her growing eccentricity in dress and habits of life. It seemed to him that she was making her own contribution to the truth of Ma'at—the very virtue he had in mind when he proclaimed himself, as he always did, as Living in Ma'at.

At this moment there was no one he could have been more glad to see. Gilukhipa in her strange blue dress; the henchman who had become her friend and helper; the basket full of delicacies for the sick—they restored his joy in Akhetaten and his trust in what it was going to mean to the world.

The Princess and Weni bowed as his chariot stopped beside them. He looked down into her face, and, noticing the engraved crow's-feet at her eyes, remembered what she had said to him as a boy—that these were the only reward for laughing at life. He was beginning to feel a special bond with people he had known in childhood. There were not many of them now in Akhetaten.

"Greetings, Gilukhipa!" he said. "What can you find to

do in the Street of the Ray? Surely no one here needs your basket?"

"You don't look far enough, Your Majesty. Your friends up here on the street could afford to eat gold if they wanted to. But all over the city poor families are building shacks on the patches of scrub left between all these fine properties. Look down this path and you'll see what I mean." Akhenaten peered between the walls, and could just see a huddle of reed huts with children and dogs swarming round them. A surge of impatience rose in him. Ordinary life was so unmanageable. It tacked hither and thither, but seemed always set against perfection.

"You ought to report it to the officials, Gilukhipa," Queen Tiye intervened. "It is their business if anyone's. Why should you be traipsing about like this?"

"Madam, you can't remember what I am like if you suppose I don't plague the officials. I go straight to Hatiay, His Majesty's chief of public works, and often make him do what I want. They've already started building some decent little houses down there—but meanwhile there's a woman who hasn't been able to stand up since she had her tenth child."

Queen Tiye sighed and shrugged. The King observed her with a kind of amusement, for he knew that she could not approve the informal ways he had introduced. She was shocked to see Pharaoh driving himself and his family about the streets. That he should be asked to look at hovels must seem to her outrageous. Perhaps, indeed, he didn't altogether like it himself. But he was the good shepherd, just as the Aten was the good shepherd of all mankind. And Gilukhipa would not allow him to forget the poor of his flock.

"Yes, dearest Mother. Don't imagine that the Princess spares the officials. I've seen them step behind pillars at her approach. And now she pursues my treasurer, begging gold for her sick-house." Akhenaten noticed that a gaggle of small children was stealing up the path from the huts, and a small crowd of bowing citizens beginning to gather at a respectful distance. "We will go to your house, Gilukhipa," he said. "It is not far, and your sick-house is the one remaining thing I want to show to my mother. We will follow you." The Princess and Weni climbed into the vehicle which she had had specially designed for her visiting. Mahu dispersed the crowd, and they moved off.

The sick-house was being built in Gilukhipa's garden; she had sacrificed her orchard for it. "As you can see, Your Majesties," she said, "the place isn't finished, and I have only a few patients." They were standing in a large, white-washed room furnished with benches and bright, peasant rugs, where, as the Princess explained, her young doctors would examine the sick. There were also great, sweating jars of cool water and chests holding instruments, drugs, linen bandages and dressings of flax. Pentu, the royal physician, and the most famous doctor in Egypt, had given the surgical instruments and the herbs and drugs—carefully chosen and compounded by himself.

Akhenaten delighted in the room. It was so simple and bare, with strength instead of the luxury and elegance he was accustomed to. He had never known anything else in the least like it, and he felt that it did indeed represent something new. Here the Aten would show his loving mercy and the sick would understand and praise his name. Perhaps in time there would not be so much suffering; the god would show Pentu and Gilukhipa what to do. Already there was much less sickness in Akhetaten than in Thebes. . . . His thoughts were broken off by words that the Princess was saying to his mother. Her harsh, deep voice always compelled attention. "Of course I understand, Madam, that my doings seem strange to you. I was born a Princess, to be sure, and have become a royal widow of the second rank. I don't expect these unfortunates to be grateful. But they are all interesting. I enjoy visiting them, and still more I enjoy fighting the officials to make them help. And beyond even that, I see it as one of the glories of Akhetaten that everyone with enough imagination can do things that have never been done before. At Thebes I thought my life was over. But here I have been born again."

The King stepped over to the Princess and took both her hands. "Dear Gilukhipa," he said, "I thank you. No

one understands my teaching better than you do. Your
actions are a witness to my words, and god shines in them.
Your sick-house shall not be held back for want of gold,
that at least I can promise you." The Princess held his
hands more tightly and she looked into his face, saying
nothing. He noticed that Queen Tiye had half turned
from them and was running her fingers along the bronze
knives, saws and spatulas in Pentu's surgical chest.

He was about to say that they should visit the few sick
who were already installed in a little half-built court near
by, when the major-domo came in, with a look of importance that was not concealed by his low bows. It was justified, for he had come to announce that the Great Queen,
the Princesses Merytaten and Meketaten and the sculptor
Dhutmose were arriving at the gate. Moreover, there were
men unloading some large objects from a cart. Weni
understood that they came from Dhutmose's studio.

Akhenaten still always felt happiness at the thought of
seeing Nefertiti, and he led the others unceremoniously
across the swimming heat of the garden into Gilukhipa's
house. They entered the loggia at the same moment as
Nefertiti and Dhutmose reached it from the street entrance.
The Queen's arm was resting lightly on the sculptor's, and
there was eagerness in her eyes and in her carriage. For a
moment the King was checked at the sight of them, the
exquisite young woman and the stalwart man with his
pleasing, ugly face. But as soon as she saw him Nefertiti
ran forward and embraced him.

"My dearest Lord," she exclaimed. "Who could have
guessed that we should meet here? I went with the children
for their sitting to Dhutmose—the portraits are going to
be all that we hoped. Then when I heard that he had
finished the doors for Gilukhipa's sick-house, I insisted
that we should bring them here at once. You will be so
much moved by them, Akhenaten. They are by far the
finest thing he has ever done." Dhutmose himself had
remained at the other end of the loggia and was now
directing four of his servants to carry the doors, shrouded
in linen covers, into the central hall.

"Your Majesty," he said, "I had no thought of your

seeing these pieces of mine before they were installed and
everything made ready for you. But now I hope that you
will look at them in the hall where the top light should
flatter them. I confess I'm pleased with what I've done—
and I believe that you will find them truthful at least. Now
let us undress them."

The two little princesses, quite naked as they loved to be
in the summer, who had run behind Nefertiti to kiss their
father and grandmother, now scampered into the hall to
help in the undressing. They tugged at the linen covers and
stood proudly beside the cedarwood doors when these had
been reared up against the pillars.

Akhenaten felt a shiver of excitement as he looked at the
panels. On one a line of sick people was shown approaching the same pair of doors. There was a man on crutches,
a woman with a growth on her breast, two blind children
holding hands—all of them with their faces turned in hope
towards the sun disc. On the other was a tumbled group of
babies and tiny children, plump and smiling as they
reached for the *ankhs* held out to them by the sun's rays.
For a moment the King responded with pure delight,
telling himself that the whole great enterprise of Akhetaten
might be justified by these carvings alone. His imagination
took him back to excursions in the *Aten Gleams*, sketching
wild duck and talking with Bak. Here in these scenes were
time and relatedness captured on the wing. They succeeded
more brilliantly than anything he and Bak had done. Yet
the inspiration was still his own, and he felt no envy.

Then there was a check in his response, as though some-
one else had intervened. He and Nefertiti, the King and
Queen, why were they not on the doors? Dhutmose must
know that Pharaoh was a part of everything within the
City of God. The Aten demanded it for his chosen son.
He realized that he was frowning—perhaps the frown that
Nefertiti had once told him was terrible. At that moment
Queen Tiye spoke out of the silence.

"This is the first thing I have seen in Akhetaten that
does not show the Royal Family. . . ."

"Oh, but it does, my Grandmother," Meketaten interrupted. "That is me," she pointed to one of the small girls

in the panel. "And that Merytaten. And we think that the poor woman is like our mother in her face."

"Dhutmose has left the upper panels blank," said Akhenaten. "He is going to put scenes of the Divine Love there. Then the doors will be complete." He added to himself, "That is what he intended."

"These two panels are marvellous," Akhenaten went on, turning to the sculptor. "No one else but you could have done them, Dhutmose. They are something new in the world, and they will be one of the glories of our city. Everyone will come to Gilukhipa's sick-house to see them."

Dhutmose gave one of his awkward bows, and stole a look at Nefertiti. The Queen did not respond. She was smiling once more, and she slipped her arm round her husband's waist. It was a position in which they had often been portrayed.

Gilukhipa sent her servants for wine, and they all went to the upper loggia which looked over what was left of the garden to the temple and palace. Akhenaten stretched himself on a couch, making room for Nefertiti to sit near his feet. He felt lively and excited, like someone who has just been rescued from peril and does not want to think about it.

"Now that the wine is poured, Gilukhipa," he said, "I will tell you all of a plan which Nefertiti and I have been making together. Tomorrow there is to be the Bearing of Tribute. Embassies have come from all our kingdoms. It is right that they should bring treasure for the Aten as the lord of all lands. But there are still many for whom these gifts are tribute paid by subject peoples to Egypt as their conqueror. This is what has to be changed."

"Yet it is a fact, Akhenaten," said Queen Tiye. "Your ancestors poured out gold and many lives to win those lands and secure our eastern frontier. Didn't Tuthmosis the Conqueror cross the Tigris and set up his victory inscription? And although your father was no campaigner, the Asians still feared his armies. When they no longer fear you, they will no longer pay you. That is my belief."

Akhenaten looked at her smilingly, for her words glanced off his conviction like straw spears. "Dear Mother. You have understood the power of the world. You have guarded Egypt as people once fancied the serpent guarded an underworld. But now that kind of power will no longer be needed. Love will take the place of fear. Why should peoples fear and hate one another when they understand that the god created them all, just as his rays sustain them all? And so this is what Nefertiti and I have devised. The day after the Bearing of Tribute we will go to the Summer Palace, and there we will celebrate the Peace of Aten. All the Ambassadors and tribute bearers will take part, and I will speak and make them understand that Egypt repents all past bloodshed, and that all people can live at peace within the circle of the sun. They will carry the message to all the four quarters, and from that day the light of my teaching will begin to radiate from this city to the farthest parts of the horizon."

"And afterwards there will be a party on the lake with boats and thousands of lamps," said Merytaten in her matter-of-fact way. "And Meketaten and I are to be there, but not our sister Ankhesenpaten because she is too small."

"And what about our cousin, Tutankhaten? He is too small, isn't he, my Father?" asked Meketaten. "I find him very babyish." The two princesses had come to stand near the head of the couch, and Akhenaten could see every exquisitely placed hair of their brows and lashes, and the tender yet firm lines of their diminutive features. They were lovely creatures, as lovely as the young deer, or the birds in his aviaries. He looked at them fondly, his eyes lingering on his favourite, Meketaten, who was both more precocious and naughtier than her elder sister, and already wonderfully sensitive to her surroundings. At the same time he felt a little sad, for he wondered whether the reactions of most people to the idea which had seemed sublime to Nefertiti and himself would not be on a level with those of the two little girls: to rejoice in the prospect of a party and to demand who was to be excluded.

"Yes. Tutankhaten is too young. And you may only come yourselves if you understand that the Peace of the Aten is a very serious thing that will change the whole of your lives." Merytaten made a suitably earnest face, but Meketaten hopped away, squatted beside her mother and lifted one of Gilukhipa's long-haired cats, holding it between her knees and her bare belly. The king watched her undulgently, feeling her enjoyment of the touch of the silky fur on her flesh.

Inevitably now the talk turned to Tutankhaten, for he was the wonder child of Akhetaten. He had been born to Tey soon after the removal from Thebes, at an age when few women expect to begin child-bearing. The tale was that she went to Pentu thinking she had a tumour, and that when the physician told her that her tumour had a heart and arms and legs, she promptly fainted. Of course, there was a great deal of speculation, but no one could seriously doubt that Tey had remained faithful to Ay, nor did it seem probable that there was anything in the rumour that the Commander of the King's Chariots had resorted to a wise woman and her potions.

Tey herself attributed her good fortune to the intervention of the Aten, and became extremely devout. When, without too much difficulty, she gave birth to a healthy boy, she saw him as a miracle child and hardly ever allowed him out of her sight. He was in fact a very ordinary infant, promising to be neither clever nor stupid, ugly nor particularly good-looking.

In spite of all the gossip and joking, everyone was really very happy on Tey's behalf—and already there was speculation as to whether a boy born so close to the royal family might not hope to be betrothed to one of the princesses. As for the King and Queen themselves, no one was more delighted by the arrival of Tutankhaten. Both of them were still devoted to Tey, and Akhenaten had come to depend heavily on Ay's loyalty to the cause of the Aten.

The impromptu party in Gilukhipa's loggia lasted for some time and became very merry. It was just the kind of occasion that Akhenaten loved, and nowadays could so seldom find time for. Bak arrived, having heard that Dhutmose had delivered the doors that all the artists knew about but none of them had seen. He admired them unstintingly, and drank to sculpture in many cups of wine. Bak had never felt any envy of Dhutmose's success at Akhetaten. He hated responsibility, and was not inclined to care about other people's advantages so long as he himself had what he wanted. He had spent two years up at Elephantine supervising the quarrying of red granite for the Aten temple. Now sculpture for the temple took nearly all his time. He had a fine house, a charming Nubian girl, and found that the life of Akhetaten suited him perfectly.

At last Akhenaten saw that he must respond to Queen Tiye's signals that she wanted to go home. He still insisted on driving her himself, and they set off for her house. For a time he made the horses gallop, enjoying the coolness of the wind. Then he slowed down and said to Queen Tiye, "After all the fine entertainment we have given you, wasn't that the best? A few people who like one another talking together. It is a simple form of Living in Truth. . . ."

"Truth!" Queen Tiye exclaimed with sudden vehemence. "Do you really think that there is truth in your Peace of the Aten? I had intended to keep quiet about politics on this visit. For you may not believe it, Akhenaten, but as I get older I like to be at one with you. Perhaps it is the wine, but now I have to say what I think. There is no peace in the northern lands now. And once they hear your policies there never will be."

Trying to check the temper that rose with this offence against his mood, the King pulled on the reins and the horses came to a standstill, swinging their feathered heads and snorting gently. "I wish you had kept to your resolution, dear Mother. You make me think that you will never understand my teaching or why it must succeed. I know it is hard for you not to have hold of the steering oar any longer. You must trust me and my light."

"So I may, but I don't trust that Syrian. That Tutu to whom you leave your foreign affairs. I know men of his kind. But I don't want to argue. I only ask how can you celebrate peace when there is war?"

"You are speaking of Aziru?"

"Of Aziru as an agent of the Hittites."

"Then I can set your mind at rest. We have exchanged many letters with the Amorite, and his Embassy is here now. He swears that he is my friend. Moreover, Aziru has met the priests and all those whom I sent to establish another city of the Aten in the northern lands. He has listened to them, and they report that he wishes to be instructed and to open his heart to my teaching. Already he has withdrawn all his forces from Byblos."

"My information is otherwise."

"Then it is not to be believed. Here are your gates. And there is the ever-correct Hapu waiting to receive you. There will be a throne set for you at the Bearing of Tribute."

The steward and her other servants came forward to bow Queen Tiye into the great house which the King had had built for her, and where he hoped she would come to live when she grew disillusioned with Thebes. As she left him, Akhenaten felt a terrible weariness. He called to Mahu to drive him to the Palace.

The sun had set. It seemed to Akhenaten that the coppery glow along the horizon was more intense, and yet more tranquil, than on other nights. "He is sending us a benediction," he thought. "He will be with us in celebrating his peace. His presence will burn in my words."

The King was standing at a western window in the summer palace of Maru-Aten. After the sumptuous Tribute-bearing of the day before, the royal household had moved down there. It was only about three miles from the centre of the city, but with its screen of palm groves, its lake and Water Court, the summer palace offered a cool retreat. The royal family lived there even more informally than they could at the Great Palace, and for that reason the princesses loved Maru-Aten. Most people, and especially their grandmother, thought that they had too much freedom at all times. But at the summer palace the last restrictions were removed. They spent much of their day with their parents, and the rest playing naked in the gardens or round the lake.

The Queen came in, followed by Merytaten and Meketaten—and by the Cypriote girl Lasia, who was now the royal nurse and companion. Nefertiti was wearing a long, pleated dress, mistily transparent, gathered round her waist by a light red sash. As she quickened her pace and came up to Akhenaten, the falling ends of the sash floated out behind her. They made him think of the ripples drawn by a graceful bird gliding on smooth water. She smiled at him without saying anything, and in silence he took her left hand and led her towards the gardens.

There were scores of people gathered by the lake; the whole court and many of the leading citizens of Akhetaten. No one spoke, and all stood facing to where a disc of beaten gold, measuring more than the height of a man across, glowed before the little temple on the islet. As Akhenaten moved through them, still holding Nefertiti's hand, everyone bowed low and he imagined himself as the divine breath bending them like wind in the corn.

It did not seem to him that he was walking by setting one foot before the other, nor that the disc with its wavering golden track in the water was no more than a sheet of metal reflecting concealed lamps. He knew that the Aten was there among them and that he was one with the god.

Now he and Nefertiti were at the lake's edge, stepping into their boat. With a few strong yet almost soundless strokes of the paddles they were at the islet and then moving together towards the temple. As soon as they were before the disc, and had turned so that the lamps were dazzling in their eyes, Akhenaten could tell that the other boats were approaching through the darkness beyond the dazzle. It had all been carefully arranged, and yet it seemed to him that it was happening spontaneously and inevitably. There were the waters of Nun. Here the islet was the primeval hill, the first created land rising from the waters. And there upon it rose the sun, the self-creator and the creator of all things. And here was Pharaoh, Son of the Sun, about to receive the men of all the lands that the sun embraced.

They were landing now, the leaders of the embassies who had come for the Tribute-bearing. There was a

Nubian, a Libyan and a man from Punt; there was an
Amorite, one of the Habiru, a Canaanite, a Phoenician
from the Lebanon and citizens of Byblos and Ugarit.
From the countries of the Two Rivers came a Kassite and a
Kardunian from Babylon, an Assyrian, a Mitannian and a
Hurrian from the far North. From the lands round the
ocean there were an Arzawan and a Luvian, a Greek from
Mycenae, a Cretan, a Cypriote and a number of others.
The King seemed to know them all without thought, and
at the same time to perceive all their lands spread out there
in the darkness within the horizons of his mind.

Their actual figures he could see only dimly as they
approached and formed a half-circle before the Aten,
their faces gilded not by the strong light that burned on
himself and Nefertiti, but only by its reflection from the
great disc. Seeing them there, he began to speak.

He began softly, speaking of the wonderful variety of
men, how they differed in the colour of their skins, the
growth of their hair, in language and in habits. All this, he
said, had been appointed by their creator, by the Aten
who rejoiced in their variousness. Then he spoke tellingly
of the mounting horrors of war. Now that it had been
revealed that the Aten was father of all men, and that all
were therefore brothers, there could be no more fighting
between people and people. With great emotion he asked
forgiveness for all the wrongs done by the Egyptians,
promising that never again would their armies march out
to conquer. When he had finished speaking, he turned and
kissed Nefertiti on her lips, knowing that as they stood
there illumined for all to see, their love expressed the
universal love of the Aten. Facing the disc, they raised
their arms in worship, and Akhenaten saw their shadows
very sharp and black on the bright surface of the gold.
Then they wheeled round to face the people once more,
and Akhenaten cried: "We have met together to seal the
Peace of the Aten, and from this place his light will be
carried through all the lands."

At this signal servants ran out from the summer palace
carrying torches and tapers and lighting little lamps that
outlined the lake and hung in the trees. Boats decked with

lamps appeared from the far side of the lake, many of them filled with girl musicians with harps, pipes and lutes. More servants poured from the palace with food and wine and great baskets of garlands and lotus flowers for the ladies. Lights appeared in two gilded aviaries where birds of every brilliant colour were revealed fluttering among golden branches.

At first Akhenaten was bewildered and shaken. He had almost to be carried to the boat, and Nefertiti supported him as they were rowed back to the lakeside. He himself had approved the sudden change of scene. It was to express the spread of light, abundance and delight through the power of the Aten. But now, while he was still lost in his vision of the lands lying one beside another in peace and understanding, he found that his great religious celebration had been transformed into a brilliant festivity.

However, as he slowly approached the place where the royal party was gathered round an elegant kiosk, Meryre, Nakht, Tutu and many others came to lavish praise on his words and on the effect of the whole occasion. Tutu said that all the embassies had been deeply moved, and were declaring that a new world had been born that night. Several ladies bowed before him who had evidently been affected to tears. Among them was Tey, who gave him her fat, warm embrace and told him how thankful she was that her Tutankhaten would never have to go campaigning.

The King and Queen sank down on cushions piled for them on the top step of the kiosk. Akhenaten leant against one of the palm-tree columns and drank thirstily. Not long ago he had been involved with the whole world, now he thought only of his wine. They kept their best wine at Maru-Aten. How delicious it was, how welcome the slight acidity, and how cooling the stream on his tired throat. His surroundings returned to him. He was aware of the aromatic smells of the plants Nefertiti had chosen for this part of the gardens. The boatloads of musicians seemed altogether delightful as they drifted by, echoing one another's tunes. And there, close at hand, was Nefertiti, looking so lovely that he told himself he might already be circling with the imperishable stars or walking in the Field

of Rushes. Even the rising babble of his guests was pleasing
to him at that moment.

Meketaten came up the steps, leading Kiki, her pet
gazelle. Without hesitation she knelt on the cushions
beside her father and lifted the angular little creature on
to his lap. Akhenaten liked the feeling of the pointed hoofs
digging into his flesh, and he fondled Kiki's head, moving
his finger gently to and fro on the bumps where the horns
would grow.

"Merytaten is at the aviaries with Smenkhkare," his
daughter said. "She is always with him nowadays, and I
heard a lot of people saying, 'What a beautiful pair!' 'They
seem to be made for each other.' Do you think they are? I
don't."

Nefertiti leant across and whispered, "We love you,
Meketaten, but it is time you went to bed."

"Is the Peace of the Aten finished, then?"

"It has just begun," her father answered. "Some day
you will be able to tell your children that you saw the
beginning of it. But they won't quite understand what
you mean, for by then everyone will have forgotten about
war."

"I shall tell them that my father was the one who
stopped war."

"Not *your* father, but *our* father, my little lotus. It is the
Peace of the Aten."

Merytaten pouted just as her grandmother would have
done. "I think it is the same thing," she said. Akhenaten
shook his head, but he smiled and gave her a kiss. Lasia
came up and led the princess away by the hand—
Meketaten leading her gazelle on its jewelled chain.
Akhenaten watched them tenderly as they paused to say
goodnight to Tiye, Ay and Tey, who were sitting on folding chairs a short distance from the kiosk. When they had
gone, he called to his mother.

"Come and talk with us. You seem quite cut off over
there on your chairs. A little conspiracy!"

"Our bones are too old for steps—even if they're padded
with cushions. And perhaps our minds are too old for your
conversation," the Queen Mother answered.

"You're putting me out of employment," said Ay in a false jocular manner. "You can't expect me to want to talk about that."

"Quite soon, I hope. But we shall find something else for you to do—if being alive in Akhetaten isn't enough for you." At this moment the King saw Mahu making his way through the crowd of guests. He was coming for a nightly ritual which Akhenaten had initiated and which had for him a religious meaning he found it hard to reveal to others. Only Nefertiti, he thought, understood what it meant to him.

Mahu's most important charge as commander of the guard was his patrolling of the city bounds. All round the crescent of cliffs, where the King and Queen had driven their chariot and where there now stood great stele charged with Akhenaten's words of dedication, sentry posts had been installed and linked by ropes. Every night Mahu and his men patrolled the whole length of this eastern boundary, while a trusted lieutenant did the same for the western circuit across the River. Every night, too, Mahu was admitted to Pharaoh's presence and reported in set words: "My Lord, Son of the Sun, I bring you good news. The City of God, the Place of Truth, the Horizon of the Aten, lies secure within her bounds."

Tonight the ritual was not to be broken. Indeed, it seemed to Akhenaten that it would have a special significance. The royal party made way for Mahu to approach the King, and all of them proved sober enough to be silent while he spoke the accustomed words. When he had finished he remained kneeling. "Your Majesty," he said, "may I give you other news? News of your people?"

With an effort Akhenaten pulled himself back from where, in imagination, he was visiting those bounds of Akhetaten. More than once he had gone there secretly with his commander, and now he saw the huge, curving line; the sentry boxes with their braziers; the men pacing in the starlight on the hard desert sand; the jackals calling from the wastes outside. And the knowledge that at the centre of it lay the Aten temple and the palace, Pharaoh and his queen. "What is it, Mahu?" he said.

"Your Majesty, here inside the wall of Maru-Aten are all your friends and all the great and fortunate. But outside, hearing the music and the din of your guests, and seeing the lights shining like an unexpected dawn, there are hundreds of your other subjects. They are standing very quietly out there among the scrub—traders, craftsmen, fishermen, gardeners, tomb-cutters—all kinds of people. They have heard you have promised the Peace of the Aten. They are looking up at the walls, wondering what is going on inside." Mahu stopped speaking, and Akhenaten hesitated. Nefertiti put her arm round him and said, "Oh, beloved. Let them come in. Have the gates opened. There is space for everyone."

Soon the banks of the lake were crowded, and jugs of wine were being passed from hand to hand. Gilukhipa went to meet friends whom she saw coming in among the rest. After her lead, most of the invited guests began to mingle with their fellow citizens. That night men and women who had never before spoken to working people except to give them orders or rebukes, found themselves chatting about children and gardens, fishing and the best places for fowling, irrigation and the latest developments in Akhetaten. Most of all they talked of the recent ceremony and the Peace of the Aten. The courtiers were astonished to discover how much the people cared about the Peace and how little about Egypt's power in foreign lands. They were in agreement with their Pharaoh.

The King and Queen did not join in the throng, but remained at the kiosk with their friends, watching the scene.

"It ought to be like this always," said Nefertiti. "We say that all peoples are children of the Aten—and yet we do not know our own people."

"Yes," he said. "Yes, that is true. But I think tonight is a very special night." He knew that he hated crowds and had difficulty in talking to ordinary people. Yet he felt sure that he loved them.

From the lakeside the noise of conversation and laughter rose until it seemed loud as the Cataracts. The royal party fell silent, overwhelmed by the sound. Akhenaten and

Nefertiti had just agreed that it was time for them to withdraw when Bak arrived at the kiosk. He had been tearing about supervising all the spectacles and lighting effects, but had found time for drinking wine. He was flushed, happy and excited, looking much as he often used to do in the early days at Thebes. He urged them to go back to the summer palace by boat. Everyone would be able to see them, and they would escape the crush.

He hurried off to make preparations, and presently the King and Queen embarked once more in their boat. Bak beat violently on a wooden gong and the noise of the party died down as though the Cataract were running dry. Ahead of the royal barque went several little boats with girls, their garlands now rather wilted, singing a song of peace which had been composed by a student at the House of Life. The girls were throwing out handfuls of flowers until the water was so thickly sown that blooms gathered at the prow of the barque like foam. The crowd of guests took up the song, then cried: "Peace to Your Majesties. Peace! Peace!" Akhenaten and Nefertiti stood up waving and making the sign of the sun. Tears were streaming down Nefertiti's face, but she seemed quite unaware of them.

When they were back in their private apartments and had been prepared for bed, Akhenaten impulsively led Nefertiti out into the courtyard. A faint hum came from the garden where the festivities had not come to an end. It was almost dark in the court, and the square of the sky above the roofs was like a cloth heavy with stars. Nefertiti was a slender white figure, seeming to shine very faintly with her own radiance. Akhenaten could smell the perfumed oils with which she had just been rubbed. He put his arms round her, and rested his cheek for a moment on the smooth hair which all day and every day was hidden by the royal headdress.

"Nefertiti," he said. "Do you feel some change in the air? It seems to me that now at last Akhetaten has been consecrated."

"I was so glad that Mahu told us about the people, and that they could all come in. They will never forget."

"At first, when I had finished speaking, I was upset that the Peace of the Aten had become no more than a party. But then it seemed right after all. Here in our city, pleasure and delight have a special meaning."

She nodded. "But now it is better to be here beneath our square of stars." Nefertiti hung quietly in his arms for a while, and then said, "They are going home. I can't hear the sound of them any more, and I can tell from the sky that the lamps are being put out."

It was true that the people were streaming home through the night; some in rich litters, some on donkey-back and some on foot. They went to the palace and the temple; to workshops and hovels; to the fishermen's quarter and the tomb-cutters' village. So the crowd split up into smaller and smaller streams, and the streams into trickles, but everyone talked and laughed all the way to their doors.

VIII

"YOUR head is most exquisitely set on your neck," said Dhutmose, turning the bust on its revolving base. "And yet it suggests a little sadness—just the faintest suggestion of a droop."

"Then it is not a true portrait," Nefertiti replied with spirit. "You know me to be the happiest and most fortunate of women. What could there possibly be in Akhetaten or in my life to make me sad?"

"I only tell you what I see here in the stone, and I have shaped the stone like a true sculptor of the Aten—under Ma'at."

"Perhaps I might be tired sometimes. That may be what your eyes and hands have discovered. I do sometimes feel weary—and my beloved Akhenaten is often so exhausted by the evening that he can hardly speak. But that has nothing to do with sadness."

"No wonder you and he are tired." Dhutmose paused while he ran his fingers along the jawline, feeling the slight hollow above it. "You bear the burden of everything upon yourselves. Above all the burden of change. It must always have been as much as a man could carry to be Pharaoh of Egypt, but in the past they lived in a mould of custom and it supported them. They did what Pharaohs had always done and what everyone expected them to do, and do again, for ever. Although some were strong and some feeble, although some went to war and others preferred to build temples, every one of them was just Pharaoh. There was a timelessness about it which must have been restful. Now Akhenaten is Akhenaten—and you are Nefertiti. Yourselves, not institutions. And you do not live in eternity but in the present. Every day Pharaoh has to take a decision about some matter that has never arisen before. Tradition is like a slave's shackle, but it is also like a pilgrim's staff."

"So it is all one—with life, and with art of the instant?"

"You can see it here, in my hands. I am making a portrait of that unique woman, the Great Queen Nefertiti. And as she is in this spring season out of all other seasons. I will not let the world forget your precise beauty at this moment. Nor even that hint of weariness."

"Perhaps I was not quite truthful just now, Dhutmose. You know that I have one sadness," said Nefertiti, lowering her head from its pose.

"That you have no son?"

She nodded. "I often think back to that night of the Peace of the Aten. It was a moment of perfection, wasn't it? I remember how we slipped out into the little courtyard we have there at Maru-Aten—with cisterns of flowers scenting the night. The square of starry sky was so near it seemed we were in a celestial tent, and although the Creator of All was making his journey in the Nether World we felt he was with us in our love. And afterwards when I was in Akhenaten's arms I told him that I was with child again, and we were both quite sure it would be a son. Akhenaten said, 'In a few hours it will be sunrise, and in a few months a new Son of the Sun will be born'. When it was another daughter, I lay for days hating her. Four daughters!"

"But why be sorry? They promise to be only a little less lovely than yourself—and at Akhetaten women are not set lower than men. The throne descends through its daughters —or did until Queen Tiye's day—so there is no difficulty there. And as things are Merytaten won't have to marry a brother. She will be happier with Smenkhkare or some young man like him than with a brother."

"All those things are true and untrue. I know that Pharaoh longs for a son so that he can pass on his divinity —and his divine teaching." Nefertiti spoke unsteadily. She had altogether given up any attempt to pose, and Dhutmose was slowly cleaning his tools. He said, "I think it would be best if Pharaoh would be content to be a man. He is surely the greatest, most beloved man in the world, and that is as much as he can bear. He cannot live as he does and yet be the god."

"You feel that, Dhutmose? It has troubled me . . . and

yet I have always known his divinity ever since I first saw him. . . ."

"Of course I feel it! As an artist I rejoice in his orders to show him as he is, in all his bodily peculiarity. And to show him embracing you, kissing the little girls, eating a cutlet. But how can I at the same time show him as a god? The old Pharaohs could be gods because they were not fully men. The godhead was in their timelessness, in their office. It seems to me that the end of Akhenaten's teaching must be that all men are brothers, united by their common flesh and their common creation . . . and the spark of divinity they have kept from that creation."

"And yet my husband *is* different from all others." Nefertiti so seldom used the word "husband" that it seemed to give an extraordinary intensity to her words.

"Let us say he is a man who has seen god—and has understood. Is not that enough? But, Your Majesty," Dhutmose abruptly changed his manner. "I have trespassed too far on this intimacy that has grown up through your coming to me here. Even in Akhetaten it is not right for an artist and a queen to come so close through words. . . ."

"Perhaps not," she looked at him with troubled eyes. "And yet you have helped me. If Akhenaten is my sun, you are the bedrock beneath my feet." The sculptor smiled at the image she had chosen, and said, "Come, let us go and see what Gilukhipa is doing in the workshop. By the sound of it she is pulling out my collection of heads."

Most of the time that she could spare from her visiting and her sick-house, Gilukhipa spent at Dhutmose's studio. Sometimes she served as one of his assistants, roughing out works or helping with casts. But more often she did her own work, asking advice when she needed it. She was becoming quite a fair sculptor.

Dhutmose had built his house exactly on the site of his old hut. It was as fine as any in the city, Attached to it he had both the large studio where he received his eminent patrons and a workshop where he cast heads in gypsum plaster. All the courtiers and wealthy citizens were eager to have portraits done by the royal sculptor, but very often he preferred to go to the quays or markets and persuade some poor stranger with an interesting face to sit for him in exchange for beer and a square meal. He had already accumulated scores of heads, forgetting all about them as soon as they were perfected.

When Dhutmose followed Nefertiti into the workshop, it seemed at first as though it were crowded with people. Having finished her own work, Gilukhipa had ransacked the stores and brought out a number of plaster heads, lining them up on the shelves and benches that ran round the room. A few were painted and had gleaming inlays for iris and pupil, but most were white and stared out with eyes that seemed all the more penetrating for being blank. Having made her obeisance, Gilukhipa asked rather cursorily, "How is the portrait going?"

"It will be my masterpiece," said Dhutmose. "The Queen is very patient."

"Meanwhile I have been disinterring your lesser works. They are as dusty as the desert in there, although I see you have them all neatly docketed. Aren't we a queer-looking lot in Akhetaten?" Gilukhipa waved dramatically towards the two main groups of casts. "Those are all courtiers and officials and people who think themselves important, and these sailors, Bedouin, peasants and such-like. The humble people look far more distinguished."

"Certainly they do, my dear Gilukhipa," said Dhutmose. "I chose them for it, while the rich simply chose me. All the same, I think it *is* true that you can detect the modest origins of some of the good men Pharaoh has converted and raised up. Look at our Mayor, for example —he still looks like a clever peasant. But what of it? I expect that I still look like the son of a Memphis butcher, but that doesn't prevent me from being a very good sculptor."

"No, Gilukhipa," Nefertiti intervened, "you of all people can't condemn the poor merely for becoming rich. Surely it is one of the wonderful things about Akhetaten that so many people have been recognized for their merit and deep understanding of the Aten?"

"Yes. Yes, of course, I expect I am being a fool. But

I doubt if the best ones are always the ambitious ones. . . ."

"Another thing you have to remember," Dhutmose hastened to add, fearing that the Mitannian was going to say something that would be offensive to Nefertiti, "is that you are used to idealized portraits. These are utterly realistic. Some are even based on moulds I took direct from the face. At Akhetaten you have to be prepared to see yourself—and others—in the light of truth."

"No doubt you are right—and I'm sure I should look a monster if you took a mould of me." Gilukhipa looked towards the Mayor and his neighbours, then laughed. "They are a sorry-looking lot, all the same. I shall go and admire your masterpiece as an antidote." She strode through into the studio.

Nefertiti stood for a moment with a stricken face, but then she drew herself up, smiled sweetly at Dhutmose and said, "They are good people, I am sure of it."

The sculptor looked back at her and said very quietly, "You must forgive me, but suddenly I have to tell you that I love you."

Nefertiti did not seem startled; she did not appear to understand the meaning of his words. "Dear Dhutmose," she replied, "you have done so much for us, and of course we love you too. All those who live under the Aten love one another."

Was it a divine stupidity? "Not like this, Your Majesty," he murmured. "Not at all like this."

In the main audience hall at the palace, Pharaoh was on his throne among the columns. He was speaking the last words of his reply to a deputation led by the Governor of Abydos. The city had been ruined by the closing of the shrine of Osiris, many of its inhabitants were starving and its buildings falling into ruin. The deputation had prostrated themselves before the throne. The Governor begged that some accommodation should be made between the old worship and the new, so that Egyptians might again flock to Abydos for the sake of the dead and the comfort of their families.

Looking down on the squirming bodies stretched before him, Akhenaten had not been able to prevent himself from seeing them in the shapes of the black reptiles of the under-world he had first encountered on the walls of the temple of Osiris. He had been disturbed, too, by the hardness of his own heart when he told the Governor that he could feel no grief for the sufferings of the cheats and charlatans who had fleeced the pilgrims and the bereaved families at Abydos. Nevertheless, because the Aten was merciful, he had promised them an increase of water for their fields so that the same cheats and charlatans could keep themselves alive if they would learn to work like other men. He even promised a year's remission of taxes. Now he ended: "I cannot listen to your plea that the dead and the families of the dead have need of Abydos, or that it was a place of comfort for my people. Nor can there be any reconciliation between your idolatory and my teaching. Those who have known the love of the Creator of All do not fear death or suppose that they can purchase their place among the blessed. Go now and see to it that the help I have promised reaches all the people, so that they may eat and enjoy the good life that the Aten has made for them."

Court officials came from behind the throne to escort the delegation from the hall. Frowning, Akhenaten watched while they were ushered out with a good deal less than the ceremony normally granted to an important Governor. Then he leant forward to speak to the Vizier, who was standing on the step below the throne. "Well, Nakht," he said, "I have shown them justice. Give instruc-tions for my promises to be fulfilled." He rose, rubbing his buttocks, for the men of Abydos had been allowed to put their case at some length, and paused for a moment, steady-ing himself on the Vizier's arm. He was recalling his visit to Abydos, and thinking how much its citizens must regret their failure to recognize a young boy on donkey-back.

Perhaps the bodily contact and the moment of silence emboldened Nakht. "Your Majesty," he said. "Beside your wisdom, mine is like a taper set against the great lamp of the temple. But is there not something . . ." Akhenaten abruptly dropped his arm, but he began again, "In the old days my family had a cenotaph and chapel at Abydos. I remember how when my father was killed in Nubia—he was still young and my mother in love with him—we went there and she was much comforted. The god had suffered . . . had been made whole . . . for simple people. . . ." Akhenaten felt a surge of anger. If the Vizier had mentioned the name of Osiris he knew that he would have struck him on the mouth. He held himself in check, but could tell from the sudden fear in Nakht's eyes how terrible his own gaze must be. "My Lord Vizier," he said in a low voice, "you have listened to my teaching, and yet you seem to have heard nothing. I will not try to reveal to you now why it is that the imagined divinity of Abydos stood for all that was dark and hateful to my Father I will only say this. I have taught all that our days are numbered. My tomb is being cut in the cliffs of the desert. But I trust in the love of the Aten. He will grant length of days to myself and those dear to me so that we may fulfil the life he has given us. So it shall be with all who understand. The sun rises in the morning, and death is for us a gate to the sunrise."

Without listening to Nakht's requests for forgiveness, the King made his formal exit between his bowing officials. His spirits were rising again, for he had arranged to follow the tedious and troublesome audience by an hour or so of pure pleasure. He was to take Nefertiti and the two older princesses to the grounds of the North Palace to see the animals there. He intended to do some sketches—he had so little time now to use his brush, and yet it still gave him the greatest delight.

As he approached the private apartments, Meryre,who had evidently been waiting to waylay him, asked for a few words.

"A few, yes, but very few. I have had a surfeit already."

"One of my priests has reported to me that last night after sunset the Governor of Abydos spent an hour with the Lord Mersure. I cannot see any good reason for them to meet. If you agree, Your Majesty, I will have the Governor stopped and questioned."

"My half-brother likes to receive visitors. He has so few

pleasures. He gets none from nature or art; he does not love
his wife and seems to care for Smenkhkare only as a valuable possession. So he must always be trying to dabble in
affairs to build up his own importance. I endure him as a
discipline—and for Smenkhkare's sake."

"Then you do not wish the deputation to be detained?"

"I have no fear of Mersure. There is nothing to show
that he bears us any ill will. My mother still trusts him.
And what harm is within his reach here in Akhetaten?"

The chariot was ready with Mahu in attendance, and
as soon as Akhenaten had, as he put it, washed off the dirt
of Abydos and taken a cup of wine, the royal family set
off for the North Palace. Akhenaten took the reins and
Nefertiti stood at his left hand facing sideways so that they
could talk in spite of the clatter of wheels and hoofs. The
two small girls were in front of their parents, where they
could see ahead and, if they felt like it, pat or prod the
horses' rumps. There was a raised block for Meketaten, as
she had complained that standing on the floor she could
not see and was half suffocated.

It was a perfect spring day, and Akhenaten chose the
riverside road that ran between the Palace grounds and
the River. Below the colonnaded walks of the Palace were
terraced gardens crossed by paths leading down to the
road and quayside. The children loved to see the crowded
shipping. One end of the quay was always busy with small
river craft, including the boats that brought vegetables
and other produce across from the fields to the west of the
River. The big sea-going ships tied up at the north end,
and there one might hear half a dozen languages being
shouted as sailors unloaded their cargoes. Today the
greatest bustle was centred on a large vessel from Syria
which was unloading timber. Ox teams with long narrow
carts were waiting to drag the cedar trunks up to the new
temple which was being built for the special use of Nefertiti. They and their drivers filled half the road.

Anticipating trouble, Mahu had gone further than usual
ahead of the royal chariot. On other streets the citizens
knew what his hurrying figure meant, and lined up at once
to bow to the passing Majesty and make the sign of the

sun. But here, with so much traffic and so many foreigners, it was very much more difficult.

The Syrians cursed and gesticulated when ordered to stop work, but Mahu got the carts backed off the road just in time to let the chariot through. The sailors lounged against the huge cedar they had been handling, making loud comments to one another which sounded far from respectful. Meketaten pointed to them and said to her father, "Look, they have hair on their bodies and arms. How hideous they are. I don't like them."

Meketaten had been fractious and difficult of late, and the King suspected that she was trying to provoke him. She was far too clever not to know that he wished her to like one kind of man as well as another. Yet he could not help being provoked—both by his favourite daughter's words and by the sailors' behaviour. He spoke sharply, and urged the horses on so that they quickly left the quay behind them.

Presently Merytaten said, "I want to see the baby hippopotamus. I like throwing food into its mouth."

"I am afraid it isn't there any longer, my darling," said Nefertiti. Then, remembering that one had always to speak under Ma'at, she added: "It died only a week after you last saw it." Meketaten at once began to cry, and her sister's face crumpled.

"Don't be sad," Nefertiti said quickly. "Let's hope that by now it is browsing in the Field of Rushes. There is something even better for you to see. A new creature. But it is a secret. A surprise which the Master of the Animals is keeping for you. We will soon be there."

The King turned the horses up the road that led to the North Palace. Although it was as much a royal house as the Palace itself or Maru-Aten, it was normally open to all the citizens. Meryre and his priests often sent new devotees of the Aten there as a part of their teaching. They were shown how to meditate on the divine perfection of plants and animals.

On the occasion of royal visits, however, the Master of the Animals saw to it that the gates were kept shut, and a little crowd was now gathered outside to watch Pharaoh and his family arrive. Many of them carried flowers, as was usual when visiting the North Palace, and they threw them before the horses as the chariot went by.

The princesses were excited by the promise of a surprise, and they jumped down from the car before their parents, and before the attendants and the Master himself were ready for them. Meketaten seemed to stumble a little, and she looked very pale, but she cried out as eagerly as her sister: "Where is it? Our Lord Pharaoh has told us that you have a marvel for us to see. Please show it to us quickly."

Their parents smilingly waved aside all formalities, and the Master led them through the court where deer were on show in their elegantly landscaped compounds, past the pool to a high tent which had been set up in an inner courtyard near the aviaries. It had, indeed, been hastily installed to heighten the atmosphere of surprise. Like all the royal tents, it had the sun disc blazoned on the roof.

Making an expectant face that was supposed to show understanding of the little girls, the Master of the Animals drew back the flap and bowed them through. The dimness inside was full of a subtle animal smell—and standing near the centre pole, to which it was fastened by a golden shackle, was a young giraffe, its large soft eyes staring apprehensively from below the heavy lashes. The princesses tiptoed forward, offering the slices of carrot which had been put into their hands. The fantastic, delicately wrought young creature backed with finicky steps until it reached the limit of its chain, then very slowly stretched out the unbelievable neck, and moved its lips, so tender and amorous, above the children's hands. Merytaten giggled as the breath and the long damp hairs brushed her palms, but her sister seemed nervous, and Nefertiti went to her side. Akhenaten stood by the entrance watching the scene intently—and it was to be engraved in his mind— the strange, elegant beast, his exquisite queen and their eager pretty daughters.

Then, without warning, the dim bell of the tent, the quiet, the balance of physical perfections, were smashed like a water jar dropped on a flagstone. A scream. For a moment Akhenaten could not tell where it came from. It seemed as though it had twisted together out of the air, out of the tension between the children and the giraffe. There was a second scream, still seemingly inhuman, yet he saw Meketaten's mouth open, her little milk teeth terribly bared. In another moment she had thrown herself on the ground.

Swiftly Nefertiti moved her towards the tent flap, out of range of the giraffe, which in its terror was swinging round on its chain, the shackled leg raised pitifully in the air.

There was a lull, the child lying hushed although with her limbs twitching. Her parents knelt one on either side of her, hoping that the attack had been an hysterical one, brought on by fear and excitement.

"He bit my head," she whispered. "The giraffe is wicked, he bit my head dreadfully."

"But he didn't, my Mother, he didn't," Merytaten said into Nefertiti's ear, the tears streaming down her face.

The King lifted Meketaten so that her head lay in his lap. He was shocked by her birdlike lightness and frailty. He could not bend down far enough to kiss her, so he stroked one of her hands.

Pentu was sent for, and the Master rushed off to fetch water and a litter to bear the Princess into the Palace. She drank eagerly and seemed better, when suddenly Akhenaten felt the small frame stiffen against him and saw her limbs contract. Scream followed scream. Merytaten dashed from the tent, covering her ears, and the King had to struggle with himself to attend on so much agony. Nefertiti saw his stricken face and said quietly and irresistibly, "Leave us, my dearest. There is nothing you can do." He did his best to lay the convulsed body on to the litter, and fled out of earshot.

Akhenaten made for the River Room. He was like a stricken animal seeking a closed place where he could escape from his kind. He was only remotely aware of the faces of servants startled by the sight of Pharaoh running through the Palace unattended. All the way the words, "There is nothing you can do" choked his mind with incredulity. The River Room was green and cool. He

stared at the painted walls, his eyes lingering on the
delicately drawn plants and reeds of the river bank, the
birds and animals and insects secret among them. Perhaps
that was why he had chosen this place as a refuge. He
remembered how he and Nefertiti had insisted that none
of the usual hunters should be depicted. Now his own body
felt as though it were full of arrows, and his mind as
though it were caught in a net.

After a time he decided that he must go to ask for news,
but as soon as he left the room he felt sure he could hear
Meketaten screaming, and he fled to the chapel. At the
centre stood the altar piece of the Divine Love. It was a
recent work, and showed the King, the Queen and the four
Princesses. The Aten shone upon them, each ray offering
the gift of life. He himself and Nefertiti appeared exalted
with a serene happiness. The sculptor was talented: one of
Dhutmose's best pupils. Akhenaten covered his face; then
stretched himself on the ground. Presently Meryre came
in, gave him water and tried to persuade him to return to
the Palace. But he insisted on remaining in the chapel. So
other priests were summoned and they celebrated prayers
and made offerings of incense. The familiar rituals soothed
the King, although they seemed empty of meaning. Then
about midnight the physician Pentu arrived to say that
Meketaten was now quiet. "Is she asleep?" Akhenaten
asked eagerly. Pentu shook his head. Before dawn he
returned to say that the Princess was dead.

In the time of anguish that followed for Akhenaten, the
actual loss of his favourite daughter was the least of his
sufferings. He had felt the tenderest affection for her; he
had played with her over the years; he had delighted in
the brilliance just beginning to show in her. When he and
Nefertiti told the news to Merytaten and the small,
bewildered Ankhesenpaten, they had all wept together,
and this was the nearest approach to comfort that he was
to feel. From the moment, only a little later, when they
watched Meketaten's light, waxy yellow corpse being
taken for embalmment, he entered a world that seemed as
dark and dry and without feeling as a deserted tomb.

When he tried to pray and commune with the god he

felt nothing. Superficial thoughts drifted through his mind, interrupted only by the mechanical repetition of the phrases "There is nothing you can do" and "He will grant length of days." When he took part in services in the Temple he seemed even further from the god and from his own godhead. As he stood at the foot of the great obelisk with the golden pyramid at its summit, he was no more than a solitary man sweating in the sun with the vast court like a desert stretching round him. The Aten had withdrawn his radiance.

In his numbness and despair he turned against his own teaching and attempted self-mortification. He lived on bread and water, spent nights on the stone floor of his private chapel, even lashed himself. But now he found that he was turning in anger against the Aten, forming prayers that were full of blame and reproaches—a kind of hectoring. Then he drank heavily for several nights and visited the harim. He sent for the daughter of a Nubian chieftain and for a fair-haired child from some land he had never even heard of. The only rewards were dreams of his father's belated lusts and a longing for Nefertiti.

For this was a part of the wretchedness of those months between Meketaten's death and her funeral. Nefertiti was as indispensable to him as before, but she had become inaccessible. It seemed to him that when he tried to approach her, she receded like a desert mirage. Yet he knew that this was not really so. He saw her watching him, wanting to come to his rescue. More than once she tried to make him talk, but then, against his will, he rebuffed her. If he could not love the Aten, if the light had been withdrawn or had never shone, how could he love Nefertiti? In his private chapel he had covered the scene of the Divine Love, for he could not bear to look at it.

One evening not long before the day fixed for Meketaten's funeral, the King went into the small court that lay between his apartments and the Queen's. He had abandoned his visits to the harim, but the night before he and Bak had been drinking until dawn. He had spent the day drowsing uneasily on his couch, and now felt washed out and empty—without thoughts either good or bad. The

gardeners had just finished their late watering; the leaves
sparkled and there was a continuous bubbling sound from
the doves courting and playing on the roofs.

Akhenaten walked softly across to the central basin
where tropical fish were circling above the blue faience.
They had been brought from some distant seas, yet there
they were, so tranquil and complete, so intently themselves.

> The birds lift up their wings in praise of you,
> The fish in the river leap before your face.

Were his words to the Aten beginning to stir with meaning
again? He stood watching the water, and for the first time
in weeks he responded, though feebly, to the air and the
light and the talking of the doves.

The fish gave a slight quiver, an almost imperceptible
lurch off course like small boats touched by a puff of wind.
He looked quickly through the leaves of the shrub that
screened him, and saw that Nefertiti had come out. The
slight sound had been made by a servant setting a stool
for her. Lasia followed with their two smallest children,
the baby just able to walk and young Ankhesenpaten who
was already growing towards the grace that was given to
all Nefertiti's daughters. Lasia had her harp with her, and
began to sing a nursery song.

When Akhenaten stepped suddenly up to them, the
baby lurched as quickly as she could to her mother's side.
In spite of everything it hurt him that she should be afraid.
Even Ankhesenpaten hung back for a moment. The Queen
did not rise as he expected, but looked calmly up into his
face. It seemed to him that she had changed in some way,
or perhaps changed only in relation to himself. Another
stool was brought, and he sat beside Nefertiti while they
played with the children and Lasia plucked and hummed
her tunes softly behind them. In appearance it was the
idyllic domestic scene which the artists of Akhetaten had
so often portrayed and its citizens emulated.

Presently Nefertiti sent the little girls away with their
nurse, then turned to Akhenaten and said without emphasis, "What is it, my Lord?" To his own surprise he

laughed, and it was not altogether a bitter or mocking laugh.

"I was in the garden," he said, "and I felt for the first time for many weeks that perhaps the god was with me again. Then I saw you through the leaves like a dream of solace. And I came to you. But it is I who must ask what it is that has been destroying me. What is it, Nefertiti?"

"You have never been an asker of questions, Akhenaten. And if I answer, it can only be from what you have taught me. I do not think that it has been the loss of our dear Meketaten—not that in itself. Nor, as people have been saying, that your teaching took no account of death. It is that you have believed that we are not as other children of the Aten. Many people have lost beloved daughters, my Lord."

"Then you do not think it is anything to be Son of the Sun? You do not believe that I was chosen of the Aten?"

"You rejected the vision of Egypt's king as a timeless figure among Egypt's gods. You left those certainties behind at Thebes. You have taught us that everything beneath the sun has divinity and is a creature of the Aten. If all men in all lands are brothers, we can only live together, using what the god had given us, each according to his powers. And your powers, as I have always known, are the greatest of any man in the world. Without you none of us would have known the Aten. We should still worship idols. You are the teacher of mankind: isn't that enough?"

"Once, Nefertiti, you worshipped me. I stood before you as the god."

"Perhaps that is true." She paused, turning over memories. "But then you have always said there must be change. That is one of our burdens. Once I worshipped you; now I love you and suffer with you. The second love is greater."

"But perhaps it is not what I must have. I am a man, certainly, and a strange looking man. My face is too long; my shoulders and shanks too thin; my belly too fat and my hips like a woman's. Because I live in truth I have had this shown to the world. But because I alone understand my Father's purposes, it is I who have created this city of

Akhetaten. It is from me that the light is spreading through all the lands. The Peace of the Aten, which can save mankind from destruction, depends upon me alone. My Father created all things in solitude, out of himself. That we know. But I have had my Queen. Our love and our family have been the symbol of the divine love. For me a cherishing wife is not enough." He spoke with a sad brutality he could not check. She did not wince or harden. He watched her with admiration.

"Under Ma'at," she said at last, "I cannot act the part of the Divine Queen. I can only be myself. The self you yourself have so largely made. But after all I believe we shall find a way."

Akhenaten stood up and looked out into the court. He felt sad and troubled. Perhaps he would never again have the conviction that he and Nefertiti made one complete and holy being. He felt sick, too. Probably his eyes were bloodshot. But he was alive once more, open to the light. The pale sky was beginning to glow. The bubbling of the pigeons had sunk to an occasional murmur: they were sitting together in pairs on the highest points of the roof—catching the last of the sun.

"I will go now and celebrate the sunset prayer," he said. "I have avoided it for many nights."

"And I will do the same. From my own window. Come afterwards to kiss the children, Akhenaten."

The royal tomb was being cut in the cliffs of a wadi that ran far into the eastern desert. It was a harsh, wild, rocky place. The King had not forbidden the construction of elaborate tombs at Akhetaten, but now they were decorated entirely with cheerful scenes of everyday life or of the worship of the Aten. Judgment and the underworld had been banished. In the same way funerals kept many of the traditional forms, but were treated as festivals. Young girls wore flowers and sang instead of beating their brows and wailing.

As the royal tomb was not finished, one of the ante-rooms had been hastily adapted to receive Meketaten.

Bak and his assistants had worked as fast as they could to decorate the walls. One of their scenes showed the King and Queen and all Meketaten's sisters weeping by her bier. This was not a usual subject, but the poor little girl had few events in her life to commemorate.

Akhenaten prepared to take part in the funeral with a bitter sense of irony. He knew that even now he would not be able to manifest the joyous spirit which he himself had decreed. His mother had come from Thebes for the occasion, and he had been glad to receive her. The fact that she would not understand his recent torments nor wish to discuss them made her company all the more desirable. On the other hand, as soon as she had arrived he could tell that she wanted to talk to him about state affairs. From the day of Meketaten's death he had entirely neglected them.

They had been carried by litter well beyond the city bounds, but now, at a point where the rocky valley steepened, Akhenaten and Nefertiti had themselves set down to walk the rest of the way on foot. Most of the court followed their example, although the Queen Mother, the princesses and a few individuals who could claim delicate health remained in their litters. The young boys and girls who had been selected to lead the funeral train tumbled as decorously as possible out of the carts that had brought them and took up their lotus flowers. Their presence did in fact lend something of the atmosphere of a festival, for their irrepressible liveliness was obvious, and their voices, when they began to sing hymns, were not suggestive of death. But no one else could feel cheerful in the company of the little stumpy coffin exposed on its bier.

The sun reflected fiercely off the rocks as the cortège toiled up the wadi, and the scent of the heat-struck flowers was sad and out of place. Akhenaten looked upwards to escape his feeling of confinement. He saw the guards who had been posted all along the cliff edges, and, circling above them, very high in the blueness, a drift of vultures. The sound of many sandals scraping on the rocks seemed more real than the chanting of hymns.

Akhenaten recognized the dark opening in the rock and

felt the sudden chill as they went inside. A linen curtain had been hung across the inner tomb to hide the unfinished chambers—the chambers of Pharaoh and the Great Queen—but stone dust was sifting out from behind it and formed a haze round the lamps and torches. Nefertiti did not seem to notice the curtain, nor to be thinking of what lay behind.

They reached the burial chamber itself, having by now left behind all but the priests and their intimate circle, and saw the granite sarcophagus waiting to receive the coffin. Standing on the far side was a sculpture of Meketaten that Dhutmose had carved from the many studies of the Princess he had made during the last year of her life. When Akhenaten saw these things, and the table beside the sarcophagus supporting Meketaten's favourite necklace, a portrait she had painted of her cat, and a little Aten shrine that he had given her for her last birthday (the only things he had allowed to be brought to the tomb), he found tears welling into his eyes.

As the high priest enacted the ancient rite of the Opening of the Mouth, Nefertiti and the two older princesses began to cry also. The little one, who had been happily staring at the lamps and the way they were reflected in the gold coffin lid, took fright and wailed so loudly that Lasia had to carry her away. So the scene that Bak had devised, and on which even now the paint was hardly dry, was never exactly fulfilled.

The heat seized them as they went out into the wadi once more. The boys and girls threw their flowers into the tomb entrance, and already before the procession was ready to move off, workmen had begun to bring blocks to close the burial chamber. Akhenaten watched them and resolved that he would never again mention Meketaten's name or think about the manner of her death.

His mother went past on the way to her litter. Scorning the attentions of servants, she was steadying herself across the stones with an ivory and ebony stick. He studied her face, still plump but netted with lines like a melon. The sensuality, which had both attracted and dismayed him as a boy, had now ebbed away to leave an impression of intense feminine will. Akhenaten looked at her with a kind of pride.

The King lay back in lassitude, thinking of nothing. He allowed his eyes to rest on the small company of guards that was marching in front, and this, together with the swaying movement of his own litter, lulled him to the edge of sleep. As they came out from the wadi, he was aware enough to notice the line of the city bounds with the sense of reassurance that it always gave him. One of the great carved boundary stones was so close that he could read a few words of the inscription as he passed. His mind drifted back to that day of the foundation of Akhetaten. Then there had been nothing but sand, stones and thorns between here and the river. Now there was the city in all its beauty and life. Then the dream of all that was to be created was in him and in Nefertiti as they drove through the desert. Now the dream had been dissipated even by its fulfilment, and he and she had become two separate people. But surely what parted them was not very much? With the tomb sealed behind him he could win her back. Suddenly, cutting across the drift of his mind, he saw that moment in Gilukhipa's house when Nefertiti came in with Dhutmose.

Now they were approaching a point where the path passed near the model township of the tomb-cutters, and Akhenaten noticed a considerable crowd gathered beside the track. Evidently they had come out to watch the royal family and all the famous people of Akhetaten go by. To his annoyance he saw that some of the guards had stepped aside and were pushing the crowd back with the shafts of their spears. One woman was struggling to hold a shaft back from her breast, and he seemed to feel the pain and indignity in his own body. He sat up and raised his hand to greet his subjects, resolving to tell the captain of the guard that this kind of officiousness was altogether against his commands.

At this moment there was a slight scuffle in the crowd, an arm appeared above the surrounding heads, and a small object arched through the air to fall just in front of his feet. For a moment Akhenaten's mind clouded with horror. It was an unheard of and most dangerous thing for anything to be thrown towards the royal person. His bearers hesitated, the Captain sprang to his side, and one of the guards thrust in among the crowd trying to seize the offender. Probably this was no more than the work of some well-meaning ignorant fellow. "It is nothing," he said to the Captain. "A gift to Pharaoh, perhaps. Tell them to go on."

From among the embroidered cushions, Akhenaten picked up a packet wrapped in a piece of worn linen cut from a loin cloth. He opened it with a feeling of some kindness, having persuaded himself to expect a humble token of sympathy from one of his subjects. Inside was a statuette of Osiris, cut in wood and painted in crude colours, the body inscribed with a spell to secure a safe passage to the Kingdom of the Dead. Violently he broke it in pieces and threw the splinters on to the desert floor.

He was appalled that so small a thing could upset him, yet absurd scenes took possession of his imagination. He saw himself going from house to house in the township teaching the Aten to the eager inhabitants. Then again he saw himself inviting them all to the Palace and speaking to them with such eloquence that they wept and adored. However, before they were back on the streets of Akhetaten his thoughts had led him on, and he was blaming himself for failing to see that the word of the Aten was taught directly to the people. Nefertiti, he knew, would agree with this, and Gilukhipa, too, from her different point of view.

As his litter was being set down outside the Palace entrance, he saw Gilukhipa herself hurrying through the groups of servants and officials surrounding him. She had a way, he reflected, of making everyone else look feeble and effeminate beside her.

"Your Majesty," she said, "I was not far behind and I saw what happened—and I know the man. What was it he threw?"

"A piece of idolatrous rubbish."

"He is a crazy creature. Some people would say he is

possessed. But he has sick children and a sick wife. The guard have tied him up and dragged him into the city. I beg you to pardon him." Gilukhipa spoke with uncharacteristic hesitation. The truth was she felt some guilt, for she had discovered from her visiting that several households in the township kept effigies of the old gods in dark corners of their little rooms.

"You must know, my dear Gilukhipa, that at any other time he would have been executed on the spot. I will pardon him, but it will do him no harm to be confined for a time. I will give instructions that a priest shall visit him and show him the light of the Aten." He saw a look of youthful pleasure and relief change her face. "So you care! You do really care! It may be that you are more the good shepherd of the people than I am, Gilukhipa."

"No, dearest Majesty," she replied, now quite restored to herself. "I have no such virtue. I know them as real men and women, that is all. And very troublesome they often are—but I do love some of them—and have sympathy for the rest."

Akhenaten entered the Palace and found that the Queen Mother, Ay and Tey and all the members of the royal house who had attended the funeral were assembled. He supposed it was customary to eat together after a funeral, but he looked at them all with weariness. Even Smenkhkare was there, he noticed, as usual keeping as close as he could to Merytaten—whose face was still puffy with tears. When the food was served he and Nefertiti shared a single tray stand between them, as they had always liked to do when they were alone. He talked to her softly about his plans to bring his teaching home to the people, and he felt that she listened with all her old admiration. When Ay leant across to say something about Meketaten, he shook his head and said that the tomb was sealed.

When the company began to disperse, he found the Queen Mother lying in wait for him. "Akhenaten," she said, "I heard you say that 'the tomb is sealed', and was glad of it. I have been waiting to talk to you. Since I arrived I have been told every hour of the day that Phar-

aoh was in his chapel, or at the Temple, or closeted with
the Queen. Now things have to be taken up again."

"Very well, Madam," he answered with a smile. "I
knew there could be no escape. Pharaoh will grant an
audience to the Queen Mother." He led her into his
working-room. This was the place where he read letters
and despatches when he had to, dictated occasional replies
to his scribes, and held his morning audience with Nakht,
Tutu and other ministers with whom he was intimate. He
had not in fact attended to any business since Meketaten's
death, but every morning the documents had been laid
before his empty chair. It was an austerely furnished room,
with a splendid symbol of the beneficent Aten in gold and
lapis lazuli inlaid on the far wall.

Akhenaten seated himself below it, while his mother
took Nakht's usual place opposite him, looking oddly out
of place on the big ebony chair. She seemed full of deter-
mination, and quite unfatigued in spite of the heat and
effort of the morning.

"My son," Queen Tiye began without a moment's
pause, "I think that you mustn't shut yourself up in this
place any longer. You have created Akhetaten, and for the
people here that may be enough. But to the rest of Egypt
you seem like a hermit. If Pharaoh is never seen, if he
doesn't go up and down the river at least once every year,
then things begin to go wrong. For all most of your
provincial officials know, you might be dead, and one of
your strange protégés sitting on the throne."

"Perhaps it is good for me to be talked to as though I
were a boy again. But you are unjust. Since we came here I
have been to Nubia and to Memphis and Heliopolis. And
every morning—in normal times—I deal with affairs of
state. You can see for yourself." He pointed to a box of clay
tablets and a basket of papyrus rolls that were on the table
between them. "Home affairs on my right, foreign affairs
on my left. What could be more businesslike?" He grinned
as he had not done since Meketaten's death.

"Yes. You went to Nubia to dedicate a temple, and
hardly stopped anywhere on the way—not even one day
at Thebes. And when you were in the North you saw only

the priests of Re, and learned men and cranks. That kind of royal progress does more harm than good. Haremhab was furious."

"Haremhab is a good soldier, but we have nothing to say to one another. Just now you said 'things begin to go wrong'. Tell me what those things are—all my reports are good."

"That is what I suspect—bad news doesn't reach you. It might disturb you and interfere with your hymn-writing and teaching—to say nothing of making you less devoted to all those upstart ministers. But my food doesn't have to go through a sieve—old though I am. The people still want to love you. They remember how you healed them; for years taxes were lightened and the administration was less harsh. And of course they liked the way you routed the Amonites and threw all the old men of power from their pedestals. Ordinary people, people who have no power themselves, will always enjoy such topplings. And I was with you so far—you know that. But for the next step great care was needed, and not enough has been taken. Some of your tax collectors do abominable things in your name—seizing whole herds of cattle, and even robbing men's gardens of all their vegetables. Others, following your wishes, are if anything too lenient. It all depends on the individual, and no one knows what he will have to pay. These are the reports I get."

"And they do not sound very serious, my dearest Mother. If a City of God has been created and the light of the Aten spread through the land with so little disturbance as this, then we have done well. The river is long, and I cannot have eyes everywhere."

"If the people begin to waver in their love, there are plenty of those whom we defied ready to turn them quite against you. There are always plotters in Thebes—the priests of Amon, the Theban nobles—the old gang. And now I think that the priests of Osiris are joining with them —and they still have power with the people. The ordinary folk need Osiris, and you have given them no substitute. They cannot face death without some help. You yourself have seemed to need help, Akhenaten. The world is saying you were not prepared for death."

He stared at her, amazed that she should dare to press on this spot. "Dear Mother. Vulgar judgments often have so much truth in them. I wish it were not so. Because I live under Ma'at I will admit that I have been made to know that I do not yet understand all the ways of my Father. But he will enlighten me, and he will never allow me to turn from his ways of light and love to those other ways of darkness and punishment. Never."

"But if it is hard for you, my son, it is impossible for Egypt. How can you hope that they will follow you? The people must be given some sops."

Akhenaten made his mind a blank to keep his anger in check. Picking a tablet out of the box, he tilted it along the light so that the crowded writing of the Babylonian scribe was picked out in shadow. Amazing that these marks could bring words from so far away. Then he spoke.

"Do you wish to tell me that Pharaoh's subjects would turn against him? This is not for Egypt—men do not revolt against god."

"I did not mean that. . . . " For the first time Queen Tiye was nervous, and the King fixed her with a questioning, ironical gaze. "But there has never been anything in the least like this before." She shot out her arms as though to indicate the whole kingdom, and he noticed how her jewelled bracelets rattled. "And no Pharaoh has behaved as you behave, Akhenaten. All the same, I mean only that you must not risk the love of the people, and you must keep the loyalty of the army."

"Is Haremhab likely to be a traitor? Or your brother Ay?" He could see that at last he had made his mother angry.

"Haremhab, and perhaps even my brother, know that an expedition should be sent to Asia. The loyalty of soldiers is in fighting."

Akhenaten picked up the clay tablet again and said with deliberate irrelevance: "Do you know that I have learned to read Akkadian, Mother? I can decipher this letter from my brother of Babylon, if you would like to hear it?"

She seemed to sweep it aside with a movement of her hand, and he reflected with a far-away affection that none of her gestures had ever changed.

"I can't read it. But I have plenty of trustworthy men about me who can. As for that tablet, Babylon is of little importance any more—you know that. But what news do you have of Aziru—your supposed friend Aziru?"

"Must we always speak of Aziru? Since he came to me last year to promise his friendship and listen to my teaching, he has stayed at home and ended his campaigning. Tutu tells me that all the lands are peaceful."

"I hear that he is hand in hand with Suppiluliuma of Hattusas. And even you, my son, can't imagine that the Hittites are our friends. They would like to end Egyptian power in Asia, push us back to our frontiers."

"And you, dear Mother, cannot understand that I would not think even that a terrible thing. What do the people of Syria or of Palestine care whether Egypt is over them or not? They only want to till their lands and enjoy the bounty of the god. And the same is true of Egypt. Was life any less good for the people when our power stopped at Sile? I believe that it was better. And as for me I do not care about worldly power. All these lands, great and small, belong to my Father, and if I am their lord it is only as his son. We do not want empires, but peace."

Akhenaten saw his mother beginning to look alarmed, and realized that he was working himself into a passion. He broke off and took some wine from his cup-bearer. Then he said, "Dearest Mother, please understand that it is not that I want the same things as you, but fail to achieve them. I want quite other things. Now I must rest. The day has devoured me like an east wind. But I give you my promise that I will send good men through the Two Lands to enquire into abuses and set them right. And as for Asia, tomorrow you shall talk with Tutu. Then, I know, you will be reassured."

He rose, and bent over his mother to kiss her just below the harsh edge of her mourning headdress. She pushed him firmly away and looked up at him. "You are trying to cajole me, Akhenaten," she said. "But I am an old Queen,

not just an old lady. Power is real, and if you don't hold
on to it, all that you care about will suffer."

"You have never believed in the power of the Aten, have
you—Queen Mother?" He gazed at her intently.

"He is not a Lord of Battles. And you have not finished
with battles yet," she answered, pushing herself up from
the chair. At that moment Nakht came into the room. He
looked strained and apprehensive. "Your Majesties must
forgive me," he said. "I am a bearer of news so bad that it
must be told at once. A messenger has arrived from
Mitanni. King Tushratta has been murdered—by one of
his own sons."

The King felt a clutch in his throat and in his chest, but
he insisted with himself that he must be calm. His voice
only shook a little when he said: "Violence is abominable.
But I cannot suffer for every royal house that is divided
against itself. There are too many crowns and too much
ambition. As for the man himself, I never admired him—
and I doubt if Gilukhipa will lament her brother's death."

"This is no ordinary dynastic affair, Your Majesty,"
said Nakht, and Queen Tiye turned her head sharply to
watch him. "I have not told you the worst. It seems that
although it was his son who actually struck Tushratta
down, it was contrived by Suppiluliuma, and he is already
beginning to take over the government. It must mean a
vast increase in Hittite power."

"Where is Tutu?" the King asked, still holding to his
calm.

"Tutu was taken ill after the funeral, Your Majesty. A
sudden sunstroke as Pentu believes."

"And that is why the messenger reached *you*, my Lord
Vizier," Queen Tiye broke in, "and why we ourselves have
come to hear of these disastrous doings? Because that
Syrian was not there to hush them?" Nakht stood silent,
running his fingers up and down the pleats in his loin
cloth. Before Akhenaten could speak, the Queen turned
to him and said, "You should never have trusted that
devious foreigner, my son. Why should he be true to
Egypt?"

"You know nothing of Tutu, honoured Mother," he

said. "If he has been at fault, it may have been in keeping things too much from me, knowing that I have enough to bear. But it is very likely that the despatch is false or exaggerated. If Tutu is better, we will hold our usual council tomorrow. And let the messenger be present."

Queen Tiye left the room abruptly. The King suspected that she had gone to look for her brother, hoping to be able to exchange views with somebody who thought as she did. The Vizier remained before him, looking even more distressed than before. "Your Majesty," he said, trying to withdraw himself from his words, "there is another thing. On his way through Memphis the messenger stopped to report. Haremhab is greatly disturbed by the news. In this letter he asks me to convey to you urgently that in his opinion an expedition should be sent at once to secure Syria." Nakht pulled a papyrus roll from his belt and held it out. Akhenaten ignored it.

"Haremhab invariably wants to send an expedition. It is his nature. It is as natural to him as pissing to other men." Akhenaten lowered his lids until his eyes showed only as long dark slits. Nakht, who was an able man but not a brave one, visibly quailed. "Those were the Commander-in-Chief's words, Your Majesty. I thought it right . . ."

"Quite right, my Lord Vizier. As I said, we will hold our council tomorrow." Then relenting, and at the same time feeling so tired that he could hardly support himself, he said, "Come, Nakht, give me your arm. I am going to my couch. The Queen Mother is indefatigable, but her son does not take after her."

Even before they were through the doorway, Akhenaten heard heavy footsteps outside. Somebody striding in bronze-studded sandals. He stood still, and almost clung to the Vizier. "No! No!" he said. "I cannot endure any more. But worse trouble is coming. Listen to its footsteps." Nakht lifted the curtain with his free hand, and they stood looking out. Ay was marching across the pillared hall as though he were on the parade ground.

"He looks as hot and angry as you looked pale and despairing, my dear Nakht. Of the two birds of ill omen, I prefer you. But to think that a few months ago I thought I was happy, and that even this morning I believed happiness might be returning." Akhenaten uttered a kind of laugh, and the Vizier braced himself to take more weight.

"But, my Lord, we know nothing. It may be some trifle —a quarrel among the chariot drivers . . . some insubordination. . . ."

Akhenaten shook his head. "*I* know. I can hear the spear in flight. Let me retreat. Back to my chair."

Ay swung the curtain roughly aside and stood in front of the King, who had not sat down but stood propped on the arm of his chair. He gave a bow as though it were some bodily exercise.

"There has been serious trouble in Thebes." The ageing soldier glared at the two unsoldierly figures before him. "But for the moment there is no need for alarm. The army was like a rock, and quickly put it down. The common people, too, went into the streets and shouted for Pharaoh. My officers, who have just disembarked, report that as soon as the Queen Mother left Thebes, that Ipy, whom we were fool enough to spare, appeared on the scene and led the outbreak. Did you know that he had escaped from your charge, my Lord Vizier?"

Before Nakht could reply, the King intervened. "No matter. Tell me what happened. Was there much bloodshed or destruction?"

"Some of the disaffected nobles tried to seize the Governor—and his house was burnt. Our men soon disposed of them. But worse still, as you will think, Your Majesty, the Temple of the Aten was attacked by a fanatical mob of Amonites. They murdered all the priests they could see, then smashed the divine images of yourself and mutilated all representations of the Aten. One of my officers who went there says that the Temple looks as though it had been trodden by giants." Akhenaten heard the sound of pleasure in his uncle's voice. Then he was aware of something heavy crashing to the ground, and of seeing the rough edges of shattered clay tablets lying close to his eyes.

Once again he was in the presence of the god. The sun burned all round him and through him, and he was made radiant but not consumed. It began to recede so that he could see the edge of the disc, then rays descending from it, and the countless hands held out in blessing. The rays narrowed and grew taut like the strings of a harp, and a humming more shrill than that of any harp string throbbed through them; the hands closed and vanished. A black figure appeared in the heart of the sun; it came nearer and showed itself to be Osiris, crudely painted. It was plain that the rays were now swords and they struck Osiris, and as the body was shivered into many parts the Ram, the Jackal, the Ibis and the Baboon rose among them and they too were destroyed. The Vulture and the Cobra fled away. The sun began to flame again, and all the heads and limbs were consumed into specks of black that danced, then twisted together into the firelit head of Amon, crowned with lofty feathers. He fixed the head with his eyes and it kindled, the feathers turning to flame. The light grew brighter and approached his face, until his vision spread into pure, singing whiteness.

Word quickly spread through the court and the city that Pharaoh had suffered another attack of the divine sickness— or, as the devout preferred to say, another visitation of the god. The news brought anxiety, but also filled everyone with excitement, and some with genuine exaltation.

These emotions quite eclipsed any response to the Theban uprising. In Akhetaten people always felt as though they were a thousand miles away from the old capital—and anyone who might have been nervous knew that the boundary guards had been doubled in number. The life of the city seemed more fervent and inturned than ever before.

In the temples the priests never ceased from offering prayers and incense, while hundreds of citizens rose before the sun to make offerings at their garden shrines—and returned to them at sunset. All Akhetaten was in perpetual intercourse with its god.

The King himself was also in an exalted mood. It seemed to him that at a time of challenge when he might have fallen back into despair, the god had taken possession of him again and his power was unbounded. At first he was troubled by headaches, but Pentu had given him some powders that dispelled them. He did not encourage visits from Pentu, however, for the physician was too inclined to treat him as a sick patient. (He remembered how his mother had made the same mistake at the time of his first visitations when he was a boy.) He had always supported Pentu in the pursuit of Ma'at in his medicine and his scorn of spells, charms and all kinds of magical flummery. But now the man was going too far. He tried out some of his preparations on monkeys; and seemed to think that every human experience could properly be treated with his herbs and powders.

Although Akhenaten felt in bodily health, he stayed for some time in seclusion. Ay and the Queen Mother had embarked for Thebes as soon as they were satisfied about his condition, and reports said that all was quiet there. As for Mitanni, a letter had come from Tushratta's murderous son sending him fraternal greetings and making no mention of the Hittites. Tutu assured him that the horrid affair had been no more than one of the family divisions characteristic of the northern kingdoms. Akhenaten found it hard to imagine how such things could be done, but he had other things to think about.

In the quietness of his room he found that his response to the divinity of the world had been more than restored to him. The days when he had moved among grey shadows already seemed incredible. One late afternoon he was looking at a bowl of wild flowers which the princesses had picked for him, when each tiny scarlet bell, each soft blue flax flower, each daisy, sprang into an extraordinary intensity of private being. Then one night, after the lamps had been burning for an hour or more, Akhenaten looked up from his reading and felt that the walls round him were reaching out to contain all the Palace with his family and servants; all the city lying there below the moon with its inhabitants, sleeping and awake; all his kingdom—until at last he knew that he was at the centre of the whole created world, flowing out into it, and drawing it into his own being. So this is what it is to be the Aten, he

212 KING OF THE TWO LANDS

thought exultantly, this is what it is to know divine love.

Yet although he had this experience of being united in love with all existence, he found himself remote from actual men and women. Nefertiti visited him every day and they were tranquil enough together, but he still felt as he had when he came upon her in the garden. Only now, perhaps, he cared less about the change in their relationship. Formerly, although he had seen their love as holy, it had been an intense coming together of himself and herself. Now when he took possession of her—which he did—he felt he was celebrating a ritual act.

When Dhutmose came to see him with his plans and problems, he did not seem able to enter into them, but only to give judgment. Even his voice seemed to come from far off. He was aware that Dhutmose felt the change and was troubled. Was this what he had often experienced in imagination, and written of in his poetry: the solitude of the Aten as he created and sustained the world? Was this what the visitation had brought him?

During these days while he remained in his private apartments, other quite different thoughts were also forming in his mind and growing stronger and stronger. As he meditated on his vision, and on the events at Thebes, and wove them together, he became convinced that it was the purpose of the Aten that he should crush the lingering memories of idolatry and the names of the old gods. Once again he saw their emblems being consumed in the fire. And when these things were in his mind, he found that he also thought of Ipy, whose life he had spared and who had betrayed him. Then he had a dream in which he was looking on at the great struggle between Horus and Seth, the story that had meant so much to all Egyptians. And then the Enemy, Seth, before his own defeat struck out the eye of Horus that was the sun, Akhenaten awoke trembling violently and with pain in his right eye. He got up and prayed until daylight, for this was an invasion from darkness, the contrary of all he had taught at Akhetaten. .

Yet still the conviction remained with him that he had to act against what was left of the old idolatry. Thebes itself dominated his imagination like a hated person. He saw the huge, tyrannous buildings still standing there with the names of Amon and the other false gods cut deeply into their walls and columns. It was dreadful that the gaze of his subjects should still fall on these symbols, worse that the sun itself should have to shine upon them every day, touching them with its rays. How had he allowed them to remain for so long? And how many idolatrous statues were still decked and tended and offered sacrifice up and down the length of the Two Lands? He believed he could feel their secret presence where they stood in darkened shrines. And all these hateful things were to be identified with his opponents, with the people who had repaid his mercy by treachery, and had smashed his temple and murdered his priests.

While Akhenaten was wrestling with these thoughts, a letter was brought to him from Ay. After the usual formalities, his uncle said that he rejoiced to be able to tell him that, in accordance with his royal wishes, Ipy and the other leaders of the uprising had been hunted down and duly put to death. "In accordance with his royal wishes?" He had never given any such command, but had he not known when Ay and his mother left for Thebes just what they intended to do? And in face of the feelings of hatred that had been invading his mind, could he deny that he had wished for the punishment of his enemies? "Enemies", the word was there in his heart, and with it the emotions that had framed it.

"Then I, too, must act." It seemed that the decision had been taken for him. The next morning he summoned his court, senior officials and priests into the audience hall of the Palace. He told them that from that day every temple in the Two Lands that had not been wholly turned over to the Aten was to be closed and guarded. Anyone found secretly officiating or worshipping there would be taken before the Governor for judgment. Moreover, that on his immediate commands men were to be sent out in every nome armed with hammers and chisels to cleanse the buildings, even those that stood empty and ruined, of the hateful titles of the ancient gods.

IX

THERE was a slight commotion at the entrance to the King's private garden. Akhenaten recognized the voice raised in stern command—it was Gilukhipa. He laid the roll he was reading back among the other papyri in the ivory casket, and turned to see what was happening.

He saw the Mitannian princess striding masterfully through the doorway, shaking off the uncertain protests of his servants and household guard. She was dressed in dark purple today, with a massive silver belt and bracelet. Her face was set in grimness beyond anything necessary to win her entry.

Akhenaten looked regretfully at the manuscripts. Since his appearance in the audience hall he had returned to a more normal way of life. But his mind still seemed a battleground of invading forces, and he was seeking to set down his teaching. It seemed to him that men's notions about the old gods had grown up in darkness and mystery from images that came in dreams and in times of ritual, passion and delirium. Now the light of the one true god had been revealed, and it must have its clear gospel. First he was reading the ancient texts concerning Horus, Re and even Kephri the scarab, for it seemed to him that in these former intuitions of the sun god, there were flashes of the true light shining through the clouds.

Perhaps he had plunged into this task partly also to escape from pursuit—like a runaway hiding in the reed beds. For he knew that Nefertiti, Dhutmose and others of those nearest to him were troubled by what they felt to be his persecution of error and by the executions at Thebes. Nefertiti had even said to him that she had never thought that the Aten would be seen to throw the shadows of punishment. Now he had to confront Gilukhipa.

"My Lord," she said abruptly, "don't blame your household for allowing me to disturb you in this way. Short of laying hands on me, they did their best to prevent it."

"Then I suppose you have something urgent to say to me, Gilukhipa."

"It is about Taty—the idiot of a man from the township."

Akhenaten stiffened and frowned. "What of him?"

"He is condemned to be sent to the granite quarries—where he will surely die. Did you agree to this, my Lord?"

Akhenaten felt a temptation to say that the affairs of a tomb-cutter were invisible to Pharaoh, but he knew that if he so betrayed himself Gilukhipa would never excuse him. The truth was that at about the time of his decision on the cleansing of the temples he had heard through Meryre that the man had refused all teaching and had blasphemed against the Aten and himself. At that moment it had seemed to him right that a small opponent should go the way of the great ones.

"Yes. I agreed. He was quite unrepentant, and said abominable things."

"He was talked at by some young priest, but he felt all along that he was condemned. His wife is desperate. She and her children have been turned out of the township. They squat all day in the dust outside his prison, begging for help."

"The woman must know that this is no more than justice."

"But, my Lord," said Gilukhipa raspingly, turning on him her most hawk-like look, "ours is a religion of love." Then, with a swift change that made him feel she dared to pity him, she went on: "Dearest Akhenaten, I am trading on an old affection. I know that. I am not doing it just for the sake of poor Taty and his wife. In the past, thousands of men were sent to the granite quarries, or to Sinai or to man the oars; hundreds probably were beaten to death for less than this man has done. But that has not been your way. That has not been the way in this city." She paused. "Who am I to teach the Master? I ask you only one thing, my Lord: that you will meet this man face to face. Not here in the Palace where you wouldn't really see him. But in the place where he is held."

Akhenaten felt a gust of angry impatience, but it seemed

to rise like an air bubble through calm water, and he found he had smiled at her and agreed to go. "We will take Nefertiti with us," he added.

They bumped along a side street in Gilukhipa's four-wheeled chariot. Weni was driving with his mistress beside him, while Akhenaten and Nefertiti sat on a hard seat behind them. Although he was muffled in a linen cloak, Akhenaten had a sense of fresh air and freedom. It was true that he had been in the habit of driving through the city, but he had kept to the few main streets and Mahu had always been there to turn the populace into lines of bowing and hailing subjects. Now he looked at people going about their affairs almost with a sense of adventure. At a crossing where they were held up for a minute, he watched an old lady lovingly arrange her little heaps of seeds and herbs and dried fruits to tempt the passers-by; then in a dark shop there was a carpenter wonderfully intent on fitting a chair leg, and an old bearded fellow, a Syrian by the look of him, sucking wine through a pipe and holding a grandchild on a little rein. "You are a clever woman, Gilukhipa," he said. "I believe you have half won your case already."

Weni pulled up his horses outside a bronze-studded door, leading into a compound attached to the guards' barracks. Gilukhipa had been there several times before, and there was no difficulty with the men at the gate, although they stared at her veiled companions. As Akhenaten uncovered his face he noticed a squad of men drilling at the far end of the big, dusty space. He realized he had not known that his own soldiers had to be drilled in this military fashion.

They approached a low white building with a guard posted. Not far away, sheltered beneath a stretched bed-spread, was a crouching woman with two small children. She looked as though she were going to run forward, but Gilukhipa signalled to her to stay where she was. A small girl escaped, trotted up and stared up at the King. When he smiled at her she rolled her eyes so that the whites showed below her dark lashes.

"She is a pretty child," said Nefertiti.

"Yes, but by bad luck she is dumb," Gilukhipa replied. Taty was sitting in the corner of a bare white-washed cell. There was a column of flies circling above his head, and Akhenaten noticed a scorpion scuttling along a rafter, but he was relieved to find no signs of ill-treatment.

"I have brought Pharaoh and the Queen Nefertiti to see you, Taty," said Gilukhipa. At these astounding words the man opened his mouth, hesitated, then rose slowly to his feet and made an awkward bow. Then suddenly he burst out: "Life—Prosperity—Health—Your Majesties. I suppose I should be grovelling on the ground like a toad?"

"All creatures have their own postures," said Akhenaten calmly. "You are here because you threw an object at Pharaoh. That in itself was heinous. And the object was one you knew to be loathsome to him. Why did you do this?"

"You had buried the little girl—hardly bigger than my poor speechless one—without any help in her meeting with the King of the Dead. You have no right . . ."

"Why are you so devoted to the idea you call the King of the Dead?"

"I was an orphan, a clever one. The priests at Abydos reared me and taught me to carve the signs. I have cut his name a hundred times." The man was terribly thin and his complexion yellowish, but his eyes were very bright above the drawn skin on his cheek-bones.

"The Aten is the Lord of the Dead as well of the Living. You have only to open your eyes to his light."

"That is how it may seem to you in your Palace with a Queen as lovely as the Lady Isis. But ordinary people are full of troubles, and of wickedness too. Great wickedness, petty wickedness. They must have judgment and the help of one who was killed through wickedness and brought to life again. You have your god; you should not take away ours."

"What never was, cannot be taken away. The Father who speaks through me is one and alone. He made you, and he made that scorpion there on the rafter. He made all things in the Two Lands and in all the lands beyond.

By his forgiveness he banishes darkness and judgment. Open your eyes, stubborn Taty."

"I will not forsake my god." The man's thin limbs were shaking and he sagged against the wall. "And now, your Majesty—tell them not to send me to the quarries. They would hardly get me alive as far as Elephantine. They can stick me with arrows out there in the compound. Or hack off my head—if that's easier."

Akhenaten stood stiffly, not knowing what he was going to do; blinded by sheer opposition. Then he felt Nefertiti's hand on his arm; it stole along like a mouse until it closed over the ball of his thumb. His body relaxed, and his mind was clear again.

"You are my subject, and my Father's subject," he said. "I have told you that the Aten reigns not by judgment but by love. And to prove this, in the very face of your transgressions, you are forgiven. Where do you work, Taty?"

"I was working in your tomb, Majesty. Cutting the signs." There was a moment's silence. Then, unexpectedly, marvellously, Akhenaten laughed. "There could be no more unsuitable place. Find him some occupation where he will see the sun, Gilukhipa." He turned and walked out with Nefertiti, while Gilukhipa remained to tend Taty —who had slid down the wall on to the floor.

Seeing the little encampment under the awning, the woman now cooking something for her husband on a pot of charcoal, Akhenaten said, "Go and give them the news, Nefertiti. Tell them they can take him away." Then he drew a fine handkerchief from his belt and added, "Give this to the dumb child. Tell her mother to wipe her lips with it and say 'Your father is saved'." He walked on very slowly, looking straight in front of him. But he heard the cries of joy and he knew when Taty's wife and children ran to join him.

When they were all back in the chariot, Nefertiti was very quiet and far away. Gilukhipa said, "It is beyond words, but I must say that I was never so happy. There was a strange thing. I was leaving Taty when his family rushed in. It seemed to me I heard the little girl calling out 'father'. . . ."

Akhenaten nodded. "I am glad," he said. "And I must thank you, Gilukhipa, for bringing me to your 'idiot'. You have helped me back on to my way. And you, too, Nefertiti, with the touch of your hand." For some time they rode without speaking; then, as the rattling ceased when they turned on to the main street, Akhenaten spoke again —more to himself than to his companions. "Yes. Women are full of their own light. But do they know where our chosen way will lead?"

The months after the forgiveness of Taty were uneventful. The King had the same sense that this was an interlude, a time of waiting, that he had experienced long ago before his father's death.

He and Nefertiti were closer to one another than they had been since Meketaten's death, but still they were uneasy. It appeared that he demanded something which she could not concede. Perhaps because of this it seemed also that her devotion was no longer entirely centred on him, but had shifted to the faith itself. They talked often of the need to spread the teaching, and Nefertiti always urged sending missions through the country to reach the ordinary people. "You have sent men with hammers," she said once. "Can you not send men with the light?"

Akhenaten hung back, although he did send more men and gold to the temples he had founded in Nubia and Amurru. He was preoccupied with his gospel—which he said might do more than a hundred missions to reach men's understanding. His other preoccupation was with the Peace of the Aten. It seemed to him that if he could show that struggles for worldly power were at an end, then everyone would have to see the glory of the god. Sometimes he paced up and down in his garden dreaming of a day when he would call together every sovereign within reach of his embassies in a glorious assembly at which each one of them would dedicate his crown to peace.

Meanwhile, there was a matter nearer home that greatly concerned himself and Nefertiti. Mersure, who was always moving between Akhetaten and Thebes, came back from the old capital after the rebellion claiming to have taken a great part in pacifying Pharaoh's opponents there. He began to visit the Palace frequently, pressing for Merytaten to be promised to his son. There was no doubt that the Princess was very much in love with Smenkhkare, and although her parents would not agree with Queen Tiye's opinion that this "was neither here nor there", they were unwilling to agree to the match in a hurry. It was now almost certain that with Merytaten would go the throne of Egypt.

The King had not grown any fonder of his half-brother. Mersure still kept his wife in their old home at Thebes, and it was known to everybody that in Akhetaten he found solace with Tadukhipa. Akhenaten had allowed the young Mitannian woman to come to Akhetaten because it would have offended against his own teaching not to do so. She was now extraordinarily handsome, and had a reputation for viciousness among those who were not as charitable as they should have been—which included her Aunt Gilukhipa.

As for Smenkhkare, Akhenaten had always been charmed by him. But Nefertiti was doubtful. She had noticed that since the Princess had ceased to be a child and had developed her first passion for this agreeable youth, he had taken to tormenting her when he thought no one of importance was watching him. He would refuse to speak to her, or send her on errands and then disappear. She could not help contrasting this with the loving respect with which Akhenaten had treated her when she was even younger than Merytaten. So she urged that they should wait. After all, there were other grandsons of Amenophis whom Merytaten might find equally pleasing—if, indeed, it were any longer necessary to keep to these royal traditions.

Akhenaten was inclined to agree with her, although he was sure she was unjust to Smenkhkare. After all, the Princess was only twelve years old, no very great age. On the other hand the Queen Mother wrote urging the match, saying that in her opinion Mersure had real influence in Thebes, and that his support would be invaluable in preventing further trouble. It seemed that his mother would never learn what kind of arguments had weight with him. Or was it that she thought he was changing?

Though Akhenaten was saddened by his failure to re-establish the old perfection of his life with Nefertiti, and although all the time he was haunted by his sense that he was waiting for greater events, this period still seemed full of promise. The more important buildings of Akhetaten were now complete. Moreover, the amount of state business that the King had to deal with seemed less—partly, perhaps, because Nakht had become accustomed to taking more decisions himself during the period when Akhenaten had withdrawn from affairs. So now there was more opportunity for him to spend his time as he wished. Quite often he went to Dhutmose's studio, where he met not only his old friends but also a number of foreign visitors. The spreading fame of Akhetaten brought adventurous people, mostly artists, from the northern lands, and even from the lands round the ocean. The talk was very lively, and sometimes it seemed that the spirit of the early days when Akhenaten was Crown Prince had returned.

One of the works that always roused the visitors' admiration was the pair of doors carved for the sick-house. They had been returned to the studio for Dhutmose to add the scenes of the Divine Love. The sculptor had never refused to obey the King's instructions, but with a kind of mild, hardly conscious stubbornness, he left the doors as they were.

But the most famous of all Dhutmose's sculptures, and the one which many foreign artists had heard of even in their own countries, was his head of Nefertiti. It stood on a high shelf in the studio, gazing out over all the company that gathered there. Nefertiti declared it to be more queenly than she was. Dhutmose said that it no longer satisfied him, as in his eyes the Queen was always growing more beautiful. He hoped that before very long she would sit for him again.

When Nefertiti went with him to the studio, Akhenaten often saw Dhutmose watching her face intently. Sometimes he felt sure the sculptor was in love with her, but then again he told himself that he was only interested in her as an artist. He found it difficult to believe that anyone else would dare to be in love with Nefertiti, although he took it for granted that everybody loved her. Nefertiti herself seemed quite unaware of Dhutmose, and Akhenaten never saw her make any response.

It was in the early summer when, as Akhenaten had expected, this period of calm was suddenly shattered. The King, Nakht and chosen members of the court were receiving some distinguished guests in the Palace colonnades overlooking the river. There was the leader of a small Kassite embassy accompanied by a noted poet from Babylon; there was a painter of noble birth from Mycenae, and an important copper merchant, with an interest in gold and ivory carving, from Cyprus. Akhenaten had invited them on this particularly beautiful morning so that they could enjoy the flowering trees on the terrace gardens.

They were looking down on the screen of boughs and blossoms that made an intricate pattern with the masts behind, when Akhenaten's eyes strayed down river and he saw a large vessel approaching, her sail fat with the north wind. The handsome cabin raised behind the sail showed that she belonged to someone of importance.

The Kassite saw the craft also, and, speaking in Akkadian, the diplomatic tongue, said, "Ah, Your Majesty. Some other great embassy arriving. Is there anywhere other than Akhetaten where one can meet such a variety of one's fellow-men—and greet them as brothers?" Akhenaten ignored this piece of edged flattery, while he, with Nakht now at his elbow, watched the ship approach the quay.

A number of unmistakably Egyptian soldiers mustered in the bows; the sail was dropped and smartly gathered in, and gang-planks went down across the strip of mud exposed at this season of the year. A powerfully built man in military dress appeared from the cabin and stepped on to the gangway with the escort of soldiers. Nakht stared intently, then murmured into the King's ear. "My Lord, it is Haremhab. I would recognize that walk of his anywhere—and the way he cuts his hair. He sent no word of his coming."

The King and the vizier made hurried excuses to their guests, putting them in the care of the chief steward. As they left, Akhenaten saw servants approaching with ribboned baskets of fruit, and the music of the group of pretty girls playing near the Palace door seemed particularly sweet and wistful.

Only an hour later, for Haremhab had insisted on the extreme urgency of his mission, a meeting was beginning in a small council room. Ay had joined Nakht in attendance on the King, but Tutu had not answered the summons. Instead, an agitated scribe appeared to report that he could not find his master. Akhenaten confronted his formidable Commander-in-Chief. Two countenances could hardly be more unlike. The King with his long, subtly moulded face, his full lips and hooded eyes that seemed always to shift from things near and particular to things far away and hidden. Haremhab with his firm, rounded face, strong, compressed lips, and eyes that stared steadily from below a grizzled fringe, cut straight and low across his forehead. It was no wonder that communication between them had always been difficult.

Seeing that Haremhab looked stiff and aggressive, Akhenaten resolved to be as informal as the situation allowed. Leaning forward and smiling, he said: "My Lord, you prefer to arrive unannounced?"

"I am here unannounced, Your Majesty, because your servant Tutu intercepts despatches addressed to your person—as well as corresponding secretly with the enemies of Egypt."

"Why do you believe these things?"

"The first because I receive no replies from Your Majesty. The second because his messengers have been intercepted at the frontier. He has been in league with Aziru, telling him that Egypt will not oppose his ambitions."

Ay emitted a wrathful grunt. "Your Majesty, have I not always said—"

Akhenaten silenced him with a gesture, then said, "Commander-in-Chief, you make this sound like treachery. But I regard Aziru as my friend. He has promised to maintain the peace, and I believe that he will do so."

"You will forgive me, Your Majesty, but we have to deal in facts and not in pretty letters that the Amorite may send to have shown to you. He is so far from being your friend that he is undoubtedly in collusion with your greatest enemy—the Hittites. Suppiluliuma is using him to stir all Your Majesty's territories into chaos so that he may pluck one ally after another. Already several cities once loyal to Egypt have surrendered. I sent you news of these things, my Lord Pharaoh, but my words were not allowed to reach you. That is why I have come to Akhetaten, bringing my tongue with me."

"It speaks with authority in its own way, Haremhab. Do not suppose that I can't recognize the ring of worldly authority. I know very well that Egypt has no abler nor more loyal servant. But my loyalty has to look beyond the Two Lands. It has been laid upon me to feel loyalty to all peoples under the sun. You know my teaching, but perhaps you cannot understand where it leads me. I do not care if the cities of the Canaanites withdraw their allegiance. Why should Egypt have power over other lands? My Father created all lands and all men, and it is his will that they should live as he made them. I have not as yet disbanded our armies, but the strength of Egypt is to be used only to make way for the Peace of the Aten."

"My Lord Pharaoh," answered Haremhab, more grimly than before, "only a savage would deny the nobility of your vision. But it is not of this world. I assure you, sire, that there to the north armies are marching. How can we betray our allies? How can I convey to you what manner of men would become their masters? Let me describe the capital of the Hittites, then perhaps you will understand. I am told by men who have seen it that Hattusas is set among mountains harsh as itself. It is defended by walls and towers of solid rock, and with gates hewn into the form of beasts, warriors and hideous gods. There everything is designed for war, with half the young men under arms. In the royal troops every man has a bronze helmet and heavy mail, and many are armed with iron. Set this beside your Akhetaten—flowery, unwalled and with play-boy soldiers who have never seen an arrow coming towards them. This, then, represents the difference between the rule of the Hittites over small peoples and that of Your Majesty's regents. If we do not march to defend our allies, there will not be peace, but a thousand times more blood-shed."

Akhenaten had been listening to the Commander-in-Chief with quick admiration. He noticed how Nakht and Ay both turned in their chairs to see how he would respond.

"My Lord Haremhab, for the first time my heart goes out to you. I did not know you had so much imagination in you." Then, observing that the soldier did not respond, but still fixed him with a military stare, his black eyes gleaming in the shade of his fringe, Akhenaten lolled back in his chair and added: "When peace is established you must leave Memphis for Akhetaten, and help to stiffen my poets here." Ay uttered another of his indignant grunts, while Nakht's lips twitched and straightened again. After a moment Akhenaten leant forward once more and spoke earnestly. "For me the picture you have drawn with such effect has a different meaning. It is because, looking into the future, I see more ambitious kings like Suppiluli-uma, more peoples devoted to war and the conquest of their neighbours like the Hittites, more fearful inventions like that of hardened iron, that I know we must have the Peace of the Aten. Now, while I am still here among you, may be the last occasion offered to men to save themselves. I do not count myself free to evade it."

For the first time Haremhab dropped his eyes. He rubbed the pommel of his dagger with his palm and said in a low voice: "Your Majesty, I wish it could be so."

"And now, to return to Aziru—for, alas, we must always return to Aziru. If cities have opened their gates to him, do we know that they did not do so willingly?"

"Sire, I have brought two men of Samyria in my ship who escaped when a thousand prisoners were put to death. If you wish it, they will tell you what they saw."

At this Nakht intervened, saying, "This may be true, but did not the King of Samyria bring this fate on himself by intriguing with the Assyrians?"

"As I see it he was our ally, and that is enough. An expedition must be sent at once."

Akhenaten stood up, ordered the council to await him, and walked slowly into an adjoining room with a window commanding the river. For the moment his mind held nothing but a general rage against the world to which Haremhab belonged. How I hate it, how I hate it—the words seemed to dance and scream within himself. He struggled to still them, looking out to his right over the Temple and all the buildings of his city so white and fair among their gardens. He pressed his forehead against the stone window-frame. God! God! Why can I not remain inviolate here? The turmoil subsided, and thoughts came back with unwanted clarity. Tutu had misled him. There was war in the northern lands. Something would have to be done.

Now his eyes rested on the river. It was about noon, and the sun was streaming along its course. He saw a clumsy country vessel stacked high with water jars, plump and smooth as eggs, moving slowly downstream. He could just see a man at the steering oar, and children playing in the bows. What do they care about the northern lands and the Hittites? Fortunate people going with the current and thinking only of getting their pots safely to market in Hermopolis. Then, as suddenly as though he had been given an order, he found that his mind was made up. He stayed for a time at the window, but he no longer saw anything of the scene outside. Then he returned to the council room.

As his three eminent servants completed their bows and sat down again, Akhenaten looked at them gently, as though in sympathy with the dismay he knew they would soon feel. "You have been kept waiting," he said, "but in these minutes I have been shown what I should do. I myself must go to meet Suppiluliuma. I will arrange a meeting in some place between our two lands. There I will show him the Peace of the Aten and man's need for it. If he will not understand, disperse his armies, call back Aziru and return all soldiers to their homes, then, my Lord Haremhab, I will allow you to lead my forces to punish these men and bring your own kind of peace to my territories."

"But, Your Majesty, the urgency is very great. It will take months for you to meet the Hittite, and then months again for me to march into Canaan. By then more kings will have fallen, more garrisons been wiped out. Sire, we cannot wait so long." Haremhab's blunt face looked more than ever stubborn and implacable.

"Things are seldom as urgent as soldiers believe once their minds are set on equipping expeditions. But I will agree to this: I will go by ship to Canaan, summoning Suppiluliuma to meet me near Ugarit. Meanwhile you, Haremhab, shall march a sufficient army into Canaan, entrench yourselves, and await my word."

Ay seemed about to make some objection. Akhenaten had always been able to silence his uncle merely by looking at him. "This is what has been decided," he said without emphasis. "And you will see that it will come to pass."

He left the room with his attendants and went straight to the private apartments to find Nefertiti. She was playing lessons with Ankhesenpaten. Between them was a boy doll, almost as large as the princess, which Bak had made for her out of a spare piece of cedar wood. He had painted the face to give that bright, impertinent look of small Egyptian boys, and the princess loved to use the doll as a scapegoat for her own sins and shortcomings.

Akhenaten smiled as he saw the three figures, but he could not resist the touch of regret. "I see you have a brother of a sort, Ankhy. Play with him while you can, for he won't grow up with you."

"He is more clever than Tutankhaten, but I like my cousin better. Cedar Boy is often extremely bad." Tutankhaten came almost daily to play with the Princess, as Merytaten was too old for her and her other sister too young. She regarded him as quite as much her property as the wooden doll.

Nefertiti had been looking anxiously into the King's

face, for she knew of Haremhab's arrival and did not suppose he would have brought good news. She told Ankhesenpaten to teach Cedar Boy how to make the sign for the first syllable of her name, and led Akhenaten over to a couch.

"Yes," he said, without Nefertiti having asked any question. "It is bad, and the worst thing is that Ma'at has been betrayed here in Akhetaten. Tutu. Tutu, whom I have so often defended—and who happens to be a Syrian." He told her everything that had passed at the council, but she heard him almost listlessly until he came to his own decision. Then she stiffened, unsightly tendons rising in her neck.

"Not that, Akhenaten. You cannot mean it. That would be madness."

"I have to go," he said, seeing again the laden boat and the sun shining down the river. "Two Kings, Kings of light and darkness. Two sources of power brought face to face. And you know, as those men did not, that I shall prevail. The Aten must prevail."

"You know the kind of faith I have in you—and it is very great. But this would not be my way."

"I know you would wish me to meet not kings but countless Tatys. But Nefertiti there is not time enough. Mine is the way to reach all hearts. Not only here in Egypt, but in all the lands."

"No time? That is strange. I thought divinity had its own time." Then she went on hastily, "Then there is your health. Will it endure such a great journey?"

"If you will come with me—in spite of your doubts—then my health will suffice."

"I can't come, Akhenaten. There is something I have been keeping from you. I am with child again. We have had so many disappointments—I thought I could shorten this one for you. You know how I have always detested what people call humour. Now I myself am made to be ridiculous. Daughter after daughter. Tragic and ridiculous together . . . tragic for you. . . ." She was laughing weakly and crying at the same time in an hysterical manner very unlike herself.

Akhenaten leant over and took her hand. He fancied that, looking through the transparent shift, he could detect a slight swelling of her belly.

"Perhaps it will not be a disappointment this time, Nefertiti. I shall carry a small hope with me, and that will help to strengthen me. Perhaps it is better that you shouldn't be with me. I shall need Meryre. And then I will take Smenkhkare as my page—he is always attentive and will look after me well. Moreover, I can observe him closely and judge whether he is worthy of our Merytaten." The King went on talking to help Nefertiti to recover herself. But she was crying bitterly now. The tears felt hot and then cool as they dropped on to his hand.

The three Egyptian ships rounded the bluff, and headed in across the bay towards the famous White Harbour of Ugarit. Akhenaten stood outside his cabin with Smenkhkare by his side. For the moment all thought of himself as Pharaoh had left him, and he was a traveller approaching his first great foreign city. At a distance he could distinguish only the high, crenellated walls and the massive gates. Then he could see the extraordinary variety of merchants' houses close-packed round the harbour. As they drew still nearer, he realized that the busy quays of his own capital, and even those of Thebes as he remembered them from his boyhood, were backwaters when compared with this ocean port. It was easy to recognize the native Phoenician vessels with their towering prows and sterns, but only a sea captain could possibly have distinguished the tangle of other boats of every shape and size, colour and rig.

"I am glad we are coming in peace, my Lord," said Smenkhkare. "For that citadel would be hard to capture."

"There are plenty more like it here in Canaan, and in Amurru. And they seem to fall readily enough if they are defended by the allies of Egypt," said Akhenaten, smiling. "What is most wonderful about Ugarit is that peoples from a dozen or more lands live here side by side; each with its own colony. Men who at home would imagine themselves to be enemies, here think only about their common interests. If they can forget war for the sake of riches, surely they can be led to do so for the light of the Aten?''

Akhenaten noticed where a berthing place had been prepared, and where a group of important personages was waiting to receive him. The breeze was just enough to let his ships slide gently in. This seemed a fitting end to an expedition which had gone with perfect smoothness from the start. Akhenaten knew that, although they had been obliged to accept his decision for a meeting with the Hittite monarch, his ministers had been convinced that it could never come to pass. Yet almost at once chance news was brought that Suppiluliuma was in the south in Amurru, the Egyptian messengers reached him without difficulty, and he agreed at once to go to Ugarit. Probably he was curious to meet the Pharaoh who was the subject of talk and fantastic stories at every court. And then, however confident he was in his own power, he must still feel some awe for the traditional supremacy of Egypt.

So it turned out that Akhenaten was preparing to sail almost before Haremhab was ready to march his forces into Canaan. However, all had been timed as carefully as possible. The voyage had been slow but uneventful, and now there was no reason to doubt that Haremhab was obediently encamped a week to the south, while the Hittites were awaiting him somewhere outside the town.

Akhenaten walked down the purple-draped gangway which had been quickly raised from the quayside, to be received by a black-bearded man swathed in purple robes who was bowing in front of him. This was Niqmeda, king of the city state of Ugarit, who took some five minutes to deliver his humble and flowery address of welcome. He said that never in all his dreams had he seen that this divine personage, the great Pharaoh, Lord of the Two Lands and of all territories beyond, would set foot on his harbour walls. That his coming was like the rising of the sun, like a gift of gold. When he had finished his eulogies he announced that his friend the King of the Hittites was encamped behind the city, adding that he too was a glorious luminary, but as the moon to the sun when seen beside Pharaoh. Akhenaten commented very gravely that he had heard that in the past the moon had been much worshipped in Canaan, but he hoped this was no longer so. This he said because he had been assured by Haremhab that Niqmeda had been induced to transfer his tribute to Suppiluliuma. The words had the effect he intended, for Niqmeda appeared a little flustered (he was above all anxious not to have to pay two masters) and passed on at once to his presentation. Servants knelt before Pharaoh with a huge roll of purple cloth and an elegant gold flask of the same dye.

"Great Pharaoh," said Niqmeda, "accept this trifling gift. It may be that in passing through my poor streets your nostrils will be offended by our rotting shellfish. I would wish that Your Majesty and your Great Queen, the glorious Nefertiti, should know the beauty that comes from so much filth, the dye which is our humble pride."

So, rather absurdly, Akhenaten's great mission began. As they drove through Ugarit to the Palace (and it was true that one quarter stank terribly of fish) he admitted to himself that this encounter with a kinglet had no place in the vision which he had cherished of the supreme opposition of peace to war. Every day of the journey he had prayed and meditated and sought to strengthen himself. Now he had to pass the time with a pompous merchant. He had consented to spend only one night as the guest of Niqmeda, while his men prepared a camp adjacent to that of Suppiluliuma. This was a comic interlude like that of the dwarfs and girl tumblers who sometimes interrupted a sacred festival. He allowed himself to enjoy the strangeness of the city.

Across the slopes above the sea-plain, a stream flowed through a shallow valley. On one side the Hittites were encamped, and now the Egyptians were established on the other. Both were small camps, manned only by the royal bodyguards—that had been a part of the agreement —and each was dominated by a conspicuous royal tent.

But in everything else they were unlike, and as Akhenaten looked at them he was reminded of the contrast Haremhab had made between Hattusas and Akhetaten. The Hittites had raised an unsightly bank crowned with stakes round their camp, and their tents were of felted wool, dark and heavy. There were a number of horses inside, and all the soldiers he could see moving about were encased in tunics of scale armour as though they were going into battle. Some of the officers were helmeted. His own soldiers had made a light marching camp enclosed by their shields, and these, with their gleaming panther and antelope skin facings and bright borders, made a gay scalloped wall that looked festive rather than martial. All their tents were white, and his own was charged with the rayed sun in gold. On his orders, his soldiers were not in battle dress, but wearing their usual white loin-cloths, some with coloured cloaks or tunics against the cool winds of Canaan.

Akhenaten looked with satisfaction from one encampment to the other. Here, he felt, was hope set against the ancient fears, life against death—it was the natural expression of all he had intended. And he was pitted against more than that sombre force across the stream. Looking inland to where the mountains lay placid below flat caps of cloud, he could see on a shoulder where five thousand men were waiting, their tents like a little town, and spires of smoke rising among them. This was a section of Suppiluliuma's regular army which had been marched down to support Aziru's ventures, but was now attending the King's command. Then away to the south, somewhere on the approaches to Byblos, were the forces of Aziru himself and of Haremhab. They, too, were waiting, immobilized, pinning one another down, waiting for the encounter of the great kings. Akhenaten was able to see the whole map, like one sketched by generals on the sand; he could feel the tension, the balance of forces. And he knew with a sudden ecstasy that he was alone against all the rest, whether they were Amorite, Hittite or Egyptian, against all that muscle and courage, that weight of bronze, those thousands of restive arrows and spears, those balanced swords and battle-axes.

As he went back to his tent from the solitary tree where he had been standing, he noticed a little party setting out from the Hittite camp. They were made conspicuous by a young, good-looking man riding on horseback—a rare accomplishment. There were also two men with spears and nets and several dogs. Evidently they were going hunting. Akhenaten asked one of his captains if he knew who the young rider might be. "Yes, Your Majesty. We learnt last night from one of their guards who came over to practise his Egyptian. He is King Suppiluliuma's son— already a hardened soldier. They say his father thinks the world of him."

Akhenaten sent for Meryre, the only man of rank whom he had brought with him, and instructed him to arrange an audience with Suppiluliuma. He was to explain to him all that was most important in the teaching of the Aten and to describe the perfection of life at Akhetaten. Then he was to present the Hittite with a massive gold *ankh*, as a sign of peace and life, and invite him to come to Pharaoh's tent at noon. "You can say," he added, "that Pharaoh has crossed the ocean to meet him, and expects that he will agree to cross a stream to meet Pharaoh. And if he is apprehensive of treachery—as soldiers, I believe, always are—you can suggest that if he will look at this camp he can see that it is as harmless as a sanctuary."

A little later Akhenaten watched the High Priest, accompanied by two officers and a young priest carrying the *ankh*, making his way across to the other camp. His slow pace, the way he hunched his shoulders and looked at the ground, showed the reluctance with which he was carrying out his mission. The King turned to Smenkhkare, who as usual was attending him, and said, "He will accomplish nothing. He has no faith. Only I have faith, Smenkhkare, only I."

"Do not say that, my lord," he replied, gripping Akhenaten's forearm and looking directly into his eyes. "There is at least one other who is with you in everything."

When Meryre returned, he told the King that Suppiluliuma had agreed at once to come to him, and had sent his royal assurances that he had no thought of enmity for his royal brother, the King of Egypt.

"But did he listen to the teaching? Did he show any understanding?"

"My lord, he listened—for a time. And he showed proper respect to me as High Priest of the Aten. But he is a soldier, a commander, a power-seeker. He has a shrine set up there in his tent, with an idol bristling with weapons. Some god of war. You will understand that the atmosphere was not congenial to our teaching. I am not fluent in Akkadian. . . ."

"I can imagine the scene," said Akhenaten grimly. "And what did he say when you had finished speaking?"

"He said it was a pretty world I had painted, but that it seemed to him a world for artists, saintly priests, women, and boys brought up in pampered courts. He said that every ruler who wanted fame and to be called great must be a conqueror, and that peace made men soft. He said that any people that was not led forward would be pushed back. Finally, he insisted that the life of the Aten might be lived in a haven on the banks of the Nile, but not in what he called the real world. I am sorry, Your Majesty. I did not do well."

"Always the same words. They spill out as monotonously as water from a shaduf. I have come a long way to discover that a man brought up in a stony stronghold among mountain barbarians turns the same phrases as men nurtured in the luxuries of Thebes or Memphis."

At Akhetaten the King often appeared in the casque crown, for it represented, he said, the peaceful might of the Aten. But now he chose to wear a soft kerchief over his hair, held in place by the simple diadem of golden ureus. The bolt of purple cloth from Ugarit was draped over his folding chair, and a bowl of late-flowering lilies filled the tent with their sweet smell. Behind the flowers was an Aten shrine. Meryre and Smenkhkare were in attendance, but there was not a weapon in sight—Akhenaten had told his page to remove even the ornamental dagger that he usually wore.

The King sat in silence, trying to keep his body relaxed

but breathing rather fast. He could hear the commands of his captains ringing through the camp, and knew that his soldiers would be making a guard of honour for the Hittite king. Then there were heavy steps on the stony ground outside, and a faint rattling and tapping of metal on metal. Akhenaten smiled for an instant.

Servants standing outside raised the tent flaps and Suppiluliuma entered. He had to stoop, for he was a moderately tall man and he was wearing a pointed bronze helmet; behind him followed two of his officers. All three men were dressed in long, tight-fitting mail tunics with fish-like scales of polished bronze, and were belted with daggers and short battle-axes, the butts spiked like brazen coxcombs. The Hittite monarch had a huge, fleshy nose which seemed to Akhenaten to project beneath his helmet like a battering ram or some other implacable instrument of war.

The two greatest of kings stood facing one another, exchanging correct formalities, each seeking his own estimate of the other. Suppiluliuma was square and muscular in every part, with shoulders like those of a good ox. His wrists, where they projected from the mail sleeve, were sown with short, brown hairs. Akhenaten was exaggerating all that was feminine in his appearance, twisting his sloping shoulders and very slightly thrusting forward his rounded hips. His arms and legs were as devoid of muscle as they were of hair. His long, white loin-cloth with its elegant pleating seemed to be flaunted against the Hittite armour.

Suppiluliuma ended his address by saying that he was honoured to welcome the glorious Pharaoh of Egypt to his shores. Akhenaten recognized this as a provocative claim to the overlordship of Ugarit and the Canaanite lands, but he had no wish to take up the challenge. He did, however, allow his eyes to slide over his opponent's helmet and mail while begging him to be seated and saying that he hoped that, clad as he was, he would not feel oppressed by the warmth of the tent. The Hittite declared himself a stranger to fatigue.

"Although, unlike yourself, I am not strong-bodied," Akhenaten resumed, watching Suppiluliuma over a cup of wine, "I have made the longer journey to this meeting-place between our territories. I have come because, although I was reluctant to believe it, I have been convinced that Aziru the Amorite has broken his promises to me and is marching against peaceful cities that are under my protection. I am convinced that he did so as your agent. I know, too, that you caused the murder of our royal brother Tushratta. I will say to you frankly, as I live under Ma'at, that I set no store by vassals and foreign dominion. Egypt is rich, and has no need of tribute. I would gladly relinquish my title to all lands beyond her ancient frontiers, leaving their peoples to live as free neighbours under the sun. But war is abominable to the god who has made all lands and all living things within them. He made an exquisite thing in man—can you not see, Suppiluliuma, what sacrilege there is in smashing these fragile vessels filled with divine wonder and delight?"

"Men must all die, Pharaoh."

"Yes, when like a plant they have bloomed and seeded. But would you set your horses in the flower beds? Because my Father has shown me the truth in these matters, I have proclaimed the Peace of the Aten. You are in bronze, my royal brother, I am in linen, but the god has given strength to his chosen son. Send orders to Aziru to return to his kingdom. Disband your army encamped there above us, tell them to strike their tents and return to their farms and flocks. I will send the same message to Haremhab. Then we can join together in the dawn of an everlasting peace. That is what I have crossed the ocean to say to you—and to demand of you, not in the name of Egypt but of my Father."

"Pharaoh, inheritor of a famous throne. I have already heard your High Priest and told him what I think of this teaching. It was not the first time I had heard such words. When I was a youth my mother would speak to me in this way, begging me not to campaign but to stay with her within the walls of Hattusas. Then lately my queen has used the same pleas when I took our son into battle. But I am a man, a king, a Hittite; I cannot listen to women. I have doubled my kingdom, made it known and feared.

My son will inherit a throne as great as yours. Yet I do not seek war with Egypt. I came here to this meeting so that we could agree on a line to be drawn between my rising power and your ancient one. But now that I have seen you, Akhenaten of Egypt, I will speak here in this tent, that has few ears and no mouths, as I would not outside. I am not surprised that you are a father only of daughters. Perhaps there is something in the water of the Nile that has thinned your blood. Perhaps some weakening spirit has taken possession of you. I do not know, but I can see that you are not one who can contend for power in the world of grown men. Send for Haremhab, a soldier whom I can understand, give him your royal command to treat with me, then return in peace to your Akhetaten, to your gardens and temples and lovely daughter of the moon."

Akhenaten had closed his eyes, and he was rocking on his feet. Smenkhkare brought him more wine, and, as he sat down, wiped the beads of sweat from his forehead.

"As a man of peace I have turned my hot anger into a cold one—more than that even prayer cannot accomplish for me. I, and my Great Queen Nefertiti also, know presumption such as yours too well. For us it is the very spirit of common minds rooted in unchanging error. Men who have passed directly from childish playing at soldiers to playing with the lives of others, who have made no break between the greeds of childhood and the greed of power and possessions, have also passed from the raw ignorance of youth to the blind conceit of age. Such poisonous green apples accuse us of lack of ripeness. My Lord Meryre has told me that you said the teaching of the Aten was fit only for women, artists, priests and delicate young men. I would reply that women bear life, artists create beauty, priests support the divine spirit, and young men finely reared have some opportunity to reflect on all these things.

"And it is in these things that men are nearest to the god. In fighting and power-lust they are more like beasts. I am told that at Hattusas you have stone lions at your gates. Why should men emulate lions? They may have a vain pride like the kings who admire them, but I have never heard that they do more than make an ugly din and grow an excess of hair on their necks.

"And even on your own terms, Suppiluliuma, you are utterly misled. You say you want glory for the Hittites, but war and aggrandizement is a destroyer of states. What is left of Sumer and Akkad, how much glory has Babylon? We remember them best for the heritage of their wise men, and for the written language that allows the rulers of the peoples to speak to one another. Warlike states perish through war. And this will worsen. Look at that axe of yours: what a weight of bronze we can now command. And your dagger with its blade of this deadly metal which your merchants are spreading among the armies. Then think of the strength and speed of the six-spoked chariots; the distance that an arrow can be made to travel from our sinewed bows. From one generation to the next these weapons grow more frightful, the carnage in battle greater. If we do not listen to my Father, embrace the Peace of the Aten, we shall destroy ourselves. And even now, if you continue as you have begun, I can see the time when the kingdom of the Hittites will be forgotten, when Hattusas will be overgrown with thorns, while Egyptians live in peace beside their river.

"So, my brother, briefly King of the Hittites, I say to you again, disband your army, recall the Amorite, turn to the Aten."

Akhenaten delivered this speech with passion, in a resonant voice, his extraordinary eyes never for a moment leaving his opponent's face. Suppiluliuma had at first seemed astonished, then angry. Now he looked up, for he had not cared to hold Akhenaten's gaze, and said in a manner that had lost its arrogance: "I know now that the blood of the conquering Tuthmosis is still in your body even if you wish to undo all that he did for Egypt. But, Pharaoh, you are mad if you think that you can turn me from my path with words. I, too, have a god, and he is in my weapons. There is my proof, my justification, my final answer. What can you do?"

Akhenaten felt emptied out, and into the emptiness surged a gust of despair. He was like a man in a glaring desert, surrounded by the white bones of an ancient battle. "What can you do?"—the question danced in the desert sky. He must not be seen to falter. He took up his wine cup and stared down into it. The desert vanished into this dark pool, and then, as though reflected from a mirror, he saw a picture. It in no way resembled the visitations of the god, but was rather as though he had glimpsed a real scene, then closed his eyes and carried it in his memory. Yet with it his sense of power returned. He stood up, faced the Aten shrine and lifted his arms slowly, as though straining against a great weight. His back was turned to the Hittite.

"Suppiluliuma," he said in a soft voice that rustled round the tent. "Suppiluliuma, you have mocked me as a father of daughters, have boasted of the coming greatness of your son. You said I could not bar your way with words —but the words which I spoke were the words of the god. Now hear me again. Your son even now is far weaker than my smallest princess. He is as helpless as a mouse in the nest with its little groping hands. He is not thinking of glory but of his mother, of the poor Queen who cares for his life and his love. . . ." Suppiluliuma looked shaken, and his officers, who did not understand Akkadian, laid their hands on their daggers as though to defend him. Then he drew himself up and said to Meryre, "High Priest of the Aten. I think your master needs your care. We will leave you."

He stepped abruptly out of the tent, but even while he still held the cloth, those inside could see his grip tighten while he took a half step back. Akhenaten moved quickly forward to stand beside him. It seemed wonderfully fresh outside, the bay was marbled with turquoise and on the mountains the cloud cap had thinned to a few ribbons. At a distance, moving slowly down the track leading from the foothills, were two men carrying something between them. Then both kings saw that another man, who had evidently been first to the Hittite camp, was running up from the stream.

"Tell them to bring the prince to me here," said Akhenaten, then returned to his seat. So great was the concentration of authority in him now that he no longer seemed to be observing events from outside, but causing them to happen. Everything took place according to the story in his own mind. He knew that Smenkhkare had come up close behind his chair and rested his hand on his shoulder, that was the only external happening.

A man's voice, uneven with panting, could be heard outside the entrance. Akhenaten could not understand why he did not follow the Hittite words, as he knew what was being spoken. Then Suppiluliuma came in and said what it seemed to him he had already heard. "He was after a wounded deer. He put his horse at a little ravine, and it seems his dagger caught in a branch and threw him. He struck his head on the rocks." When he had spoken he stood as rigid as a statue, and all waited in silence for what had to happen.

The two bearers pushed their way in, the rear one still with a dead gazelle slung across his back, the head dangling pitifully and blood on the nostrils. They had made a rough litter with a cloak wound over hunting spears, and on it the Prince was lying with a cloth shielding his face.

"Lay him down in front of me," said Akhenaten, and as the men did so he leant down and turned back the cloth and observed him closely. The young man's handsome face was quite unmarked, but a large swelling showed through his hair. He opened his eyes, then at once emitted a terrible cry, followed by sobbing whimpers. His father knelt beside him, awkwardly. Then the prince babbled something while continuing to sob. Suppiluliuma's expression changed; before he had appeared dismayed or even disgusted, but his face puckered and tears seemed to spurt on to his big nose. With a sudden, curiously pathetic movement, he took off his helmet, now so plainly absurd, and looked up at Akhenaten. "He says he cannot see . . . that he is quite blind, my Lord Pharaoh."

Akhenaten nodded. "He is as I said, more helpless than a new-born mouse." There was something in the repeated mention of this little creature that seemed shocking to those who understood it. The Prince contrived to roll over on to his face, muttering a few words. "He is calling on his mother?" Akhenaten said. "He has forgotten distance."

He knew that everyone was waiting for him to make the drama roll forward again, yet he delayed it with a kind of cruelty. "Cover him with the fur robe from my bed, Smenkhkare. He will be glad of a second darkness." Then, very deliberately he took another drink of wine before turning to Suppiluliuma, who was still kneeling before him, the muffled form of the Prince lying between them.

"You understand now that the words of the god are powerful, just as his eye is all-seeing? There are tears on your face, Suppiluliuma, yet your son is no more than blinded. You must have caused a thousand deaths, ten thousand, without a single drop of this salt water. Is it that you do not care about other men's sons? Or is it that you cannot picture anguish until it is there before you?"

The Hittite shook his head dully. "It is terrible to see, my Lord Pharaoh. And my ambitions are blinded with him. Tell me what I should do."

"It is not for you to do anything, but for the god. The god through his chosen son. The Prince is in darkness; do you now see the light?"

Again Suppiluliuma shook his head, but he stared up at Akhenaten. "I can feel the power that is in you, Pharaoh," he said submissively.

"Then if you will be obedient to my Father's word, accept the Peace of the Aten, I will open your son's eyes so that he may see light, and then a second light, and, when the time comes, rule peacefully over his own land, the mountain land of Hattusas."

In silence Suppiluliuma unlatched his belt, handing it with its dangling weapons across the prince's body. "There is my promise," he said.

Akhenaten rose, and no one who saw him at that moment could deny his peculiar grace. He spoke softly to Meryre, then said, "We two, the Pharaoh of Egypt and his High Priest, will show ourselves humble servants of the Aten. We will expose this death-dealing Prince to his life-giving rays, begging the sole god of the lands to open his eyes." They picked up the litter, quite unaware of any weight, and carried it out into the sunlight, all the rest following behind. Meryre stationed himself at the Prince's head, Akhenaten at his feet. Then abruptly Pharaoh snatched back the fur robe and struck the exposed face on both temples, while the High Priest cried in the loud voice that he used in the great Temple Court at Akhetaten: "Hail to the Living Aten." Deftly Akhenaten took the Prince's hands and pulled him to his feet, saying, "Look and you shall see my face."

For a moment the two men stood almost touching, then the prince uttered a groan and said, "Eyes! Eyes! Whose are those eyes?" Suppiluliuma ran forward and supported him with a kind of tenderness. "Tell him to douse his head in the stream; then while he is kneeling there to give thanks to the Aten." It was only now, when Akhenaten spoke in his ordinary voice, that all those who had been involved in the drama realized at what a pitch it had been played. Once again leaning on Smenkhkare, the King went back into his tent.

When Akhenaten woke from a sleep, the sun was so low that he could see the full silhouette of the guard standing outside. It was very quiet, and when he raised himself he found that only Smenkhkare was with him. The youth came over and prostrated himself before the bed, kissing the ground. Then, still bowed down, he said, "Dear lord, Divine Pharaoh, let me worship you. I do not deserve the joy of having witnessed what you have done.. Except that I have always had faith. I have known the godhead in you even when others doubted it. Yes, when others more fortunate wavered, I have known you always as Son of the Sun."

Shadows advanced up the tent, and Meryre and the captain of the royal guard came in. "You have woken at the right hour, Your Majesty," Meryre said when they had made their obeisance. He was flushed and excited, and seemed to have forgotten the deportment of a High Priest. "While you slept we have been to the Hittite camp, seeing that all your commands were carried out. An officer has gone to the army with orders that they march northward at dawn tomorrow, and that every man shall return to his home. I myself read the message which the King's scribe wrote to Aziru telling him to end his campaign and withdraw to his kingdom. And with my own hands I set up an Aten shrine in place of the idol—which the captain has taken away and smashed with hammers. Now, my lord, with your consent, I will get out my brush and write to Haremhab. We should find him back in Memphis before us, not one of his soldiers having drawn a sword or bow. Your Majesty, how can we rejoice enough?"

Soon Niqmeda sought an audience, and poured out tributes to the divine Pharaoh's miraculous achievements and his own rejoicing at the prospects of peace. Ugarit, he said, was in microcosm what the whole world would now become—a pattern of prosperous neighbours. After the kinglet had been dismissed, Akhenaten said, "Peace will indeed be good for his trade, but that man is so worldly, so used to the tricks of merchants, that he has no more faith in the Peace of the Aten than in the sweet waters of a mirage."

As the sun set Akhenaten and Meryre ate and drank together, with Smenkhkare waiting on them with sedulous attention. They talked of the past, of every step forward that they had taken towards this triumph of the Aten. They even ventured to recall the dark days of Meketaten's death when, as they said, it had seemed that the sun was eclipsed. From time to time, but not too often, Smenkhkare intervened with a few words of wonder and praise. At last, when the lamps were beginning to dance and dazzle in his eyes, the King pulled his page down beside him and said that they would announce his marriage to the Princess Merytaten as soon as they saw her again.

The next morning, when Akhenaten and Meryre went out, heavy-headed but still exalted, to deliver the sunrise prayer, they found that all the dark tents on the ridge above had gone, and that the first columns of men were already moving northward. "This morning," the King said, "there is no need for our prayer. For today that sight will be feast enough for my Father as he stands on the horizon. Let us wait until the first rays touch them as they march away."

He stood looking up towards the hills, his face full of

triumph. The sun rose over the sea, and in its clear light the grey lines took particular shape. He could distinguish chariots and foot soldiers, catch specks of colour.

Then, just as he was about to turn away, the columns halted. Tiny figures, presumably officers, were running between them. Some hitch, he thought, perhaps some trouble with the baggage trains—he knew so little of the affairs of armies. But then he noticed that a small group of men was coming fast down the hillside. Meryre moved closer beside him, but they did not speak for several minutes.

"It is Suppiluliuma," said Akhenaten. "I can recognize his helmet."

"Probably he is coming to take his leave of you. Or perhaps he is simply returning to his camp and will not march with his army." Both explanations were reasonable, and yet neither could believe in them.

Suppiluliuma had officers and guards with him, and a man with a sweaty, grimy face and torn shoes. The Hittite king crossed the stream and came straight up to Akhenaten. It seemed as though he expected to find him standing there.

"Now I know the value of your promise, divine Pharaoh." As he spoke, his own words fed Suppiluliuma's anger so that he reddened and became almost inarticulate. "Common traitor, rather. Give me ungodly men. You speak of truth with your eyes turned up to the heavens. And all the time you are plotting to outwit me. Does your god then not believe in truth for Hittites and strangers?"

Had he studied to do it, he could not have found more appalling words. Akhenaten took hold of Meryre's arm. He was shaking violently and could not speak. Meryre said quietly, "Sire, His Majesty has no knowledge of any treachery. He does not know what has happened, or why your promised withdrawal has been halted."

"Does not know? Then he is childish, is not in command. This man has come from the south," the Hittite pointed at the sweaty traveller. "He brings word from Aziru that while he was waiting peacefully for the outcome of our meeting, losing easy chances of victory, your general

Haremhab attacked him. He fell treacherously on one of his battalions, killing scores of Amorites before they could pick up their arms. Against such aggression, Aziru could not fail to fight back. He says he is outnumbered two to one, and I am sending my army to his help. If the Egyptian Pharaoh is not in command of the Egyptian general, then there is nothing more to be done here."

"Wait, I beg you to wait." Akhenaten was still trembling, and his voice sounded as though he were suffocating. "There has been some mistake. Or some small provocation, perhaps. A messenger is already on his way to the general Haremhab with my order for his immediate return to Egypt. All can be put right if you will only wait."

"How can I wait? These treacheries began many days ago. Perhaps by now Aziru is holding out desperately, waiting for reinforcements. You, Pharaoh, may be able to forget and betray your allies. I cannot."

"Suppiluliuma," said Akhenaten huskily, "I will accept your insults because the greatest things are now threatened by the meanest. You and I have power not only over our peoples, and all peoples, but over those not yet born. Yesterday, in the light of the god, you made a solemn pledge of peace. And present peace would be a father of future peace, just as we are fathers of our sons. All this you would sacrifice to what may well be nothing but error, and which at worst involves the folly of a petty king and a general nervous in a foreign land. Hold back your army, and I, Pharaoh of Egypt, will remain here as your hostage."

Suppiluliuma gave Akhenaten a look which showed the return of some half-comprehending admiration. "It is too late, Pharaoh," he said. "Can't you hear it is too late?" Carried very faintly on a landward breeze came the sound of trumpets. They looked towards the slopes and saw that once again the columns were marching. But now it was towards the south, and their standards were raised.

"We will send messengers," said Akhenaten. "We will send more messengers." Meryre helped him back to his tent.

Yet at noon it was a messenger who came to him. He brought a written despatch from Haremhab. It said that the general had held absolutely to their agreement, keeping his men within their entrenchments, making no threat to Aziru. But it had been his duty to send out reconnaissance parties. They had brought back reports, many reports, that Aziru was moving his forces to places of advantage where they could entrap the Egyptians, and advance against Byblos. Moreover, one party had vanished, and he had reliable information that it had been ambushed, the men tortured and put to death. For the safety of his troops he had therefore been forced to go out against Aziru. Fighting was in progress, and he was confident of victory.

The disaster was so complete and irrevocable that Akhenaten was stunned. So much force had already poured from him in the struggle with Suppiluliuma, and now that his joy was gone there was only emptiness. He was like a man whose Ka has left him and gone far away. He sat sagging and speechless in his tent, ignoring his companions and their attempts to reach him.

He tortured himself by imagining Haremhab taking the fatal decision. News had soon reached them that the supposed ambush had never taken place, but had been composed of lies, nervousness and the expectation of bad faith. If only he could have been there!

They do what they are commanded not to do, these soldiers, and then cry: "Look what has happened—it is as I said, war is inevitable." He began to build up such rage against his Commander-in-Chief that he thought of seizing him, striking him, ordering his execution. I have the will to do wrong and not the strength nor the means. This is what it is to be the divine Pharaoh. And yet I did prevail. I did prevail.

The voyage back was beset with troubles. First the wind veered and they had to take refuge in Cyprus, where they were held for a week in a miserable little port. Then a storm struck them when they were halfway between the island and the Delta. They were blown almost as far as Gaza and had to beat slowly westward again.

By now the three vessels were separated, and when at
last the King's ship reached the longed-for entry to the
Bubastic branch of the Nile it was alone and short of
provisions. Even now the extraordinary ill-luck persisted.
The dependable north wind failed, and the Delta was
wrapped in mists after a heavy rainfall. The weary crew
had to row for two days through the low, shrouded landscape. They saw nothing but reed-beds, occasional poor
fields and vineyards, and here and there a small, abandoned temple of one of the old gods of these northern
nomes, already made ruinous by stone-robbers and overgrown with weeds.

During the greater part of this miserable voyage Akhenaten remained on his couch. All through the storm he was
sick, and even afterwards could not eat the unsavoury food.
Smenkhkare was always trying to wait on him and to say
things he supposed the King would like. In particular he
insisted on the greatness of his victory over Suppululiuma,
and its proof of his divine power. Usually the King listened
silently to this, and seemed glad to accept it. Then one day
he turned on the young man and shouted: "Do you think
I am like one of those women who is always demanding
admiration for her hair or her eyes or her breasts—only
that I demand it for my divinity? You had better be silent.
You understand even less than the others. . . ." Then later
he sent for him and said that he was grateful for Smenkhkare's understanding and love.

But in spite of his grief, his feeling of betrayal and of
anger against Haremhab that still sometimes seized him
like a pain, slowly Akhenaten began to return to himself.
He longed to be back in Akhetaten, to be again within its
protective bounds and among his own people. Perhaps after
all he had been deluded into believing that he must go out
to challenge the world for the Peace of the Aten. He told
himself that when he had listened to the god in his own
tranquillity he had not doubted that the light was to
spread outwards from Akhetaten. Now he must give the
rest of his life to bringing this to pass.

As the King's strength and power ebbed back, he found
he was thinking more and more often of the child that

must have been born while he was away. Was it at last a son? What had been no more than a small hope, grew day by day into a conviction. He told himself it might not be so, and yet he could not doubt it. By the time that, to the delight of everyone on the ship, they could look out on to the familiar banks of the river, Akhenaten believed that he had seen Nefertiti with a male child in her arms. It seemed as clear as the picture of the Prince's fall that he had seen in his wine cup.

In his eagerness to be back, he gave orders that they should sail straight past Memphis without declaring themselves. He spent much of each of these last days on deck under an awning. Sometimes he talked softly with Meryre, and occasionally consented to play a game of draughts with his page. But inwardly he was waiting for the appearance of each riverside temple, each fort or town, which marked the stages back to Akhetaten.

X

NEWS of the King's return had spread through the city. Although no one knew just what had happened at Ugarit, there were rumours of some great marvel that had taken place there. Yet at the same time it was being said that Haremhab was fighting in Canaan. Not many people understood enough to care whether things had gone well or badly: the great thing was that the King had come back. At Akhetaten he was generally held in affection as well as worshipped, and when word came of the ship's approach, everyone who could turned out to welcome him.

Akhenaten was greatly stirred when he saw the people massed along the river bank. As he stepped ashore there was a tremendous hail of greeting and the bank of faces swayed and wavered. Yes, it was true that he should never have left the Horizon of the Aten. This was where he belonged, and where the god intended him to complete his work.

Nakht was on the quay, with the Chancellor, Ay and other members of the court. In another group that quickly surged forward were Dhutmose and Bak and many of his friends. Almost with his first words he asked the Vizier where the Queen was. In his imagination he had seen her waiting for him with their son in her arms.

"She has not long been up since her confinement. She thought it better to receive you at the Palace," Nakht replied.

"I had feared she might be ill," Akhenaten said, but did not ask any further question.

He was carried up through the terrace gardens in an open litter. He responded with real emotion to the familiar cries of *Life! Prosperity! Health!* that followed him all the way. It seemed to him that they had never before had so much meaning in them, or been uttered with such sincerity and love.

Nefertiti was waiting for him at the Palace entrance,

with her daughters and Lasia just behind. She was wearing her close-fitting royal headdress, and the clear perfection of her face and shoulders was exposed against the dark doorway. She appeared poised against his coming as though against a strong wind.

As he stepped down from the litter, with a touching hesitation she made the correct obeisance, then ran forward to embrace him. He opened his arms, feeling that all was well. The girls came to demand their share of the hugging, and for a few minutes they were like an ordinary family when the man has returned home. Then with great eagerness Akhenaten swept Nefertiti into his working-room and stood with her below the golden sun on the wall.

"Bring him to me here so that we can first look at him together below the rays of the Aten," he said, scrutinizing her face and smiling happily.

"My dearest, has nobody told you? I have borne you a daughter." Nefertiti spoke with absolute simplicity, and without apparent fear, defiance or wish to appeal. Akhenaten could see that she had suffered to attain this state; she made him think of a piece of the finest linen that had been hammered on the washing block until it was cobweb-fine and pliable. Yet he did nothing to check the groan that seemed to be wrung from him. And he left Nefertiti alone as he walked stiffly over to his official chair. His head felt dull and heavy, and he supported it on his hand.

"I should have known that this, too, would be denied me. What have I done? What have I failed to do?" He looked at her standing there before the gold and lapis, straight, pale and delicate. He had walked away from her and yet she did not appear forlorn. How quickly Nefertiti recovers her figure after childbirth, he thought to himself inconsequentially. Then, seeing how tranquil she seemed, although he knew very well it did not mean indifference, he felt a great desire to hurt her. "Is it I who have failed?" he said. "Or is it because you no longer worship as you did? Because you do not give what a king can ask of his queen?"

"I do not know, my Lord. These mysteries are beyond me. I only know that I wanted a son with all my being—

and for your sake, Akhenaten. I made daily prayers and offerings. I stooped to foolish feminine devices—playing often with Tutankhaten, and going to Gilukhipa's sick-house to handle the boy babies. Every day I exposed my body in the sunlight. Then, rather before her time, the little girl was born." Her head was drooping now, and Akhenaten felt a kind of pity, and yet he said, "You did all these things. Right things and foolish things. But had you true faith in me? And through me in my Father?"

"My Lord Pharaoh," she replied, still gently, "I cannot tell if my faith is what you demand or what it should be. But I believe in your greatness, your teaching, your power to save the world."

Akhenaten was ashamed. Why had he gone back over these arguments, tormenting both of them, and so soon after his joyous return? "Oh, Nefertiti. To think of the per-fection we have known together! Nothing has happened, and yet we cannot meet. We are like a couple with the Love Feast spread between us. We can see the wine, the delicacies, and know how sweet it would be to sit down to eat together. But we can't move forward. We are tied as though we were in a dream."

"And you have no son, and I think will never have one now. Do you wish to see your daughter, Akhenaten?" He shook his head.

After this the King and Queen lived together in a muted fashion which each felt came from the other. Akhenaten was seldom inconsiderate, and he refrained from further reproaches. They were brought together mainly as parents, and in their ritual life at the Temple. But although these shared responsibilities sometimes allowed them satis-faction and a fleeting awareness of one another, their relationship was worsening. Akhenaten became more obsessed with the belief that Nefertiti was depriving him of a source of power that she had given in the past and was now withholding. The same belief made him turn instead towards Smenkhkare.

It was not only because Smenkhkare had never lost an opportunity to insist on his faith in the King's divinity and his unique power as Son of the Sun, but also because he had witnessed the triumph over Suppiluliuma and shared the joyful celebration which had followed. In Akhetaten, too, it was Smenkhkare more than anyone else who spread the story of the curing of the Hittite prince and the submission of his father. He made it clear that if the Peace of the Aten had been delayed it was entirely due to the war-minded obstinacy and disobedience of Haremhab.

The whole court was exalted by the Ugarit story, and by the time it reached the rest of the city it was being said that the prince had been raised from the dead. Some insisted that when Suppiluliuma called back his army and sent it against the Egyptians, the sun had been darkened for an hour. Among the courtiers and the King's friends, only Ay realized how complete the final failure had been. Like the rest he saw that the outcome would have been quite different if Haremhab had behaved with restraint, but then as a soldier he had never in his heart believed in the possibility of lasting peace between the peoples. As he insisted again and again in private to Tey, "War could only have been a matter of time."

Almost everyone else at Akhetaten was prepared to trust that the Peace of the Aten would begin when Haremhab returned to Egypt. The King had sent an absolute order to his Commander-in-Chief to disengage at once and withdraw his army. He instructed Nakht and the Chancellor that whatever happened nothing was to be paid from the royal treasury for the despatch of further expeditions. There was one personal matter that made all thought of what had taken place in the north even more hateful to Akhenaten. A reliable report had been received that Tutu had fled to join Aziru, and was now claiming the reward for his good services.

The King made up his mind to end all immediate involvement with his neighbours, old allies and supposed enemies alike. He declared that so far as he was concerned Egypt was now restored to her ancient frontiers, and that if Egyptian sway was to continue further afield, it would be through missions of goodwill that could help to prepare the way for the spread of his teaching.

It was inevitable that as soon as was decently possible

after the King's return, the question of Merytaten's marriage would be raised once more. Mersure arrived from Thebes, and at once sought an audience. First he told the King at some length of the success he had had in keeping the peace in the old capital, and winning over many of the disaffected nobles. He made it clear that he was the leader of an influential group, many of them the sons of men killed as a result of the uprising, which was now controlling affairs in Thebes. As he built up this picture of himself, Akhenaten watched him closely, wondering whether what he said was true, yet hardly listening to his actual words. He disliked the man's quick eyes and his studied, unfeeling movements.

Mersure changed his manner, becoming suddenly more intimate. He said, "All this, and my ability to be of service to you, make me the more glad at the good news Smenkhkare has told me. I mean the promise you gave him at Ugarit that his marriage with the Princess Merytaten should not be delayed much longer. My son feels his lack of merit so strongly that he has left it to me to urge his case. He says that your wishes are all that are of importance to him. But I am not so patient, dear brother. It seems plain to me that our children should be given to one another very soon, so that all Egypt may see that the succession is assured."

"Then you have stood the situation on its head, Mersure. If I am in favour of this marriage it is because of the love and good opinion I have for your son. The reasons you have advanced carry no weight with me."

"Yet there is another thing that surely must. Isn't it true that here in Akhetaten young people are encouraged to marry for love?" Mersure gave one of his flat laughs. "Your eldest daughter has an open nature. I spoke to her more than once in your absence, and she did not try to hide from me how eager she is to become Smenkhkare's wife."

"Merytaten has grown up under Ma'at, and so does not attempt to conceal the truth. Her love must count very much with us; that also is true. But there is no need, my Lord Mersure, for you to come here with pleas and arguments. Indeed, if anything would turn me from this match it would be your urging it. But my promise has already been given to Smenkhkare, and it is only a question now of agreeing with the Queen Nefertiti how soon it can take place."

Nefertiti was in fact still uneasy about Smenkhkare, but it was only too evident to her that Akhenaten's estimate of him had soared, and that his mind was made up. Merytaten herself began to lay siege to her feelings to win consent for an early marriage. She told her mother that she knew Smenkhkare might be a capricious husband, but that this would make no difference to her love. All she wanted was to be with him and to bear him children. For a time Nefertiti hesitated, thinking that to give her full blessing and take part in the festivities would be an offence against Ma'at. But in the end she gave way, and even persuaded herself that her judgment of the young man might be quite wrong.

As soon as Queen Tiye heard that the marriage was to take place she announced that not only would she come for the occasion, but that she would come to live in her house at Akhetaten for a long time—or perhaps for good. Akhenaten was overjoyed when he read her letter, for he felt that with his mother near at hand and Smenkhkare drawn into his family circle, his estrangement from Nefertiti would be made tolerable. After what he now brooded over as his betrayals, it seemed to him that he could count on the Queen Mother's support in his everyday life, Smenkhkare's in his divine life.

Meanwhile, during the time before the marriage was to be solemnized, the King allowed himself one exquisite solace. He determined to give the young couple jewels and furniture that would express as perfectly as possible the spirit of their faith and the ways of Akhetaten. The work was too light-hearted in purpose to appeal to the genius of Dhutmose, so the King put Bak and his best palace craftsman in charge of the work.

On objects of every size from couches and chairs and great gold vessels and plates to jewels and trifles such as spoons and inkpots and jars for cosmetics, they celebrated their delight in the whole created world. They put into visible form all the images and ideas that Akhenaten had expressed so gloriously in words. They showed men of every race pleasuring themselves together; they showed "all cattle great and small" frisking in the sunlight; they showed the fish leaping and the birds raising their wings in praise of the Aten. Most often of all they showed the royal pair holding hands, kissing, walking blissfully in their garden. And here there was no need to wait, or to fear pests and blight—the trees and flowers sprang into full magnificence of leaf and bloom and fruit.

Almost every day Akhenaten found time to visit the workshops with Bak. He loved to see the trays of turquoise, agate, carnelian and malachite, the little stacked ingots of gold and silver, the tusks and the big blocks of ebony and cedar wood. And still more he loved to see the artificers in action: the smiths with their miniature furnaces, drawing, beating and moulding the precious metals; the jewellers cutting the stones and building up the designs cloison by bright cloison; glass paste being poured, wood and ivory carved and polished. As he said, it was almost like building the city over again, but here everything was under their hand and could be made perfect.

When all the furniture was completed and the caskets filled with jewels, they were moved into the wing of the Palace that had been done up and extended for the Princess and her husband. Now for the first time Merytaten was allowed to see all the treasure that had been made for her. She was enraptured, hugged her father, kissed Bak, and declared she was the most fortunate of all girls in the world. Then she showed every piece to Smenkhkare, and delighted in them even more than before.

The festivities that followed the marriage were equally brilliant and joyful. Ever since Meketaten's death the whole city had shared in a series of shocks and anxieties. Now the citizens seized upon this uniting of the handsome pair, whom they could expect would one day rule over them, as the occasion for wild rejoicing. Perhaps there were still anxieties below the surface, like the black catfish that lurked in the deepest channels of the Nile, but if so they only increased the general excitement. For several days the Horizon of the Aten was a place of wine and garlands, music, dancing, love-making and the giving of presents. Even the workers' township was provided with ribbon-decked poles, sides of beef and huge jars of beer.

When it was all over, Akhenaten determined to withdraw as much as he could from affairs and devote himself to writing his gospel. He told Nakht to open the state business to Smenkhkare, and to instruct him in the new ideas of government that they had shaped at Akhetaten. He also arranged that Merytaten and her husband should take the place of Nefertiti and himself in some of the lesser Temple rituals. He was pleased to find Smenkhkare ready to devote himself to just the kind of official duties that he had always found most wearisome.

Akhenaten now took to paying regular visits to Queen Tiye's house. The first time that they were there alone together, he poured out the story of his meeting with Suppiluliuma as it appeared from his own point of view. Tears came into his eyes when he described the final disaster, and the Hittite army turning, as he put it, "from peace to war."

"Your intervention did no harm," was Tiye's final comment. "The situation is no better and no worse than it was before."

Well though he knew his mother, Akhenaten was still amazed that an event which for him was of such tragic importance that he could hardly bear to contemplate it, should be dismissed in this fashion. But her total incomprehension no longer maddened him. On the contrary, he found it soothing and restful. Far more completely than in his boyhood, his mother now offered him a calm anchorage.

It was not long before Akhenaten found that he was most in the mood for writing when he was at the Queen Mother's house. He had all his materials transferred there from the Palace. Each morning on arrival he drank cooled pomegranate juice with his mother while they talked of trifling practical affairs of a sort he would once have refused to notice. Then he retired to her loggia and his writing.

He worked very slowly, often spending a whole morning in musing, sometimes entirely lost within himself; sometimes rousing enough to respond to his surroundings. At these moments he became aware of the winter sunlight, of the movement of leaves and the play of their shadows on the loggia floor. Most of all he responded to the wintering swallows as they swept past three or four together, leaving faint syllables of meaning in their wake.

In his hymns to the Aten he had been able to pour out his vision of the solitary creator and his manifold creation in free poetic images full of his own wonder and delight. Now he had to set out everything that had been revealed to him not only about the nature of the god, but also about the way that men must hope to follow if they were to be united with him at last. He knew that this teaching must not be like the dry precepts of the old priests and sages, but must be simple and yet woven of poetry—for that in itself was a part of the faith.

Although on some days he wrote little or nothing, on others his brush seemed to run over the papyrus as though it were alive. Then he knew that the god was present and his work was good; everything about him danced to the tune of his excitement, and he would whistle and call in answer to the swallows. One thought often returned to him: that when at last he had finished his task, it would re-unite him with Nefertiti. She would recognize his words, know the source of their truth, and understand that together they could make them speak to every man and woman, however humble. He fancied their meeting in various delectable spots—by a pool, under a fruit tree, within earshot of a fountain. Then always he would give her the rolls; she would need to scan only a few lines, look up at him—and they would be restored to one another.

Towards the end of the winter season, Akhenaten was possessed by a fever that confined him to the Palace for as much as two weeks. When he felt strong enough to visit his mother's house once more, he entered unexpectedly and found her lying awkwardly on a couch with her head back and her eyes closed. Looking at her with fresh eyes, he realized that she had grown thinner. She sat up quickly, greeted him as usual and asked him how he was.

"My legs are even feebler than usual, thank you, dearest Mother. The fever has been driven out by some of Pentu's powders. Yes, I am better, but I think it is I who should be asking after your health . . .?"

"I am well enough. A little tired, perhaps. It's much colder here than at Thebes, and I think the air doesn't suit me. That is all. Tey is here already, with her golden heart, fussing round me. Please do nothing to encourage her."

At this moment Tey came in, carrying a tray with several little bowls and dishes.

"Ah, Your Majesty, dear nephew! I am so thankful that you are recovered and that you have come here." Akhenaten saw that she wanted to embrace him as usual, but that the tray was preventing her. Because of his pang of fear, this seemed extraordinarily comical. "As you can see," she went on, "I have been cooking little dishes for her with my own hands—coddled eggs and such things— but still she doesn't eat heartily as she used to do. And I have been telling her that she should send for Pentu, but she says she is perfectly well. Perhaps she will listen to you, Akhenaten."

In the end the Queen Mother's will prevailed. But when after another week she could not conceal the fact that there had been no improvement, Pentu was called in.

The royal physician examined his patient very carefully indeed, particularly sounding her chest and stomach. He said that it was too soon to make a diagnosis, but Akhenaten could see that he was troubled. He left her some herbal drugs, said that she was to eat light foods and not rise before noon. "I am obliged to eat lightly, and it is years since I rose before noon," was Tiye's only comment.

Before long, although still insisting that there was nothing seriously wrong with her, the Queen Mother sent to Thebes for her own physicians. As soon as they were installed they began to treat her with all kinds of spells and weird concoctions, so that her rooms came to look like a magician's shop. All this distressed Akhenaten, and made

Pentu very angry. Nevertheless, for a time she did seem rather better.

Then one day after walking some distance to prove her strength, Tiye collapsed and had to be carried back to her house and to remain in bed. Until now Akhenaten had tried to believe his mother's protestations, and had remained hopeful. But he could no longer fail to see how bad her colour and breath had become, and how fast she was losing weight. Yet still she told him that she would be quite well again when the full spring had come. He could not guess whether she really believed what she said, or whether she was moved by some fine sense of politeness. He was afraid that the first was true, and that nothing would make her prepare for death.

At this time when the King had most need for support and comfort, he found that Smenkhkare, while he was very solicitous for him, had begun to speak against Nefertiti. He implied that she was not standing by him in his distress, and hinted more strongly than he had done at Ugarit that she was being false to him in withholding her faith. Nefertiti did nothing to dispel these impressions. She had always been sensitive, proud and uncertain in her relationship with Queen Tiye when the King was involved.

Akhenaten was himself becoming nearly prostrate with nervous exhaustion and sleeplessness, and one day when he was with his mother and she still insisted on talking about her recovery, he burst out that she must know that she was dying, and should prepare for the journey. She was as angry as her weakness allowed, and afterwards would not admit him to see her.

When the hot weather had just begun, Queen Tiye was evidently failing. Pentu succeeded in driving out the Theban doctors and making the sickroom seemly again. Akhenaten was recalled, and he could tell that she was glad to have him beside her. Sometimes he sat at the head of the bed supporting her, and she would whisper how well she felt in this position. As he sat there, aching and wretched, he wondered at himself. He had always avoided sickness when he could, and now he thought of nothing but holding this stubborn, emaciated, sour-smelling old lady.

He could see that there was not much time left. Then one morning when she had appeared unconscious on his arrival, she roused herself and spoke more strongly than she had for a long time. "Akhenaten. You made a fool of yourself when Merytaten died, You must promise that you won't do the same for me. You'll miss me. But I think you can rely on my brother and on Mersure." Then, after a pause, she said, "If you don't mind, Akhenaten, I don't wish to be buried here. Pharaoh had a chamber made for me beside his own in the Valley, and that is where you should put me." Akhenaten was dreadfully torn, and yet he could not help rejoicing. It seemed it had been politeness after all. He murmured his promise, and gave her the blessing of the Aten. She died just before the next sunrise.

Akhenaten felt a sense of personal loss unlike anything he had experienced over the death of his daughter. The last months had brought them as close together as they could ever be, but even over the years when he had seldom seen her, he had always been conscious that she was there, his opposite and sometimes his opponent, who gave strength to his sense of himself. After the sheer loss of her being, this perhaps was the worst of his distress. The vision that usually sustained him of his kingdom and of all the lands and their peoples spread out beneath the sun, with himself—Pharaoh—at the centre of the pattern, for the time at least had left him. And with it went the courage and force needed to complete his gospel.

Yet as though the final promise she had asked of him remained as a binding command, Akhenaten did not give way to despair. "You must not make a fool of yourself," he repeated, with a tender inward smile. He and his mother had always spoken different languages.

The great wheel of the Egyptian year brought back the hot weather and then the inundation. Most of the peasants up and down the valley were idle once more while the muddy waters worked for them. The inundation was a good one, and Akhenaten knew that even if he felt adrift and depleted, his subjects would find his life in the waters, and would be praising Pharaoh for the promise of good crops. He looked out from the Palace windows on to the wide spread of the river, and told himself that when it receded and the grain was being sown, he would be able to take up his work again. And now much of his hope and faith, bruised by so many blows, were turned towards his gospel and the light that it would bring.

The royal family was to move as usual to the Summer Palace. Nefertiti acquiesced in going, but she did not show any of her usual delight at the prospect of escaping to the private paradise that they had created at Maru-Aten. Smenkhkare declared that nothing could give him greater satisfaction than to leave his duties and be with the King in tranquillity. "Too much business," he said, "had cut him off from the things he most cared about." Perhaps Ankhesenpaten showed the greatest expectation of pleasure, for she was just at the right age to enjoy the gardens, the water court and the lake; she could take command of her small sisters, and quite soon Tey was to bring Tutankhaten to stay with them.

Akhenaten found Nefertiti more remote than ever when they were established at Maru-Aten. What angered him most, and then shamed him for feeling anger, was that she did not appear to be unhappy. She spent much of her time with Lasia and the children; she had long sessions with the chief steward about the development of the gardens; when Tey arrived she was ready to accept her foster-mother's company. This made matters worse, for Akhenaten could not help noticing that his kindly aunt was beginning to look at him reproachfully.

Smenkhkare was very ready to offer the devotion that Nefertiti seemed to deny him. He made him feel that he perfectly understood what he was suffering from the loss of his mother. He declared that so long as they were at Maru-Aten his one desire would be to prove his faith in the divine power, and his love of the King himself. Moreover, Akhenaten found that his son-in-law was always there when he wanted him, ready to listen, to row his boat or drive his chariot.

One day the King went to the temple in the Summer Palace to make thanksgiving offerings for the inundation, which had now reached its height. Serving the Aten had never become a matter of correct procedure for Akhenaten and now his emotion, his sense of participation in the divine life, was deeper even than usual. He was thinking of the waters that would soon begin their slow ebbing, and of his hope that when the earth emerged again as on the day of creation he would be able to take up his work.

As he turned from the altar and began to lead the procession of priests back to the gate, he noticed far across the court a figure lying prostrate on the flagstones in front of one of the statues of himself. He saw the man rise a little to kiss the granite feet and then lie down again, exposed to all the force of the summer sun. He stared intently, believing he knew who this worshipper was, and as they neared the gate he sent one of the young servers to bring back a report. When the boy returned, delighted by an excuse to run in the precinct, he puffed out, "It is the P-Prince Smenkhkare, Your Majesty. I did not dare to address him: he did not seem to know that I was there."

Akhenaten stood quite still. They were pouring water on his hands, and the fans rustled softly above his head. He could see Smenkhkare only as a little horizontal line of brown and white, but in his imagination he pictured his outstretched form in all its physical perfection. And towering above it the figure of himself. This is not idolatry, he thought, this is the pure love of the Aten. Surely with love such as this I can succeed. Then he thought of Nefertiti, and of their union, and of all the scenes of the Divine Love which had been set up throughout the kingdom. In the end the understanding of man is stronger, he reflected. They only can see the full light.

The purification was finished, the sandalled feet about him were beginning to shuffle and to grit the desert sand that still always blew on to these pavings. He moved forward again and went out through the shadow of the great gate where the flags were swinging gently on their poles.

It was the evening of the same day that Mersure arrived at Maru-Aten. Reluctantly the King allowed him to be admitted. In his fervent and yet dreamy mood the whole essence of the man was offensive to him.

"What is it, Mersure? What is it that can justify your disturbing me here and at this hour?"

"My dear brother! I have hesitated too long, not wishing to add to your difficulties. But today I have received a letter from Smenkhkare's honoured mother that has decided me not to delay any longer. She says that talk has now reached Thebes and caused disturbances. The mob believe that such things will offend the god, and that they will suffer."

"What things, Mersure?"

"Can it be true that you alone do not know? I am told that they sing of it in taverns. It is that the Queen betrays you with your trusted servant Dhutmose."

"And why should I believe what is sung in taverns?"

"Sire, my poor brother. I have long known it to be true, and I have brought a witness of its truth. Tadukhipa. She went sometimes to Dhutmose's studio in search of her aunt. If you will see her she will describe to you . . ."

Akhenaten felt sick and faint, not because of what Mersure was telling him but from disgust at the occasion, at the baseness of it all. As for what this creature before him had said about Nefertiti, it seemed to him that if it were true he knew it already, and if it were not it made no difference.

"See Tadukhipa! See her! I hope never again to have to know of her existence. There is no need for me to see anyone: no need. And understand this, Mersure, whatever may happen after this, you and your words, your sewage stories, have played no part in it. Pharaoh alone is the source of his own acts." As Mersure withdrew, Akhenaten marvelled that so vile a father could have a noble son.

Nefertiti was sitting on a block of stone in Dhutmose's studio while the sculptor walked up and down beside her. It was the first time she had ever gone there alone. She had found him putting some small touches to the new head of

herself which had been set aside since she had left for
Maru-Aten. Before anything else she had looked at it and
said, "I see I am getting older, Dhutmose." And he had
answered, "But more beautiful, more fully occupied by
life. Isn't it so?"

Now she had told him all that she knew of what had
happened, which was not everything. "I do not know
whether he believed Mersure. When he spoke of him his
voice and his face were quite strange to me. For a time he
hated Haremhab, but this was contempt. He said that it
made no difference. That it had been shown to him that
he could no longer rule with me beside him. That I had
long refused to be his Queen . . ."

"I feel such a villain. Why did I have to tell you of my
love? What made me do it but vanity? I had to display the
creation of my heart before your eyes. I wanted you to
admire it. Yes, the vanity and folly of an artist."

"All you did was to make me dream of myself as an
ordinary woman. It was very wonderful, but only a dream.
I know that people have thought that I was not a woman,
although some have held me to be more, others less. You
offered me reassurance. But, Dhutmose, I do not even
know whether it was this dream that divided me from
Akhenaten. He changed also. Once his idea of divinity
was a light within him, pure light that illuminated everything and made it real. But then . . . then . . ." She was
thinking of Meketaten. "Then it hardened. We had to be
King and Queen far above the earth. There I could not
follow him. And yet, was it so? He met Taty face to face
and saved himself. And with his mother. . . . Oh, Dhutmose, it seems to me now that the failure has been all mine.
Perhaps, too, he was right that it was my lack of faith that
denied us a son."

"One thing I can see," said Dhutmose glumly. "You
still think only of him. And one thing I cannot understand
is how a man could have you and part from you. But I am
just a handyman of stone and mallets. Why should I
understand the King and Queen?"

"Why indeed, when it seems they do not understand
one another?"

"As an ordinary man I will say that I am angry that Nefertiti should cleave to the King and not to me. And angry that I shall have to go away from the city I have done so much to make. But as we have all tried to live under Ma'at, I have to admit that everything comes from your Akhenaten. Even my love and what you have called your dream. Think of it. I am the son of a butcher; you the daughter and wife of Pharaohs. Only in the light of his idea could such a man and woman have known one another as we have known one another."

"Yes, that is true. And there again I have failed. At this moment it seems to me that in all my striving after Ma'at, I have been true to no one."

"Don't accuse yourself. That would be the worst treachery to the spirit of the Aten. It's as I said before. Akhenaten released change, and change is like a whirlwind—you cannot stable it in your courtyard. It is a glorious idea to all creators, an abomination to most Egyptians."

Nefertiti looked up quickly and her voice trembled a little. "I have never forgotten what you said to me up there in the sunset. Up there on the cliff when Akhetaten itself was still only an idea. About the forces of the world ranged against Akhenaten. Now it seems to me you think that they are going to win."

"In a sense they cannot win. I see all this city, and all the lives within it, as a work of art created by the King. And as that it is eternal, like the circling of the stars. So that it doesn't matter if its own life, and all those lives, are cut short. They have been made. That is what counts."

"So you think that even our city will not endure—will be forgotten?"

As she sat there looking at him with so much tragedy in her, Dhutmose longed to seize her up; to run. "Nefertiti, how much you are yourself. So purely yourself," he exclaimed, then went on: "I believe that wherever there has been great creation it lives and has power. Think of the pyramids. They are pillaged, battered, their line of kings has gone. Yet men turn to them, they fill the imagination. Akhetaten is frail, yet much greater than the pyramids."   .

Nefertiti smiled and seemed comforted. Then she said, "One thing I will not ask you, Dhutmose. I will not ask you about the power of the Aten. For there I have my own faith."

"Isn't it all the same? Yes, the Aten is for ever. And now you will go to the North Palace and remain there with the children. You will know how to live, and Ay and Tey will protect you. As for me, I shall quit in my own good time. And although I can't stay to protect our Akhetaten, I shan't take anything away. I shall leave all my work here —all those citizens rich and poor. And reigning over them I shall leave your head, Nefertiti." He put an arm round her and led her across the studio until they both stood looking up at his masterpiece. "How good it is," he said. "What love I put into those cheekbones—and how they responded! Perhaps I shall leave even this half-carved piece, although I itch to go on with it. For then it will wait here with just the faintest hope that I might come back to finish it."

"Dear Dhutmose! But will you take nothing with you— after all these years and all that you have made?"

"I shall take those first lucky fishing-rods. I shall take gold, for I am a practical man and don't wish to suffer any more than I must. For that will be enough. And I shall take one small figure of you that I made for myself and for nobody else."

He put on her light cloak, kissed her slowly, and led her to the door. There was a curtained litter waiting to receive her.

"Goodbye, Dhutmose."

"Goodbye, Nefertiti."

The fan-bearers closed in behind her, and the sculptor turned quickly back.

The litter, with curtains drawn, was carried all the way from Dhutmose's house above the wadi to the North Palace, yet very few people in the streets guessed who was inside. Looking out through the chinks, Nefertiti saw a house in the merchants' quarter with furniture piled in the garden. She guessed that the owners were moving back to Thebes.

Having taken his decision, Akhenaten determined to live by it. He assigned Maru-Aten to Smenkhkare and his daughter, and said that before the sowing time began he himself would return to the Great Palace. Without waiting for any request—although he did not doubt that Mersure intended to press for it—he proclaimed Smenkhkare as king to rule beside him. Co-regencies of this kind has been established many times before, although not for the reasons that moved Akhenaten.

Partly because he thought it would please Smenkhkare, and partly to make it clear to the people that his son-in-law was indeed to be a king with a throne only a little lower than his own, Akhenaten prepared to have the coronation celebrated with traditional ceremony. For this purpose he had a magnificent Festival Hall built to the south of the Great Palace. He also transferred to Smenkhkare the sacred names which had belonged to Nefertiti. He did this not out of cruelty, but to show that the young sovereign had in every way taken the place of the Queen in the worship of the Aten.

One morning when he left his rooms where he spent most of his time while he remained at the Summer Palace, he found workmen balanced on planks and ladders in the main hall of columns. Merytaten and some of her ladies were seated near by watching what was going on. Stone dust was falling on to the polished floor. He beckoned to his daughter, and Merytaten crossed to where he was standing.

"Smenkhkare ordered this to be done?" he asked sadly, pointing to the place where the royal cartouches were being chipped away.

"Yes, honoured Father. And my name and titles are to go into the place of my mother's. We knew this was what you would wish."

"And you yourself thought that it was right?"

"Of course, my Lord. I am now the only King's Great

Wife—or will be as soon as Smenkhkare is crowned. And since the Queen has betrayed you, we want nothing to remind us of her." Merytaten spoke with great complacency and had a virtuous air. The truth was that Merytaten was completely dominated by her husband, and agreed with him in everything. She had always been a simple, unimaginative girl, and now she seemed to have no personality of her own. She was subdued, but satisfied with her condition. Akhenaten seldom saw her.

As though to give himself pain, he went on through the water court and towards the lake. Just to walk seemed a labour. He passed slowly through the court. He and Nefertiti and several young painters had enjoyed themselves there devising the intricate pattern of tanks at the foot of the columns. Each had real plants below the surface, and most naturally painted waterside plants above. Even now one would swear they were real. They had stocked the tanks with tropical fish brought back by the royal ships. He noticed that many were empty; it had taken loving care to keep these brilliant morsels alive. He went to a point where he could look out over the lake. The gold disc was still there on the island, reflecting the rays of the sun, for they had set it in stone to be a memorial to his declaration of the Peace of the Aten. As he leant on the balustrade, a flowering creeper swinging shadows across his face, he closed his eyes, turned day into night, saw them both standing there before the disc, and remembered the sense he had then of commanding the whole world.

On his way back, the thought emerged clearly into his mind that he was disturbed by Smenkhkare's action in having Nefertiti's cartouche erased. Worse that he should have given the order without consulting him. But then he reflected unhappily that it was very much in line with the things that he himself had decreed; moreover, Smenkhkare had never hidden his condemnation of Nefertiti or his desire to banish her from their lives.

The Festival Hall was finished in time for the coronation to be held at the proper season—with the beginning of the new year's sowings. Among the many noble, wealthy and influential people who attended were friends of Mersure's

from Thebes whom he declared to be one and all devoted
subjects and servants of the Aten. Akhenaten did not know
them, as all had come into their estates or won office since
he had left Thebes. Although they tried to behave correctly, he could not fail to discover that they knew almost
nothing of his teaching. However, the fact that they had
come to show loyalty to Smenkhkare made them tolerable
to him.

In spite of all the eminent visitors, and the beauty of the
coronation ritual which Mersure and Akhenaten had
created for the first Pharaoh to be crowned under the full
sway of the Aten, there was a lack of spontaneous rejoicing
in the city itself. The fact was that most ordinary people
were quite confused as to what was happening at court, or
what was meant by Smenkhkare's accession. No proclamation had ever been issued about Nefertiti, and as every
family in Akhetaten had tried to model itself on the royal
family, and had set them at the heart of their worship, they
were not prepared to feel any very great enthusiasm for
Smenkhkare and Merytaten. No one except a few courtiers thought of altering the carvings of the Divine Love
in their household shrines.

Among those who did not attend the Coronation were
Ay and Tey. They now lived at the North Palace with
Nefertiti, and their relationship with the court was a
delicate one. Both of them, and Tey in particular, were
naturally outraged by the treatment of their beloved
foster-daughter. In spite of what Nefertiti herself said,
they attributed this entirely to the plotting of Mersure.
Ay was not himself a subtle politician, but he understood
something of the lines of power, and he knew that he was
contending with Mersure and that some day there might
be an open struggle between them. He was confident that
his understanding with Haremhab was worth ten times
more than any schemes that Mersure could make in
Thebes.

For these reasons Ay had no intention of accepting any
duty to Smenkhkare. On the other hand Pharaoh must
command his loyalty, and he could not altogether escape
from his long if reluctant respect for Akhenaten himself.

Moreover, most important for the honourable soldier he felt himself to be, there in his sister's son was the source of legitimacy.

This was where Tey s understanding began, and where the whole of her feminine will joined in with her husband's. Their Tutankhaten must marry Ankhesenpaten; the god had clearly intended it even when he seeded her womb. So Ay continued to stand by Akhenaten, and did nothing to weaken the support of the army.

Akhenaten played his part in the Coronation with conflicting emotions. He felt a quickening of his spirit when he was able to look at Smenkhkare, now with the double crown on his head and the uraeus serpent resting on his brow, seated so near him on a throne one step below his own. (Merytaten had not been granted the full role of Great Queen, for it was through the being of the two Pharaohs that the sacred love of the Aten was to be manifest.) Nevertheless, as the rites were slowly enacted, he could not save himself from memories of his own crowning, or from imagining Nefertiti as she endured these hours away in the North Palace. And when the moment came for Smenkhkare to salute him as an expression of the Divine Love, he could not feel the same worship in the young man that he had recognized when he saw him prostrate in the temple at Maru-Aten.

As soon as the Coronation and the somewhat subdued festivities that followed it were over, Akhenaten felt ready to return to the writing of his gospel. He had moved back to the private apartments of the Great Palace, and seldom left them except to officiate with Smenkhkare in the Temple. It still seemed to him that he had to finish his task of bringing the light from the inmost part of his being, but that as soon as this was done it must be carried from Akhetaten throughout all the lands. As a small token of his intentions, he sent Smenkhkare to Memphis to dedicate a new temple and make everyone there and at Heliopolis aware of the missions that were to follow. In spite of all that had happened, when he allowed himself to think of this future time, which he now named to himself the Spreading of the Rays, he could not forget Nefertiti and his old hope that this understaking, with which she would have so much sympathy, would bring them together again.

At first he failed to win the presence of the god as he had known it during his best days at his mother's house. Sometimes he fell into low moods such as he had never before experienced when he brooded on the blows he had had to bear. Sometimes he could not resist going out into his garden and watching the thousand small existences and happenings that were going on there—a thing which all his life he had loved to do, but which he felt ought now to be denied. Gradually as his isolation and solitariness increased the power came back to him, but now he was less excited than before and more intensely gathered in to his work, more grossly involved.

He was resting in the garden after a spell of writing when he saw a large snail surging steadily along the path and then turning among the leaves. He admired the lines of the shell, and remembered how for some people the spiral was a symbol of the sun. The head of the creature neared a twig, and how quickly it drew back those horns through which he was sure it was able to perceive everything in its proper world. He reached out his hand to cover the snail, and it shrank until almost nothing of it showed beyond the edge of its shell. He picked it up and turned it over. With a last wince the snail settled into its retreat, a dark mass of life with a paler frill undulating round it. "It reminds me of myself," he thought as he felt the smooth, firm coil between his fingers and thumb. "Once it walked along the paths of the world, but now for a time while the god holds it in his hand, it draws back into a smaller and smaller space until the whole of itself, and all that it has fed on and known through its perceptive horns, is held in this thick density of being." Then, more fancifully, he told himself that the gluey stuff that was oozing from it might be for the snail like the words he was sweating on to the papyrus—but then he shook his head and tossed it gently into a flower bed. "Let it feed upon lilies before the birds get it," he said aloud.

Akhenaten liked to feel that his gospel was approaching completion as the corn grew and ripened in the fields, and during all this time, even in his solitude, he felt at one with everything and had no human loneliness. He gave some days to reading what he had written, and he knew it would speak to men's hearts as he had never yet been able to speak to more than a few. There was little more to be set down—perhaps twenty lines, perhaps a hundred.

Now he began to be restless and seemed unable to give himself to these final passages. He was exhausted and empty. Smenkhkare had returned from his mission to Memphis a short time before, but had paid only a formal visit to report on the new temple and to bring letters from the priests and scholars who were the King's friends in the northern cities. Akhenaten was not disturbed by his not coming again, for he had made it plain that he was engrossed and had to remain in retirement for a little longer yet. Now he sent for him, saying that he was tired and needed to be with him before he could finish his task.

Smenkhkare did not appear until the next day, and then he seemed strangely careless, and brought none of the assurance of faith and worship that Akhenaten needed for replenishment. With strong feeling he read him some of the finest of his words, but the young man was reluctant to discuss them, and indeed was hardly attentive. At last the King asked him what was the matter; had something happened in Memphis to trouble him?

"Nothing at all, Akhenaten. All my news is good, and I have never been in better spirits in my life. Soon I shall be happy to share it with you."

"Why not now? I love to hear anything that means your happiness."

"Don't be impatient, Akhenaten. I am waiting for a visit from my father. And I can promise you it will concern your happiness as well as mine." Smenkhkare laughed in a way that Akhenaten had never heard before.

"Mersure?" he said. "It is an extraordinary thing if he can be concerned in any happiness of ours." Smenkhkare laughed again and soon withdrew, saying he had many affairs to attend to after his return. "It seems that you neglected everything," he added as he went out.

His bodily condition was so bad, that for some time after

this visit from the young Pharaoh, Akhenaten lay limply on his couch, his legs trembling and his heart knocking erratically against his ribs. Yet when he tried to discover why he had such a sense of menace his mind was confused. What had Smenkhkare said or done to afflict him in this way? He knew that his extraordinary absorption in his work had affected his mind as well as his body—and a young man full of affairs of state might well not be able to understand the importance of the words he had read to him. "He did, after all, speak of my happiness," he insisted to himself.

By the next day he had almost regained his confidence, and was sitting over a solitary meal listening to his favourite harpist, when Merytaten arrived in his apartments. She slipped in quietly, leaving her women outside, and it was not until he looked into her face that Akhenaten realized that anything was amiss. Servants ran forward with a chair, and the King himself poured her a cup of wine. There was something inert about her, and her eyes were all the time looking at something not present. She was like a woman taking part in a rite who has taken drugs and is half stupefied, half excited.

"I am glad to see you, daughter," said Akhenaten gently.

"Then you should not be, dear Father. There is nothing in me to make anyone glad—except that I have at last discovered how worthless I am. But I am not going to do anything about it. I cannot. I am no better than a slave. There seems no spark in me that can be blown into courage. I have come only to say that I am sorry." She took a gulp of wine.

"Sorry for what, Merytaten?"

"Sorry for what is going to happen: for your undoing, my Lord. I can only say as an excuse that I have long thought that my parents were mad. Yes, it is your fault too. What right had you to upset everybody because of your ideas?"

Her father sat looking at her, not saying a word. At last she showed some feeling, as though coming round from her wooden fixity. "But this is not at all what I wanted to say. You may be possessed, but you were always good to us. Too good, dear Father. You have not understood that most people cannot deserve goodness. So I have come just to say I am sorry. Not to ask forgiveness. I must go back; there is nothing else I can do."

"It seems to me you are frightened, Merytaten. If you wish to stay, we can protect you." Akhenaten found that he was incapable of asking any further questions.

"It is worse than that. I must return, but also I want to return. My life is with Smenkhkare. I am sorry." She got up and hurried away, dry-eyed and without ever having so much as touched her father's hand.

Akhenaten signed to the harpist to play again. He sipped wine, peeled and ate a fig with exceptional care and delicacy. He had no thoughts, but through the mists of his mind there rose one clear resolve. He would finish his gospel. Some time passed—he had no idea how long—then he went to the room where he liked to write, took the last roll from among the others in the casket, uncovered his ink and took up the brush with the fish handle. The words were there, the words he wanted. He wrote fast, though with long sullen pauses. He threw the brush down and tried to read what he had written. Was something wrong with his eyes? Then he realized that the sun had set and his room had more shadows than light in it.

The servants came and lit the wicks in two large bowl lamps on tripods. Now as he read his exultation rose, and when he had finished his eyes kindled and seemed to glow without help from the lamp flames. Into this quietness came his house steward, anxious and questioning. Was he to admit Mersure and his son . . . his Majesty . . . he knew they were arriving at the Palace.

Akhenaten looked at him with a curious smile and said, "We cannot deny Pharaoh. And it would not become us to deny his parent. Bring them both to me here." At that moment, with his great work triumphantly finished, he felt himself to be invulnerable. He leant back in his chair and did not move when Smenkhkare entered, followed by Mersure.

Both of them bowed, and then the young man came

forward, knelt, and kissed his foot. "I come to salute
Pharaoh, the great teacher, the saviour of mankind—and
my benefactor to whom I owe everything." He gazed up
with a countenance expressing the faith and devotion that
he had always manifest in the past. Akhenaten responded
with sudden joy as though someone had opened a door on
the sunrise. He had been wrong. Deluded. A foolish,
ageing creature imagining evil in the heart of the one who
loved him most. He reached forward and cupped Smenkhkare's face in his hands and quoted softly, " 'Thou drivest
away darkness, Thy dawning is beautiful on the horizon
of the sky'." Then he said, "Smenkhkare, you are with me
then? My gospel is finished; together we can illumine the
world."

While he was still gazing into the smooth young face and
liquid, worshipful eyes of his disciple, every feature
changed as though some demon had taken possession of it.
Even before Smenkhkare had wrenched away his head,
jumped up and turned laughing to his father, Akhenaten
had realized the treachery and wanton cruelty that had
been prepared for him. He felt not only anguish as though
his testicles had been kicked, but a kind of terror at the
coming of this evil stranger.

"Didn't I tell you that I could do what I liked with him?
That he would still swallow any flattery?"

"Flattery?" Akhenaten whispered to himself. "Flattery?"

"Yes, look at him!" Smenkhkare went on, still speaking
to his father. "He has always gone after anything I cared
to throw him like a starving dog. You can almost see the
ribs and the hanging tongue. Even that performance in the
Temple. God, what a bore it has been. I have earned my
crown—and never forget that, honoured Father."

Mersure stepped forward, looking as though even he
found this scene too much for his stomach. "You have
deserved this, Akhenaten. It is shameful for any man to be
so easily duped. We shall leave you to repent your vanity—
and the folly of thinking that your visions were worth more
than Egypt; that your childish dreams were fit to supplant
the ancient wisdom. . . ."

"What do you care about Egypt? Or about wisdom?"

Akhenaten's voice was steady. "Let us remember Ma'at, even if your truths are abominable."

"Perhaps you are right, half-brother. But I care about power—power over Egypt and an end to misrule. You yourself, willingly and unasked, gave my son the crown that Thebes is now ready to accept. The priesthood of Amon has come to terms, and the nobles are waiting to show their allegiance. The army will acquiesce, for although Haremhab and Ay are not fond of me, they know that things cannot go on as they are. Tomorrow we shall sail for Thebes, and what a welcome your loyal subjects will give to the young King and Queen! As for you, stay here and enjoy your Peace of the Aten. You can still call yourself Pharaoh if you wish. But the horizons of your rule will be narrow, dear half-brother."

Akhenaten was holding on to his chair, bracing himself against faintness. He ignored Mersure, and said, "You duped me, Smenkhkare, and I am not ashamed that you found it so easy. Hitherto I have had no great imagination for baseness. You may think that you have also broken me, robbed me of power. But it is not so." He looked towards the casket. "I have here something that will command men when you are a homeless bird, lost and forgotten. . . ."

"So that is it," cried Smenkhkare. "The rubbish that you would read to me. To punish you for that, and to save you from clinging to dangerous dreams, I will dispose of it for you. It's all about light, isn't it? Well, let it make some." He seized up the papyrus rolls, roughly shook them out and held them over one of the lamps until they kindled. Then he dropped them in the bowl of oil, and a flame swathed in black smoke leapt to the ceiling. Akhenaten's faintness was mounting, while the young man had fed his own excitement. "Where is your god now? Does he burn with his gospel?" The last thing Akhenaten could distinguish was the room full of black ashes, swirling like a cloud of flies.

Nefertiti was still living in the North Palace with her daughters and Tey and Tutankhaten. Ay was there only occasionally, calling in on his journeys between Thebes and Memphis. Privately he said that he could dethrone Smenkhkare when he liked, but he wished to give him and his father time to discredit themselves. One thing only had concerned him at Akhetaten, and that was to secure that Ankhesenpaten should be betrothed to his son. As soon as Akhenaten had sufficiently recovered from the collapse of mind and body that had followed Smenkhkare's treachery, Ay had exacted the royal consent. Nefertiti had no wish to oppose the arrangement, although she was astonished to discover how ruthless even Tey could be when her ambitions for Tutankhaten were involved. At least the two children were fond of one another, and this marriage could mean that the dynasty would continue with Akhenaten's seed.

Ankhesenpaten herself was delighted by the betrothal. She had become a strong-willed, imperious child, and the family disasters had made her precociously aware of her position and prospects. She had been ready to blame her sister for her conduct, and thought it only just that she should have a chance of succeeding her. In spite of her own situation, Nefertiti was able to feel anxiety for her eldest daughter. But for the present there was nothing to be done—and Merytaten had after all chosen her own way.

Many people were astonished that Nefertiti did not surrender to bitterness or despair. Some said that it only proved what they had always believed—that she was not fully human. Part of the truth was that she had suffered so much even before Akhenaten had forced her to leave him that she was already armed against such invasions. But far more her resistance was due to her faith in the light, which had not been dimmed by anything that had happened. To other people she seemed cool and detached, but she lived with hope and a sense of waiting.

She lessened her unhappiness by working with Gilukhipa. Now that building, planting and tomb-cutting were at an end, and every month merchants left the city, dismissing their servants, there was a big increase in poverty and sickness. Some working people, it is true, moved up to

Hermopolis or even further afield, but among those who stayed, many turned to Gilukhipa for help.

Akhetaten had become very quiet, and was beginning to look shabby. Much of the original building had been hastily done, and now paint and plaster flaked away and no one bothered to restore them. When families left they invariably pulled out the valuable roof timbers and shipped them with their furniture. Their houses fell into ruin in the midst of parched gardens and slowly dying trees. Even at the Palace some of the magnificent inlays fell out and were not replaced.

The life of the city that had grown and flowered faster than any other was now withering almost as quickly. Yet it did go on. Ay and Nakht together contrived that a share of the taxes and dwindling foreign tribute should reach Akhenaten's treasury. This made it possible for the more sincere and less ambitious of the courtiers and officials, and hundreds of priests of the Aten, to continue much as before. As for the artists, who had always been treated like nobility at Akhetaten, most of them remained and passed their days according to their temperament. Some worked quietly for their own enjoyment, while others took to riotous living. Among these was Bak, who had become a drunkard. He and his hangers-on often made disturbances in the streets at night, but Mahu and his men treated them leniently for the King's sake.

All these people who had decided to stay at Akhetaten accepted the view that the true Pharaoh was still among them, and that their city was still the capital of the Two Lands. Unlike the merchants and others who had gone away full of abuse, they felt nothing but sorrow and sympathy for Akhenaten. Indeed many of them had a constant faith that the Aten would raise him up once more, and the whole city be restored to greatness.

Yet reports and rumours about their Pharaoh were not encouraging. He seldom appeared publicly in either the Palace or the Temple. He was said to be living in a kind of trance, speaking very little and often not understanding what was said to him. Then it was made known that he had recovered, and even that his divine powers were

stronger than before. But while people were still convinc-
ing themselves that he would now expel his son-in-law and
resume his rule, the shocking news spread through the city
that Akhenaten had left the Palace and gone to live in
some humble house—no one at first quite knew where.

After this, great events developed fast. All Akhetaten
went out into the streets and celebrated when messengers
from Thebes announced that Smenkhkare was dead, and
that Mersure had escaped into hiding. The young Pharaoh
had been found lifeless in his bed, but nobody doubted
that he had been smothered, and that Ay and other army
officers were behind it. Quite soon Ay himself arrived at
Akhetaten, and there was a tremendous rush to prepare
the Great Palace for him and his family. Tey tried to
persuade Nefertiti to return to the Palace with them, but
she calmly insisted on staying where she was. Nor would
she take any part in the crowning of Tutankhaten and
Ankhesenpaten, although she said prayers and made
offerings for them. She had had enough of crownings.
Besides, it did not appear to her that under Ma'at the
accession to the throne of two children could have any
meaning. Ay would be the effective ruler, and Ay now
that he had so much worldly power had become a stranger.

Nefertiti did not condemn her foster-parents for what
they were doing. Nevertheless, when she heard of the
lavish preparations being made for securing Akhenaten's
throne to their son, and of the gold that was being heaped
on officials to buy their loyalty, she could not help recalling
a day during the first flowering of Akhetaten when they
had called Ay and Tey to the Palace and had given them
gold collars beyond counting to show their gratitude and
affection. The princesses had crowded on to the balcony
with herself and Akhenaten, and had passed up the gold
necklets one after another. The occasion had been like a
warm family party, but with the whole court and many
others looking on and applauding. Her foster-parents had
taken great pride in having the scene recorded in their
tomb, and she wondered whether it shamed them at all to
think of it displayed there in bright colours on the wall.

She decided that it did not, because like most people

concerned with the outer world, their past life very easily became unreal for them. If practical circumstances demanded that they should change their outlook and beliefs then they did so, and could no longer suppose that they had ever thought differently. Soon she was forced to accept the truth of this still more sharply, for even in her retirement she saw and heard enough to realize that Ay intended to make an agreement with the old order, and particularly with the priests of Amon. She saw that for the sake of legitimacy he intended to have his son crowned first at Akhetaten, but that as soon as that was secured the Aten would be betrayed.

Akhenaten found that he could clearly remember just when he emerged from the dazed state of sleep-walking in which he had existed after the hideous destruction of all his hopes. He had been sitting, as he often did, in a chair, supporting his head on his hands and allowing a meaningless procession of thoughts and images to drift through his mind. Then his fingers began to feel his skull, the firm rounded box of it. He ran a fingertip round his eye sockets, sliding the flesh on the edge of the bone until it hurt him a little. Yes, there he was, there in his own familiar body. He looked up and saw a blue dish of pomegranates that his servants had placed on a stand beside him. One of them was cut open, and the pink pips looked firm, real and inviting. He picked them out one after another and crunched them between his teeth, enjoying their slight resistance. From that moment the reality of himself and his surroundings came back to him, and he began also to understand his situation.

Now that he saw things clearly and once again felt that he was living in truth, he understood that he had failed in everything. Some of the failures were caused by other people, but he saw that this made no difference and he no longer brooded over betrayals. He also opened his heart completely to accept the fact that he had done wrong in many ways, although he needed more time to explore their nature. Having accepted his failure and wrongdoings, to his own astonishment he found that he had an altogether new kind of lightness—something far more intense than anything he had experienced after the most sacred rites of purification.

After a few days of this, he decided that his existence in the Palace was not only useless but absurd. When his courtiers bowed and prostrated themselves, when the priests prepared him for his kingly rituals, he wanted to laugh. In every way his life as Pharaoh had become a pretence.

At first he thought that he would move into his mother's old house, but he saw that in such a setting he would have to live the life of a retired prince, and that was not what he wanted. He found himself thinking about the man Taty. He remembered that Gilukhipa had told him that she had arranged for the troublesome tomb-cutter and his family to manage a market garden. In spite of his early resistance, Taty had become an ardent convert to the Aten.

Akhenaten took Nakht and Meryre into his confidence, telling them to continue the government of the city and the temple as they had done while he was ill. He also sent a letter to Ay informing him that he was about to relinquish such power as he had, and giving his consent in advance to any steps that Ay might think necessary. He had by now learnt enough of the situation to be confident that this would lead to the accession of Tutankhaten—and that seemed to him the best thing that could happen.

As soon as he arrived at Taty's place he knew that he had made the right choice. It was on good soil near the river on the southern edge of the city. One sight of it showed that Taty had become a superb market-gardener. All the care and precision he had put into incising the animal and geometric forms of the script, he had now evidently directed into making these perfect plots of leeks and onions, beans and lettuces, and into training those fig trees and sycamores. Only the clump of date palms that hung over the small white house had defeated Taty's ordering hand.

Akhenaten had left the Palace quite alone and on foot. He recalled those other rare occasions when he had gone out secretly among his subjects, but then he had gone as a king disguised. Now he had left his kingship behind him. He found it tiring to walk along the streets, and it was most strange to have no servants at his elbow. Never before in his life had he moved anywhere without attendants. It was a new form of nakedness. He had no gold with him, either.

As he looked about the garden with sober pleasure, Akhenaten noticed Taty stooping low to weed a plot of onions. He had not warned him of his coming, yet when the man straightened himself and saw him opening the gate, he did not make any sign of astonishment. And when Akhenaten asked if he might come to lodge and work with him, he agreed quite calmly as though he understood just what had happened. He was immediately practical, and said, "I have just started to grow flowers as well as vegetables. One of the best men who raised flowers for entertainments and festivals has recently left the city, and although trade is declining, it is worth while for me to take his place. You can be in charge of the flower garden."

"Thank you, Taty, but I can't quite agree to that," Akhenaten replied. "All my life I have enjoyed gardens, but I have never known how they were made. You will have to take charge and show me exactly what to do."

"You will soon learn. And the exercise will do you good. You can see how much my health has improved through working in the sunlight." It was quite true that Taty was better covered and more muscular, as well as calmer and more stable.

His authority over his family was so good that they, too, appeared to take their former Pharaoh's arrival for granted, and treated him only with normal good manners and respect. The child who had been dumb, now a pretty and talkative young girl, attached herself particularly to Akhenaten, working with him in the flower garden and waiting on him when he would allow it. He had a room to himself which at first struck him as amazingly small, but of which he soon became fond. He took his meals with Taty, and often talked with him in the evenings. Then their daytime roles were reversed, for it was most often Akhenaten who taught and Taty who listened.

Although at first it made him ache all over, he found immense satisfaction in gardening. He knew that he was a slow worker because he had no skill, and moreover he sometimes stopped to watch birds and insects or to examine the forms and habits of the plants themselves. On the other hand he never allowed himself to be absent-minded, but devoted the whole of his attention to doing everything correctly. Living in this way his body and mind, which had been exhausted, were slowly mending.

"I thought I had to lose everything. One thing after another. Besides, how dared I hope that you would want to see me again, Nefertiti?"

"Your doubting it is the only thing I find hard to forgive."

"Perhaps I began to hope when I learnt that you were holding back from Ay and Tey and their affairs. But I didn't allow myself to think of it. Then when I looked up from my staking and saw Weni helping you down from Gilukhipa's chariot, it seemed as though I had always expected you."

Akhenaten and Nefertiti were sitting together on the little terrace outside Taty's house.

"It was Gilukhipa who gave me courage to come," Nefertiti said. "She knew that I was thinking all the time of Ay's policies and what they might mean for you. Then this morning, when I had finished giving out the bandaging linen, she almost shouted at me, 'You are a fool, and I've no more patience for you. He is better and you know where he is. Be off with you.' It did not take me long to get here."

"And now, because of your goodness, there is nothing to keep us apart. You have proved right in everything. I had to cease to be a king to learn I was not a god. Or I learnt I was not a god and so ceased to be a king. If I had allowed you to open my eyes, I should have been saved my worst errors—perhaps even my failure. The only claim I can make for myself is that I did act at last. And now here I am as Taty's under-gardener—a man with divinity in me like other men. But I am true to the Aten in that I don't regard what has happened as a punishment, but as a way of learning."

"You know I have never doubted that you were greater than other men, and now your greatness seems to shine brighter than ever. And I was not right in everything. Far from it. I turned away from you when perhaps a true woman would have won you back. That was an error less than yours, only because I am less than you. And now, Akhenaten, may I come back to you? May I return to you as your wife? Or do you wish to be here by yourself? I could understand it if you did, dear husband."

"Come back, Nefertiti, and there may still be time for me to redeem one of the worst of my wrongdoings. But there is something I must say to you first. It would be sweet to think that we could live and work together here as man and wife. Ordinary people. But I believe that this, too, will be denied us. I am marked out by what I have been; even by what I am. I shall be made to finish my way. Do you still want to go along it with me?"

Nefertiti did not say anything because it did not seem necessary. She laid her hand on top of her husband's long one and said, "Look. Our hands are both coarser than they used to be. Mine from bandages and poultices and such things, and yours from the soil. But they still seem to like one another and to fit together well."

Two more rooms were quickly added to Taty's house, and Nefertiti moved there with the little girls. She gave them lessons in company with Taty's children, and helped in the market garden. It was doing well in spite of the fact that Tutankhaten and his court had withdrawn to Thebes and the city was in decline once more. Akhenaten was already becoming a good cultivator, and he felt none of the impatience that he had done in the old days when he looked at the gardens of Akhetaten. He liked to be bound to the movement of the seasons. The only hardship was that when he sowed seeds or planted out seedlings he wondered whether it would be granted to him to see them bud or come into flower.

He and Nefertiti lived very simply together. They celebrated the sunrise and sunset prayers with Taty and his family, but seldom spoke of the great matters that had always concerned them. Akhenaten once declared that he got as much satisfaction from making his Syrian roses grow as he had from seeing his Temple rise, but Nefertiti shook her head and said that was going too far. They were a couple who shared a secret without wanting to talk about it. And the secret was not only their love but also everything they had believed, done and suffered together since Nefertiti had come to his bedroom with her cat. They had no regular visitors except Gilukhipa. Mahu made occasional rather formal calls, and they discovered that he had moved into a house within sight of Taty's and always had one or two of his guards in the neighbourhood.

It was summer, the flood was at its height, and Akhenaten and Nefertiti had to admit that for the first time they missed lofty rooms and wide stone floors, pools and fountains and ceaseless fanning. Taty came back from market with a heavy look. He lifted the empty panniers off the donkey's back and leant them against the wall, then sat down with Akhenaten and Nefertiti on the terrace while his wife brought water.

"There has been a proclamation made at Thebes. There seems no doubt of it. I didn't believe it at first, but everyone is agreed."

"You had better tell us what it is," said Akhenaten, touching his eyes and lips with cool water.

"Pharaoh and the Queen—as they call themselves—have changed their Aten names to Amon. Pharaoh is now Tutankhamun. It seems that passions are being worked up, and people expect that worshippers of the Aten will be persecuted."

Akhenaten and Nefertiti looked at one another sadly, but with complete calmness. "She could not help it," she said, thinking of Ankhesenpaten. "There was no one she could turn to."

"No, not even Tey—dear Tey whom we have loved. By now she will not be clear in her mind that there is any difference between Aten and Amon." Then he turned to

Taty. "Don't be afraid for your family. They can't perse-
cute everyone; there have been too many of us. And I
command you to do nothing to bring down trouble on
yourselves. It is my last royal command, Taty, and you
must obey it. Did you learn anything else?"

"All the temples are to be repaired, and the priests to go
back to the old ways. It is said that Pharaoh is having
scores of idols made and decked out in jewels to be set up
in the chief sanctuaries. That is all that I have heard—and
it is enough."

That evening Akhenaten led Nefertiti by the hand to sit
on the bench under the palm trees. The western sky was
still burning, but the north wind was enough to make a
harsh rattling in the fronds, and the air was cooling a
little.

"We both knew it would come to this," he said, "and
yet it is hard to bear when at last it comes. Soon there will
be nothing left of what we have made. They will plunder
the gold, and even the stones and the timber, and Akhetaten will return to the desert. Only the Aten is for ever."

"That is what Dhutmose said. Those were his very
words." She looked up, and at the mention of the sculptor's
name they smiled at one another. "But Dhutmose also said
that Akhetaten was greater than the pyramids, and that
the idea of it would endure, and fill men's imagination."

"I don't see how that can be. To whom can the jackals
and hyenas speak? But it is of no importance, so long as the
sun rises again and again in people's hearts until at last
they understand." They sat in silence for some time, the
bats flittering above their heads. They could hear dogs
barking, and Taty and his wife talking inside the house.

"The most difficult thing," he said at last, "is the thing
that our poor Merytaten said to me. 'What right have you
to upset everybody because of your ideas?' But we have
learnt to accept that also, haven't we, Nefertiti?" She
slipped her arm very softly round his waist, and held the
elbow that she encountered.

"Yes, my dearest love. As you alone saw, there has to be
change. It is like the sunrise. It will come again and
again."

After a few days there was news of rioting in Heliopolis. The people there demanded the restoration of the Pharaoh Akhenaten. Then it was not long before the arrival of Ay's men. He had sent a hundred strongly-armed guards as well as a captain, fearing that there might be trouble within the Horizon of the Aten. The ship tied up below the empty Palace. There was no shipping there any longer, and sand and straw blew about the quays.

As soon as Akhenaten heard that this party had been sent to arrest him and escort him to Thebes, he sent for Gilukhipa. "I will put her into your care," he said. "If she works with you she will not be very unhappy. And our daughters must be hidden among your child patients for a time. It can easily be done. Very few people will be sure that they are alive. Then you can look after them and all the other children as well," he added, turning to Nefertiti and kissing her.

He ordered Taty back into the house, but agreed that Gilukhipa and Nefertiti should go down to the boat with him. "There is plenty of water between here and Thebes," he said. "And the Egyptian people have always believed that their Pharaoh was in the flood."

But it was not to happen in this way. Akhenaten walked out through the gate where the captain and a few of his guards were waiting. The captain moved forward in an officious manner, pushing himself between his captive and the two women. At that there was a shout from the house across the way and out ran Mahu, armed with a spear and axe.

"No, Mahu! No!" Akhenaten cried. "Not for me! No!" But the man had thrown all his heart and force into the assault, and nothing could stop him. So at the last instant Akhenaten stepped in front of the captain and Mahu's spear went through him.

They carried the body back into the garden, and Nefertiti, who hitherto had made no sound, said, "Let him lie there, for a moment, under the Syrian roses." Then Gilukhipa said, "Do you remember how, on the day when he dedicated the city, he said that wherever he died he would be returned to the Horizon of the Aten, and 'there shall be made for me a sepulchre in the eastern hills'? Afterwards it was written on every one of the boundary stones. That wish at least he can have."

"Yes, we will bury him here in the tomb near Meket-aten," Nefertiti answered. "But perhaps one day he will be carried to the Valley of the Kings, for in a way that is where he belongs. But it is very hard to know what will happen. Come Mahu, it is you and your men who must carry him."

JACQUETTA HAWKES is the younger daughter of Sir Frederick Gowland Hopkins, O.M., Nobel Prize-winner and discoverer of vitamins, who was a cousin of the poet Gerard Manley Hopkins. She grew up at Cambridge, and from an early age was determined to study archaeology, being drawn to it partly by a visual enjoyment of things and of styles, partly by a growing awareness of the poetry of history. She read archaeology and anthropology at Newnham College, Cambridge, and for a year afterward had a research scholarship. Miss Hawkes excavated at a number of sites in England and elsewhere, and published papers in specialized journals and a monograph on the archaeology of Jersey. Early in the war she entered the War Cabinet Offices, later transferring to the Ministry of Education when she became British secretary to the British National Commission of UNESCO. She has, however, more recently renewed a relationship with UNESCO in collaborating with Sir Leonard Wooley to write the first volume of the *History of Mankind.*

During this period Miss Hawkes published *Prehistoric Britain* (written in collaboration with Christopher Hawkes) and *Early Britain* in the "Britain in Pictures" series. Thereafter she resigned from UNESCO and from the Civil Service in order to devote herself to writing, in which she found herself growing more and more absorbed for its own sake.

Miss Hawkes is the author of *A Land,* an interpretation of man's relationship with nature, and *Man on Earth,* a poetic and informative book about the emergence of the human species. She has also written *A*

Woman as Great as the World, a collection of short stories, and *Providence Island,* a novel. She is now married to J. B. Priestley, noted author and critic, with whom she collaborated on *Journey Down a Rainbow.*